Starting Over

Book 1 in Starting Over Series

By Evan Grace

Starting Over

Limitless Publishing, LLC
Kailua, HI 96734
www.limitlesspublishing.com

Formatting: Limitless Publishing

ISBN-13: 978-1495920349
ISBN-10: 1495920348

Dedication

To my bestie's Mel V. and Stacy for not letting me quit when some days I wanted to delete my story and say forget it. Thanks for believing in me.

Prologue

Bellamy Carmichael stared at herself in her bathroom mirror for a long time, frowning at her reflection. She was finally eighteen years old, but wasn't she supposed to feel different? She looked the same and she talked the same. She had waited for a long time for this moment—to become an "adult." Now she had nothing holding her back from finally putting her plan into motion.

She was going to seduce the only man she had ever loved: Luke Carter. She couldn't help the smile that touched her lips and her stomach was fluttering when she thought of him. Sure, her brothers had lots of good looking friends, but Luke was always different. He never treated her like a pest the way the others did. He always included her in whatever they would all do. Taking a deep, calming breath, Bellamy still wasn't sure how to execute her plan. She had wanted this and him for so long and now that it was time, the butterflies in her stomach wouldn't let up. Bellamy was at a loss on what to do, so she started with the one thing she knew would help her chances and that was how she looked.

She'd saved her money from her part-time job at Luke's mom's bakery and teaching at her mom's studio. She went out the day before to buy a pink satin bra and panty set; the bra fit her like a glove and hugged her just right, the panties were a barely-there piece of matching silk that sat low on her hips and felt smooth against her skin. Having a dancer's body that was lithe and flexible was sure to entice him, or at least she hoped it did.

After Bellamy finished slipping on the lingerie, she slipped on her sundress, the color of pink grapefruit. The bodice hugged her breasts down to her waist, the neckline dipped down low enough that she showed a decent amount of cleavage and the hem stopped at her mid-thigh.

Normally she wouldn't have chosen a dress so provocative because her dad would've thrown a hissy fit and made her change, but luckily her parents were with the Carters on their boat. She slipped on a pair of white-sequined flip-flops and walked back into her bedroom.

She gathered her stuff just as her best friend Stacy Hutchins burst through the door. "Oh my god, Bell... you're fucking hot!"

Bellamy's giggles burst past her lips at her friend's constant potty mouth.

"Thanks. You're not too shabby yourself."

Stacy was several inches taller than her and had a body that made Bellamy envious. Stacy had nice large breasts (after years of friendship they'd seen enough of each other's bodies). Her tiny waist and full hips were that of a centerfold, and the girl had legs for days.

Her skin tone was light olive that only got darker in the summer to match her long dark hair and eyes. She always wished she looked more like Stacy.

Bellamy stood in front of her vanity to check herself over. Her hair was brown with natural red highlights; it hung down past her bra strap and had a slight wave to it. She loved the color of her eyes. They were a cross between blue and gray. She hated the fact that with all of her sunbathing she only had a hint of a tan, but she was lucky to have that at all. In looks they couldn't be more different, but Stacy was the sister she never had.

Her friend was also wearing a sundress, but hers had a halter top and was dark lavender.

"Bell, I've got to ask, are you still going through with this plan of yours tonight?"

She knew her friend just worried about her getting hurt. "I've never been surer of anything, Stacy. Luke can't ignore me now, I'm eighteen. I've seen the way he's looked at me and I know he's got to be at least feeling something like what I am."

"But Bellamy, you're a virgin. How are you going to hide that fact from him?"

Bellamy swallowed the lump in her throat. She'd heard enough stories to know that it was going to hurt the first time, but with Luke, it'd be totally worth it.

"I know, but it'll only hurt for a second, right?" Bellamy placed a shaky hand to her stomach.

3

"Yes, that's true, but don't you think he'll be mad if he finds out during?" Stacy had been trying to talk Bellamy out of this for days.

Bellamy just shrugged her shoulders. She'd just cross that bridge when she came to it.

"All right. If you're absolutely sure, let's go get your lover boy," Stacy said as she looped her arm through Bellamy's and pulled her into the hallway.

It was finally time for her to make her move.

***

Luke Carter sat in his truck outside his best friend Dustin's parents place waiting for him to come out so they could head over to the Red, White and Blue festival.

Just two months before he'd graduated from the University of Southern Florida. He'd gotten his Bachelor's in business and got his Master's in Architecture. He had busted his ass to finish so he could come home and start working with his dad and Charlie, Dustin's dad.

Luke had been best friends with Dustin and his twin Dylan since they we're in diapers—or at least that's what pictures showed—but they had. Where there was one, the other two were usually right behind.

They'd all been in Kindergarten when Dustin and Dylan's baby sister, Bellamy, came along.

He couldn't help himself and looked up to the Carmichael's second story window that he knew belonged to her. Bellamy had been their little pain in the butt for a long time, and it wasn't until she hit her teens that Luke noticed she was changing.

She'd always been a pretty little girl, but by the time she'd hit fifteen she was a knockout, and he hated that he even thought that. Luke always knew she was gonna be trouble and she was. Bellamy followed them endlessly and it had always been harmless, but once she hit her upper-teens it became way more.

He knew she always had a little crush on him, but the older she got the more flirtatious she became. Even though Luke thought she was beautiful, she was also the baby sister of his best friends. Add in the fact that he was six years older than her, and he felt like a sicko for even looking at her.

Luke had moved back home a month ago and got a little apartment on the edge of town. It had surprised Luke that he really hadn't seen a whole lot of her since he'd been back. He'd catch glimpses of her coming and going, but he hadn't really spoken to her. He'd missed her birthday/graduation party the week before because he flew out to see his older brother, Jason, and his new wife.

Now he was staring at her window like some creepy stalker. Luke was so caught up in his thoughts that when Dustin hopped in his truck, Luke started.

"Jesus! You scared the shit out of me!" Luke exclaimed, clutching his chest.

"Well, you're the one who was sitting there in la-la land. What gives?"

Thank the Lord above that Dustin didn't realize that Luke had been staring at Bellamy's bedroom window. "Nothing, man. I was just thinking."

"Okay. Whatever you say. Now let's go find some chicks."

Luke started laughing at his friend as he pulled out of the driveway and headed towards the riverfront.

***

Bellamy walked around with Stacy most of the late afternoon, talking to friends and flirting with boys. She hadn't seen Luke yet and she was becoming worried that he may not even show up. A boy they'd graduated with, Rick Davis, had had a bottle of rum in his truck, so once Bellamy had a soda in her hand he led her to his truck and poured a generous amount of the strong clear liquid into her glass.

She needed all the help she could get and the alcohol seemed to be a good way to ease her nerves, especially if Luke did show up. Sure enough, as she finished her second drink, she happened to look up to see him standing by the beer tent.

Luke looked gorgeous. His dirty blond hair was cut close to his scalp. She could see the light five o'clock shadow dusting his jaw and his green eyes sparkled as he scanned the crowd.

He was wearing khaki cargo shorts and a white t-shirt that showed off his tanned, leanly muscled arms. Bellamy always appreciated his nice ass, too.

She couldn't help the nervous giggle that fell from her lips as she watched him.

Bellamy had to make her move soon, because if she didn't do it, she wouldn't at all. She knew there were tons of girls there probably dying for his attention, but Luke was hers.

She motioned to Stacy and started running through the crowd towards him. Bellamy saw him turn towards her as she called his name. She didn't think she just launched herself at him. With her arms around his neck and her legs wrapped around Luke's waist, Bellamy hugged him tight.

"Hi, stranger," she said brightly.

The smile he gave her made Bellamy think that Luke was a little nervous. "Uh, hey, Bell. What's up?"

"Nothing. Just hanging out with friends and I saw you standing here by yourself, so I wanted to come see you. I'm mad, you know—you missed my party." Bellamy tried her best pout, but she knew it didn't look genuine.

"I know I did, but I had to go see my brother and sister-in-law. You got my present, though, didn't you?"

Bellamy had been surprised when Luke's mom, Lola, brought a gift that was from only him to her party. She'd gone up to her room, sat on her bed, and opened the little box. It was a simple gold chain with a little teddy bear charm on it with her birthstone—an emerald—where its heart was. The card that came with it said:

I know it seems a little childish, but I knew you probably wouldn't want to take TT with you to college, so I got you something to remember him by. Bellamy, you're going to do great and can't wait to hear all of your crazy stories.
Yours,
Luke

TT was the teddy bear her brothers got for her as a gift when Bellamy was born, and even now, at eighteen, she still slept with him.

"Of course I got it. I can't believe you did that. I think by far it was my most favorite present." Bellamy nervously licked her lower lip as she brought her hand around and rubbed her thumb across Luke's lower lip.

She looked up and caught a flash in his eyes of something. Bellamy wasn't sure what that something was, but it made her heart beat faster and an ache start between her legs.

Neither one of them said anything for what seemed like forever, but a throat clearing behind Bellamy had her turning her head to see her brother Dustin staring at them. She felt Luke stiffen against her and he gently let her down.

"Why are you harassing him, brat? Don't you have things to do?" Dustin said, his lip quirking up in the corner.

"I'm not harassing him, you ass! I haven't seen him since he's been home and I just wanted to say hi." Bellamy didn't hide the irritation in her voice.

She watched her brother lean forward and take a whiff. "Really, Bellamy? Have you been drinking?"

"Maybe. Don't you dare say anything to Mom and Dad! I kept all of your secrets from them, so you better keep quiet." She turned to Luke. "See ya later."

"See ya," he muttered.

Bellamy couldn't help herself and stuck out her tongue as she walked past her brother and back towards Stacy, who was still talking to Rick.

She just had to give it a little more time and soon her brother would be hooking up with one of his random skanks and then Luke would be alone. Oh god, she hoped he was. If he decided to find his own girl for the night it would kill her.

Bellamy grabbed her hair and twisted it up on top of her head as she followed Stacy and Rick over to a group of their friends. When she turned her head, Bellamy found Luke watching her and the ache started all over again.

***

Luke didn't know what the hell had just happened, but he sure as hell was glad Dustin interrupted when he did. He'd been about two seconds from claiming her delectable mouth with his. When the little hellion had licked her lower lip and eyed his mouth like a treat, it took every ounce of strength to keep from getting an erection.

Her body had been warm and soft against his. The desire to claim her had struck him so hard that he started counting back from 100 to try and think about anything but her, nudity, and sex. Luke shook his head to clear her from his thoughts and followed Dustin to meet up with some of their friends.

***

After the fireworks were over, Luke felt like just going home. Dustin had found himself some action, so he was going home with her, but dammit if Dustin didn't ask Luke to make sure Bellamy got home safely since Dustin knew she'd been drinking.

Luke said bye to Dustin and his "date" and took off in search of Bellamy. He'd walked around for a good twenty minutes before he finally spotted her and when he did he saw red. Some little prick was pawing at her and from the look on her face she wasn't happy about it.

He walked up as Stacy came marching over and started telling the guy to go away. Luke grabbed Bellamy and pulled her back against his chest, staring daggers at the other guy who looked older than Luke was. "Dude, she's taken, so move along."

Luke watched as the guy stared at the two of them for a moment and quickly said, "Sorry, man, I didn't realize." He started walking away from them and got lost in the crowd.

"Did he hurt you?" Luke couldn't keep the irritation out of his voice.

"No-o-o, he just—he just scared me. He wouldn't take no for an answer." He could feel her trembling as she said it.

Against his better judgment, he pulled her towards him and wrapped his arms around her protectively. He wanted to groan when she wrapped her arms around his waist and held on tight. Her body fit perfectly against his, the top of her head only reaching his shoulders. Her citrusy scent was invading his senses as he started feeling his groin tighten.

Luke quickly stepped back. He had to get her in his truck and get her home. Then like the sick fucker he felt he was, he was going to jerk off until no more sexual thoughts of Bellamy entered his mind.

"Dustin wants me to take you home. Are you ready to go?" He watched her turn to look at Stacy and then turned back to him.

"Yes, I'm ready."

Luke put his hand to the small of her back and led her to his truck. Once on the road, silence filled the cab until Bellamy started fidgeting in her seat. "What's the matter?"

"Um, I have to use the bathroom really bad and I don't think I can wait until we get to my house." The look on her face showed her distress.

"Okay, well my apartment's closer, so we can stop there."

Bellamy smiled at him as he turned and headed for his place.

Once they got there he led her inside. His mom had decorated a little for him. Luke wasn't too worried about it because he was going to start saving up to buy his own place. The walls were the standard white, but his mom had added some colorful prints to the walls.

11

Luke noticed Bellamy looking around curiously. She turned to him. "I like your place. I can tell Lola had a hand in the décor."

"Thanks and you know how she is, she's got to add her touch everywhere." He scrubbed a hand over his face. "The bathroom is down the hall, first door on the right."

He watched as she smiled and then turned to walk down the hall. As soon as he saw the door shut he went into the kitchen to grab himself a beer.

***

After Bellamy closed the door, she leaned heavily against it and took some deep breaths. Her pulse started racing as sweat started to dot her upper lip, but her little act about needing to use the bathroom worked out perfectly. Her brother had mentioned where Luke's apartment was, so she knew he'd offer to bring her here instead of taking her all of the way home.

She walked to the mirror and gave herself a once over. Bellamy shook out her hair and then opened her purse to grab her travel-sized toothbrush and quickly cleaned her teeth. She then spritzed her body with a little of her body spray, dabbed some powder on her face and put a touch of lip gloss on.

When she was satisfied she straightened her shoulders, took a deep, cleansing breath and slid the straps of her dress off of her shoulders. Slowly the material eased down her body until it hit the floor. She kicked it off along with her flip flops and looked herself over in the mirror.

"You can do this," she whispered to herself, over and over. Bellamy knew it was now or never. She eased the door open slowly and as quiet as she could she padded down the hallway.

She found him sitting on the couch watching TV. She put one hand on the wall and one on her cocked hip as she waited for him to notice her. It didn't take more than a few seconds before he looked up at her. His eyes widened and she felt her blood heat up as Luke's eyes quickly slid down her body and then back up.

"B-Bellamy, what are you doing?"

She tried to give her sexiest smile and then slowly made her way towards him. Bellamy added a slight sway to her hips that she hoped Luke appreciated. As she got closer to him, he quickly stood up. His face may have looked panicked, but she could see he had become aroused.

It was huge, how was he supposed to get that in her body? Bellamy reminded herself to breathe and to keep telling herself that people made it work all of the time and to quit being a scaredy-cat.

"Bell, we can't do this," Luke whispered. His voice sounded pained.

She walked towards him until they were almost touching. Bellamy reached out her hand and touched his chest. She could feel his heart pounding against her fingertips. She let her hand make its way down to his erection, letting her hand glide right over it and looked at him in surprise when it pulsed against her palm.

"Bell…" was all he said to her before he grabbed her face and slammed his mouth down to hers.

Luke's lips were frantic against hers. She could taste the beer that he'd been drinking. He used his thumbs to open her mouth and swiped his tongue against hers. Bellamy couldn't help the whimper that left her lips. She gingerly touched her tongue to his, stroking it slowly. Bellamy had been kissed before, but the couple of times it'd happened they tried to suck her face off. Luke knew what he was doing, it felt like he was taking the time to cherish her and savor every kiss.

She felt Luke turn them until he was lowering her onto his sofa, the material soft against her back. Luke lowered his lips to a spot behind her ear that caused her to shiver as he kissed and nipped at the sensitive skin. As his lips traveled lower, Bellamy felt her pulse pounding as her body heated up.

The sensations were all so new to her and it was causing a major sensory overload.

He reached her silk-covered breasts and swiped his tongue against one peak and then the other through the silky material. The feeling was so amazing she gripped his head. She felt her core start to throb, the feeling so incredible that she was convinced she'd orgasm with him never touching her down there.

Before Bellamy could react Luke popped the front clasp of her bra bearing her breasts to him. Her first instinct was to cover herself, so she gripped the arm of the sofa behind her. Bellamy didn't realize that that move thrust her breasts right into his waiting mouth.

First one nipple, then the other; she felt them hardened to almost painful points. She looked down and saw Luke's eyes on her as he sucked one nipple into his mouth. His tongue wet and rough around the tip, every pull of his lips caused the ache between her legs to grow. She couldn't help the cry that she released and let her head fall back.

Bellamy felt her panties dampen so much that she was sure she was going to leave a wet spot on the cushion. He groaned her name as he made his way down her body, kissing and nipping her untouched skin.

She got nervous as he grabbed the sides of her panties and began pulling them down her legs. Again Bellamy gripped the arm of the sofa to stop her natural reaction and that was to cover.

"You're so beautiful." Bellamy opened her eyes to see Luke staring at her. Her body flushed all over when she watched him remove his shirt. Then he lowered his mouth to the spot between her legs that scared the shit out of her. She let out a surprised yelp at the first swipe of his tongue and by the third Bellamy was pushing her hips up to get closer to him.

She had never experienced anything like this in her life. Sure Bellamy had masturbated a little, but the orgasms she experienced were little blips. Now, well—now she felt like she was going to burst at the seams.

Bellamy let out a deep groan as Luke's lip suctioned her clit; she couldn't help but tense up as he eased one finger inside of her. She felt his groan as he worked the digit in and out of her. Bellamy was coiled so tight that when the dam broke she saw stars. One little nip of his teeth and rubbing a spot inside of her had her crying out with the most intense feeling she felt in her entire life.

Little aftershocks rocked her body as he gently nuzzled her and then started to kiss his way back up her body. When his lips finally met hers she could taste herself on him. It was different, but oh so good. Luke kissed her like a man possessed. Before Bellamy could even completely come down she could feel his penis lined up at her entrance and thrust inside of her in one powerful move that had her crying out.

The quick tearing of her virginity wasn't as bad as the uncomfortable feeling of being stuffed so full. Bellamy's eyes started to tear up as she tried to adjust to the intrusion. Luke broke their kiss and looked at her with questions in his eyes.

He brushed a strand of hair out of her face. "I'm sorry, I didn't mean to be so rough. Are you okay?"

The pain and uncomfortable feelings were fading away and as he slowly starting rocking his hips, thrusting in and out of her, Bellamy could feel that warm feeling start to build up again. "Pl-Please, Luke. I need you."

That was all it took before he started to pick up the pace. It was so much better than she'd ever imagined and she didn't want him to stop. Luke bent down, capturing a nipple between his lips and sucking it to a painful point.

Their moans and groans mingled with each other as he grabbed one of her legs and placed it over his shoulder, causing him to sink deeper inside of her. There were simultaneous groans as his penis hit her deep inside. He slid his hand down her body and started rubbing her clit in little circles.

Bellamy's cries became more desperate and she could feel an orgasm so much more powerful brewing that it scared her, but she was afraid to tell Luke to slow down, so she braced herself, grabbing on to Luke's shoulders and pulling him down for a kiss.

Thank god she was limber and flexible because she felt like he had her all twisted. He moved his lips along her jaw and all the way up to her ear. With a tiny nip and a lick he whispered, "Let me hear you come, baby." Luke pinched her clit and she exploded all around him. She opened her mouth to scream, but no sound came out.

She felt her body trying to pull Luke deeper, but his control had seemed to snap because he started pounding into her with an almost animalistic growl until finally he buried himself deep and groaned against her neck as he came and came.

Bellamy stroked Luke's hair as he laid there with his head on her chest until both of their breathing started to slow back down, neither one of them saying anything until Luke finally broke the silence.

He leaned his forehead against hers and smiled down at her. "You okay?"

She just smiled and nodded. She wasn't sure what she was supposed to do after this. Well... she knew what she wanted to do. She wanted Luke to carry her to his bed and let her sleep with him tonight—and maybe forever too—but she didn't know how to tell him that.

She couldn't help but wince when he pulled out, but when he looked down she saw his face pale.

"Bell, please tell me you weren't a virgin. Please tell me I didn't just take the virginity of my best friends' baby sister. Tell me!" he shouted as he pulled away from her and quickly put his clothes back on.

Bellamy started to tremble and quickly tried to shield her body with her hands. She felt her face flush with embarrassment and humiliation.

"I'm sorry, Luke. I wanted to tell you, but I knew this is how you'd react." She took a deep breath. "I've waited so long to turn eighteen so we could be together. Please, you have to believe me! I wasn't trying to deceive you, but I wanted so much for you to be my first."

She sat up, wincing from how sore she was already. It made her feel nervous and vulnerable when he didn't say anything. He just stood there, staring off into space. Bellamy quickly grabbed her panties and slipped them on, followed by her bra. She ran her fingers through her hair as she waited for some sort of response from him.

She watched as he quickly moved away from the sofa and went into the bathroom, only to come out seconds later with her purse, dress, and shoes.

"You need to get dressed right now and then I'm taking you home." She watched him walk into the kitchen and she could hear him in the refrigerator. There was no mistaking the hiss from a bottle as the cap was removed and thrown into the sink with a recognizable clink.

She slid her dress back on and slid back into her flip flops. She opened her purse for a rubber band and pulled her hair up into a messy bun. When she was finished, he came out with his keys in his hand. "Come on, let's go." She didn't respond, she just followed him out of his apartment and back to his truck.

***

Damn, damn, damn. He fucked up so bad that he didn't think anything was going to fix this. A fucking virgin! When he'd thrust inside her he felt the resistance, but stupid him had just thought it was from lack of experience, but he knew when he'd pulled out of her and saw all of the blood, he'd panicked.

He could hear Bellamy crying softly in the seat next to him, but there were no words that he could say at that moment that wouldn't make him sound like a complete asshole.

By the time he pulled into her parents' driveway he was surprised that his molars weren't ground into dust from grinding his teeth so hard.

She didn't make any attempt to get out of his truck right away, she just stared straight out the front windshield.

"Luke, I'm sorry." Her voice was barely a whisper.

He sat there for a moment, trying to choose his words carefully, but he was so angry that he just didn't care.

"You're sorry? Bell, what you did was so not right! You could've told me you were a virgin. Wait…you know what? I never should have touched you in the first place." He could tell she was crying harder by the way her shoulders started shaking. "This was a mistake and it never should've happened. Your brothers are my best friends and this could ruin it, but you know what? It's not going to ruin anything because we're going to pretend that this never ever happened. You better get inside. We're never going to talk about this again."

She didn't even look at him before she opened the door and jumped out of his truck. Before she could even walk away he started backing out of the driveway. It took everything in his willpower not to turn and see if she was still standing there.

If he saw her tears it would undo him even more. As he drove down the street with her house growing smaller in the distance, he felt an ache start to build in his chest. He struck his steering wheel as hard as he could, letting out a string of curses that his mom would've bopped him on the head for if she'd heard them.

Luke knew one thing for sure and it killed him for even thinking it, but that was the most intense sexual experience of his entire life. And it was never going to happen again…Ever.

***

Bellamy was thankful her parents weren't home when she let herself into the house. She ran up to her room, stripping off her clothes and jumping into the shower.

She scrubbed every inch of her skin trying to erase the memory of him, but it was no use. She could still feel his hands and lips all over her body and it just made her cry harder. As she finished washing, she felt something warm run down her leg and when she reached down to check she knew right away that it was his semen mixed with her blood. "Oh god!" she groaned. They didn't use any protection.

She had just had her period a little over a week ago, so she figured she was in the clear. Plus what were the chances of getting pregnant the first time?

After her shower she braided her wet hair and threw on a nightgown and climbed into bed. She grabbed TT and snuggled up against him. Bellamy felt the metal around his neck and grabbed the necklace that Luke had given her. The sobs started again as she ripped it off of her bear and threw it across the room. She didn't want to ever see it or him again.

Chapter 1

6 years later

"All right, ladies, let's cool down and stretch and I'll let you cut out a few minutes early," Bellamy announced to the students of her favorite class.

She grabbed her towel to wipe off her face before she started the cool down following the Kettle ball class that she taught two times a week.

After a series of stretching and breathing exercises, Bellamy let her class leave and she began wiping down the mats and Kettle balls. Bellamy began working at *Fitness Anytime* three and a half years ago when she finished college. As a personal trainer and part-time fitness instructor she just about lived in the gym.

When all of the equipment and mats were cleaned and put away, Bellamy made her way towards the women's locker room. She exchanged pleasantries with many of the patrons as she made her way to her long awaited shower.

Bellamy had just made it to the door when one of the other trainers, Josh, stopped her. On the inside she was rolling her eyes, but pasted on a fake smile.

"Hey, gorgeous, have you finally decided that we really need to start dating?"

Sure...the guy was good looking. He was at least six and half feet tall. Josh was built, but not overly so like some of the men who worked out there. His golden blond hair was buzzed very short and he had brown eyes that had little flecks of gold in them.

Personality-wise the guy was a moron and self-centered. Josh was the type of guy that would be flirting with a girl one minute and staring at himself in the first shiny surface he could find the next.

If the conversation wasn't about sports he usually didn't know what he was talking about.

He'd been pestering Bellamy for a date for the last several months, but she wasn't interested. The year before, Bellamy had dated another trainer, and when it didn't go well it became an uncomfortable work environment until Mason had quit and gone to another gym, which suited Bellamy just fine.

"Josh, you know I don't date coworkers."

"Oh, come on, you know we'd be perfect together. Two gorgeous specimens like us, we'd turn heads wherever we went." He gave her a smile that she knew he used on many women in the place, but she was just not interested.

"Seriously, Josh, I'm flattered...really, but it's just not going to happen." She quickly slid by him and disappeared into the locker room, breathing a sigh of relief.

"Was Josh at it again?"

Bellamy looked up and smiled at Stephanie, who was one of Bellamy's favorite clients. The mother of three had been one of her first clients when she got into the personal trainer game. Bellamy had worked hard to help her lose all of her baby weight and then some. Now Stephanie was studying to be a personal trainer herself.

"You know how he is. The man can't take no for an answer," Bellamy responded with a heartfelt smile.

"So you're heading home soon?" Stephanie asked her.

"Yeah, I'm heading out tomorrow. I'm looking forward to seeing my family."

Bellamy was going home to Beaufort, South Carolina. A home that she loved and missed, even though it was only forty-five minutes away. Six years ago she left and only went home when it was absolutely necessary.

She built a good life for herself in Savannah and the apartment she shared with her best friend, Travis, was her home now.

***

After Bellamy said goodbye to Stephanie and promised to come to dinner soon, she showered, got dressed, and headed out to meet Travis and his partner Brad for dinner.

She walked into the little Italian restaurant that was by their apartment and a spot that the three of them frequented often. Bellamy spotted Brad right away as he stood up and waved to her. His light mocha skin was flawless under the low light of their table. Bellamy quickly kissed his cheek and then did the same to Travis when he stood to greet her too.

Travis pulled out her chair and Brad pushed it in for her as she sat. They all quickly ordered their meals. Bellamy ignored Travis's eye roll when she ordered her usual, Salmon and a spinach salad. "Oh, don't start, Travis. I already told you that my mom is going to do nothing but shove food down my throat when I go home, so I'm gonna be good until then."

"Yeah, yeah, I know. Although I am looking forward to Ruth's cooking when we get there. How was work?" he said, reaching up to push a stray lock of hair out of Bellamy's eyes.

They'd always had an easy affection towards each other. They'd been best friends for almost as long as she'd been gone from home. He was with her through a lot of heartache that Bellamy had been through that first year. She didn't know how she ever would've survived had it not been for him.

When things first started getting serious between he and Brad, Bellamy had been scared that he wouldn't need her anymore, but the three of them had become a unit. Bellamy loved Brad and loved how good he and Travis were together. It made her envious of what they had, but Bellamy knew she had issues that stopped her from committing to any sort of relationship with anyone.

They ate their meal as they made easy chit chat, but Bellamy was just waiting for Travis to bring up the one thing that had her hesitant about spending two weeks back home. After six years she was finally going to get some closure with the only man she was ever going to love and the man that broke her heart.

As she finished her meal, she noticed that both Travis and Brad were staring at her. "Okay, you two. Just spit it out."

Travis spoke up first. "So are you going to do it? Are you going to tell him?"

Bellamy took a big drink of water and grabbed her napkin, shredding it as she thought about her answer.

"That's the plan. I'm not looking forward to it, but I've put it off for too long already. Maggie says it'll give me closure, and maybe him, too. All I know is that I'm ready to move on. You know— really start dating."

Maggie, Bellamy's therapist for the last five years, had really helped her through the darkest time in her life. Now Bellamy was ready to finally start living the life she should be. Granted, she had a job she loved, friends that she loved too, but she longed to have a relationship of her own.

"Sweetie, it's going to be fine, and when you're ready you'll meet a nice guy and you never know what could happen," Travis said as he picked up her hand and kissed it.

"Yeah, Bell, Trav is right," Brad said. "Do what you need to do when you go home and just be open to whatever happens. I believe everyone has that one person that they're meant to be with forever and you'll find him when you're meant to."

Bellamy grabbed Brad's hand, squeezing it. "Thank you, both of you. I don't know where I'd be right now if I didn't have you. I'm grateful that you guys are taking time to come see me and my family during your vacation. I'd be lost without you."

"No, you wouldn't. You don't give yourself enough credit, Bell. Look at what you've gone through and came out of. Not everyone would be so strong."

Bellamy could feel her eyes tearing up and quickly blinked them away. She didn't understand all of the faith Travis had in her since he'd seen her fall apart more times than she could count, but she was happy that he was in her life.

She leaned over to hug him close. "I love you."

"I love you too, sweetheart."

After dinner, Brad had invited Bellamy to go to the movies with him and Travis, but she declined. Now she was standing in her closet trying to decide what to pack.

She grabbed several of her sundresses, varying in styles and color. Once Bellamy laid them down on the bed, she started to pull out her sandals to match. It was going to be nice to dress girly for a change, instead of her normal everyday clothes that usually included a tank top, t-shirt, and shorts.

Bellamy went to her jewelry box and start rifling through it, pulling out earrings and necklaces that she may need. She was ready to close it, and then she saw *it* laying at the bottom.

Bellamy took a deep breath, reached down, and pulled out the necklace Luke had given her six years ago. The color had changed from aging, the metal slightly tarnished. She gripped it tightly in her hand as she thought back to that night that seemed ages and ages ago. Her mom had found it after Bellamy left for college and had sent it to her, not even realizing that Bellamy had never wanted it found.

She rubbed her thumb over her birthstone that was set in the spot where the heart would be. Bellamy made a quick decision and stuck it in with the rest of her jewelry she was taking. She shook off the melancholy and began packing.

***

Luke had had a busy week. He'd been working long and hard to finish the plans for their latest renovation project. Three months ago, when they were just getting to the busy part, he at least had time for a social life. It was a boring social life, but at least he had the option then.

Now he was lucky to be in bed by eleven. This project was his baby and it could change their business forever. He wanted every last detail to be hammered out. The sooner the better, so now he was working day and night. Luke stared at the plans on his drawing board in his home office. He had worked every summer for his dad and Dustin's, learning everything he could about the construction/renovation business until he graduated college and joined their dads' building and remodeling company six years earlier.

He and Charlie, Dustin's dad, were the two that drew up the majority of the plans, while Dustin and his dad were the ones to head up the construction part. They worked as a well-oiled machine and had built quite a name for themselves in the last decade.

One of their biggest projects to date was starting up this week. They'd be doing the renovations on an old plantation and bringing it back to its former glory. The Bartlett plantation had been vacant for the last thirty years and was in complete disrepair. This would be their most challenging project, but they'd all been looking forward to it. If it turned out the way they planned, this job would get them a lot of recognition.

He was so engrossed in his plans that when a small hand touched his arm, he started.

"Oh, baby, I'm sorry." Luke couldn't help but smile at the petite little woman in front of him.

"It's all right, Mom. What brings you by?" he asked as he set his pencil down to give his mom his full attention.

"Well, first, I'm sorry to just walk in, but I knocked and knocked and your front door was wide open. I also wanted to remind you that we're having dinner at Ruth and Charlie's this coming week. You know Bellamy's coming home tomorrow. Ruth's beside herself too. I think this will be the longest that that little girl has been home in the last six years."

As soon as Luke heard her name all of these images of her came rushing back to him. Everything surrounding that fucked up day. Her jumping into his arms at the festival, giving her a ride home, taking her virginity and then the disaster that followed when he realized what a huge mistake he had made.

Luke hadn't given her too much thought the last couple of years. It was always easy not to think of her when he'd been with someone, but Luke had been single for almost a year now.

He never understood it either. One day… not one single thought of Bellamy, then he'd see something or hear a song that brought the memories rushing back. Luke didn't know if he was completely prepared to see her again, but he was older and, he hoped, wiser. He'd be friendly, but that was it. No matter how good she looked or how much of attraction might be there, he wasn't going to touch her at all.

"Dustin mentioned it already, so I'll be there. Let me know if I need to bring anything."

"I think they're all set, but I'll call you if they need anything. I'm so excited about seeing my girl!" The smile on her face was enough to know that his mom's excitement was genuine. She'd always had a special relationship with Bellamy.

"I'm sure! You are Mom, after all. Are you on your way home from the shop?" His mom owned a little bakery off of Main Street and she was a fantastic baker.

"Yep, I just had to do my weekly order since I probably won't get to it tomorrow. I'll get out of your hair—and sorry again that I just barged in. You need to quit working so much. You need a life, sweetheart."

Oh goodie! She was on that kick again. His mom was afraid that he was becoming a workaholic. She was ready to see him settle down. He wouldn't feel so much pressure if his older brother and his wife weren't spitting out kids every time they turn around.

"I have a life, Mom. This project has just been a little more time consuming than any of us anticipated, and since we start this week, I'm just making sure everything is how I want it."

"All right, sweetie, don't work too hard." She kissed him goodbye and was gone before he could walk her out.

"Crazy woman," he muttered to himself with a smile on his face.

Luke was most certainly a momma's boy and he was comfortable enough with it that he didn't really care if his friends tried to give him shit for it. He almost told his mom about Bellamy back when it happened, but because their families were so close, he was worried that it might affect the lifelong friendship their parents had. And that's why he'd kept it to himself for the past six years.

Later that night after Luke had showered, he sat on his bed with his towel wrapped around his hips. He was exhausted since he'd been working fourteen-hour days for the last few weeks. They'd all agreed to cut down on the work load for the next two weeks. Dustin's twin was being deployed right after the Fourth of July and they had lots of stuffed planned before Dylan shipped out.

It was a good thing, but also a bad thing because it meant that he'd be seeing a lot of Bellamy. They were both adults, which made him sure they could be around each other. Luke couldn't help but wonder if she had a boyfriend. It wasn't any of his business, of course, but he didn't know how he'd feel about seeing her with some other guy.

He shook his head. "Great! I'm going mental already." Good, he was talking to himself now too…Fantastic.

Luke pulled open the top drawer of his night stand and pulled a picture out of the bottom of it. It was a picture of Bellamy, Dustin, Dylan and himself at that first Christmas after she'd left for school.

He'd purposely brought his girlfriend with him to be a buffer. Luke remembered, especially now, looking at the picture how sad Bellamy had looked when he introduced them. She'd lost that sparkle that she always had in her eyes. If anyone had noticed, no one ever said anything.

Bellamy had even worn a big bulky sweater to hide her body from him.

He shoved the picture back in the drawer and slammed it shut. Why couldn't he get her out of his head now? They had barely seen each in six years and he couldn't forget the fact that she had manipulated and deceived him. Then he'd been a complete asshole to her.

It was probably a safe bet that she'd avoid him like every other time she was home. To be honest, he almost wished that she would because it would make things easier.

Chapter 2

The drive from Savannah to Beaufort was uneventful. Bellamy had done the drive so many times she could've done it in her sleep. The scenery was breathtaking. Bellamy smiled as she took it all in.

She looked at the time displayed on the stereo. She'd be at her parents' house in thirty-five minutes. She was thrilled to see her mom and dad, especially her twin brothers, Dylan and Dustin. Although six years separated them, they were thick as thieves. Bellamy was the baby and loved following her brothers around, especially because of one person...Luke.

To keep some of her growing anxiety at bay she flipped through the stations on the radio and found Three Days Grace "Never too Late" flowing through the speakers. "Hm...Never too late, huh?" she mumbled to herself. Her family and his had no idea what happened between them the summer right before she went to college. She shook her head as she drove, driving those thoughts out of her head. She couldn't afford to think of the past now. What good would it do? It didn't help or change anything that happened. She was finally, after all this time, ready to move on with her life. If she ran into Luke, which was bound to happen, she'd be…friendly. A tear slipped down her cheek when she thought about the way things played out. Their daughter would be five, getting ready for Kindergarten, no doubt wrapping everyone around her little finger.

It didn't matter that an umbilical cord that was too long managed to wrap around and take the life of her little girl. Eventually she'd tell Luke. Oh, she tried over the years, even after learning she was pregnant during her second week of college. She tried. Too many times she'd call only to hear the laughter of women in the background. It stung and it hurt, but what did she expect? Luke had made it clear after the night they slept together and he took her virginity that it was a mistake. He told her that his friendship with her brothers was too important and he wouldn't make that mistake again.

After that she spent the rest of her summer at home, waiting to go away to school. Her best friend, Stacy, knew what had happened and she had tried to get Bellamy to go out with her, but she felt like her heart was broken, so she stayed at home to sulk. Like Luke wanted, no one but Stacy knew what had happened.

As she drove down the highway, finally those thoughts got out of her head. Her cell phone rang and when she picked it up, she smiled when she realized that it was Travis. "Hey, Trav. Whatcha doing?"

"Nothing, sugar. You home yet?"

"Nope I should be there in about twenty minutes. Where are you?"

"I'm on my way to get Brad, and then it's off to Charleston to see my folks. We should be down to see you on Friday, so be prepared to do some dancing. Oh, your mom called and invited us to stay with you guys, but I insisted that Brad and I would be fine in a hotel."

"Sounds fantastic. Tell Brad that I can't wait to see him." She laughed when she heard Travis grumble into the phone. "Oh, sweetie…you know I always look forward to seeing you, too."

"Don't you forget it. We'll see you in a week."

"Sounds good. Drive safe. I love you."

"Oh, Bell! I love you, too."

Travis was very high-strung and needed someone who could even him out, and that's what Brad did. Whenever the three of them were together, good times were meant to be had, and she couldn't wait.

As she drove into Beaufort, she smiled when she drove through downtown. She knew with it being close to the Fourth of July that the town was filled with tourists. The Fourth was always a big celebration.

On every lamppost and building, American flags were flying and red, white and blue banners hanging on the awnings of every single business. When she was younger, her dance class, taught by her mom, used to perform on the main stage during the festivities. They always drew the biggest crowd. Her mom was a dancer from the time she was three until now. Granted, all her mom did now was teach, but even at fifty-four she still was a graceful dancer. Her brothers would tease her endlessly about all of the costumes she wore. As Bellamy got older, her main focus was on contemporary dance.

Bellamy didn't dance much these days unless she was in a club, but every now and then she'd get the urge and go down to the gym where she worked and let loose. Even now she still remembered most of the routines she did back then, even though there were days when she couldn't remember if she ate or not.

Before she knew it, Bellamy was pulling down her street to her family home. The house her parents had built for them was stunning. It was an old Colonial home that her dad and Patrick had renovated and turned it into a work of art. It was white with a large wraparound porch, with a balcony on the second floor that was part of her parents' bedroom. The backyard had a beautiful stained oak deck that led out to a luscious garden that was home to several different shrubs and flowers.

Bellamy climbed out of her Prius and went around getting her suitcase out of the trunk when she heard the front door bang open. She looked around the trunk and smiled at her mom as she started running down the steps.

"My baby girl's home!" she squealed as she ran to her only daughter.

Bellamy came around her car to run towards her mom. They embraced each other and Bellamy realized she needed this time with her family.

"Oh, Momma! I've missed you so much," Bellamy gushed.

Ruth stepped back from her daughter, still holding her hands. "Oh, honey, you look fantastic. Look at your hair—it's gotten longer since you were here for Christmas." She cupped her daughter's face in her hands and leaned forward to kiss her on her forehead. "Come on, baby, let's take your bag in the house. When we get you settled I thought we could go surprise your brothers and Daddy for lunch. Are you hungry?"

"I'm starving, going out sounds fantastic."

Ruth led her into the house and up the stairs to her old room. The room she grew up in never changed. The walls were the same pale lavender that they were when she painted them in high school. She had a queen-sized, four poster bed with a soft oak finish. She glanced at her vanity that still sat in the corner; it was part of the set that came with her bed. Her bench in front of the window still had the same cream and lavender pillows scattered all over it. She couldn't hold back her grin when she walked over and plucked her teddy bear up. She turned to see her mom putting her clothes in her dresser. Bellamy might've been biased, but she always thought her mom was beautiful. Her hair was a deep auburn that she wore in a bob that came to her chin. She was the only one in the family with brown eyes. She had the same turned up nose like Bellamy as well as full lips. Her mom was taller than Bellamy and had the body of a dancer: lean, long muscles and a narrow build.

"You don't need to do that. I can take care of it."

Bellamy watched her turn and smile. "Oh, honey, I don't mind. Is it so wrong I want to take care of my little girl when she's home?"

"No, of course not. Thank you," Bellamy said as she sat down on her bed. "So, Momma, where's Dylan? I figured he'd be here."

"He's with the boys, working. You know how he is: He can't just sit around and do nothing."

Bellamy smiled because that sounded just like her brother. He was always restless and could never just sit and do nothing. Her mom came over to sit with her.

"So, honey, how's your job? Are you helping folks get physically fit?" her mom asked as she ran a hand absently over Bellamy's hair.

"Of course. I've been getting busy. Lots of word of mouth referrals, and I've been teaching a few aerobics classes, too. Oh, and I talked to Travis on my way here. He and Brad should be here Friday."

"I don't know why he doesn't want to stay here with us. He insisted that he and Brad would just stay in a hotel." Bellamy knew her mom was looking at her closely. "So, are you seeing anyone?" Her mom's heart was in the right place, but she didn't realize that after Luke and then losing baby Rose that she had dated very little. She didn't think her mom wanted to know that her only dates these days were with a gay couple or her battery operated boyfriend.

"No, Momma, I'm not. I-I just don't have time."

"But, honey, in high school you always had tons of dates."

"I know, it's just been hard. I work too much, plus it's just hard to take any relationship I try to have to the next level." After losing the baby, she had opened up to her mom a lot. Obviously her mom had no idea who Rose's father was, but Bellamy's therapist, Maggie, thought it was a good idea to be open with her mom, and in turn, Bellamy would confess to her mom the intimacy issues she had with men.

Ruth put her arms around Bellamy, squeezing her tight. "I know, baby. There does come a time when you have to try and move on. I know you tried to keep everything that happened away from me at first, but I'm your mom and I want to be here for you. Have you ever told the father about Rose yet?" She hadn't meant for her mom to find out about the baby the way she had, but when the doctor told her the baby was gone and she'd have to deliver her, Travis thought her mom should be there for her. Ruth never judged and never asked questions. She just held her daughter and helped her deal with the pain and grief of losing a child the way she had.

"No, I haven't told him, but I will soon. That's at least the plan while I'm home. What does it matter, anyway? She's gone, and she'd been gone before I really ever had her." She turned her head to keep her mom from seeing her eyes glistening with the tears that threatened to spill over.

"Oh, honey, I didn't mean to upset you. Whether you tell him or not, I'll support you. Now why don't you freshen up and we'll leave in ten minutes, okay?"

"Sure, Momma, that sounds good," she said with a smile. Her mom hugged her and left her alone in her room. Flinging herself back on her bed, she stared at the ceiling. She was beginning to regret coming home already, but she had to remember this wasn't about her and it wasn't even really about Luke. She was home to visit with her brother before he left to go to a war zone and to spend some much needed time with her family.

Ten minutes later she met her mom downstairs in the kitchen. Bellamy's mom was digging through her purse and didn't notice Bellamy was standing there.

"Momma... You ready?"

"Oh, sweet lord, you scared me, honey," her mom said, clutching her chest.

"I'm sorry. I didn't realize you didn't hear me come in."

"That's okay, baby. I guess I'm just used to being home alone most afternoons. Are you ready?"

"You bet. When does Daddy think I'm getting in?"

"Oh, I told him you wouldn't be here until tomorrow morning," she said with a mischievous grin.

"Well, I guess it's a good thing that I didn't tell him when I was coming when I talked to him yesterday, huh?" Ruth grabbed her purse and then Bellamy's hand as they headed out to her mom's Charger. Bellamy still couldn't believe that her brother convinced her mom that she needed a souped up Dodge Charger. She had to admit it was a beautiful car. It was sleek black, with black leather interior and when her mom started it, the engine purred like a kitten.

Her dad and Patrick's office was only about ten minutes from her parents' home. The drive felt longer than it was because Bellamy couldn't contain her excitement seeing her family. When they pulled into the lot Bellamy forgot all about being nervous seeing Luke. All she wanted was to wrap her arms around her dad and hold on tight. Ruth stopped Bellamy before they got out of the car.

"Now, honey, be prepared to get the life squeezed out of you. You're all your daddy has talked about for the last two weeks."

"I can't wait, Momma." Bellamy threw open the door and started walking towards the office when she heard those familiar voices.

"Look what Mom brought us, Dylan. I thought we got rid of the little brat."

"I thought so, too. I guess we're gonna have to throw her in the dumpster and let the trash man deal with her."

Bellamy started to squeal as both of her brothers stalked towards her. She knew if they got their hands on her she'd for sure end up in the dumpster. So she did what she did best: scream for her mom and took off running. In a matter of seconds her brothers had her surrounded, all six-foot-three of them.

"You boys play nice or I'll beat you both," she heard her mom shout. Bellamy knew her mom wouldn't help her because she just stood there smiling as she said it.

"Come on, guys, please don't throw me in the dumpster," she pleaded. "Look at me—I'm a lot smaller than the two of you."

She looked at both of them and could see the mischievous twinkle in their eyes. Before they could do anything she wrapped her arms around Dylan hugging him tight. "Oh, Bell, you know that's not playing fair." He wrapped his muscled arms around her, squeezing her tight. "How ya doing, peanut? I've missed you. Don't ask me why, but I did."

She smiled against his chest. "I missed you too, Dilly."

"Oh, I see who your favorite brother is," she heard Dustin grumble from behind her.

She turned around and launched herself into her brother's waiting arms. She braced herself because she knew what was coming next, and he didn't disappoint her. Bellamy thought she was going be sick when he started spinning her around. She could hear her mom's voice calling out for Dustin to stop.

Dustin didn't stop until she heard that familiar deep timbre of a voice. "Dammit, Dustin, put your sister down before I put a foot up your ass."

Bellamy smiled as Dustin put her down and she turned to see her dad standing next to her mom. She took off in a sprint. "Daddy!" she hollered right before he grabbed her and pulled her into a big bear hug.

"Oh thank goodness, my baby girl is home." He pulled Bellamy back to smile down at her. "God, darling, I'm so glad. You look like your momma. You just keep getting more and more beautiful."

Her dad was fifty-six, but he still looked fantastic. His chocolate brown hair was starting to become more silver, but it was still just as thick and wavy as when she was younger. His blue-grey eyes were surrounded by the wrinkles that only seemed to add to his handsomeness and always seemed to have a year-round tan from being outdoors all of the time. She always thought he looked so rugged, like a cowboy. Besides a little bit of a belly starting, he was still pretty trim. Charlie pulled her in again for a big bear hug. "Oh, my sweet baby girl, I've missed you so much. We don't get to see you very often, but I'm glad you're here."

Bellamy smiled against her dad's shoulder. "Me too, Daddy." She had to admit that when she was younger there were advantages to being the only girl, and she hated to admit it, but she exploited them a lot.

"Well, well... look at who we have here." She turned to see Patrick walking towards them.

"Patrick!" she called as she ran over to hug him.

"How are you doing, sugar?"

"I'm good. Just glad to be home." When she looked up at him she could picture what Luke would look like in twenty years. Patrick stood about six feet two inches and was built like a man who spent a lot of time doing manual labor; he still had bulging muscles in his arms, and a barrel chest. Like her Dad, he was carrying a little extra weight in his midsection, but it only added to his character. His hair was a mixture of the same sandy-blond hair that Luke had, but with more silver coming through. His eyes were the palest green, and they made her remember all of the times when she was younger looking at Luke.

She quickly shook her head and plastered on a smile. "So y'all planning on taking me to lunch, or what?"

Bellamy heard her dad laugh as he joined them. "Come on, my starvin' girl. Ruth, she's gonna ride with Patrick and me." He turned to look at her brothers. "Boys, you ride with your momma and make sure she doesn't speed in that speeding ticket with wheels."

"All right, Dad. we got her," Dustin shouted as Bellamy watched them load into the Charger.

"Come on, Bellamy. Let's get something to eat," her dad said as he helped her into his truck. Patrick slid in next to her and as they pulled out of the lot, he pulled out his cell phone.

"Hey, honey, it's me. Bellamy's here and we're all heading to Frank's for lunch, can you meet us?" He listened for a minute. "Good. Hey, will you call Luke and see if he can meet us, too?" He paused and neither he nor Charlie must've noticed Bellamy stiffen up. "Okay, baby, we'll see you soon." He hung up and turned to look at Bellamy. "Lola is sure excited to see you, sweetheart. It's been so long since we've all been together. It'll be nice to catch up."

She sighed and put her head on Patrick's shoulder. "Yeah, I'm glad I got to get away longer than a few days. How's Jason? I got an email from him a couple of months ago, but I really haven't heard from him lately." Jason was Luke's older brother who moved to Seattle with his wife Sherry.

Jason was nine years older than Bellamy, but he always looked after her when she was growing up.

"He's been plenty busy, that's for sure. Sherry's pregnant again. I swear they're gonna have a half-dozen kids before Luke has one." Bellamy felt a wave of nausea sweep over her and quickly tried to hide it. "Jesus, sweetheart, are you all right?" Patrick asked as he turned towards her.

"Yeah, baby girl, you don't look well. Are you okay?" Charlie asked as he started to pull over.

She shook her head and cleared her throat. "I'm okay, really. I'm just kind of tired. I didn't get much sleep last night because I was so excited to see everyone." She feigned her excitement.

Charlie nodded and pulled back onto the road. A few minutes later they pulled into Frank's Tavern. "Are you sure this is where you want to eat, baby girl?"

"Oh yeah, Daddy, they have the best burgers and fries. God, I don't think I've eaten a burger in over a year." Her dad and Patrick shared the same shocked expression.

"Oh no. Well, we'll have to have Frank make you the best burger you're ever gonna eat," Patrick said as he opened the door to the tavern for them.

Once inside they found her mom and brothers already having tables moved together. She was just about to sit down when she heard the door and slowly turned around. She was thrilled that it was Lola standing there, beaming at her. Bellamy raced over to her mom's best friend and greeted her with a big hug. "Oh, Lola, you look fantastic."

She leaned in smelling the sweetness of goodies that she had probably made earlier. "Oh, and that smell; were you making those yummy cinnamon rolls I love?" Lola certainly didn't look like a woman who ran a bakery. She was a tiny, petite woman that only stood about five feet four inches and couldn't have weighed more than one hundred and ten pounds. Her light auburn hair was cut in the cutest pixie cut and she had the most intense brown eyes.

She grinned at Bellamy. "Of course. Your momma asked me to make up a special batch for you, so you could have them for breakfasts while you're home."

"Oh, that sounds heavenly. You do realize that I'll have to work out hard while I'm here on vacation," she said with mock horror.

Bellamy saw Patrick come over to kiss his wife. "Hi, baby. Did you get ahold of your son?"

"Our son is stuck at a jobsite. I swear he's becoming a workaholic like you," Lola said, laughing. As she walked away, Bellamy saw Patrick reach out and swat her on her rear end.

Everyone gathered around the table, all talking at once. She was able to relax now that she knew Luke wouldn't be showing up. She just wasn't ready to face him. Bellamy could guess that he hadn't spared her a thought at all since she left for school, and no matter what feelings she still had for him after all of these years she'd deal with them. She was very good at pushing those feelings to the back. At least that way she wouldn't have to feel anything.

***

When Luke hung up with his mom he immediately felt bad for lying. It was so much easier to tell her he was working then to tell her the truth: that he wasn't ready to face Bellamy. They'd seen each other over the past six years, but it was always brief. Either she made a point of avoiding him or he had a girlfriend at the time and didn't want to rub it in her face. He knew he hurt her back then, but what did she expect? Her brothers were his best friends and Dustin had asked him to make sure Bellamy got home safely that night. So what did he do instead, he took her back to his apartment because she said she couldn't wait to go to the bathroom.

He'd behaved himself until she'd come out of the bathroom in her bra and panties. When the hell had she gotten so damn hot? He remembered the way she looked, her light brown hair curling down to the middle of her back. She was chewing on her pouty lower lip, which he knew she only did when she was nervous. Her legs were so long and lean from all of her years of dancing, and when she started to walk towards him he couldn't stop watching the slight sway of her hips. His gaze slowly moved up over her narrow hips, to her flat-toned stomach. Her breasts weren't huge, but the way she filled out the pink lace bra she wore made him shift his weight to ease that ache that started in his groin while he stood there panicked, watching and waiting to see what she'd do.

He knew what he should've done. He should've told her nicely to go put her dress back on and take her home. She was the little sister of his best friends, and if they had any idea the kind of thoughts that were going through his head they would've beat his ass. Did he listen to that little voice in his head? Hell no. Instead he stepped closer to her and when she'd lifted her hands and started touching him he didn't think at all. He lifted his head and cupped her face in his hands before he slammed his mouth to hers. Her lips were soft and pliant against his. He tilted her head to the side so he could deepen the kiss. She'd moaned against his lips as he eased her mouth open with his lips and with tiny flicks his tongue entered her hot mouth. Her tongue dueled with his for what seemed like forever. The feel of her mouth fused to his was more intense than anything he'd ever experienced before. Luke broke the kiss to ease her onto the couch. He'd kissed her everywhere. Luke laid down on top of her. He'd kissed the side of her neck, smelling the flowery scent that lingered on her skin. His hand slid down and unhooked her bra. Luke felt her stiffen for a second before she began to relax again.

He kissed his way down her body...The ringing of a phone brought him out of his thoughts. Jesus—he had to get a grip and quit thinking about that night and her. He picked up his cell phone and looked at the caller ID.

"What do you want, Zach?" Zach Peterson had been friends with him, Dustin and Dylan since they were kids.

"Well, hello to you, too. What crawled up your ass?"

"Sorry, I was just in the middle of something. What's going on?"

"Nothing. I talked to Dylan earlier and I think we're gonna go to Shooters tonight and play some pool. You wanna come?"

"Yeah, that sounds good. What time?"

"Why don't you meet us at Dustin and Dylan's folks' place at seven?"

"All right, I'll see ya tonight." He hung up. He knew showing up tonight he could possibly run into Bellamy and he figured he'd have two choices. First, try to talk to her and apologize for something that happened six years ago or just pretend that nothing happened. Either way, he knew he was fucked.

***

The rest of the day was uneventful for Bellamy, which she didn't mind. When she got home she sat out on the deck by herself, reading and drinking a glass of lemonade her mom made for her before she left for work. She'd told her she only had a couple of classes to teach and then she'd be home to start dinner. Bellamy had insisted to her mom that she could start dinner, but Ruth had told her that she was on vacation and that she wanted to take care of her.

She must've dozed off because she felt someone pushing on her shoulder.

"Bell, wake up."

Bellamy smiled when she looked up into her brother Dylan's face. Dylan was so much different than his twin. Dylan could be very intense at times—maybe that's why he went into the Marine Corp. He was also very protective of her, especially after an accident that happened when she was just ten years old. At times she didn't mind, but sometimes it drove her batty. She reached up and fingered the scar beneath her hair line that ran from her temple to behind her ear.

"Hey, Dylan. What time is it?" She sat up and stretched.

"It's five o'clock and dinner's almost ready." He sat down in the lounge chair next to her. "So how ya doing, kid?"

"I'm good. Glad I was able to make it home to stay for a few weeks before you go." She couldn't help but frown. "I'm gonna miss you, Dyl. How long do you think you'll be gone?"

She watched his gaze soften as he looked at her. "A year at least. I'll be up for reenlistment when I get back, but I think I'm gonna be done after this."

"Really? I thought you were gonna stay in until you could retire."

"I was, but Dad and Pat are probably gonna retire in the next couple of years. So I thought I'd stay here and help Dustin and Luke run the business."

"It'll be nice to have you closer to home."

Bellamy got up from the lounger and turned to look out on the backyard.

"Bell, can I ask you something?"

"Sure, what do you want to know?"

"How come you haven't really been home much until now?" Bellamy's shoulders tensed and she turned her head away from him.

"I-I just have been extremely busy, that's all. I've come home for the holidays. Doesn't that count?"

"Yes, you've come home, but you split so fast it's like you weren't really here at all."

She turned to look at him, plastering on her best fake smile. "I know. I've just—I've just been really busy. You know I have lots of clients who depend on me to help them get into shape. Between my clients and the classes I teach, I work 9-10 hour days sometimes. What's with the twenty questions? I'm here, aren't I?" She tried to walk around him to get in the house, but he grabbed her and pulled her into a hug.

"Hey, I'm just glad you're here, okay? Don't get all defensive. I was just giving you crap. Now let's go eat, I'm starving."

Bellamy knew Dylan meant well, and it just made her feel guilty because she did high-tail it out of town as soon as she could when she came home. As they walked in the back door, Dustin was heading in the front. "Ahh...I see I'm right on time. Smells good, Momma." Bellamy watched as Dustin bent to kiss their mom on the cheek. He then walked around the table to hug his dad. "Hey, Pop, I know you saw the finished plans for the old Bartlett Plantation, I think it'll be great when we're done."

"Yeah, this will be our biggest and best restoration project we've done. Pat and I think this job is finally gonna get us some attention. I'm proud of you, Son. You boys have worked mighty hard at getting us this job and I know when I'm ready to retire you boys will do us proud."

Bellamy smiled when she noticed Dustin blushing. He was very laid back, but when something was important to him he gave it his all. Most people who met him always thought he was pretty boy that could get everything and every girl he wanted. Little did they know her brother had to work hard to get to where he was now. She took a moment to look around the table. It made her heart swell to be sitting with her family and enjoying her mom's delicious cooking.

They made small talk as they started passing the dishes around. When the fried chicken stopped in front of Bellamy, she couldn't contain the moan that escaped her lips. Her brothers both looked at her and started laughing hysterically. "What? It's been too long since I've had Momma's fried chicken. This looks delicious."

Ruth smiled as she watched her daughter fill her plate. "Well, eat up, honey. You're too skinny as it is."

"Momma, I'm a personal trainer. I have to keep in shape," Bellamy said as she started to dig in.

When dinner was done, Bellamy started clearing the table and loading the dishwasher. She was so stuffed she felt like she needed to lay down for a while. Dustin walked in carrying the rest of the dishes.

"Thanks," Bellamy said as she grabbed the bowls from Dustin.

"No problem. You look good, Bell, even if you are a stick," Dustin said with his signature smirk.

"Oh really? Check out these." She flexed her arm and laughed as her brother took in the muscles in Bellamy's arms.

"Geez, girl, you've got some guns on you."

"I've started weight training three times a week. It looks good if my clients see I work out as hard as I make them." She turned back around to finish loading the dishwasher. She smiled when she felt Dustin's arms come around her for a hug.

"I'm glad you're home, brat. I think we're gonna go have some beer and play pool. Do you wanna come with?"

Bellamy turned around, "Thanks, but I'm kind of beat, so I'm just gonna stay home tonight. Maybe this weekend we can go?"

"Definitely, but if you change your mind we're leaving in thirty, okay?"

"Okay." She kissed Dustin on the cheek as she made her way out of the kitchen. She grinned as she found her parents sitting together on the sofa. They had just celebrated their thirty-third wedding anniversary. She always counted herself lucky because so many kids she grew up with came from broken homes. She and her brothers' tight circle of friends were among the minority where their parents were still happily married. Bellamy wasn't delusional; she knew sometimes things were hard with her mom and dad, but for the most part things were good.

She tried to sneak by her parents, not wanting to interrupt them playing kissy-face with each other.

"Bellamy Ann, is the kitchen all cleaned up?" Ruth asked as she snuggled up to her husband.

"Yep, it's all done. Thanks again for a delicious dinner. If you need me I'll be in my room." She walked over kissing both of her parents before she ran up the stairs.

***

Ruth turned, and when she knew Bellamy was upstairs, she turned to Charlie. "I'm worried about her. I talked to Travis last week and he said that Bellamy hasn't been on one single date in the past few months. I know he didn't want to tell me, but he's worried about her. He says she works all of the time and that this is the first vacation she's really ever taken. Should we talk to her?"

"Honey, I know you're worried, but let's just see what happens when she's home these next couple of weeks before we jump the gun, okay? She's almost twenty-five years old. We have to trust that she's taking care of herself. Okay?"

"All right. It's just she's our baby and I can't help myself." Ruth never told Charlie about Bellamy and the baby—she had promised her daughter she wouldn't. Bellamy had slipped into such a bad depression after losing the baby and leaving the hospital without Rose. Ruth had never kept anything from Charlie, but she didn't think he would understand. She was afraid that Bellamy would never come to her again with anything if she betrayed her trust.

***

Charlie sometimes didn't understand why Ruth was always worrying about Bellamy, sure she was their baby and the only girl, but when she was home visiting, sometimes he'd catch Ruth staring at their little girl with such concern. Maybe it was just that mother/daughter bond that he had with their boys. All he knew was that his baby was home and if there was a problem they would figure it out soon enough.

***

Bellamy was sitting in front of her window reading a romance novel when she happened to look down and saw Luke standing there. He smiled at her and waved. For a second she didn't know what to do or how to react. Her nerves started going crazy and she had to concentrate to keep her hands from trembling. She slowly raised her hand to wave and gave him a half-smile. She pushed her window open further to talk to him.

"What are you doing here, Luke?"

"Your brothers and I are going to Shooter's. Do you want to go?"

She shook her head and stepped away from the window. Bellamy half-ran, half-stumbled into her bathroom, checking herself in the mirror. Her makeup had worn off, but she still looked okay. Bellamy ran her hand through her hair and quickly pulled it up into a loose bun. The whole way down the stairs she told herself that she was just gonna talk to him for a second and then go back in. The rational part of herself told her that she could be an adult about it, but the eighteen-year-old that she was once tried to rear her head into a desperate need to run. Bellamy opted for the grown-up approach, and as she walked towards the front door, she had to stop the butterflies that seemed to have taken up residence in her stomach.

***

Luke was standing at the bottom of the steps when Bellamy walked out of the house. One look at her and he had to remind himself not to stare and to breathe. She was wearing a white tank top that didn't hide the fact that she wasn't wearing a bra. She must've noticed him staring because she quickly wrapped her arms across her chest. Bellamy had on a pair of tiny pink knit shorts that made her legs look tanned and long. Her feet were bare with the exception of a tiny ring on the second toe of her right foot. She stopped at the top of the stairs, looking uncertain and chewing on her lip.

"How ya doing, Luke?" Bellamy finally said, her voice so quiet Luke had to strain to hear it.

"I'm good, Bell. You gonna come give me a hug or what?" He wanted to take it back as soon as he said it. The way her eyes widened made him think that maybe it was too much, too soon. Especially since he had yet to apologize for the way things went down back then, but he wanted to hold her.

***

Bellamy walked slowly down the stairs towards him and before she could say or do anything, his arms hesitantly wrapped around her. He looked like he'd just gotten out of the shower. His ash-blond hair had that, messy "I don't care" look. He smelled so good—like summer and soap was the only way she could describe it.

She felt his breath on her ear as he whispered, "God, Bell, you look great."

Bellamy hurried and stepped away from him. "Ah, thanks. I'll see ya around." She couldn't seem to get away from him fast enough. As she ran back into the house Bellamy sighed with relief as the door shut behind her.

***

He wasn't sure why he wouldn't let her go when she tried to pull away from him, but the minute she put her arms around him he didn't want to let her go ever. He shook his head and kept chanting "mistake" over and over in his head. Her brothers, especially Dylan, would blow a gasket if he tried to get involved with her. It was obvious though that she only spoke to him to be nice. It was clear that she remembered what had happened between them, and why wouldn't she?

Luke took her virginity and then all but kicked her out of his truck when he took her home. God, he had to get out of his own head. He needed a beer and he needed to get laid. Yeah, that was his problem. It had been awhile since he'd been with anyone. Maybe he just needed a casual hookup. No strings, just someone to scratch his itch and to help keep his mind off the one person he knew he could never have.

"Hey, man, what was up with my sister? You guys seemed kind of serious," Dustin said as he put his phone back in his pocket.

"Uh, nothing. Just saying hi. We ready to go?"

"Yeah, we're just waiting on Dylan."

Just as he finished talking, Dylan came bounding down the stairs. "You pussies ready to go?"

Dustin and Luke flipped him off as they walked towards Luke's truck. As he climbed in he saw Bellamy standing in her window. She gave him a slight wave and then walked away. Yeah, he definitely needed to find some action.

***

Bellamy was lying on her bed when her cell phone rang. She dug it out of her bag and flipped it open.

"Hello."

"Hey, my sexy best friend."

"Oh, Travis! Where are you? Are you in Charleston?"

"Yeah, we just got here about an hour ago. My mom says that next time we come you better be with us or we're not welcome." He was laughing as he said it. His mom, Gail, was a very sweet-natured woman who was very accepting of her son's lifestyle. Bellamy adored her. His dad, Tom, was just starting to come around over the past year, and he and Brad seemed to get along wonderfully.

"Tell Gail that I'll try to come see her before I head home. How's Brad? I figured he would've called me."

"He was going to, but mom put him to work as soon as we walked in the door. She thinks just because we're gay that we automatically cook."

"But don't you?" Bellamy said with a laugh.

"Yes, but geez, stereotype much? Seriously, though, I'm just glad Mom and Brad get along so well. But what I want to know is have you seen Luke?" She knew he was going to ask her.

"Yeah, I actually saw him about thirty minutes ago. Dammit, Travis, I want to know how I can still feel something when I look at him after he threw me out like I was some cheap slut. I know why he did what he did. He loves my brothers and didn't want to screw up their friendship, but it still hurt. Not to mention the fact that I'm going to have to tell him about Rose."

"Bell, honey. I know it wasn't easy for you to see him, but you have to let the past go. Yes, you will tell him about Rose, but just enjoy your time at home. Brad and I will be there Friday and we'll take you out dancing, and you can just forget about him for a while, okay?"

She wiped the tears that were starting to spill over. "Yeah, you're right. I'll see you guys Friday. I love you, Travis."

"I love you too, honey. We'll call when we're on our way. Bye."

"Bye." She closed her phone and sat back on her bed. She could do this; she could spend some quality time with her family and before she left she'd tell Luke about Rose. And let the chips fall where they may.

Chapter 3

The guys showed up at Shooter's and when they walked inside they were welcomed with the music blaring from the jukebox and cue sticks striking balls. While Dustin went to grab a pitcher of beer, Dylan and Luke went to meet their friends who were already there waiting. They all had remained friends with all of the guys they grew up with. Zach was sitting with their friend Bobby Adams, and Skeeter was flirting with a couple of girls who didn't even look old enough to be there. Luke just shook his head and sat down across from Zach.

"Hey, I thought you were meeting us at their place?" Luke mentioned as he motioned to Dylan who sat down in the chair next to him.

"Yeah, I was, but I got held up so I called Dustin and told him I'd just meet you guys here. So who wants pizza? It's my treat," Zach said, pulling out his wallet.

"Well, in that case, hell yeah, I want pizza," Dustin said as he sat down with a pitcher.

They placed their pizza order and went to the pool tables to play a few games before they ate.

Dylan and Zach played the first game while the others stood off to the side, talking.

"So, Luke, my Dad said he was really impressed with the plans we put together for the Bartlett project. Everything still a go for tomorrow?"

"Yeah, before I left today I arranged for the crew to meet us there to start gutting out the inside. They should be bringing the trucks over around two tomorrow so we can get rid of all the old stuff. They won't start bringing over supplies until next Monday, but that'll give us plenty of time to get most of the stuff cleared out."

"Work, work, work—is that all you guys talk about?" Skeeter asked as he came walking up.

"No, dickhead, it's not. What were you doing talking to that jailbait? What were they, sixteen?" Dustin asked with a smirk.

"For your information, they were twenty-two, but I'd rather talk to your sister. I heard she's back in town. From what I hear, she's smokin' hot."

Dylan turned to look at Skeeter, who winked at him. They were all aware of Dylan's protectiveness of his baby sister, and before he could say anything, Luke grabbed Skeeter by his shirt. "Don't you fucking talk about her. Stay the hell away from Bellamy."

"Whoa, man, relax, I was just talking shit." Skeeter swallowed hard. Luke watched Skeeter's eyes dart around to the others.

"Luke, back off, man," Dylan said, stepping in between them. "Skeeter, just cool it. You can just stay away from my sister. You got it?" Everyone knew that Skeeter wouldn't try anything with

Bellamy, but sometimes he needed to be reminded that she was off-limits.

"Yeah, I got it. Jesus, man, like I'd be stupid enough to try anything with her," Skeeter said as he backed away.

Dylan grabbed Luke and they walked away from the others. "What was that all about, man?"

"Dude, she's your little sister and he doesn't need to be hanging around her, that's all."

Dylan stared hard at him. He was worried that Dylan would see through his bullshit. The truth of the matter was that he wanted to be the one with her. Dammit—he really needed to quit thinking about her.

"All right, well—let's go play some pool," Dylan said as he slapped Luke on the back.

When they walked back over, Luke sucked it up and apologized to Skeeter. Luke knew he was harmless, but he just wanted it to be known that while she was back that he was to stay away from her. All that kept going through Luke's head was "mine." He was going to have to try harder to get her out of his head, but he had a feeling that it wasn't going to be easy. Especially knowing she was in town and after feeling her body pressed against his. He shook his head and slammed his beer.

Chapter 4

Bellamy got up early the next morning and thought she'd go for a run to clear her head. She had been restless all night, tossing and turning with dreams of Luke and of Rose going through her head. It had been a long time since she last dreamt of either one of them. Bellamy knew it was because she was there to get closure.

She shook her head to clear her mind, threw on a sports bra and her running shorts. Bellamy went into her bathroom to pull her hair back in a ponytail and brush her teeth. When she was done she headed downstairs and ran into her Dad getting ready to leave for work.

"Morning, Daddy. You're up early." She sat at the bottom of the steps putting on her running shoes.

"Yeah, darlin'. I'm meeting Patrick at the office to make sure everything is ready for the Bartlett renovation to start today. You going for a run?"

"Yep, I want to get it in before it gets too hot." She stood up kissing her dad on the cheek. "I'll see ya later, Daddy."

She grabbed her iPod and headed out of the door.

***

"Are you seriously gonna let her walk out of the house in that? She might as well run in her underwear," Dylan said, standing next to his dad as he scowled at the door.

"Son, I'm seriously not bothered by it, so why are you?"

Dylan shrugged his shoulders. "I see the way guys look at her. I just want her to be careful, that's all."

"Dylan, I know you feel like you have to protect your sister, but she's a grown woman you have to trust that she can take care of herself." With that he patted his son on the shoulder and strolled out the door.

***

Bellamy was already three miles into her run when she saw a truck drive by and start to slow down. She pulled out one of her ear buds just to be on the safe side. Bellamy slowed her pace when she heard the truck turn around. She felt herself begin to panic when she heard a door open and slam shut.

"Bell!" a voice called from behind.

She turned to see Luke walking towards her. Her pulse was already up from her run, but seeing him made it go up even more.

"H-Hey, Luke, what's up?" She felt her legs tremble as he got closer. He looked amazing. Again his hair was wet and disheveled, but it really worked on him. His green eyes seemed brighter in the sunlight. He was wearing a blue t-shirt with the company logo that fit snug across his broad shoulders. His body in the past six years had definitely become more lean and muscled. Luke's jeans were worn with the knees looking frayed and he was wearing a worn looking pair of steel-toed boots.

"I was just on my way to the office when I saw ya." He couldn't help but take in the sight of her. Her body had definitely changed in the last six years. It was obvious she took excellent care of herself. Her little sports bra and skintight shorts left little to the imagination. Bellamy's body was lean, but not overly muscled. It just proved that she worked out a lot. He couldn't help but stare as a drop of sweat rolled down between her breasts. Luke was just happy she didn't seem to notice him ogling her. "Do you have any plans later?"

"Ahh, no. Why, what's up?"

"Would you like to have lunch with me? I thought maybe we could go down to the Waterfront and then we could catch up." Was he really asking her out? He'd lost his damn mind. After the long talk he had with himself, he was doing the opposite of what he should've been doing. He could tell he made her nervous when he asked her. She wouldn't even make eye contact with him.

"Listen, Bell, its okay if you don't want to. I just thought it'd be nice to hang out."

He was relieved when she looked up at him and cracked a small smile. "No, it's fine. Lunch would be nice. What time do you want to meet?"

"Well, how about 12:30. Do you want me to come get you?"

"No, that's okay. I've got some stuff to do before I meet you."

"Okay, well, I'll see you later," Luke said as he started walking backwards toward his truck.

"Bye, Luke." He watched as she stuck her ear buds in and started walking away from him. He caught her turning to glance at him and with a small wave, she turned.

He watched her as she ran down the road. "God, she's got a rockin' body," he muttered to himself. He couldn't stop staring at the way her ass moved in those barely-there shorts. He felt himself get half aroused, and wanted to kick himself. As he walked back to the truck he tried to think of anything non-sexual to get his body to stop reacting to her. Maybe it wasn't smart to ask her to lunch, but he just wanted to clear the air. He wanted to apologize for hurting her. He had to make her understand why he acted the way he did. He turned his truck around and headed to the office. At least it was gonna be a busy morning, so he wouldn't sit and think about her, especially in front of Charlie and her brothers.

***

When Bellamy got back from her run she found a note from her mom saying she was heading to the studio and she'd see her that night for dinner. She smiled when she found Lola's cinnamon rolls waiting on the counter for her. She grabbed a plate out of the cupboard and put half of one on her plate. While she waited for it to warm up in the microwave, she grabbed a glass of juice. She stood at the counter while she ate, and savored every bite she took of the cinnamonny goodness. Lola was certainly a master in the kitchen.

Bellamy couldn't believe she told Luke that she'd have lunch with him. She shook her head. What could they possibly talk about? She knew she needed to apologize for her deception that night, but she wasn't ready to tell him about Rose yet. She didn't really need to tell him because their baby didn't make it. Telling him wouldn't change the outcome, but she knew it's the right thing to do. Bellamy had struggled with this decision for over five years. Would he want to know? Would he even care?

She put her plate and glass in the sink and went upstairs. It was only nine o'clock, so she decided that she'd relax and do some reading. Bellamy stripped out of her sports bra and shorts and quickly showered. Then, since she was alone, she just crawled into the bed naked. As she eased under the cool covers, her thoughts drifted to Luke. She could still see the way the sun was shining off his hair. She could smell that masculine scent of his body when she'd breathe deep.

Before she realized what she was doing she'd eased her hand slowly down her body, moaning as her fingers slid over her clit. She moved her fingers in tiny rhythmic circles. Her breath was coming out in short pants, her other hand slowly crept up to pinch and pull at her nipples. She slid her hand down to slit and found herself swollen and wet. She eased one finger inside of herself, thrusting it in and out. Bellamy could close her eyes and still feel the way it felt to have Luke inside of her; stretching her to the point of pain, but it felt so good. He was always the star of her fantasies. No matter how much Bellamy tried to think of others, the face she'd conjure up always turned back into Luke's.

Her hips lifted from the bed as she started thrusting them harder. Bellamy added another finger and took her hand from her breast and brought it down to her clit. She was writhing on the bed between the dual stimulation she was giving herself. Bellamy had become quite proficient at getting herself off quick. Granted, she always felt empty afterwards. In a matter of seconds her hips shot off the bed as her climax hit her hard and fast. She groaned low and deep in her throat as the pulsing caused her to start pumping her hips until the ripples started to slow. Bellamy could feel the walls of her pussy squeezing her fingers as she started to catch her breath. "Oh wow!" She panted as she lay there spent. She'd never come that hard before. She shook her head and rolled to her side to read her book.

***

Bellamy woke up after an hour, not even realizing that she had dozed off. She groaned as she got up and stretched. She got a pair of panties out of her drawer and went to her closet to find something to wear. She had brought several sundresses, so she decided on a baby blue one that was made of soft cotton. It had thin spaghetti straps, the bodice was form-fitting and the hem hit a few inches above her knees.

She pulled out her jewelry and grabbed the necklace from Luke. Bellamy stared at it and then made her decision. She grabbed TT and slid the necklace around his neck. She stared at it for a moment, then she laid him on her bed and went into her bathroom to freshen up. Bellamy thought about the lunch date as she brushed her teeth. She didn't know honestly how it was going to go, but a part of her was looking forward to it.

When Bellamy was done she moisturized her entire body. It was supposed to be extremely hot and humid, so she opted for just a little blush and lip-gloss. She styled her hair, tying her riotous curls back loosely. She slipped on a pair of white flip-flops and went downstairs.

When Bellamy looked at the clock it was only eleven, so she decided to head over to her mom's dance studio. Bellamy pulled up in front of the little dance studio that her mom started when her brothers were both still in diapers. It made her smile to remember all of the times she spent there as a girl and up until she went away to college.

Bellamy walked into the small studio, looking at all of the pictures on the walls. The first one she got close to was of her mom holding her brothers in front of the big window adorned with the words *Ruth's Dance Academy.* She couldn't believe how young her mom looked. Granted, she was only twenty-two when the boys were born. Her dad must've been taking the picture because he wasn't in the shot with her. As she scanned the photos, she saw all sorts of little girls, with the occasional boy, in various costumes. Bellamy felt her smile broaden when she saw a picture of her mom holding her. She couldn't have been more than a few weeks old. Her brothers were standing on each side of her and her mom smiling.

Ruth had told Bellamy she was a surprise. After the twins and starting the dance studio, they didn't plan on any more children. She glanced at more photos, laughing at one of her and her best friend Stacy in their little leotards and tutus. The one that caught her attention the most was one of Bellamy and her mom. They both had on black leotards, pink tights, and matching black leg warmers. It was amazing how much Bellamy resembled her mom, except for having her dad's blue eyes. They shared the same slender build, auburn hair and slightly turned up nose. Bellamy was around fifteen in that picture. They stood side by side with an arm around each other while Bellamy clutched a trophy in her hand.

Bellamy walked around the corner to find her mom standing in front of the mirrors doing different ballet poses. Bellamy had asked her once why she didn't try to dance professionally, but her mom simply said that it wasn't what she wanted. She wanted to get married, have a family, and teach.

Ruth glanced over and saw Bellamy standing there and smiled. "Hi, baby, what're you doing here?"

Bellamy walked in to hug her mom. "Hi, Momma I just thought I'd come visit you. Is that okay?"

"Of course, honey, I was just surprised to see you that's all. You look beautiful. What're your plans today?"

Bellamy didn't know if she should tell her mom about her lunch date with Luke, but then again, she didn't know that Luke was Rose's father. She'd probably just assume that they were just catching up since he missed lunch the day before. "Uh, I'm meeting Luke for lunch today."

Her mom smiled at her. "Oh, really? That's nice. Are your brothers going?"

"No, I don't think so. We're gonna get something to eat and catch up. So when's your class starting?" Bellamy was hoping that her mom didn't pick up on the quick subject change.

She had turned to look at the clock. "Oh, in about thirty minutes. Wait until you see this little group. There are only four little girls, all of them are three. They actually remind me a lot of when you and Stacy started. Which reminds me: have you heard from Stacy lately?"

Stacy and Bellamy had been best friends since they met in dance class. After the summer they graduated from high school they drifted apart, and didn't talk very often. She knew that Stacy was living in Chicago and was a photographer for a magazine there.

"No. I think the last time we talked was last year when she called me on my birthday. How are her mom and dad?"

"Well, Gary had a heart attack last week." Bellamy couldn't hide the fact she was worried. "He's okay, honey. Lola and I took some food over for Renèe this past weekend, but Gary was still in the hospital. Stacy is in town helping her mom get the house ready before he's released."

"Oh, wow. Maybe I should go over and see if they need any help."

"That's sweet, but why don't you let them be for right now while they get him home and settled."

"Yeah, maybe you're right. Once they get settled maybe I can go see them."

"That's probably a good idea. They've had a rough time."

Bellamy watched as her mom's little students started filing in. It brought back fond memories of all of the dance classes and performances she did growing up. Her mom never pushed her to do any of it. Bellamy was a stubborn child, and if she didn't want to do something, then no one could make her, but she loved dancing. Her mom wasn't a strict teacher, but she insisted that the moms of the students sit in the waiting area during the class. She said it helped prevent the kids from getting distracted. Bellamy sat quietly in the corner as her mom lined the little girls up and went through a very simple dance routine to the "Good Ship Lollipop." It was cute to sit and watch as they watched her mom with such an intense look in their eyes as she went through every little step.

She tried not to think about it, but Bellamy kept thinking about what it would've been like to have her mom teach her granddaughter all of the moves she was showing these four little girls. She swallowed the knot forming in her throat—she had to stop thinking about it. She'd started going to therapy six months after losing Rose. It had helped her a lot, but sometimes certain things would bring it back. Her therapist Maggie had told her that it wasn't unusual to have certain things set her off, but instead of holding them in, she had told her to cry, scream and yell if that helped get it out. Travis had been her rock through all of it. Now being home, being near Luke was causing some of her sadness to resurface. She just had to get through the next couple of weeks and then she'd go back to her life in Savannah.

Before she knew it, her mom's class was over and the mothers had all come in to get their kids. Ruth had walked them out, chatting with them. When she came back, she walked over to her daughter.

"Baby, are you okay? You seemed to be in your own world there for a little bit."

"I'm fine, Momma I was just thinking about stuff. Sorry I missed your class." Bellamy smiled at her mom and then pulled out her phone. "Oh, I better get going if I'm gonna meet Luke. I'll see you when you get home tonight. I love you."

Ruth grabbed her hugging her tight. "I love you, too. Your daddy's making steaks on the grill for dinner."

"All right, that sounds fantastic. See ya, Momma," Bellamy said as she walked out of the studio. She got into her car, put on her sunglasses and headed towards the Waterfront.

***

Luke glanced at his watch and saw that he had to leave in fifteen minutes for his lunch date with Bellamy. "It's not a lunch date," he kept telling himself. Who was he kidding? Luke was looking forward to seeing her. He knew if Dylan found out where he was going and who he was meeting he'd insist on joining him. Dylan's motive would be to make sure Luke didn't try anything with his little sister. If only Dylan knew that something did happen between them six years ago, and Luke wanted Bellamy to forgive him for how it ended.

Why was he still thinking about her, about that night? He couldn't help but think about when he'd finally stripped them both down and settled himself between her thighs. The look of innocence on her face as he bent down to kiss her. He couldn't take it and had quickly positioned himself and thrust into her with one stroke. He kissed her as she cried out and tensed under him. Luke stopped until he felt her body relax under his and she started kissing him harder. He started thrusting into her with slow measured strokes.

Luke reveled in the feel of her as she started contracting around him and moved his hand down between them, stroking her clit until she cried out his name as she started coming. He'd started pumping into her faster and harder until he felt the tingle shoot up from his balls straight to the tip of his cock. Luke had collapsed on her with both of them struggling to catch their breath. When he finally pulled out he had panicked when he saw the blood. He remembered demanding answers from her. Bellamy had a look of fear and humiliation on her face. He had quickly gotten dressed and told her to do the same.

"Luke?" He turned to see his Dad staring at him.

"What'd you need, Dad?" he asked.

"Nothing, son, you just seemed distracted, that's all. We're all going to lunch before we head over to the Bartlett Plantation. Do you wanna go?"

He shook his head. "Nah, I've got stuff to do. I'll just meet y'all over there in an hour or so."

"All right, we'll see you there," Patrick said as he left Luke's office.

After he heard them all leave, Luke went to the bathroom and splashed water on his face. He gave himself the once-over, finger-combing his hair. God, he was nervous thinking about the conversation he needed to have with her. Did he bring it up first thing or did he wait until they were leaving? All Luke knew is he didn't want Bellamy to feel bad about anything. The whole situation was his fault: he had no self-control that night. He'd freaked out on her because, even though she was a virgin, that had been the most intense sexual experience he'd had in his whole life. He was so fucked up about it and a part of him thought maybe that's why he reacted the way he did. Thinking back, that had caused most of the panic. He could deal with Dustin and Dylan, but he just couldn't deal with what he felt being inside her. Knowing she wanted him to be her first had humbled him when he thought about it now.

God, he didn't even use a rubber that night—he'd never done that. Luke was always in control; even when his teenage hormones were raging he never was stupid enough to sleep with someone without protecting them both. But with Bellamy he lost all of the control he thought he had. Thank god he didn't get her pregnant. That would've definitely killed his friendship with Dylan and Dustin. He jumped in his truck and started to head towards The Waterfront.

***

Bellamy decided to ask to be seated out on the patio. It was already hot, but under the umbrella it wasn't bad. The Waterfront was right on the Beaufort River and it was a sight to behold. She ordered water while she waited for Luke and took a deep breath, inhaling the flowery, fragrant aromas that tickled her senses.

Bellamy was nervous as hell waiting for Luke. She stared out at the river, watching several sail and motor boats go by. She smiled remembering when her brothers had saved up their money the summer before she turned twelve and bought a beat up old sailboat. Her parents had been adamant about her staying off that boat. Bellamy was a very good swimmer, but her parents worried about her, especially when it came to her being near water. With her parents at work, Bellamy took every opportunity she could to go off with her brothers.

At eighteen, they were great about taking Bellamy around with them. Their friends didn't seem to mind her tagging along, either. Now at twenty-four, she's pretty sure they'd tell her it was so they could pick up chicks. She probably looked like a fool staring out at the river smiling like an idiot.

"Bell?" Bellamy turned to see Luke standing there smiling at her. She couldn't help it when her stomach felt like it was doing flip-flops. She stood up when Luke walked around the table to hug her. Bellamy felt her breath catch when he pulled her close. Damn, he smelled good. She couldn't place it, but it was some sort of musk.

Bellamy pulled away. "Hey, Luke. How are you?"

The smile he gave her made her knees feel weak. "I'm good. You look amazing."

"Uh, thanks," she said with a bit of nervousness in her voice.

Luke held her chair as she sat back down. God, when he walked up and saw her staring out at the river with the smile on her face he couldn't help but just stand there and watch her. He couldn't believe how in six years she'd grown into a beautiful woman. She looked the same, but different. Yeah, this was definitely gonna be harder than he thought.

Their waitress came and took their drink orders. Bellamy decided on a glass of sweet tea and Luke ordered a Coke. When the waitress walked away, Luke looked at Bellamy intently. She must've sensed it because she looked up at him.

"Thanks for meeting for lunch today. So, do you have any big plans while you're in town?"

"Not really. I guess just relax and spend some time with Dylan." He saw her frown, but just as quick it was gone. "My mom has been pushing me to come home for an extended vacation for a long time, so this seemed like the right time. Your mom and dad look great. Lola made me a batch of her famous cinnamon rolls, so of course I had to eat one of those for breakfast today."

She was so cute. She always started rambling when she was nervous.

"Yeah, it's a wonder Jason and I didn't become obese having a mom who can bake like she does. What'd you think of your mom's new car? I still can't believe Dustin talked her into a Charger."

"I know, it's weird seeing my mom in anything other than that blue minivan that she drove forever, but I guess she's not really driving around kids anymore. Daddy made it sound like Momma's got a lead foot."

"Yeah, your mom's gotten several speeding tickets in the past six months. Your dad threatened to take the car away from her, but you know how she is; she's stubborn and told him that if he took her car away he'd be sleeping on the couch." Luke smiled when he watched Bellamy cover her mouth to stifle the laugh that burst out of her mouth.

"Oh, my god! I'd just love to see Daddy try to take that car from her." The waitress had brought their drinks and quickly took their orders. "So why didn't Daddy try to kill Dustin since he's the one who convinced her to get that car?" she said, trying to hold back her laughter.

"Well, Dylan and I wondered the same thing, but you know Dustin—he missed his calling as a car salesman. Somehow he convinced her that she needed that Charger. I think at first it was so he could drive it, but your mom is too smart for that and won't let anyone touch it."

The more they sat and talked, Bellamy felt herself relax little by little. Before the night that everything changed, they would sit and talk all of the time. When she was younger Luke would come for sleepovers with the boys and he'd always bring her a rose from his mom's garden. They were Bellamy's favorite, and as time went on the little crush she had on Luke turned into love, or at least what she thought love was. She knew at times he felt something towards her, especially as she got older. She'd catch him several times just staring at her. She wasn't sure what she saw in his eyes, but it would make her heart start pounding in her chest.

They both smiled when the waitress brought out their food. Bellamy couldn't help but stare at the burger and sweet potato fries Luke had ordered, they smelled delicious. She looked down at the turkey wrap she ordered for herself and wished she would've gotten something like his, but she knew her mom would be all about feeding her, and since she couldn't workout like she did at home, she'd have to be careful.

"So how's the business? Patrick and Daddy said that you and Dustin are doing a fantastic job?" she said as she picked up her wrap to take a bite.

"It's going really good. I don't know if your dad or Dustin have told you, but we begin renovations on the Bartlett Plantation today."

"I've always loved that property. Gosh, I remember walking around it when I was younger. It definitely has potential to be beautiful like the pictures I've seen of it. You guys must be thrilled."

"Yeah, we are. This is pretty much Dustin's and my baby. Charlie and my dad have handed off the reins, so to speak." Bellamy could tell this job really mattered to him.

"Well, I'm sure they're going to be so proud of you guys when it's all done. I know I can't wait to see what your plans are." She took a sip of her tea.

"Why don't you stop by to see it? We're gonna be gutting it for the next week, but you can come take a look around the inside today if you want."

"Yeah, okay. Maybe I will. Can I try one of your fries? They just keep looking at me," Bellamy said with a teasing smile.

"Here you go. Eat as many as you want." He passed her the basket and watched as she grabbed a few fries.

"Mmm. These are so good." She moaned as she slipped a fry in her mouth. Bellamy took the last sip of her tea and then grabbed her glass of water.

Oh, Jesus, he felt himself get half-aroused watching her eat those fries. It didn't help when she started moaning as she was slipping them into her mouth. He couldn't be mad; she didn't realize what she was doing to him. It was apparent he was a guy who got turned on by someone eating.

Their waitress came with the check and to clear the plates. Luke grabbed the check and pulled out his wallet.

"Luke, how much do I owe you?" Bellamy asked him as she pulled her wallet out of her purse.

"Bell, I asked you to lunch, so it's my treat, okay?"

She put her wallet away. "Thanks. I've had a nice time."

Luke got up from his seat and came around holding out his hand to Bellamy. "You're welcome. Now let's go for a walk down to the river.

Bellamy slipped her hand in his as he helped her up. She tried to pull her hand away from his, but he just held on tighter. Neither of them said anything at first until they reached a path that led out to one of the piers. When they reached the end, Bellamy stared out across the water. It was a hot day, but there was a wonderful breeze coming off the river. The wind whipped Bellamy's ponytail around as she became lost in thought. She didn't know where she and Luke would go from here, but after Bellamy talked to him about Rose, she'd probably have her answer. She felt him staring; she slowly turned her head to look at him. Neither of them said anything.

Bellamy felt her heart hammering away in her chest. *God, he's beautiful*, she thought to herself. The way the sun was reflecting off of his hair, his green eyes looked so clear and he was covered in light stubble, like maybe he decided not to shave this morning. Before she had a chance to react, Luke stepped towards her.

Luke lifted his hand and brushed some of Bellamy's hair back that came loose from her ponytail. Her hair felt so soft beneath his fingers as he tucked the loose strands behind her ear. He let his hand slip behind her neck, holding her in place as he lowered his mouth to hers. Luke touched her hesitantly with his lips at first, but when he felt her body start to lean into his, he deepened the kiss. Her lips were as soft as he remembered them. Luke felt Bellamy's hands touch his chest, grabbing the material of his shirt.

Bellamy couldn't believe that he was kissing her. She loved the feel of his lips against hers at first, but then everything came back to her and she knew that it was a mistake. They had too much history for this to be happening now. She came to her senses and pushed him away. "Luke, stop!" She stepped back from him, breathing hard.

Luke looked at her with confusion, and then turned away. "Bellamy, I'm sorry, I don't know what came over me," he said as he turned back to face her. "Really—this isn't why I asked you to lunch. It's just we never really had a chance to talk about what happened between us, and I just didn't want you avoiding me anymore. You don't know how bad I feel about the way I treated you, but you have to understand your brothers are my best friends and, hell, I'm closer to them than my own brother. If they knew what I did they'd kill me for sure. You know how protective they are of you."

Bellamy's mind was reeling. What could she say to that? And this definitely wasn't the time or place to tell him about their daughter, but she did have things that maybe she should say.

"Listen: I understand why you did what you did. I know how important Dustin and Dylan are to you. I'll admit it wasn't the way I'd envisioned myself losing my virginity, but that's in the past and what feelings I have for you…"

"Feelings you have?" His eyes went wide.

"I-I meant had. Jesus, I've gotta go. Um, thanks for lunch." She turned and ran down the pier.

"Bellamy, don't go!" He called after her, but she just kept going. He caught up with her as she was getting in her car. "Bellamy, wait, please don't leave—talk to me."

She rolled down her window. "Luke, it's nothing, okay? I just—I just mixed up my words. You just caught me off guard. I've gotta go." She rolled up her window and knew he stood there watching as she drove away.

Luke got in his truck and shook his head. Why the hell did he kiss her? All that did was make him want more, and did she still have feelings for him? He knew when she was younger she had a crush on him, but did she feel more, and does she still?

Chapter 5

Bellamy got back to her parents' house thankful they were working. She didn't want to deal with anyone right now. She walked upstairs to her room, flopping down on her bed. Why did he have to bring it up? She absently rubbed her hand over her stomach. God, she remembered the first time she felt those tiny flutters, and then when they became hard kicks and rolls, but then she remembered when they suddenly stopped. She needed to stop thinking about it. "Why did I agree to see him?" she whispered to herself.

She rubbed her palms over her eyes trying to stop the tears before they spilled over. Bellamy had had enough. She was tired of getting like this. This was all part of her moving on with her life and she needed to start now. She jumped up from the bed and grabbed a pair of running shorts and a sports bra. Bellamy decided she was just going to run and run until her mind was rid of all the thoughts going through her head. She quickly changed, threw on her shoes, and ran out of the house.

***

Luke showed up at the Bartlett Plantation ready to get started, and he wanted anything to take his mind off the way lunch had gone with Bellamy. He still could've kicked himself for kissing her, because now he wanted more and he knew he couldn't have it—at least not with her. It'd be too complicated.

When he climbed out of his truck he noticed workers everywhere. They'd hired extra help so they could gut the place quicker. Their goal was to begin the renovations the following week. He climbed up the stairs and walked down the wraparound porch finding his Dad and Charlie towards the back of the house.

"Hey, guys. What'd I miss?"

"Where ya been, son?" Patrick asked.

He looked at Charlie and then back at his Dad. "I-uh, was having lunch with Bellamy."

Both men arched an eyebrow and looked at each other. "Well, you know that little girl of mine used to follow you around like a lost puppy. I swear Ruth used to say that she would've rather had another set of twins like the boys than have another little spitfire like Bellamy was."

Patrick's body shook with laughter as they listened to Charlie. "You know, I think you're right. I love that girl like she was my own, but she sure was a handful. But what did you expect being around boys all of the time, especially this one," he said pointing at Luke. "If he would've told her to jump in the river she would've done it without batting an eyelash. Did you guys have a nice time?"

"Yeah, we did. It was nice to catch up with her since I really haven't seen her too much when she's been home before. Well, I'm gonna leave you boys to do whatever you're doing. I'm gonna go find Dustin and see what's being done." He walked away, thankful his dad didn't start questioning him anymore than he had.

Luke walked in the house and found Dustin and Dylan looking over the plans. They both looked up when they saw Luke approach.

"Hey, guys, how's it going?"

"It's going," Dustin said. "I was just showing Dylan all of the plans we have for this place."

"So what do you think, Dylan? It's gonna be pretty amazing when we're done, don'tcha think?"

"Yeah, I'd say so. So what are the owners gonna do with this place when you guys finish?"

"I think they said they were gonna sell it. They're an elderly couple and I think they're moving to Florida, so they want to sell it and be done with it. What time is the dump truck gonna be here?" Luke asked as he walked around the dining room.

Dustin looked at his watch. "They should be here in about thirty minutes or so."

"Good. I'm gonna go ahead and help the guys upstairs." Luke said as he started walking away.

"We'll be up in a minute," Dustin called out to him. He turned to his brother. "I wonder where he was. He seems distracted."

"Yeah, I noticed that, too. Maybe it's female troubles," Dylan said with a shrug.

"Yeah, maybe. Let's get this party started," Dustin said as they started heading up the stairs.

***

Bellamy felt her head clearing, finally. After running five miles, she realized she was near the Bartlett Plantation. She knew she should just keep going because Luke was there, but so were her dad and brothers. Bellamy started to jog down the road leading to the plantation, taking in the lane lined with elm trees and rhododendrons. It was such gorgeous landscape and the smells were wonderful. She decided to cut through the trees to get to the house quicker. She kept jogging as Lady Gaga was pumping through her ear buds. When she reached the winding driveway, she slowed her pace to a brisk walk, looking around at all the greenery that surrounded the driveway. *Wow it's really gonna be gorgeous when they're done,* she thought. As Bellamy came up on the house, she stopped to admire it. It was smaller than a lot of the other plantations, but it was still just as extraordinary. It was two levels: the first was several feet off the ground with winding stairs that led up to a huge wraparound porch. It had French doors at the front with several long skinny windows. She glanced to the side and saw Patrick, Luke, Dustin, Dylan and her dad all coming out of the front doors.

They all stopped when they saw her. Her dad's smile dropped all of sudden as Luke, Dustin and Dylan all came rushing down the stairs, waving their arms and yelling. She stopped, pulling her ear buds out hearing them yell for her to move. It was then she heard the beeping and turned to see a huge dump truck backing up right at her. Her body froze; she couldn't get her brain and legs to function together. All of a sudden it felt like she was flying through the air, and when she hit the ground a heavy body was wrapped around her.

"Bell, are you okay?" She shook her head and looked into Luke's eyes.

"Yeah, I think so. What the hell happened?" Before Luke could answer her the place erupted in chaos. Dylan and Dustin were yelling at the truck driver and Charlie and Patrick ran over to help her and Luke off the ground.

Charlie had pulled Bellamy away from Luke and into his arms. "Jesus, baby girl, are you okay? Do you have any idea how scared I was when I saw that truck backing up right towards you? Your Momma would've killed me if I let anything happen to you."

"Daddy, I-I'm okay. Just a little shaken up is all." She snuggled up closer to her Dad because she was afraid her legs would give out if she let go.

"Bellamy, I swear you'll do anything for attention," Dylan said as he came over and pulled her into a hug.

"Oh, you know me. I just love to make an entrance." She laughed against his shoulder. Bellamy pulled away from Dylan as Dustin wrapped an arm around her shoulders.

"Luke, are you okay?" she asked as she patted her brother on the arm and walked towards Luke and Patrick. She noticed blood running down his arm.

"Yeah, Bell, I'm fine; it's just a nice scrape. How are you?"

"I can tell already I'm gonna be sore tomorrow. Thanks, though. It probably would've hurt a lot more if the truck hit me instead."

Patrick started laughing and wrapped his arms around her. "Well, honey, I think you took ten years from my life, but I'm glad you weren't hurt. How did you get here?"

"I was running and I wound up near here, so I thought I'd stop by to see the place before you guys start." She paused as she wiped some gravel from the back of her shorts. "I think I'm just gonna head back to the house. I think I just want to go soak in the tub for a bit." She walked over to kiss her dad on the cheek. "Bye, Daddy, I'll see you tonight. Bye, boys. Bye, Patrick." She waved to them as she turned and started walking back down the driveway. She didn't get very far before Dylan was beside her grabbing her arm.

"Come on, I'll drive you home."

She turned to look at him and saw the others all standing there gawking at her. "I'm fine. I don't need a ride." She said it loud enough for all of them to hear her. Bellamy could hear Patrick's barky sounding laugh.

"Oh, Charlie, your girl is stubborn."

"Yep, just like her momma. Luke, will you please give my stubborn daughter a ride home? I'm afraid if Dylan drives her home she may kill him," Charlie said with a laugh.

"Yes, sir. I'll get her home." Luke walked over and jumped into his truck. Bellamy was at the end of the driveway by the time the guys let Luke leave. Luke noticed she was limping a little. He just had to do what he did. When he saw that truck heading right towards her, he, along with everyone else, panicked. Luckily he was faster than the others. Otherwise it could've been a lot worse. Air tackling her seemed to be his only option to get her out of the way quick.

"Bell!"

She turned to see Luke pulling up beside her. "What do you want?"

"Your dad asked me to give you a ride home. Get in the truck."

Bellamy shrugged and walked around, climbing in. "Thanks. My hip is bothering me a little."

"Yeah, I noticed you were limping. Sorry about tackling you. I just didn't know a quicker way to get you out of the way of the truck," Luke said as he glanced over at her. His eyes followed to where she was rubbing her hip bone. "Are you gonna be okay?"

"Yeah, nothing a hot soak in the tub won't cure," she said with a slight smile.

That was not the image he needed right now. Bellamy naked lying in the bathtub, he shook his head trying to get the image out of his head.

Before Luke knew it he was pulling into her parents' driveway. Luke had pulled his truck up to the walkway so Bellamy could slide right out onto the path up to the door.

"Do you want some help?"

Bellamy turned towards him. "Nope, I'm good. Thanks for the ride." He watched as she slid out of the truck and crumbled to the ground.

"Shit!" he shouted as he jumped out to help Bellamy up. He watched as she tried to get up; shaking his head he came up and scooped her up in his arms. She squirmed, but he held her tighter. "Quit fighting me, Bellamy Ann. Do you have to make this difficult?" he said as he carried her towards the house.

"I'm not trying to be difficult. I can just take care of myself." She had no choice but to put her arms around his neck, bringing her face close to his. God, he smelled good. It was still the same musk scent that she could smell earlier mixed with a little sweat. Bellamy knew she needed to get a grip.

"Where's the key to the door?"

"Um, it's in a little pocket on the inside of my— my shorts." She looked straight ahead, keeping herself from looking at him.

"Okay, here's what were gonna do; I'm gonna put you down, but I want you to hold on to me and I'll get the key out. Is it in the front or the back?"

"The back," she croaked, her cheeks heating up with embarrassment.

"Um, okay. Here, let's put you down." He lowered her until her feet touched the ground. Luke kept his arms around her waist just in case she went down again. "How ya doing?"

Bellamy looked into his eyes, willing herself to look away. "I-I'm fine…I think. It's just sore." She held on to him as he turned her towards the door.

"Now I want you to grab on to the frame. Which side is the pocket on?"

"It's on the right side," she whispered.

Luke could tell she was trying to keep the weight off her left hip. He grabbed her hips. Holding her steady, grabbing the top of her shorts and pulling them down just a bit until he saw the hidden zipper. Luke told himself not to look, but he couldn't help it. Her body was lean muscle and he sucked in a breath when his fingers made contact with the smooth skin of her ass. It took him a few seconds, but Luke snapped out of it quickly and pulled the key out. He slipped it in the lock and opened the door for Bellamy.

Oh god! When she felt his hand come in contact with her skin she about melted into a puddle right on the floor. He was standing so close to her now she could feel his warm breath on her neck. It caused goose bumps to raise all of her skin. Bellamy hobbled through the doorway and turned to look at Luke. "Thanks for helping me home."

"You're welcome." She watched him turned to walk away, but he turned back around. "Bellamy?"

"Yeah."

"Can I take you out Friday night, maybe dinner, and we can maybe go see a movie or something?"

Bellamy didn't know what to say at first. She stood there chewing on her lower lip, which was a bad habit she had tried to break a long time ago. "Um—I'd like to, but I have plans Friday night. Maybe Saturday?"

Luke stood there not saying anything for a few seconds. "Saturday it is. I'll call you later to make plans."

She smiled at him with a hint of shyness. "That sounds good. Bye, Luke."

Bellamy shut the door, leaning against it trying to gather her wits. "I must be a masochist. I think I need my head examined," Bellamy muttered as she limped upstairs. She went into her bathroom and started running her bath water. As the tub was filling, Bellamy went into her room to strip out of her clothes. She examined her hip in the mirror and noticed some small scratches, but couldn't see any bruising yet.

Bellamy limped into the bathroom, slipping into the hot water and shutting the faucet off. She settled into the tub, letting her body relax. Now if only she could get her mind to shut off. She just wanted to know why she said yes to a date. Was it a date? Maybe he just wanted to make it up to her. She shouldn't even care, but she did. She never stopped loving him even though he didn't love her. Bellamy knew she was walking on a slippery slope with Luke. Maybe she just had to see if those feelings she had were the real thing or just some school girl crush.

Bellamy just had to make sure she protected her heart because Luke broke it once already, and after losing Rose, she wasn't sure it ever totally healed.

***

The whole drive back to the jobsite Luke kept trying to get his shit together. He would've been fine, but as soon as he held Bellamy in his arms he was overcome with desire so strong that had she not been hurt it's possible he would've fucked her right there on her parents' porch. What made it worse was getting that damn key out of the pocket on the inside of her skintight shorts. The feel of her skin—even just that brief touch—caused him to become half-aroused. Luke was just glad that by then she was standing with her back to him.

Bellamy had always had a nice body from all of her years dancing, but now it was firm and tight. "Jesus. I need to get a grip," he muttered to himself as he pulled back into the Bartlett Plantation. The last thing he needed was for Bell's dad and brothers to see him with an erection. Luke climbed out of his truck and found Charlie and his dad carrying some plaster out to the dump truck.

"Hey Dad, hey Charlie. How's it going?"

"It's going good, son just trying to get things moving along. Did you get Bellamy home all right?"

"Yeah, but her hip was giving her trouble. I had to carry her to the house. She said she was gonna soak in the tub for a while to see if that helped. Is there anything that I can do here?"

Charlie came over and patted Luke on the back. "You're a good man, Luke, getting my girl home. You'd be doing me a real big favor by going back over to our place and keeping an eye on her until Ruth gets home."

"Um…okay, but what about Dustin or Dylan?" Luke said, trying to hide the fact that being alone with Bellamy could be a big mistake.

"I know, Luke, but if either one of them show up she's gonna be all in a tizzy thinking they hover and drive her nuts. It's not a problem, is it?" Charlie said with a questioning glance.

"No. No problem, Charlie. I'll make sure she has everything she needs until Ruth gets home," Luke said starting to walk to his truck.

"Thanks, Luke. I owe ya one. Don't forget we're having steaks on the grill and Ruth's making her homemade fries, so be prepared to feast," Charlie hollered.

As Luke was driving back to Bellamy's, he gave himself a pep talk that he was simply there to make sure she was okay, and to get her anything that she needed. He would not touch her for any reason. Why did Charlie have to ask him to do this? Why did he say yes? Luke was going to have to work on his self-control. He wasn't expecting to have this sort of reaction to her seeing her again. He pulled into the driveway telling himself, "don't touch her, just don't touch her" over and over. Now if he could just make himself get out of the truck.

***

After the bath, Bellamy felt somewhat better. Her hip was still really sore, but at least she could bear weight on her leg. Bellamy managed to blow dry her hair, pull it up in a chignon and moisturize her body. She dressed in a pair of purple cotton shorts and a black racer back tank top. Bellamy decided to go downstairs and see if she could find an ice pack in the freezer, Bellamy was sure she would. Her mom seemed to always have everything that they ever needed. She scrounged through the freezer and didn't find anything. "Well, shit," she muttered. Bellamy was just getting ready to make herself an ice pack when she heard the front door open.

"Bell?"

"Luke? Is that you?" *Oh god, what is he doing here,* she thought. She quickly checked herself over in the toaster when he came walking in.

"Hey," was all he could say when he walked in the kitchen and found Bellamy leaning on the counte,r getting an extremely prime view of her legs and ass.

"Um, what are you doing here? Aren't you supposed to be working?" Bellamy said as she slowly walked to the refrigerator. She winced as she opened the freezer, reaching for the ice.

"Here, let me help you. I'm here because your dad thought it was safer to send me than one of your brothers." She gave him a quizzical look.

"He was worried about you." Luke gave her a devilish smile when she rolled her eyes.

"I swear they're going to continue to treat me like a little girl until I'm fifty." Bellamy went over to the cupboard trying to get a baggie down. Luke came up behind her and grabbed it for her. "Thanks."

"Is it so wrong that they love you and want to make sure you're taken care of? Face it, Bell, we all look out for you. It's just the way it's always been. I'm sure there are worse things you could be dealing with than having a family who loves you and watches out for you." He grabbed her by the elbow. "Come on, let's get you settled in the living room."

God, it felt right taking care of her like this. Luke shook his head—he must've really wanted his ass kicked by his best friend. Dustin, he had a feeling, would be fine with any sort of relationship between him and Bellamy. Dylan, on the other hand, would be difficult, and he couldn't blame him. After that summer with Bellamy's accident, Dylan had turned super protective of her. Not that he couldn't blame him. Luke could still sometimes see her in his mind when he and Dustin found her floating face down in the pool. When Dustin had pulled her out, they were both sure she was dead, and when Dustin had resuscitated her and she started coming around, Bellamy had reached for Luke.

Now here she was, this beautiful woman, and they were alone.

Luke helped Bellamy to the couch and handed her the homemade ice pack. It felt so nice to have him taking care of her. Bellamy had become very independent in the last six years. Moving away from home and having to rely on her own strength to get through the mess that her life had become had been important to her. Luke was always her weakness, even when he didn't even realize it.

Bellamy laid on her good side on the couch while Luke settled in her dad's recliner.

"Luke, you really don't need to stay. I'm settled here and Momma should be home in a couple of hours," Bellamy said as she eased her head onto one her mom's pillows.

Luke looked at her with a smirk. "Bell, your dad asked me to come stay with you, so I have no intention of leaving. Your dad also promised me a steak dinner. So, sorry darlin', but I'm staying."

"Fine. Do you want the remote?" she asked, holding it out to him.

"You can pick something to watch as long as it's not some girly shit," Luke said with a smirk.

Bellamy turned on the TV and started looking through the guide, stopping at one of the movie channels. She smiled when she saw *The Fast and the Furious* was on. "Do you remember when you and my brothers took me to go see this?" She asked as she turned it on.

***

Luke smiled: of course he remembered. Ruth and Charlie had made them take her and her best friend Stacy to see it. It was the summer before her sophomore year in high school. They'd been home from their first year in college and Dylan had been home for his first leave from the Marines. In the theater, Bellamy and Stacy had sat a row in front of them, and he kept catching himself watching her. Bellamy was always flipping her hair behind her shoulders and looking behind herself at them, smiling. It was the first time he realized that she wasn't a little girl anymore and started seeing her as a young woman. He really needed his head examined.

"Yeah, I remember taking you. After it was over, all you talked about was how hot Paul Walker was," Luke said with a laugh.

"Well, he was and he still is. You know, when I was younger I always thought you looked like him—except taller, of course." Oh God, did she really just say that? Bellamy hid her head, trying to hide her embarrassment from Luke.

"So, Paul Walker, huh? I'm kind of flattered, Bell." He smirked.

"Oh, geez, just drop it. Better yet, why don't you go ahead and leav… Oh ow." Bellamy exclaimed gripping her hip.

"What is it?" Luke asked, crouching down in front of her.

"I-It's just, I moved it wrong, but it hurts like a bitch," Bellamy seethed as she tried to ice it down.

"Here, lift your head," Luke told her as he sat on the couch. He put the pillow in his lap. "All right, lay your head back down," he said as he moved his hand down and held the icepack over the area. She tensed up for a moment before she let herself relax. "Is this helping?"

"Um, yes," she whispered. Bellamy felt a warm wave travel through her body as she tried to focus on the movie. After a few minutes, the pain was going away.

Neither on them said a word as they both sat there watching the movie. It was such an intimate moment between them. Bellamy felt like she was being tortured, she had so many emotions running through her. This was how she had always hoped their life would've been, but Luke had made it clear that he never would've hurt her brothers like that. For now, she'd enjoy this moment because she knew that it'd be over soon and she'd be alone again.

Bellamy had tried dating after she lost the baby, but it wasn't easy. Every time her dates would try to get physical with her, she'd freeze up and they usually never called her again. Travis had tried to help her deal with it, but he couldn't totally understand what she was going through. Her therapist had told her the reason the dates had never gone well was probably because Bellamy still had feelings for Luke. Whether Luke knew it or not, they were forever tied together because of the daughter they had lost. Maggie had suggested Bellamy come home and tell him about their daughter and that it would give Bellamy some closure.

Now, laying there with her head in Luke's lap felt so right to Bellamy, she realized that the only way she could move on was to give it one more try with Luke. Bellamy was going to have to get past his defenses when it came to her brothers, and if nothing happened, then she'd know she did all she could.

Luke was in hell. Having Bellamy lay with her head in his lap was pure torture. He could smell the scent of her shampoo—it was some sort of floral scent that kept wafting into his senses. Luke tried to pay attention to the movie, but he kept catching himself looking down at her. He could see that her eyes were starting to flutter shut. *Thank god*, he thought.

Once she was out, he could slip off of the couch and sit on the other side of the room. Far away from her, he could feel his self-proclaimed self-control slipping rapidly. Bellamy was hurt, but did that stop his erection from throbbing inside of his pants? Hell no, it didn't. Luke leaned back further into the couch and felt himself start to get sleepy too. He could hear Bellamy's soft even breathing and it started to lull him to sleep.

***

Ruth had been so worried when Charlie had told her what'd happened to Bellamy at the jobsite. She had wanted to cancel her classes to come home and take care of her, but Charlie had insisted that Bellamy was fine and that he'd sent Luke to look after her. That had seemed to relax Ruth. On her way home from the studio, she called Lola and told her what happened and to calm her own nerves. Lola had told her she'd bring one of Bellamy's favorite desserts, cheesecake with strawberries. Ruth had hung up with Lola as she pulled into the driveway.

When Ruth walked into the house she froze, Bellamy and Luke were both asleep. She walked around to stand in front of the couch. Bellamy was lying down with her head in Luke's lap. Luke had pillowed his head on the back cushion with his hand resting on Bellamy's hip. Ruth stood there trying to decide if she should wake them or not, but Bellamy's eyes started to flutter open.

Bellamy looked embarrassed. When she tried to sit up, Luke's hand on her hip kept her from doing so. "Hi, Momma. Did you just get home?"

Ruth smiled at her daughter. "Yes, baby, I did. Your daddy told me what happened today. Are you okay?"

"Yes, Momma, I'm fine. It's a little tender where I hit the ground, but considering the alternative, I'll take a sore hip." Bellamy leaned up, pushing on Luke. "Hey, wake up, sleepy."

Luke came awake quickly, looking confused. "Hi, Ruth. Sorry I fell asleep," he said, looking sheepish.

"Oh, honey, after what you did today you can do whatever you want," she said as she bent, kissing him on the forehead.

"Well, you know—I've always been faster than Dustin and Dylan. I'm just glad she's okay," Luke said as he gave Bellamy a quick glance. Luke got off the couch and then reached down, helping Bellamy stand up. She put her full weight down and let out a sigh of relief.

"Oh, thank you. It's definitely feeling better," Bellamy said as she walked over, giving her mom a hug. "So Momma, I hear you're making homemade fries tonight."

"You bet, darlin', and I just talked to Lola; she's bringing one of your favorite desserts," Ruth said as the three of them walked to the kitchen. "Luke, honey, would you like a beer?"

Luke sat down at the table next to Bellamy. "Yes, please."

Ruth went to the refrigerator and pulled out a bottle of Fat Tire for Luke. She twisted off the cap and brought it to him. "Here you go. Bell, do you want something to drink? I have your favorite wine."

"Yes, ma'am."

Once they all had their drinks the three of them settled around the table. Luke and Bellamy had given her the whole story on what happened, just in case Charlie left anything out. Ruth could only shake her head, grabbing her daughter's hand and squeezing it tight. "I swear, Bellamy Ann, you get yourself in more trouble than either one of those boys."

"Oh, Momma, I do not. I can't help it—I'm prone to unfortunate mishaps." She paused, taking a sip of her Pinot Grigio, letting the fruity flavor please her palate. "You know I don't go looking for trouble, it just seems to find me," she said, pretending to pout.

"Oh, don't listen to your mom, the boys and I managed to get ourselves into our share of predicaments, but we were smart enough not to let anyone else find out." Bellamy looked at him and stuck out her tongue.

"Well, Luke, would you care to share with me some of these predicaments?" Bellamy watched her mom give him that stern, motherly look she used to scare the pants off the boys.

"Just keep your mouth shut," Dylan warned with a smile as he came walking into the kitchen. He bent down to kiss his mom on the cheek and surprised Bellamy by doing the same to her. Luke got a punch in the arm. "Jesus, dude, that fu—I mean, that freakin' hurt," Luke said as he grabbed his arm and feigned pain.

Chapter 6

Bellamy smiled at the chatter that was all around her. Lola and Ruth were slicing potatoes and the men were grabbing the beers and steaks and heading out to the deck so Charlie could fire up the grill. She continued to sip her wine while her mom and Lola prepared the fries. "Momma, please let me help you. I don't like to feel useless."

"Baby, you just sit and relax, we've got it all under control. Don't we, Lola?"

"Of course we do, Bell. Did you see what I brought for dessert?" Lola said, smiling at Bellamy.

"Cheesecake with strawberries, it's one of my favorites. So how's business, Lola?" She asked.

"It's real good, darlin'. You know how it is during the summer. It's my busiest time of year next to Thanksgiving and Christmas. How about you, honey? How's the personal training business?"

"It's good. I've been supplementing my income by teaching some aerobic classes at the gym, too. Hey, maybe one day you and Mom can come down to the studio and I can put you two through one of my most popular classes. It's called Stripped and it combines dance with well, uh—some strip-tease moves."

She laughed when Lola and Ruth both stopped and looked at her. "Seriously, it's a fun class, and before you ask, no—there is no removing of your clothes. My classes are always packed on the nights I teach it. Of course no men allowed, but trust me, you'll love it."

"Well, sign me up," Ruth said with a huge smile.

"Sounds like fun. I'm in, too," Lola said, bumping her hip into Ruth. "I think it'd shock the hell out of Pat and Charlie if we told them we were gonna learn how to strip." She giggled like a young girl and wrapped her arms around Ruth.

Bellamy gave them a questioning look when Lola whispered something into Ruth's ear and they both turned red. "I don't even want to know what you just said. I'm pretty sure it'd scar me for life." With that Bellamy picked up her glass of wine and walked out onto the deck, ignoring her mom's laughter coming through the sliding door.

As soon as Bellamy shut the sliding door, the men all turned to smile at her as she went to sit down on one of the lounge chairs. Dustin walked over and sat down next to her. "How ya doin', kid?" he asked, nudging her with his shoulder.

"I'm doing okay. Just a little sore, but better. Did you guys get much work done after the incident?" she asked as she put her head on his shoulder.

"Yeah, we put a nice dent in it today. Next time you want to come take a look around make sure to wear full-body armor." He smirked as he wrapped his arm around her. Bellamy couldn't help but snuggle closer to her brother. Even with the big age difference, the three of them were close. She happened to glance up to see Luke staring at her. She felt her cheeks heat up from the heated look he was giving her. Bellamy nervously licked her lips and let out a sigh when she swore she saw him clench his teeth. He quickly looked away and jumped in a conversation Dylan was having with their dad and Patrick.

Luke felt his cock start to stir when he looked at Bellamy. Her curls were coming out of the knot she had them in, it made him want to grab onto them as he thrust his tongue into her warm mouth. He'd bet anything that she tasted sweet from the wine she'd been drinking. This was definitely the wrong place and the wrong time to be having these thoughts about her. Jesus, her dad and brothers were all right there, and if they'd been looking at him they would've noticed the way he was watching her. When she licked her lips she was looking right at him and it about did him in. Luke had no choice but to ignore her, otherwise he was gonna do something really, really stupid.

***

Dinner was so delicious and Bellamy felt so full. The men had all retreated to the family room to watch a baseball game, as the women sat around the table drinking their wine. Bellamy smiled at the banter between her mom and Lola. They were so much alike, yet so different. Ruth was tall with a dancer's build, while Lola reminded Bellamy of a pixie. The two women grew up together and had always had a sisterly bond that no one seemed to understand but them. Both women had found the loves of their lives and Bellamy was beginning to think she'd never have hers.

"Bell?" her mom asked, looking at her strangely.

"I'm sorry, Momma, what were you saying?" Bellamy said, looking between both women.

"Honey, I just asked if you wanted some dessert, but you just sort of blanked out on us."

"Oh, yeah, I was just thinking about something." She paused, taking a sip of her wine. "I would love some dessert."

After the women finished their dessert, Bellamy delivered dessert to the men while they were watching the ball game. Her dad and Patrick were sitting in the two recliners facing the big screen, while Dustin, Dylan and Luke were scattered throughout the room. She walked over to her dad first, handing him a slice of Lola's cheesecake. "Here ya go, Daddy. Momma said you couldn't have a full piece," she said with a wide smile.

"Oh, and why is that, little girl?" her dad said with eyebrows raised.

"I don't want you to lose your girlish figure, honey!" her mom shouted from the kitchen.

The family room erupted in laughter as everyone stared at Charlie. Bellamy stood back as her mom came sauntering in and stopped right in front of her dad with a gloating smile. He grabbed her, pulling her onto his lap. Ruth squealed as he kissed the side of her neck. Her mom quickly got off of his lap when everyone started whistling and catcalling.

Bellamy watched her dad smack her mom right on the butt, her mom walking away.

"Oh, my god, Dad!" Bellamy laughed as she turned her head

"What?" he asked innocently as he watched his wife walk out of the room.

She rolled her eyes and walked over handing a plate to Patrick. He smiled up at her when she leaned down and kissed his cheek. "Thanks, darlin'."

Bellamy passed out the rest of the plates and made her way back into the kitchen where her mom and Lola were sitting drinking coffee. The women both turned and smiled at her as she sat down across from them. Bellamy had wondered how her mom had managed to keep her secret from her best friend and her husband. She felt guilty that her mom had probably lied to her dad when Travis had called her, frantically begging her to come to Savannah and not tell anyone she was coming. Bellamy was scared that if her dad ever found out that he'd be devastated and furious that Ruth had kept something like that from him. She knew she needed to stop worrying about it, because if he hadn't found out in 5 ½ years, then he wouldn't find out now.

"Baby, what's on your mind? You looked sad for a second there," Lola said, reaching across and grabbing Bellamy's hand, giving it a gentle squeeze.

"Oh, uh—n-nothing. I just was wishing I lived closer, I miss seeing y'all." She paused, taking a sip of her mom's coffee. "I mean, I know I'm only forty-five minutes away, but with work I'm too busy to come home more."

"Oh, honey, we understand. Your momma and I were just talking about how good it was to have everyone together. Of course, we're missing Jason and my sweet little grandbabies, but that's life, honey. Sometimes our lives take us in different directions." Lola grabbed her purse pulled out a little photo album. "Here are some recent pictures of my little angels; Gracie is 6, Tucker is 4 ½ and little Maisy is 2. Now they're expecting baby number four. Sherry swears that after this one they're done, but that's what they said after Tuck was born, so we'll see."

Bellamy smiled as she flipped through the album. Her grandchildren were all beautiful, and Tucker looked exactly like Luke did at that age. Granted, Bellamy wasn't even born yet, but she'd seen enough pictures growing up. Jason and Luke looked a lot alike, but where Luke was more muscular, Jason was lankier. Gracie and Maisy both looked like Sherry. Bellamy had only met her a few times. They had sable hair and eyes the color of sapphires and they were the size of peanuts. Bellamy passed by pictures upon pictures of their beautiful family. They looked so happy together. It made her a little envious of what they had and what she desperately wanted someday for herself.

Bellamy handed the album back to Lola. "They're getting so big and so beautiful. Do you guys get to see them much?"

"Not like we would like to, but I was lucky enough to be out there for all three of the babies births. See, Sherry's momma died when she was a young girl, so I've tried to be there for her like she was my own. I'm just hoping that I'll be there for the fourth, too." Lola smiled so big and giggled as Ruth put her arms around her.

"Don't let her fool you, Bellamy. Lola probably has her plane ticket bought for, I'm guessing, two weeks before Sherry's due date, so she won't miss it."

Lola looked at Bellamy's mom with a shocked expression and started laughing. "How did you know? Did that rotten husband of mine tell you?" Lola narrowed her eyes at Ruth.

"Uh, no, but after you almost missed Gracie's birth, you conveniently started booking your trips before her due dates, so how would I think this one would be any different?"

***

Everyone started to leave shortly before nine since it was only Tuesday and everyone but Bellamy had to work tomorrow. Bellamy walked her brothers out, as Dylan was staying over at Dustin's so they could head to work early. She stood with them in front of Dustin's truck.

"So, Bell—what's your plans Friday night?" Dustin asked as pulled her into a hug.

"Well, Travis is supposed to get into town, so we might go out. Why, what are you guys doing?"

"Nothing yet, but maybe we'll meet you guys out."

"Sure, I'll see y'all tomorrow and we can make plans." She kissed both of her brothers goodbye and walked back into the house; it looked like Luke and his parents were getting ready to leave as well.

She walked over to Lola, giving her a hug and a kiss goodbye. "Thanks for the cheesecake. It was wonderful as usual."

"You're welcome, sweetie. I'm sure I'll be seeing you soon."

Bellamy was then pulled into a hug by Patrick. "Glad you're home, little girl. No more dropping by the jobsite, you hear?" He winked as he said it. She watched as Patrick grabbed Lola's hand as they walked out the door. She turned and found Luke standing right behind her.

"Jesus, you scared me." Bellamy put her hand to her chest to stop her heart from beating right out of it.

"Sorry, didn't mean to scare you. Come here." Luke's voice seemed deeper when he said it. She took a step towards him. His hand came up and he tucked some of her loose curls behind her ear. Bellamy stood there, dumbfounded. As much as she still wanted him, she was pretty sure his feelings about hurting her brothers still rang true, but it didn't stop him from slowly wrapping his arms around her in a tight hug. She felt like she had no control over her body as her arms wrapped around his waist.

Luke could feel the blood rushing from his head straight to his cock when he felt Bellamy's body melt into his, it felt so right every time he held her. Every time it made him feel that he never wanted to let her go. He couldn't help the torment he felt, knowing how he had hurt Bellamy and it was partially his fault that she didn't come home very often. Luke couldn't help it when his lips started moving before he could make his brain work. "Bell?" he whispered. "I want you to come over tonight. Will you?"

Bellamy pulled back from him enough to look into his eyes. "Uh, why?"

"I just thought we could hang out for a while." Luke didn't want to beg, but he felt like he was close to doing so.

"O-okay, sure. When do you want me to come over?"

"Why don't you just follow me over now?" Luke stepped back from her and turned towards the dining room. "Bye, Ruth. Bye, Charlie. Thanks for dinner."

Ruth came walking out with Charlie in tow, "Oh, honey, you are so welcome. Drive safely." Ruth kissed his cheek and squeezing him in a hug.

Charlie came over and clapped him on the shoulder. "That was some quick moving today. I hope you know how grateful I am that my little girl is safe."

Luke wanted to say that Bellamy was not safe from him, but that would've been so bad. For a moment he could've sworn he saw a glint of recognition in Charlie's eye, but maybe it was wishful thinking; wishful thinking that if he had Ruth and Charlie behind him, then it'd be easier for the boys to be accepting.

"I'm just glad that I was able to get to her in time. See ya tomorrow at work, Charlie. Bell, I'll be waiting outside for you." With that Luke walked out and stood in front of his truck.

***

Bellamy looked at both of her parents, who were wearing the same questioning look. Her dad was the first one to speak. "You going to Luke's?"

"Yeah, he wants me to come over and hang out for a little bit. Why, is it a problem?" Bellamy asked.

Her dad looked at her mom and then back at Bellamy. "No, no problem at all, darlin'. Just be careful driving home. Have a good time, sweetie." He kissed his daughter on the cheek and headed back towards the kitchen.

Once her dad walked back to the kitchen, her mom turned back to Bellamy. She walked closer, wrapping her arms around her. Neither of them spoke for several seconds, her mom spoke first. "Baby, just be safe. Do you have condoms?"

Bellamy pulled back from her mom. "Momma, that's not why I'm going over there. Luke just wants to hang out." She whispered so her dad wouldn't hear her. "What gave you the idea that I was going over there to sleep with him?"

"Oh, honey, I'm not blind. I saw the way the two of you were watching each other tonight. Luke had that look in his eye that I've seen many times in your father's. Lola noticed it too, and, honey, it's no secret that when you were younger that you had such a crush on him. I honestly couldn't be happier if the two of you ended up together," she said, shrugging her shoulders.

Bellamy could feel the heat rising in her cheeks; she was flabbergasted by what her mom had just said to her. "Okay, but we are not getting together and I'll probably be home in a couple of hours. So don't worry about me." She kissed her mom then grabbed her purse.

Bellamy smiled when she saw Luke standing in front of his truck waiting for her. "Just follow me. I've got a house over on Parker Street."

Bellamy nodded as she walked over and got into her Prius. When they were on the road heading towards Luke's house, Bellamy had a long pep talk with herself. "I'm just staying for a drink; maybe a movie, but nothing more," she repeated herself over and over all the way to Luke's.

***

Luke kept checking the rearview mirror, making sure Bellamy didn't change her mind. He saw the apprehension in her eyes when he asked her to come over; Luke just wanted to be alone with her for a little bit. He pulled into his driveway, leaving Bellamy enough room to park behind him.

Luke cut the engine and jumped out, walking over to Bellamy. "Hey, Bellamy." He grabbed her hand, helping her out of the car. He continued to hold it as he led her up the front walk and onto the porch.

"Oh, wow, Luke, I love this little bistro table," she exclaimed as she walked over to look at the wrought iron table and chairs. The cushions had red, yellow and orange stripes; she ran her hand over the material.

"Well, if you like the porch, you'll love the inside." Luke grabbed her hand, giving it a squeeze and led her into the entry way. He had dark oak finished hardwood floors accented by a deep wine runner that went right down the middle of the hall into the living room.

His living room was his favorite room. Along the farthest wall there was a stone fireplace. The mantel was made of marble; a huge round mirror fixed to the wall above it. His couch, loveseat and chair were overstuffed and made of rich brown leather. In the corner of the room was an entertainment center that held a large flat-screen TV. The walls were dark sage green with off-white trim. Bellamy turned to look at him with wide eyes.

"Luke, it's so beautiful," Bellamy said with awe in her voice. Did you decorate it yourself?"

He came to stand right next to her. "No, I redid the floors and painted. Mom did all of the decorating."

"How long have you lived here?"

"About two years, but I've owned it for three. See, between work and trying to fix this place up, it ended up taking longer than I'd hoped, but I'm happy with it now. Come on, I'll show you the rest." Luke led her into the kitchen and she noticed that all of his appliances were stainless steel.

Bellamy was surprised how clean it was considering he was a bachelor. She loved his breakfast bar that had three barstools on the side leading to the dining room. Bellamy walked around the counter to check out the dining room. It wasn't decorated like the living room was—the walls were the same sage green and the trim was the same off-white, but there weren't any pictures on the wall and the dining room table was made of an unfinished oak. Bellamy could see that it was a work in-progress, but she could certainly see the potential. She walked back into the kitchen and Luke was opening a couple bottles of beer.

"Here, Bell." Luke handed her the bottle as he continued the tour. He led her down the hall and quickly showed her the bathroom. It was decorated in pale blues and yellows. The shower stall was tiled and had a frosted glass door. Other than that it was a typical bathroom. They ventured further down the hall; the first door they came to opened up to Luke's office/home gym. The walls were a plain white. An expensive looking stereo system took up one corner with a weight bench; free weights and a punching bag took up another. He had a desk right in front of the window; she smiled because she couldn't see the top, which was covered in what she would guess to be sketches.

"Sorry it's such a mess, but your brother and I have been working night and day trying to get the plans done for the Bartlett place. Come on—one last room to show ya." Luke grabbed Bellamy's hand and led her down the hall to the last door.

When Luke opened the door to his bedroom, Bellamy smiled; it was totally a man's room. There was nothing on the walls, and as far as furniture went, there was a huge bed, a dresser, a nightstand and, of course, a flat screen mounted on the wall. Bellamy looked at Luke and smiled. "So I take it you didn't let your mom decorate your bedroom, huh?"

"Um, yeah, I didn't really want to ask her to decorate this room for me. I'll get to it eventually." Luke led her back out to the living room.

"Well, you should be proud of what you've done here: it's gorgeous, Luke." Bellamy glanced at the clock and took a sip of her beer. She knew the smart thing to do would be to thank him for showing her his place and walking right out of the door, but of course she felt herself listening to the hormones that started raging like she was eighteen again. This may be her one and only chance to be with Luke and she really wanted to take it. Bellamy gave Luke a sideways glance and noticed that he was watching her. "Luke, why am I really here?" she asked, her voice no more than a whisper.

Luke felt a sense of pride when he saw how much Bellamy liked what he had done with his house, and now she was standing in his living room looking as uncertain as he felt. Before he knew what was happening, he was walking towards her. He took her beer and sat in on the coffee table. Luke smiled when he saw that her cheeks were flushed and her eyes were glassy. "Do you really want to know why you're here?" Luke asked with his lips so close to hers he could feel her breath tickle his lips. "Answer me, Bellamy," he whispered against her lips.

Bellamy felt like her head was spinning, his breath soft against her lips. She tried to answer him, but she couldn't force the words out and all she could do was nod her head. Luke leaned his forehead against hers and before Bellamy could react, Luke took her lips in such a possessive kiss it caused her whole body to tremble. His lips were full and soft against hers. She could feel his hands slide up into her hair and Bellamy let him turn her head so he could deepen the kiss. She felt his tongue tickle her lips, so she opened her mouth to him, letting her tongue lightly touch his.

Luke could've sworn he growled when he felt Bellamy's tongue touch his. He used his lips to push hers further open and plunged his tongue into her hot mouth. He took the clip that was holding Bellamy's hair up out and tossed it on the floor, letting the silken curls slide through his fingers as it fell down her back. He felt her pulling his T-shirt out of his khaki shorts and felt all his blood rush straight to his cock.

When Luke pulled away so Bellamy could take his shirt off, he was panting, but so was she. "Bellamy, tell me you want this as much as I do," he whispered as he leaned into her with his lips against hers. Luke let his hands slide from her shoulders until he was cupping her breasts in his hands.

Bellamy moaned when Luke rubbed his thumbs over the hardened points of her nipples. "Yes; god, yes," she panted, and that was all it took for Luke to step back, wrap one arm behind her back and an arm under knees, lifting her to his chest with a desperate yearning. He took her down the hall to his room and sat her on the edge of his bed. Bellamy felt her stomach drop as he grabbed her tank top and pulled it over her head. Luke pushed her back on the bed, settling next to her. Bellamy turned her head so she was facing him. She felt her heart melt when he cupped her face with his hand, stroking her lower lip with his thumb.

"Jesus, Bell, when did you get so gorgeous?" He leaned forward, taking her lips slower this time. Luke felt Bellamy's hand sliding down his chest, rubbing and stroking along the way. His cock was so hard it felt like it was going to burst, so when Bellamy's hand slid down to rub his erection, he couldn't hold back anymore. Luke crushed his lips to hers as he rolled on top of her and settling between her thighs. He rubbed his cock, which was still encased in his shorts against her shorts-clad pussy. Luke loved listening to her moan as he started touching her everywhere.

Bellamy felt Luke's hands slide over her stomach until he reached her lace covered nipples; she arched into his hands as he rubbed his thumbs over the sensitive peaks. Bellamy felt him flip the front closure of her bra open, her chest rising and falling fast. Bellamy opened her eyes, and what she saw took her breath away. Luke was studying her like he never wanted to forget her body. He must've felt her watching him because he looked at Bellamy with such an intensity that she felt herself trying to wiggle out from underneath him and away from those piercing green eyes.

As Bellamy was wiggling beneath him; he grabbed both of her hands, dragging them until they were above her head. Her wrists were slim enough that he was able to hold on with just one hand. Luke could feel Bellamy's rapid heartbeat as he let his free hand slide down her neck until he reached her breasts. He touched and tasted each breast with delicate touches of his fingers and his tongue. He could feel the heat radiating from between Bellamy's thighs as she was writhing beneath him. Luke pushed himself up and pressed his lips to hers. "I have to be inside you now, Bell," he whispered against her lips.

As soon as he said it Bellamy thought she was gonna lose it. "Oh, p-please, Luke," she moaned. Bellamy watched beneath her lashes as Luke slid down her body taking her shorts and panties all the way down her legs and tossing them on the floor. She watched as he got up and pulled a foil packet out of his nightstand, and when he took off his shorts and boxer-briefs, Bellamy felt her mouth begin to water. Luke's body was her definition of male perfection; his shoulders were broad with defined muscles bulging in all of the right places. His chest was covered in a light sprinkling of hair— a darker blond than the hair on his head. His abs were well-toned with light blond hair that looked like a trail leading straight to his cock.

"Oh, my," Bellamy whispered, then slowly licked her lips. He was huge; how was she supposed to take him? Was he really that big? The one and only time she'd ever had sex with him or anyone else for that matter it hurt, but she assumed it was because it was her first time. Bellamy brought her attention back to Luke's face as he was putting the condom on. Once it was in place he crawled back between her legs, surprising Bellamy by taking a quick swipe with his tongue between her saturated folds. "Luke!" She cried out as he did it again and again.

"Oh, Bell, you taste so good," Luke groaned with each pass of his tongue. She was so wet for him. He could see her juices running out of her and down the crack of her ass. Luke felt her body tremble as he started making small circles around her clit. He was dying to push her over the edge, but he felt her grab his hair. "What is it, baby?" he whispered.

Bellamy was squirming. "You. Inside. Me. Now. Pleeasse!" she cried. Bellamy hated the sound of desperation in her voice, but she couldn't take it any longer. She watched as Luke pushed himself up and over her. Bellamy watched as he stared down at her. Luke's chin was wet from her juices. He was breathing as hard as she was. Bellamy grabbed his head and brought him down for a scorching kiss. She could taste herself mixed with his unique flavor. While he was kissing her she felt his hand move down her body until he spread her legs further apart—she felt the tip of his cock rubbing against her clit, causing her to moan into his mouth.

"Are you ready for me?" Luke said against her lips. Bellamy nodded her head and kissed him. As he started working his cock inside her, he moaned.

"You're so tight, baby. Let me know if it's too much."

"J-just keep going. I-I want to feel all of you." Bellamy wrapped her legs around his waist trying to pull him in deeper.

Luke was losing all control. He was trying to be gentle, trying to take it slow, but when he looked into her pleading passion-filled eyes he snapped. Luke grabbed her hands again and held them next to her head—taking her lips in another soul-stealing kiss. As he kissed her, he reared back and thrust his hips to impale her in one long stroke. Luke's lips swallowed her cry and he stopped moving for a second to let Bellamy's body adjust to the intrusion.

"You doin' okay? You are so fuckin' tight. I'm afraid once I start moving it'll be over too quick."

Bellamy smiled up at him touching his lips with her fingertips. Her pussy felt stretched to the max, but it didn't hurt anymore. She just wanted him to move. "I'm good. Please, just make me come," she pleaded. He wasn't even moving inside of her, but she felt the pressure building that she knew she wasn't going to last long either.

Luke pulled half-way out and rolled his hips as he pushed back in. God, she felt incredible. This was supposed to be just a one-time thing to get her out of his system, but he had a feeling that this was just going to make that hunger he felt for her so much stronger.

He knew she was getting close—he could feel the walls surrounding his cock start to squeeze and release him. Luke wanted her to come before he did. He started slowly stroking her in and out. Luke started rolling his hips, so his pelvic bone came in constant contact with Bellamy's clit. Her moans and cries were getting louder and louder. He bent down, taking her nipple between his lips, sucking it into a hardened point. When the contractions started, he bit down on it and Bellamy exploded.

Bellamy felt like her body was falling apart. She swore she was screaming, but the blood roaring in her ears made it difficult to tell for sure. Her vision was blurred and she realized tears were running down her face. Luke had let go of her hands and she had buried her fingernails in his back. Bellamy felt Luke swell inside of her as his thrusting became deeper, harder and faster. She lifted her head off the pillow and started kissing and licking at his neck. She felt him slide his hand in between their bodies and started strumming her clit again.

Luke took her lips and began hard-thrusting his tongue into her mouth. When he felt the ripples start around him he pounded into her, and with every stroke, Bellamy cried out over and over until he felt his balls draw up tight as he came. He could feel her walls contracting around and milking his cock. Luke didn't think he'd ever come that hard before. When his breathing started to slow, he realized that he was laying with his head on Bellamy's chest and she was stroking his hair. "Bell?"

"Uh-huh." Her words were coming out breathless.

"Do you want me to get off of you? I-I don't want to squash you," Luke said as he put his head back down kissing her neck.

"Mmm...Don't move. I like this." She smiled against the top of his head.

Neither one spoke for what seemed like a long time. Bellamy was afraid if she did it'd ruin the moment. She never realized before what she'd been missing. Granted, she only had one time, but she didn't plan on it being that way. Bellamy didn't pine away for him these past six years. She loved him, but she didn't sit around waiting for this moment to happen. Bellamy just never felt right taking a relationship to the next level with anyone. Maybe that made her a sucker, but she didn't care. And if this was her only chance to be with him, then she'd make the most out of it.

Luke pushed himself up on his arm as he looked down into Bellamy's sleepy eyes. She had the most beautiful grin on her face. He rested his head in his hand as he started running his fingertips over her stomach. If this had been any other girl, he'd be herding her to the door, giving them the excuse that he had to get some sleep before work. Luke wasn't trying to be a dick, but he didn't want anything more than just a casual fling. He'd had relationships when he was younger, but they wanted the kind of commitment that he wasn't ready to make yet.

Bellamy turned to her side so they were face to face. She lifted her hand, rubbing it against the stubble on his cheek. He could tell she was sleepy. He wondered if he should send her home so her parents wouldn't worry.

"I'm gonna get cleaned up. Do you want something to drink?" Luke said as he leaned down to kiss Bellamy on the lips.

"No, I'm okay. I think I'll just get dressed and go home." She started to sit up, but Luke leaned over, pushing her back down. He decided that she wasn't going anywhere.

"Nope. I want you stay here just like this," Luke said. "I'll be back in a second." Luke turned and walked out of his room. He disposed of the condom, threw on his underwear, and went to the kitchen to get a drink. Why did she want to leave? Maybe she thought he was trying to get rid of her when he said he was gonna get cleaned up. Luke shook his head as he grabbed a carton of orange juice and took a generous gulp out of it. He closed it and put it back and hurried back down the hall. When he walked into his room he couldn't help but smile: Bellamy was fast asleep in the middle of his bed.

She had the look of innocence while she slept. Her light-tanned skin was so smooth and soft. Bellamy's sweet lips were red and swollen from the kisses they shared. Her hair was in complete disarray with long curls spread all over his pillow. Luke climbed in next to her. He lifted her legs so he could pull the covers out from under her. He stripped out of his boxers and grabbed Bellamy around the waist pulling her back against his chest.

Luke smiled. He knew she must've been out because she didn't make a peep when he moved her. He moved his hand down her arm and let it rest on her hip. He buried his face in her hair smelling the sweet fragrance of her shampoo. Luke felt his eyes get heavy, so he let sleep claim him.

***

Bellamy wasn't sure what time it was when she woke up, but it couldn't have been morning since it was still dark out. She turned to see Luke sprawled out next to her on his stomach. He was facing her with a hand draped over her hip. Bellamy couldn't help but roll over to him. She felt his arm tighten around her waist, pulling her closer. Luke rolled to his side so her back was against his chest. Bellamy felt too good lying with him like that, she knew she could get used to it, but she knew that it wasn't that way for him. Did he tell her that? No, but she would never do anything to ruin his friendship with her brothers.

Bellamy had to get out of there. She didn't want any awkwardness between the two of them in the morning. The truth was, she could stay in his arms forever, but that's not how it was meant to be. She lifted his arm and slowly slid from under it. Bellamy froze when she heard Luke moan, but all he did was mumble something and then roll over. She walked around the bed until she found her clothes lying in a little pile. It only took her about thirty seconds to get dressed. She tiptoed down the hall and found her flip-flops right where she had left them.

She slipped her feet into them, grabbed her purse, and snuck out the front door. Halfway home she realized she was being a big chicken shit and she should've just stayed, but it was too late now.

Chapter 7

Bellamy woke up around ten in the morning. She was grateful that neither one of her parents woke up when she got home. When she had fallen into bed it was around four o'clock. Bellamy had to squint her eyes against the sun shining through her window. She sat up rubbing the sleep from her eyes and when she stood up, her muscles felt deliciously sore, which brought back last night with Luke quickly. Bellamy had never come that hard before, but when your only way to get off is with a sex toy, what could one expect? The real thing was so much better, and maybe when she went back to Savannah, she could try dating again since it was always the physical intimacy that held her back. She wasn't gonna start sleeping around, but if she met someone she liked, then she'd consider the physical stuff.

Bellamy took a shower and stayed in a long time, letting the hot water loosen her muscles. Once the water started running cold, Bellamy got out and wrapped herself in a towel. Travis and Brad were still supposed to be coming Friday. Bellamy decided to check her phone to see if they called. She grabbed it out of her bag and saw that she had three voicemails. The first one was from Travis checking in to say he'd call her Friday when they left Charleston. The second one surprised her. "Bellamy, do you want to explain to me why you weren't here when I woke up this morning? I expect a phone call to at least tell me you're okay. Call me." Oh wow, so Luke wasn't happy to find her gone this morning. Bellamy didn't know why, but it kind of made her wet. She listened to the last message. It was her mom wanting to have lunch with her today.

Bellamy decided she better call Luke first. She was overcome with a major case of nerves as she waited for him to answer or his voicemail to pick up. It ended up being the latter. When it beeped she decided to have a little fun with him. "Hey, Luke, it's me. Sorry I didn't wake you when I left this morning, but, you see, if I would've…well, let's just, um—yeah, never mind. So on that note, I had a pleasant time with you and I'm sure we'll talk later." She smiled as she hung up, and got ready for the day.

***

The whole drive in to work gave Luke entirely too much time to think about last night. He couldn't remember a more intense sexual experience; well, he could, but it was the only other time he'd slept with Bellamy. Why did she get under his skin like that? Why did she leave without saying goodbye? Luke couldn't believe the message that he had left her this morning when he realized she was gone. He sounded like some barbaric fool, but that's what she brought out in him. He felt the need to claim her, the need to beat his chest and the need to bring her back to his home and never let her leave.

It gave Luke a jolt of lust this morning when he got out of the shower and noticed that her fingernails left scratches all across his upper shoulders and back, because he knew he caused her to have such intense pleasure that she lost control. He had to get himself together as he pulled onto the Bartlett Plantation. The last thing he'd need was for anyone to suspect that he and Bellamy had sex last night.

He got out of his truck and as he was walking around back he ran into Dylan, just great. "Hey, Dylan. What's going on?"

"Nothing much. Dustin and I just got here ourselves. Man, you should've gone out with us last night. My brother is a hoe." Dylan laughed at his own comment.

"You're just learning that your brother is a slut? That's all right. One of these days he's gonna meet a woman who will bring him to his knees and I can't wait to watch." Luke laughed.

"So what'd you do last night?" Luke knew Dylan was gonna ask him, and now he was gonna have to lie.

"Nothing. After I left your folks' place I went home and watched some TV, then went to bed. Pretty boring shit," Luke said with a shrug of his shoulders.

"Yeah, you act like your eighty, not thirty. Come on, let's see what the plan is for today," Dylan said as they went around the back to find the others.

***

By eleven, Luke was ready for lunch. He thought about calling Bellamy and asking her to meet him, but the guys would get suspicious if he ditched them. He pulled out his cell phone and smiled when he saw that he had a voicemail from Bellamy. As Luke started listening to it he felt himself get hard, the little minx was speaking with a sultry tone, but when she said she had a pleasant time that's what did him in. She used a voice so saccharine sweet and phony he was gonna paddle her tight ass the next time he saw her. Luke deleted the message and hit her number. Payback was a bitch.

***

Bellamy had met her mom and Lola for lunch at a little sandwich shop by Lola's Bakery on Main Street. She was running late, so they were already seated waiting for her. Bellamy sat in the chair in between the two women. Leaning over, she kissed her mom on the cheek and then did the same to Lola.

"Sorry I'm late. I didn't get up until an hour ago." She watched as Lola and her mom shared a knowing glance. Bellamy grabbed the glass of water in front of her hoping it'd hide the fact that she was blushing.

"It's fine, sweetie. Your mom was just telling me that you went to Luke's last night. What'd you think of his house?" They both watched her, waiting for an answer.

"Um, well, it's beautiful. I really like the color of the walls and the furniture. My favorite was the kitchen; I loved the stainless steel appliances."

Her mom smiled at her and then at Lola. "You did do a fantastic job decorating it. When will you help him finish? I know you still have his dining room, office, and his bedroom to do."

"Oh, well, he already told me his bedroom is off-limits as far as decorating goes, but I may start putting together ideas for his dining room. Bellamy, you should help me."

Bellamy couldn't help it when she started choking on the water she'd been trying to drink when Lola suggested such an asinine thing.

"Baby, are you all right?" Ruth asked as she patted Bellamy on the back.

"Y-yes, Momma. I'm fine, it—it just went down the wrong pipe. I'm sorry, Lola, you want my help decorating Luke's dining room? I don't know anything about that kind of stuff; I really don't know that I'd be any help." Bellamy exclaimed; hoping for some sort of distraction or change of topic.

"Well, I just thought it'd be nice for us to spend some time together while you're home. I don't really expect you to help me it'd be more keeping me company," Lola said as she smiled with a twinkle in her eye.

Bellamy felt like such a jerk. She'd forgotten all of the times that she'd hang out with Lola at her house or down at the bakery when Bellamy was younger. Ruth had told Bellamy that since Lola didn't have a daughter of her own she tried to spend time with Bellamy as much as possible, plus she was Bellamy's godmother and loved her like her own. It was Lola who taught her how to bake and to sew, and when her brothers were tormenting her too much she'd stay with Lola and Patrick for the weekend being spoiled rotten.

"You're right, Lola, that sounds like a great idea. I'll bring the liquor," Bellamy proclaimed with a big smile.

"Now you're talkin'," Lola said as she grabbed Bellamy's hand, clearly thrilled that they were going to get a chance to hang out together.

Bellamy's phone rang. She picked up her purse, digging it out and smiling when she saw it was Luke…Oh god—Luke was calling while she was with his mom and hers.

She tried to keep her face straight as she answered. "Hello?"

"Well, hello to you. So why didn't you stick around this morning?" Luke's deep voice caused Bellamy's pussy to spasm and right in front of the moms, no less.

"Yes, Brett, I know you prefer I do your training, but like I told you, I'm on vacation right now, as a matter of fact I'm sitting right across from my mom and her best friend, Lola."

"Oooh, you're with the ladies, huh?" Luke chuckled softly into the phone. "I can't stop thinking about last night, the way it felt to have my cock shoved inside your tight, hot pussy. It's getting me hard just imagining the noises you made as you started to come…twice."

Holy shit. Bellamy was seriously gonna kill him when she saw him next. She watched her mom and Lola out of the corner of her eye. They seemed to be talking quietly to each other. Bellamy plastered her fake smile back on her face just in case they started watching her.

"Ah, Brett, that's so sweet of you to say. Of course I'll get you in shape before your wedding to Chad. So don't worry, we'll get rid of your so-called beer belly in no time flat. But I should be going and we'll talk more when I get back."

"Oh, don't you dare, little girl; beer belly? I don't know if my marriage to Chad will work. See, I've got this girl who I've got to get naked again and I don't think poor Chad will like it. But what I want to know is, will you like it when I get you naked again?"

Bellamy's body tensed as she felt a warm flush work its way up her neck to her cheeks. She clenched her thighs together so the ache between her legs would stop.

"I'm waiting." His breathing was heavy and uneven.

Bellamy cleared her throat. "Y-yes, I'd like that very much, B-Brett," she stammered.

"Well, it's a date then. You're mine Saturday night, Bellamy, and that's a promise." Luke hung up before she could reply. Did that conversation really just take place? Oh, wow. She was in so much trouble. She picked up her water, taking a huge drink, hoping it'd cool her off because her body was on fire.

"Was that one of your clients, honey?"

"Yes, Mom. Brett's high-maintenance, and with his wedding coming up, he's driving me crazy," she said with a laugh. Bellamy was just lucky she didn't have to answer any more questions because their sandwiches were delivered.

***

Friday afternoon Bellamy decided to go home and take a nap. She'd been helping her mom get ready for her recital and getting up early to help Lola at her bakery. In between all of that she'd spent time with her brothers and talking to Luke a lot on the phone and texting. She knew Travis and Brad were gonna be taking her out, so she was going to have to rest up.

Returning from helping Lola at the bakery and then running some errands for her mom, Bellamy pulled in the driveway and saw Patrick and Dustin's trucks. They must've decided to have lunch at the house instead of going out. She knew Luke was in there, but she didn't think she could face him after the previous night, and worse, after his little phone call.

Bellamy decided her best course of action was to sneak in and go directly to her room. She walked up the front steps and slowly eased the front door open.

Bellamy poked her head in and she could hear the men talking in the back of the house. She knew they must be in the family room. Bellamy stepped silently into the foyer, kicked off her flip-flops, and walked silently down the hall. She smiled to herself when she heard her dad's booming laugh, and in turn the others started laughing, too.

Bellamy started up the stairs, taking them one at a time, hoping that the men were too engrossed in whatever they were doing to hear her. Once at the top, she walked down the hall to her room. Just as she walked inside, she heard the bathroom sink turn on and then off. When the door opened, her eyes widened as Luke stepped out of the bathroom. Neither of them moved at first, they just stood there looking at each other.

"Hi," Bellamy said, her voice no more than a whisper.

Luke had seen Bellamy pull in the driveway and ran up to the bathroom, waiting for her. He smiled when he saw the look of surprise on her face when he emerged from the bathroom. Luke could see the blush that was spreading up her neck to her face. When she whispered "hi" to him, he didn't say anything, he just started walking into her room, shutting the door behind him. The closer he got to her, the more nervous she seemed to appear. Finally they were less than an arm's length away and Luke could smell the fragrant scent of Bellamy's shampoo that had somehow become an aphrodisiac to him.

"So I hope you know that the wedding's off between me and Chad, but don't be sad because I'm over him," Luke said with a wicked grin.

Bellamy couldn't help but start laughing. "I-I'm sorry, but your mom and mine were sitting right across from me. I figured you wouldn't want them to know who I was talking to." She noticed him start to frown. "But that was fine with me; I didn't really feel like playing fifty questions with them."

"Yeah, there definitely would've been some questions. I do, however, have a question for you…"

"Sure," Bellamy answered slowly.

"Was it really only pleasant? Because, I'm sorry I thought it was pretty fuckin' great," Luke said, feeling uncomfortable with the admission.

Bellamy looked down at her feet for a second and then back at him. "Um, yeah, I'd say it was pretty fuckin' great, too."

Luke grabbed her with one arm around her waist, hauling her against him and crushing his lips to hers. His other hand grabbed her hair and held her mouth to his.

Bellamy eased her mouth open, letting the tip of her tongue tickle Luke's lips. She heard a growl that started deep in his throat as he opened his mouth and let his tongue enter her hot, eager mouth. His tongue felt so good against hers. He moved his head to deepen the kiss as she grabbed onto the front of his shirt, like she was holding onto a life raft.

"Luke! Where are you, man? Did you fall in?" They both stepped back from each other to the sound of Dylan's voice.

"Shit! Sorry, Bell, I've gotta go. Remember what I said, though: you're mine tomorrow night." He leaned down, kissing her one more time.

"I won't forget. I'll see you later," Bellamy said as she sat on her bed, watching Luke walk out of her room. She gingerly touched her lips, savoring the tingles that were left behind. Bellamy knew for sure at the moment that she was a masochist. Why else would she sleep with the one man that ever mattered to her...again. It made sense that when they made love she didn't freeze up like she had with the other men she tried to date.

At least this time he was smart enough to use a condom, since that one forgetful moment had changed Bellamy's life. Unfortunately, it'd change Luke's too, as soon as she told him about their daughter.

Bellamy felt terrible keeping it from Luke, but she was scared. She knew in her heart that she still loved him, and it was hard enough accepting that fact. Once Bellamy told Luke about losing his baby, he'd hate her for sure. Maybe, for once, Bellamy wanted to enjoy one part of her life that she knew she'd only have for a short time, and maybe that'd make him hate her even more, but it was worth the risk. After she told him, and the dust settled, she had a feeling that she'd have the closure her therapist always told her she needed. Losing Luke in the process would be awful, but considering she didn't really have him in the first place, she'd have to just get over it. Now if she could just keep her heart out of whatever was going on between them she'd be okay...Maybe?

***

"What the hell took you so long?" Dylan asked as Luke walked down the stairs.

"I had to make a phone call, and since you dicks were being so loud, I stayed upstairs. Are you guys ready to go?" Luke really hated lying to Dylan, but he didn't want to deal with the whole, "none of you assholes better touch my sister...Ever." Dylan had made that declaration right after Bellamy's eighteenth birthday. Maybe, just maybe it'd be different because it was him and not one of their more wild friends. Luke decided to just see what happened between him and Bellamy, and if there ended up being something to tell, well—then he'd face them and hope that they still remained friends.

When Dustin, Charlie and Patrick met the boys in the hall they all headed out to the trucks. "Hey, when did Bellamy get home?" Charlie asked as they started loading up.

"I don't know, Dad, but I didn't hear her come in. Luke you were upstairs, did you see her?" Dylan asked as the others turned to look at him.

"Uh, no, I didn't see her. She must've slipped by me when I was on the phone." Luke shrugged as he climbed into Dustin's truck. They seemed appeased by his answer and all followed suit getting into the trucks.

Charlie and Patrick climbed into Patrick's truck. As they pulled out of the driveway, Charlie glanced at Patrick. "So have you noticed anything between Bellamy and Luke?"

"You know, now that you mention it, Lola told me last night that she caught them staring at each other pretty intensely."

"Ruth told me that same thing and after you guys left," Charlie said. "She said that she was going out to say bye to Luke and found them having some sort of moment. She did go to his place last night too, and I know she didn't get home until way after two."

"Does it bother you that your little girl and my boy may be involved somehow?" Patrick looked worried when he asked.

"Hell no, it doesn't bother me. You know I love that boy like he was my own. I'm actually kind of glad, because I know Ruth was worrying about Bellamy. I guess Bellamy's friend had let it slip to Ruth that Bellamy hasn't dated anyone in a long time. Anyway, Luke's a good man and whatever is happening between them, I certainly won't mind or complain."

"What about Dylan and Dustin? Well, maybe not so much Dustin, but you know how protective Dylan is of Bellamy. How do you think he'd react if Luke and Bellamy started dating?" Patrick glanced at Charlie as he pondered that question. He couldn't think of anyone better to be his daughter-in-law than someone he already cared for and loved. Lola, the night before, was already speculating how beautiful their children would be and where a good place for a wedding was. Patrick just hoped that two meddling moms and overprotective brothers would all just back off and let whatever was happening happen on its own.

"Honestly, I don't know how that son of mine would act, but I tell you what: if he loves his sister and he loves Luke, then he should just accept whatever is going on. Otherwise he could lose them both and that'd be the dumbest thing that boy has ever done." They ended their discussion as they pulled into the jobsite.

After the guys all left, Bellamy changed into a t-shirt and climbed into her bed. She couldn't remember the last time she had been so exhausted; granted, she didn't get much sleep the night before. It didn't take long before she slipped into a deep sleep.

***

Travis and Brad had tried reaching Bellamy twice after they left Charleston, but it kept going right to voicemail. Travis was really looking forward to this visit. He loved Bellamy's mom and dad—they had been nothing but nice to him. Her brothers, being the jock looking types, never treated him different, and he knew it was because of Ruth. Travis and Ruth had become extremely close after Bellamy lost the baby. Ruth never told Bellamy, who was dealing with her own grief, that Travis had been devastated about Rose. When Ruth had stayed with them while Bellamy recovered, Ruth had found Travis sobbing out in the parking lot of their apartment the night they brought Bellamy home. Ruth didn't say anything to him, she just wrapped her arms around him and held him until the tears stopped.

Travis had planned on helping Bellamy raise the baby. He'd offered to marry her and officially be Rose's father, but Bellamy told him no. She had said that as much as she loved and appreciated him that it'd be terrible for him. He hated that she was right. Bellamy was still trying to get the courage to tell the father and hoping that he'd be involved with the baby.

The closer they got to Beaufort, the quieter Travis got. "Trav? Whatcha thinkin' about?" Brad reached over squeezing Travis's hand.

Travis glanced at Brad smiling. He loved the way the sun seemed to make Brad's fresh-shaven head gleam. Sometimes he didn't know how he got so lucky to find Brad; they were opposites in so many ways, but then so similar. Brad's skin was light mocha, his eyes were a dark hazel. He was a sharp contrast to Travis's light-olive toned skin, chocolate brown eyes and ebony hair. Brad loved dancing, all types of music and socializing, whereas Travis only danced when forced, listened to rock music and preferred the solitude of home. Somehow it worked and they'd been together for two years.

"Nothing. It'll just be nice to see how Bell's doing. I think she's finally ready to tell Luke about Rose." Travis looked then switched lanes. They were twenty minutes from Bellamy's home.

"Why does she have to tell him at all?" Travis gave him a knowing look. "Yeah, I know—she needs closure with him, but god, she's gonna have to relive it all over again. I know I wasn't around then, but you both told me about it and I can't imagine it's any easier for her to talk about it now than it was two years ago when she told me. So do you think we're gonna get to meet him?"

"Yes, I'm sure we'll meet him. He's best friends with her brothers, and it's Dylan's going away party, so I'm sure he'll be around."

"Well, if he hurts her, so help me, I'll beat his ass," Brad muttered under his breath.

Brad was very laid-back, but if he was provoked or someone he cared about was hurt, he turned into a mean motherfucker. Travis knew Brad loved Bellamy like she was his sister and they both had watched her grow so much stronger in the last two years. Travis would be damned if he let anyone cause her to have a setback.

"I don't think you'll have to worry about that. I'm pretty sure if her brothers knew what happened between them they'd take care of it before you could. But you play nice; I'm sure if he had any idea what Bellamy went through he would've been there. Brad, I love you, but we can't interfere. This is for Bellamy. She needs to do this when she's ready."

"Okay, you're right. I'll behave," Brad told him as they drove into Beaufort.

***

Bellamy woke up from her nap feeling refreshed. She sat up stretching when she heard a horn honking over and over. She got up and walked over to the window, looking out to see Travis's midnight blue Mustang pull into the driveway. Bellamy squealed as she flew down the stairs and out the front door. She jumped into Brad's arms as Travis yelled as he got out of the car. "Uh, Bell, why aren't you wearing pants?"

Bellamy looked down and realized that she was in just a t-shirt and panties. "Oh my gosh! I just got up from a nap. I'm so excited you guys are here." She loudly kissed Brad on lips and ran over to Travis, throwing her arms around him. He grabbed her around the waist and threw her over his shoulder and started towards the house.

She smiled at Brad, who walked behind them. "Brad, have I ever told you how sexy I think you are? Travis smacked her hard on her exposed ass. "Ouch," she yelped.

Brad chuckled behind them as they walked into the house. Travis sat Bellamy down on her feet and gave her the once over, his eyes widening. "What the hell, Bellamy; you had sex with him, didn't you?"

Bellamy looked at him with a shocked expression. "I, uh—what are you talking about?"

"I don't know, but I can just tell. You've got that 'I've had sex' look."

"There is no such thing, Travis, and you know what? Yes, I had sex with Luke and I just may do it again. It's been six freaking years. I know it's just sex, but I'm going to enjoy it while it lasts." Bellamy pushed by him and started walking towards the stairs.

"Bellamy, wait!" Travis said. "I'm sorry, okay? I just want you to be careful."

"I promise I am. I'm protecting my heart this time and it won't matter once I tell him about Rose.

He'll probably never speak to me again. So for once in my life I'm being selfish and going after something I want, because in another week, we'll be back in Savannah and I'll probably never see him again." She turned on her heels and walked up the stairs with Travis and Brad following.

"Honey, Travis didn't mean to sound like an ass. You know we're here for you no matter what," Brad said as he sat down next to Bellamy on her bed, wrapping an arm around her shoulders.

Bellamy looked up at Travis as he stood there. He walked silently to her and sat on her other side. Bellamy smiled at him as she pushed some of his ebony bangs off of his forehead. "Trav, I know you're just lookin' out for me, but I'm a big girl and I promise not to break. Okay?

"Okay, honey, now we want details, and don't you dare leave anything out."

Bellamy smiled as she settled in the middle of her bed with Brad on one side and Travis on the other. She told them about her lunch date, the incident at the jobsite and a little that happened the other night, but that was all. Bellamy didn't feel it was necessary to give any details about what went on with her and Luke in private, because that's what it was…Private.

"All right, all right, so you're not gonna give us details. But honestly, how was it?" Travis asked, picking up her hand and kissing it.

Bellamy put her head on Travis's shoulder and sighed. "It was incredible. That's all I'm gonna say. So where are we going tonight, boys?"

Brad put his arm around her shoulder. "Well, we thought we'd go to Club Xtreme tonight. We'll have some drinks and do some dancing. Did you bring The Outfit?"

Bellamy smiled. "Of course I did. It better fit me because Momma's been feeding me too good." She patted at her stomach.

Travis and Brad got off the bed and helped Bellamy up. "All right, honey , we're gonna go get checked in at the hotel and relax for a little bit. We'll be back at eight to get you, so be ready," Travis said as he and Brad walked to her doorway.

Bellamy threw on her robe and walked over, kissing Brad on the cheek and then kissing Travis. "Oh, I'll be ready, boys." She winked and then led them downstairs as they said their goodbyes. Bellamy watched them pull out of the driveway and then went back upstairs. Her boys were in town and she was so excited to spend the night dancing with them.

Tomorrow, though—that was another story. She couldn't help but wonder what Luke had planned for her. Bellamy knew it was a mistake, but she'd already made so many where Luke was concerned. What was one more?

***

Bellamy was in her bathroom putting the finishing touches on her hair. She usually always wore it showcasing her natural curls, but tonight she decided to flat-iron it until it hung smooth and sleek past her shoulders. She checked her make-up, which was minimal, but decided on a cherry colored lip gloss.

Bellamy walked back into her room took off her robe and began to get dressed. She pulled on her black lacy Victoria's Secret cheeky panties, smoothing them into place. Bellamy pulled on her black mini-skirt, checking in the mirror that her ass wasn't hanging out. The next piece was a deep red corset-top that she never would've picked out for herself. Two months ago, while she was out shopping with Brad, he saw it in a window display and made her try it on. She had to admit that it was beautiful. It cinched in right above her belly-button, showing off just enough of her stomach. Bellamy loved how it lifted her breasts, making them look fuller then they were. She put on the last piece of the outfit: a pair of black peep-toe stiletto pumps.

Bellamy took one last look at herself in the full-length mirror in her bathroom. She always felt a little uneasy when she wore the outfit, but Travis and Brad had insisted she looked hot in it, and they were tired of seeing her in her usual tank-top, cotton shorts and flip flops. She grabbed her black coach wristlet and went downstairs to wait for Brad and Travis.

When Bellamy arrived she was surprised to find it empty. She knew her parents were home because her mom had come up and talked to her after her shower. She went into the kitchen, looked out the sliding door, and saw her parents talking animatedly to Travis and Brad. Bellamy stood there for a minute observing them. Brad was wearing a hunter-green t-shirt that stretched tight across his muscled chest and tucked into a pair of faded jeans that fit his lean legs, hugging in all of the right places. She smiled as she watched him sit down and put his arm around her mom, both of them laughing at something her dad had said. Travis was leaning against the railing, watching and smiling at Brad. His brown eyes always seemed to be intense when he was looking at Brad. His ebony hair was a little shaggy, his bangs tapered across his forehead.

Travis's body wasn't as muscled as Brad's, but Brad spent a lot of time in the gym. Travis preferred just a simple plan of running and eating right. They were certainly a beautiful couple. Bellamy envied what they had. She knew they struggled at times, but it only seemed to strengthen their relationship.

Bellamy was lost in her thoughts when she saw Travis waving from the deck. She shook her head, smiled and walked out to the deck.

"Hot momma! Ruth, does your daughter look great or what?" Travis beamed at Bellamy.

"Yes, she does. My goodness, honey, you look fantastic. The boys just told us you're going dancing." Ruth stood up, walking over to her and grabbing her hands.

"Uh-huh. We're going to Club Xtreme. Are you sure I look okay?" Bellamy smiled at her mom with a hint of uncertainty in her eyes.

"You look great, but you'd look better if that skirt went to your ankles and your shirt actually covered your stomach." Her dad laughed from behind her.

"Oh, honey, don't listen to your daddy. You'll always be five in his eyes. But yes, you do look beautiful. You guys have fun and be careful." Her mom kissed her while Brad and Travis shook hands with her dad. Her mom giggled like a school girl when Travis and Brad both kissed her goodbye. Bellamy gave her dad a peck on the cheek and followed the boys around the house to Travis's car.

Ruth grabbed Charlie's hand and pulled him into the house. "Well, Mr. Carmichael, we're all alone for the night. What do you suppose we do about it?" Ruth let out a squeal when Charlie picked her up and tossed her over his shoulder. Her laughter flooded the empty house as he carried her up to their bedroom.

Chapter 8

Luke grabbed a pair of jeans out of his dresser and was putting them on when his cell phone rang. He looked at the caller ID and saw that it was Dylan calling. "What's up, Dyl?"

"Nothing. You meeting us at Dustin's?"

"Yeah, I'll be there in twenty. So what's the game plan?" Luke said, holding the phone with his shoulder as he slipped his jeans on.

"Well, my whore brother wants to go to Club Xtreme tonight and check out the single ladies. I'd rather go play pool, but he's convinced Zach that we needed to go hunting for women. So there ya have it." Dylan chuckled.

"Club Xtreme…All right, let me finish getting ready and I'll be there." Luke hung up and went to his dresser and pulled out one of his vintage rock t-shirts and threw it on. It fit snugly across his shoulders. He looked in the mirror, rubbing his hands through his hair. He didn't care if his hair looked disheveled because he wasn't trying to impress anyone. The only person he cared about was Bellamy and she had plans tonight. He'd shaved in the morning, but already his face was covered in a light five o'clock shadow. Luke grabbed a belt and his Dr. Martens out of his closet.

When he was done getting ready, he shoved his wallet in his back pocket, grabbed his keys and took off out the door. The whole way to Dustin's he wished he was going out with Bellamy. He couldn't get her off of his mind. Every time he closed his eyes he could see her naked body stretched out under him. He could smell the floral scent of her shampoo, and he felt like he could still taste her on his lips.

Luke flashed back to the present as he pulled up in front of Dustin and Zach's house. When he got to the door, Zach opened it, letting him in. "What's up, Luke? You ready to do some dancing?"

"Yeah right, dude, I'm just along for the ride," Luke said as Dustin handed him a beer when he walked into to the living room.

"Just as long you don't try to cock-block. I'm in the need for some action," Dustin said as he sat down on edge of the couch. "What's up, Luke?"

"Nothing. Are we gonna go soon?" Luke said and then took a long pull of his beer.

"Yeah, we're just waiting for Dylan to get off the phone." Luke raised an eyebrow in question. "He's talking to Chris. Dylan hasn't talked to him in a while and Chris wanted to tell him all about his new wife Betsy."

"His wife? Huh. Well, good for him. Why didn't he invite Dylan to the wedding?" Luke asked. "I thought they were really close." Chris Edwards was Dylan's friend who served with him in the Marines.

"Yeah, I guess it was a spur of the moment thing. Nobody knew they got married until they got home from Vegas. Why anyone would want to get married is beyond me. I love my freedom and I love not having to answer to anyone," Dustin exclaimed.

Luke had no idea why Dustin was anti-marriage Luke certainly wasn't looking to get tied down anytime soon, but Dustin always swore that he'd never take the plunge.

Dylan came out, slipping his cell phone back in his pocket. "Well, that crazy bastard is something else. He calls to talk to me and then decides that he wants Betsy and me to talk. She stammered through most of the conversation, but whatever. As long as he's happy, I guess. So you guys ready?"

They all said yes as they made their way out to Dylan's truck. Luke would've rather stayed home and had Bellamy come over. "So what's Bell up to tonight?" Luke tried to play coy as he asked.

Dylan turned to look at Luke. "Her best friends Travis and Brad are in town, so she went out with them tonight. We told her we'd try to hook up with them later."

Luke didn't like the idea of Bellamy out with two guys. Sure he had no claim to her, but he sure as hell wished he did right about now. Tomorrow night he'd have to question her about these guys. He had no right, but he didn't really care. He'd occasionally heard Ruth or his mom mention this Travis, but nothing more than just how much they liked him and how good he was for Bellamy. He was good for Bellamy, not those yahoos. He shook his head, trying to get those possessive thoughts out of his head. Luke had it bad for her and he just needed to accept it and keep her in his bed. He'd just have to suck it up and deal with Dylan, man to man. and prove to him that he'd be good to his sister, because hell—he was already half in love with her.

***

Bellamy sat with Travis at a table near the dance floor while Brad was at the bar getting their drinks. It was only a little after eight o'clock and the club was already packed. It was the weekend before the big Fourth of July festival that they had every year and it always brought lots of tourists around the area, giving all of the local businesses tons of traffic, including the clubs.

Brad came back to the table with Bellamy's gin and tonic and his and Travis' beers. The music wasn't very loud at first, so they were able to talk without trying to shout over the music. Bellamy took a sip of her drink and smiled at Travis. "Thank you for coming this week. I know you both have been super busy, and I just wanted you to know how much I appreciate it."

"Sweetie, I don't know why you keep thanking us. We wanted to come, plus your mom practically begged me to come visit." He smirked.

"Yeah, yeah, my mom loves you. You're a real kiss-ass, you know that?" Bellamy laughed.

"You're right, Bell, and it's not just your mom. Mine calls him, not me, her son," Brad said, rolling his eyes.

"Okay. Enough with the 'let's give me shit all night' game you two love to play." Travis pretended to pout. Bellamy jumped off of her bar stool, walked around to Travis and wrapped her arms around him.

"You're such a good actor, brat! Oh, I love this song. Who's gonna dance with me?" Bellamy stood between them, waiting. Brad stood up and grabbed Bellamy's hand. "Trav, you coming?"

"No, you guys go ahead. I'll come out in a little bit."

Travis loved watching them dance together. In the two years he'd been with Brad, he watched as Bellamy and Brad developed a very special relationship. He sometimes worried that if things with Brad didn't work out that he'd lose Bellamy in the process. Travis knew that was ridiculous, but he occasionally was plagued by his own insecurities. He snapped out of it to watch Brad wrap his arms around Bellamy's waist, moving to the beat of the music.

Song after song, he watched them gyrate on the dance floor. He could tell that Bellamy was having a good time because she had the biggest grin on her face. Brad was protective over her, so a lot of times when they went out dancing he'd hang all over her. Travis didn't care because it kept guys away from her. He knew they needed to step back and let her take care of herself, but she seemed to bring out their possessive nature.

Brad had ahold of Bellamy's hand as they walked back to the table. "You two were looking good out there." Travis smiled proudly as he said it.

Bellamy wrapped her arms around his shoulders. "I don't want you feeling left out, Travis," Bellamy murmured against his ear.

"Honey, I swear you're not leaving me out. Brad loves to dance and I don't, so you're actually helping us both out." Travis watched as she walked back to her seat and took a large drink from her glass.

"So where are your brothers, Bellamy, I thought they'd be out with us tonight?" Brad asked.

"Oh, crap!" she exclaimed. "I was supposed to call them so we could meet up. Let me step outside and I'll call them quick."

"Wait, Bell, you're not going outside alone," Brad said as he stood up. "Trav, we'll be right back."

Bellamy knew there was no point arguing with Brad, so she let him lead her out of the front entrance of the club. She pulled out her cell phone and hit Dustin's number on her contact list. Bellamy held the phone to her ear as she listened to it ring and ring. Dustin didn't answer, so she left him a message telling them where they were. She closed her phone stuck it back in her purse.

"No answer?"

"No, but I told him where we're at, so maybe they'll show up."

They started walking back to the door. When they came back in the club, the lights were flashing and the bass was pulsing through her body. Bellamy was walking behind Brad when an arm snaked out a seized her around the waist.

Bellamy yelped and saw unfamiliar eyes staring at her. "Um, hi. Could you let me go, please?" The guy was looking at her like he'd eat her up in a second, causing her heart to start beating a frantic rhythm in her chest. He was a mountain of a man; in her heels she came up to his shoulders, but he seemed as wide as he was tall.

"Maybe I don't wanna let you go. I'm dying to know what's under that little skirt of yours," he whispered against her ear.

"N-no, thanks. I just want to go back to my friends." Bellamy felt his grip loosen a little and she used that opportunity to slip away from him. She scrambled to catch up with Brad. She turned to see the guy who grabbed her staring at her while he whispered something to the guy next to him. A chill ran down her spine seeing the two of them stare at her with a scary intensity. Bellamy knew she should've told Brad about the guy grabbing her, but she knew he'd go after them and she just didn't want any trouble.

They got back to the table, finding that Travis got them another round of drinks. She sat down, grabbed her glass and took a huge swallow letting the crisp flavor chase away the nervous feeling in the pit of her stomach.

"So did you get a hold of the guys?" Travis asked.

"No, I got Dustin's voicemail, but I did leave a message telling them where we're at, so maybe they'll show up."

They all sat and finished their drinks as they watched people crowd the dance floor. When

Bellamy was done with her drink, she grabbed Brad, pulling him to his feet. "Come on, let's dance. You coming yet, Travis?" Bellamy asked.

"Not yet, you guys go tear it up. I'll come out in a little bit," Travis said. As he watched Bellamy and Brad go to the dance floor, he went to the bar.

***

The guys got to the club around nine-thirty. They'd decided to stop at Shooter's first to have a pitcher of beer and play a quick game of pool. Luke wasn't a big fan of the club scene anymore. It was one thing when he was younger and he was trying to get laid, but now it wasn't. He followed the guys to the bar where Dustin ordered them a round of beers.

Dustin passed out the beers while they all stood there. "Do you guys want to find a table or just stand?

"I doubt we're gonna find a table," Luke said. He had to raise his voice for Dustin to hear him over the music. They followed Zach and Dylan to the end of the bar that was by the dance floor Luke looked around seeing people everywhere. He had to admit there were a lot of good looking women there, but it was only one that kept running through his mind

Luke stood next to Dustin, who was scanning the club. "Hey, isn't that Travis?" They all turned to where Dustin pointed to a guy with short black hair who seemed to be watching the dance floor intently.

All Luke could think was that Bellamy must be here. He wanted to walk around and look for her, but decided to wait and see what was going on with this Travis.

Dylan called out to the guy sitting at the bar. "Hey! Travis!"

Luke watched as the guy turned to them, smiled, and started walking over. "Hey, Dylan, how are you, man?" Travis asked while giving Dylan the usual guy half hug, half handshake. Travis turned and did the same thing to Dustin.

"We're good, man, just glad you could make it here for a visit and Dylan's party. Come here, I want you to meet a couple of friends of ours." Dustin led Travis over to Zach and Luke. "Guys, this is Travis, Bellamy's best friend. Travis, these are some really good friends of ours, Zach Peterson and Luke Carter."

Travis shook Zach's hand first. "Hey, man, nice to meet you."

Zach nodded. "Yeah, you too."

Travis stuck his hand out towards Luke. "Luke, it's nice to meet you."

"It's nice to meet you too, Travis. Is Bellamy here?" Luke asked, trying not to sound eager.

"Holy Shit!" They all turned to Zach, who looked like he wanted to swallow his tongue. Zach pointed towards the dance floor. Everyone turned to look and saw Bellamy dancing with some guy that none of them knew. Bellamy was dancing with her back against his chest—the guys' arm was wrapped possessively around Bellamy's waist, his hand coming to rest on her exposed stomach. They moved sensuously together and drew several looks from other people on the dance floor.

"Travis, please tell me that's Brad, otherwise I'm gonna have to kick someone's ass," Dylan muttered.

"Yeah, that's Brad. Doesn't she look hot?" Travis exclaimed.

Luke said absolutely nothing as he watched Bellamy on the dance floor. She looked amazing. Luke could've sworn that if she moved just right he could see her ass. He could feel his dick start to harden just from looking at her. Luke knew that the guy dancing with Bellamy was with Travis, but that still didn't stop the desire to walk out there and pummel him.

She was smiling and laughing, and he wanted to be the one that was out there with her. Maybe he'd dance with her later. He knew Dylan would probably be a problem, but he knew he might as well get it over with now. Luke needed Dylan to know that even if it was while she was home that he was going to be involved with her. He caught Travis glaring at him out of the corner of his eye. Luke wondered if Travis knew what happened between he and Bellamy all those years ago.

Dylan walked over to Dustin. "Why in the hell did Mom and Dad let her leave the house looking like that?"

Dustin looked at his brother, shaking his head. "Man, I know you feel the need to protect her, but you've got to stop. She's a grown woman, and I'm sure that's why they let her leave looking like that.

You know you'll end up pushing her away if you don't stop."

"Shit, I know you're right, I just can't help myself." They both looked out at the dance floor watching their baby sister having a good time.

"I know, but back off a little, let her do her thing and just trust that she'll be all right. Now, let's go do a shot," Dustin said, pushing Dylan towards the bar.

Travis watched Luke stare at Bellamy with such an intensity he almost thought he should be worried, but he had a feeling that Luke had feelings for her. He decided to let it be for now, so he went out to the dance floor and smiled when Bellamy's face light up when she saw him.

Bellamy grabbed Travis by the shoulders and the three of them moved in unison, letting the music flow through them. Travis hated to dance, but Bellamy loved when he'd do it for her and Brad. The three of them swayed to the beat. She felt Travis and Brad get closer to her. Bellamy always figured it was their way of dancing together, but not. Bellamy happened to glance to the side and saw him, Luke, standing by the bar watching them, or maybe he was just watching her. She nervously licked her lips, watching him watch her. God, she loved him and wanted him so much it made her heart ache. "Only Girl in the World" was pulsing through the speakers as her eyes stayed locked on him.

She felt Travis's lips near her ear. "He looks like he wants to eat you alive, Bell. Let's give him a little show."

Bellamy swallowed any nervousness she was feeling as the three of them started to undulate their hips. She let the beat of the music flow through her body, losing herself to the music and having Luke watch her.

Luke kept telling himself to look away, but he couldn't; it wasn't until he felt someone standing next to him that he turned away. Dustin was standing next to him with a questioning look on his face. "What's up, Dustin?" Luke tried to sound nonchalant, but he could hear his own nervousness come through.

"Nothing, just seeing if you were ready for another beer. Zach's buying the next round."

Luke held up his beer bottle, seeing that it was almost empty. "Yeah, let's go." He followed Dustin to the bar, where Zach was passing out beers. They all were standing around shooting the shit when Travis and Brad walked over to join them. Travis went through all of the introductions, and out of the corner of his eyes Luke saw Bellamy walk down the dark hall to the bathroom. He excused himself and followed silently behind her, waiting in the hall when she entered the ladies' room.

***

Bellamy used the restroom then went to the sink to wash her hands. She checked her hair and clothes in the mirror. She pulled out her lip gloss and quickly applied another coat to her lips. Bellamy was satisfied with how she looked, so she opened the door and walked back into the hall. She felt someone tap her shoulder and when she turned, Luke was standing there.

Before Bellamy could react, Luke pushed her against the wall, taking her mouth with a fierce passion. She clutched his shirt and kissed him back as hard as he was kissing her. Bellamy felt Luke's hand slide up her leg until he reached her ass. She felt him rub and squeeze it, causing her to moan into his mouth.

Luke pulled his mouth away as his hand slid around the front until he cupped her mound. He smiled when Bellamy whimpered against his lips. "Bell, you look so fuckin' hot. It's taking all of my self-control not to rip your panties off and fuck you right here against the wall." He watched her head fall back as he slipped his hand beneath the fabric of her panties, finding her hot, swollen and wet. Luke found her clit and rubbed his finger in tiny circles around it. It didn't take long before he could tell she was close to coming, but the men's room opened when someone walked into it.

"Shit! I'm sorry, baby, as much as I'd like to have you come all over my hand right here and now, I'm afraid we'd probably get kicked out of here." He bent his head, capturing her lips in a soft, sensual kiss, but just as he started to pull his hand out of her panties, she grabbed his hand, holding it right over her pussy as she started to climax right there.

Bellamy couldn't believe that she just had an orgasm outside the bathrooms. She closed her eyes. As the pulsing stopped she felt embarrassed because it was more the sincerity of the kiss that triggered her release. When Bellamy cracked open her eyes, Luke had a shocked expression on his face. She felt her cheeks grow hot under his stare, "Oh my gosh, I—I s-should g-g-go." Bellamy tried to get past him, but Luke wrapped an arm around her.

"Jesus, Bellamy, that was the sexiest thing I've ever seen." He rubbed his thumb over her swollen bottom lip. "Tomorrow can't get here soon enough." Luke leaned down and kissed her one more time before he let her walk back to the group first.

Bellamy felt like she was walking on rubbery legs when she spotted Travis and Brad talking to Dylan and Zach. She smiled at them, but felt awkward when Travis gave her a knowing look. Bellamy walked over to Dustin, wrapping her arms around his waist.

"Hey, little girl." He stared at her for a second and then whispered into her ear. "Uh, Bell, your lipstick is smeared."

Bellamy quickly wiped around her mouth. "Is it better?"

"Yeah, and don't worry, I'm not even gonna ask."

"Thanks." Bellamy watched as Luke joined the group.

Luke noticed Dustin look at him closely and then back at Bellamy. He really hoped that neither he nor Dylan saw what he and Bellamy were doing outside the bathrooms. Dustin turned to him. "Luke, your lipstick matches my sister's."

Luke quickly scrubbed his mouth with the back of his hand. "Shit, I'm sorry, Dustin, I can explain."

Luke and Dustin turned to see Bellamy watching them with a worried look on her face. Dustin smiled at her and then turned back to Luke. "Listen, she's a grown woman, but so help me, if you hurt her in any way, shape, or form, I won't stop Dylan from kicking your ass. When he's done, it's my turn, and you know I can be a lot meaner than him."

Luke let a nervous laugh escape his lips, but his expression turned serious. "Dude, you know I'd never intentionally hurt her. Please don't say anything to your brother because I want to do it myself."

Dustin clapped him on the back. "Yeah, okay. Have fun with that."

Bellamy let out a sigh of relief. She wormed her way through the group and wrapped her arms around Dylan. "Hi, big brother. You gonna come dance with me?" Dylan didn't like people knowing that he was a good dancer. Their mom used to have him dance with Bellamy when Ruth was trying to teach her different styles of couples dancing. Throughout high school Bellamy had become extremely good at the jive, as well as Dylan. Dustin would tease them incessantly about it, but then he'd grab their mom, swinging her around the studio floor. Dancing was just something that they all enjoyed doing together.

"Sorry, Bell, but I'm gonna have to pass." Dylan smirked as he turned back to Brad and Travis.

Bellamy walked over to Dustin, Luke, and Zach who'd just joined them. "All right, who's dancing with me?" She tapped her foot, waiting for a response.

Dustin and Zach looked at each other, then her, both shaking their heads. "Fine, what about you, Luke?'

"Uh, maybe later?" Luke said, looking uncertain.

Bellamy rolled her eyes at them. "Fine, I'll go dance all by my lonesome." She laughed as she walked right through them to get to the dance floor. Bellamy found a spot right at the edge of the dance floor so Luke would get an eyeful. She smiled when Ke$ha's "We R Who We R" starting bumping through the speakers. Bellamy let the music flow through her as she started letting her hips sway sensually from side to side; her arms floating above her head. She let her head fall back and her whole body started moving to the music.

Bellamy let herself get lost in the song, not caring if anyone was staring at her; well, everyone but Luke. She turned slightly and caught sight of Luke staring at her she flashed him what she thought was a seductive smile. She knew it must've worked because she saw him shift his weight. Bellamy let her eyes drift down to the obvious bulge in his pants. She continued her visual assault on him, slowly licking her lips as she let her eyes drift closed. When Bellamy peeked at Luke from beneath her lashes she swore he moved closer to the dance floor. As the song went on she let her body sway, moving her hips to the beat of the music. Bellamy decided to be bold so she extended her arm, motioning to Luke in a come hither motion.

***

Luke had to fight every urge he had to fuck her right then and there. He tried to let his gaze move to other women on the dance floor just for a brief reprieve, but with every thrust and swivel of her hips he was lost. He stood there contemplating whether or not to go out there with Bellamy. She was turning him on intentionally with the little dance she was doing. He turned to see Dylan having some deep conversation with Brad and Travis. Dustin and Zach were talking to a couple of girls at the bar. He turned back to Bellamy and strode out to the dance floor, pulling her to the middle. Some song about finding a lover came on and the beat was good enough that Luke knew he could handle it. He wrapped his hands around Bellamy's waist as they started dancing.

As Bellamy started moving, Luke felt her press her stomach firmly against his expanding dick. He felt her start to undulate in small circles against him and it was driving him out of his mind. Luke gave in and started moving in unison with her, enjoying the feel of her body pressed snugly to his. Bellamy smiled up at him and it lit up her whole face. He couldn't help but return it. It was safe to say that he was so far gone for this woman and he decided he just didn't care anymore.

***

Bellamy gazed up into Luke's green eyes and felt her heart start to flutter. She let her fingers slide up into his hair; it felt soft and silky beneath her fingers. She loved that he wore his hair a tad too

167

long because that messy look really, really worked for him. She smiled when she pressed her body more firmly against his. Bellamy could feel his arousal as she rubbed against him.

Although her experience was severely lacking, she still wanted to do so many naughty things to him. She'd learned a lot watching porn, but there was nothing like hands-on learning. Bellamy just hoped that her severe lack of experience wouldn't show because then she'd have to confess that he'd been her one and only lover. He'd been her first and she wanted him to continue to be her first for everything. She could only pray that he'd want to be her last, too.

Bellamy sighed when Luke lowered his head to let his lips tickle the side of her neck. She slid her hands down to the back of his neck, letting her nails graze his skin.

"Bellamy, I swear, if you don't stop doing that I'll have no choice but to drag you out to your brother's truck and fuck you," Luke growled in her ear.

She turned her head, smiling, placing a small whispering kiss on the corner of his mouth. Bellamy then leaned into him to whisper in his ear. "I wouldn't mind," and gave him her most demure smile.

Luke was ready to drag her out of there when Travis came out to the dance floor. "Hey, you two, we're all gonna head to Shooter's."

"Sounds good," Bellamy said as she and Luke followed Travis off the dance floor. All of the guys turned and smiled at her when she walked up. "So, boys, you ready to get your asses kicked at pool?" Dustin, Dylan and Zach all turned their heads, laughing. "What? Why are you laughing, you jerks," Bellamy said with a feigned pout.

"You are the worst pool player I've ever seen. Plus, you cheat." Dustin laughed.

"I don't cheat. I can't help it if you boneheads get distracted easily." Bellamy turned to Travis and Brad. "I don't cheat, do I?" She gave them puppy dog eyes.

Brad held up his hands in surrender. "Uh, I plead the fifth." They all started laughing when she came at him wrapping her arms around his neck.

"Brad, you're such a brat." She let go and started walking in the direction of the door, calling over her shoulder. "Fine, I'll just sit and watch like a good little girl." Brad and Travis ran to catch up with her telling the guys they'd meet them at Shooter's.

As the three of them walked around to the side of the club, Bellamy couldn't help but smile as Brad grabbed Travis's hand. She loved them both so much and hated that they couldn't be more open in their relationship when they were out in public. Not only were they a gay couple, but an interracial one as well. Bellamy smiled when Brad turned towards her and held out his other hand to her. She'd been so worried when he and Travis started dating that she'd be tossed aside, but they immediately had hit it off and Brad never made her feel like a third-wheel.

"Well, isn't this sweet, we've got two queers and what—your little whore groupie," a deep voice mumbled from behind them.

Bellamy felt Brad tense as the three of them turned to face whoever was behind them. Brad pulled Bellamy behind him and Travis protectively. Her eyes widened in recognition, it was the guy from earlier. Bellamy counted five guys standing there, they were all big guys, but none were as big as the one who seemed to be their leader.

Travis spoke up first. "We don't want any trouble. We're just trying to leave."

The leader smirked, "Oh, they don't want any trouble, boys. Well, by all means, we'll just let you leave so you can fuck each other in the ass." His friends started laughing as they stood there.

Bellamy felt Travis and Brad turn her around and each grabbed a hand. It happened so fast none of them had time to react. She watched horrified as Brad and Travis were shoved forward, but before Bellamy could rush towards them an arm snaked around her waist and a hand covered her mouth as she was lifted off the ground. Bellamy struggled against the guy holding her, but he was too strong.

"Put her down, dickhead!" Travis yelled. "She hasn't done anything."

The big guy smiled. "Oh, she's done plenty: strutting her ass around in this outfit and then leaving with you queers. My friends and I are gonna show her what real men can do." Bellamy felt his hand slide up from her waist to cup her breast. The other guys all started to get in front of their friend. Bellamy couldn't help the tears that starting running down her cheeks.

Bellamy watched Brad take a step forward with his fists clenched. "Put her down, asshole!" He then threw the first punch, and all hell broke loose. Bellamy tried to scream past the hand covering her mouth as Travis and Brad started taking on the four guys. She fought against the hold that the guy had on her, but he tightened his grip and started walking backwards from the fight.

Before she knew what was happening, Bellamy felt her back connect with a truck. Her heart started pounding when she saw the look in his eyes. He had his big body pushed up against hers.

"Looks like it's just you and me, so I'll make it quick." He leaned forward, licking the side of her face

Bellamy felt her adrenaline kick in and she started fighting him with all of her might. His hand slipped down so it was only covering half of her mouth, she opened and clamped down on his hand as hard as she could. Bellamy went wild in his hold, kicking and hitting at him until he dropped her. She brought her knee up and connected with his balls. He dropped to the ground with a grunt. Bellamy ran around the truck and jumped onto the back of one of the guys charging at Travis.

"What the fuck!" Bellamy heard him yelp. She grabbed his hair in both hands and pulled as hard as she could. She felt him try to buck her off of his back until she was lifted off of him by the big guy. Everything went to slow motion as the guy whose hair she pulled turned and grabbed her legs as she started to scream.

***

Luke and Dylan led the way out of the club. They were starting to walk to the truck when they heard a scream. Luke looked at Dylan. "What the fuck was that?" When they rounded the corner they all froze. Luke saw Travis and Brad fighting with three guys, and then they heard the scream again. Luke felt his blood start to boil and anger pulse through his body as he saw two guys grabbing and struggling to get Bellamy in between two trucks. When reality set in, all four men went charging after them. "Bellamy!" Luke heard himself yell as they got closer. He grabbed the guy holding Bellamy's legs by his shirt, pulling him away from her. The guy swung, but Luke ducked in time and landed a right hook right his face.

Bellamy felt herself begin to panic as the two men started dragging her away, but all of a sudden the guy holding her legs was gone. She fought the hold of the other guy until he was gone, too. Bellamy curled into a ball to protect herself until strong hands grabbed her. "Bell?" She looked up into Dylan's eyes. Bellamy couldn't help the ragged sob that escaped from her throat. She heard the guy who had grabbed her start to groan as he lay on the pavement. Still sobbing, Bellamy felt like she was having an out of body experience. She pushed Dylan away from her and stood up, and with a primal cry she ran over to the guy still lying on the ground and started kicking him in his side over and over. "You bastard! Don't you ever touch again!" Bellamy was ready to go at him again when arms wrapped around her.

"Baby, don't." She turned her head. Luke bent his head down and gently put his lips against her ear. "Calm down, baby." Bellamy felt her legs give out as Luke sat on the ground, pulling her into his lap. She snuggled into him as he wrapped his arms around her, speaking into her ear. Bellamy swore that she heard the sounds of sirens getting closer.

***

The police had come and taken everyone statements, but the assholes that had attacked Bellamy, Brad and Travis managed to slip away while everyone was checking on Bellamy.

The whole time the police were talking to Bellamy, Luke didn't let go of her. When they finally finished, he turned her so they were face to face. Luke could feel her trembling as he held her. He grabbed her chin, tipping her head up. "Baby, are you okay?" Bellamy gave him a watery smile and nodded. He hugged her tighter to his chest as he rubbed her back. Luke watched as Dylan approached them with a pissed off look on his face, but it didn't stop Luke from continuing to hold her.

"Bellamy Ann?" Dylan all but barked at her.

Bellamy let out a heavy sigh as she turned to her brother. "What, Dylan?"

Dylan walked up to her. she could tell he was upset.

"What just happened here wouldn't have had you worn something that actually covered your body. Five minutes more was all it would've taken and we would've been too late to stop them from assaulting you. You've got to be more careful, dammit!"

Bellamy could hear the rest of the guys groan and try to get Dylan to shut up, but she was seeing red and she didn't care. "Oh, I see. I didn't realize that I asked for that. Stupid me! I'm sick and tired of you trying to run my life." She ignored him when Dylan started to open his mouth. "Yeah, yeah, you still hold some guilt from something that happened when I was ten years old. Dylan, I'm almost twenty-five: get the fuck over it!" Bellamy couldn't help that sobs racked her body. "You've got no idea what I've been through…Jesus! Travis, please get me out of here." Travis and Brad came over to her, wrapping their arms in a protective embrace around her as they led her to Travis's car.

Dylan and Dustin stood side by side as they watched Travis and Brad lead Bellamy away. "I didn't mean to upset her…I just freaked out. You and I both know given the chance those guys would've grabbed Bellamy and would've been gone before we even realized what the hell happened. I didn't mean it when I said it was her fault because of how she's dressed."

Dustin clapped a hand on his shoulder. "I know you didn't. She's pissed off right now, just let her cool off and then you can apologize. Let's just go back to the house and chill." They all started walking back to Dylan's truck when Luke pulled out his phone.

Brad helped Bellamy get settled in the front seat of Travis's Mustang. The sobs had quieted, but she still was angry and hurt. She heard her phone ringing. She pulled it out of her purse expecting to see that it was Dylan, but instead it was Luke.

"Hi," was all she could get out.

"How ya doin', baby?" His voice was soft and gentle when he spoke to her.

"I'm okay, I guess."

"Well, we're getting ready to go back to Dustin and Zach's, and then I'm heading home. Come over?"

"You really want me to after what just happened?" Bellamy hated how whiny her voice sounded.

"Yes, I do. I just need to see you. I'll be home in about ten minutes. Will you come?" He sounded eager for her to come.

"Yeah, I'll be there." She closed her phone and looked at Travis. "Can we grab something quick to eat? I'll tell you how to get to Luke's afterward."

After stopping at a drive-thru, Travis pulled into a parking spot and turned to look at Bellamy as she quietly ate her burger. "Bell, are you sure you want to go over there right now?"

"Yes, Travis, I'm sure. Please don't worry about me, okay?" She smiled when he grabbed her hand and gave it a squeeze.

"All right, if you're sure, but you call us if you need us." Bellamy nodded at him and then back at Brad. "All right, Bell, how do we get to Luke's?"

***

When Luke got home he unlocked the house, turned the porch light on, and sat on the steps waiting for Bellamy to get there. He wasn't expecting anything to happen between them tonight. He just wanted to spend some time with her since she was so upset after her fight with Dylan. He saw headlights turn down his street and saw the Mustang slow to a stop at the curb. Luke watched Bellamy lean over, hugging Travis. She opened the door and climbed out, hugging Brad when he got out of the backseat to get into the front. Both guys waved at Luke as he stood up, walking to Bellamy. He'd do anything to see that sad look vanish from her face.

When she reached him, Luke pulled her into a hug. "Come on, baby, let's go inside." He kept an arm around her waist as he walked her inside. Luke led her into the living room. "Why don't you find a movie for us to watch and I'll get you something to drink."

"Okay," Bellamy said as she watched him walk out of the living room. Bellamy picked up the remote, turning the TV on so she could see if there were any movies coming on. She absently went through channel after channel, but nothing was jumping out at her. Bellamy started going through the movie channels when she saw a movie she wanted to see: *Unfaithful* with Diane Lane and Richard Gere. She'd never seen it before, but she thought Richard was hot so she'd give it a chance. She kicked off her shoes, tucking her feet underneath her when Luke came walking back in with two sodas and a bag of popcorn.

Luke sat down next to Bellamy and smiled when she snuggled into him. "So what movie are we watching?" He asked as he grabbed a handful of popcorn.

"*Unfaithful*, is that okay?"

"Um, sure. I've never seen it. Do you want me to shut the lights off?"

"I'll get them." Luke watched as Bellamy got off of the couch and hit the switch to turn the lamps off. He put his arm on the back of the couch while Bellamy sat back down and snuggled into him again.

They both sat in silence as the movie started Bellamy's hand was absently stroking his chest, and Luke was dying. She didn't even realize that his dick was so hard and she was practically in his lap. It felt nice sitting there with Bellamy in his arms. Tomorrow he'd talk to Dylan, he figured better to face him head on about his feelings for his sister. He closed his eyes hoping that this wouldn't throw the friendship they had away. Luke had to be prepared that it could come to that because he was pretty sure he couldn't give Bellamy up yet.

He groaned to himself as he watched the scene where Diane Lane's character and her lover were in a public restroom going at it. Luke felt Bellamy's body tense next to him. He watched her out of the corner of his eye. Her lips parted and she slowly licked her lips. Luke could've sworn he saw her clench her thighs together. His sweet little Bellamy was getting turned on by the hot sex scene.

Bellamy was so turned on by the movie she had to slow her breathing, otherwise Luke would know for sure, but that wasn't necessarily a bad thing. She let her hand that was on his chest start sliding down. Bellamy reached under his shirt, softly stroking his stomach, she heard his breathing hitch and in one fluid motion she turned herself over so she was straddling his lap.

Luke opened his mouth to say something, but Bellamy silenced him with her mouth. The kiss was soft and tender and Luke let her control the pace. He wrapped his arms around her back, his hands stroking lightly over her exposed skin. As she kissed him, she started pulling his t-shirt up. Luke leaned forward so she could get it over his back then he leaned back so she could pull it all the way off. Luke startled Bellamy when he cupped her face with both hands. "Bell, you don't have to do this. This isn't why I asked you over."

Bellamy leaned forward, kissing his chin and down his jaw. "I know. I want this." She continued kissing him. She licked and nipped as she made her way down his neck to his chest. She kissed and licked every inch of his chest. Bellamy could feel the steady beat of his heart as she slowly lowered herself, her lips never leaving his skin. She knew what she wanted to do next, but she was nervous. Bellamy wasn't sure if he'd figure out she didn't know what she was doing. She had seen it done enough on the porn she watched. She had accidentally walked in on Travis doing it to Brad once, but seeing it done by two people who cared about each other was so different. Brad whispered words of love as Travis lost himself in the act. She didn't stay to watch the finale because she didn't want to embarrass them or herself.

She was just gonna have to do it and hope she didn't look like an idiot. Her trembling hands started to undo his belt. She undid the button and then slowly started lowering his zipper. Bellamy yanked Luke's jeans down, with his help, to his knees. She pulled down his boxer briefs, licking her lips at the sight of his huge, glistening erection.

Bellamy slowly reached out, trying to wrap her hand around the base of his cock, he was almost too big around for her hand. She leaned forward, sticking out her tongue, and let it glide over the smooth head. Bellamy moaned at the first taste of the salty, musky fluid that oozed from the tip of his cock. She continued to swirl her tongue round and round, licking him from root to tip. Bellamy braced herself: it was now or never. She opened her mouth, sliding down around his cock until it hit the back of her throat. Her gag reflex caused her to ease off until he was only half-way in. She moaned when she felt Luke's hand slide into her hair. Bellamy pulled almost all the way out when she swirled her tongue around the tip and then closing her mouth around him again.

The sucking sounds Bellamy was making were causing Luke to lose his mind. He could tell she wasn't experienced at giving blowjobs, but her enthusiasm made up for it tenfold. "Bell, baby, you better stop or I'm gonna come in your mouth." She mewled around his cock and started sucking harder. He let his fingers sift through her hair, but then grabbed her head, stopping her. "N-no, baby, I want to be inside you when I come." Luke grabbed her and pulled her on the couch.

He leaned over her, kissing her deep. He loved that it had her whimpering. Luke started kissing her down the same path she had taken. She groaned when he reached that sensitive spot where her neck met her shoulder. Luke reached around, finding the zipper that held her top together. He continued his assault on her neck, then gliding his tongue down to the tops of her breasts. When he had the top undone, he pulled it down until her breasts were free. They were firm and perky, her nipples a dusky shade of pink.

At the first swipe of his tongue over her stiff peak, she cried out. His other hand rubbed over the other nipple, lightly pinching it between his fingers. The gentle pull of his lips around her flesh made her squirm, rubbing her pussy against his leg, the need for release was becoming overwhelming. Luke slid lower, kissing and nipping at her stomach all the way down to her mound. "Come here," he whispered. He helped her slide her rear-end to the edge of the couch. Luke grabbed her panties and slid them down her legs and off. He grabbed her legs, pushing them up until her feet rest on the couch. Luke smiled at his handy work. She was open to him and the glow from the TV let him see her luscious pink folds.

Bellamy watched in awe as he held her thighs open and lowered his head. She saw his tongue take a slow, gentle swipe of her pussy from the bottom to the top. Bellamy couldn't help the moan that escaped from her lips. She couldn't take her eyes off of him as the tip of his tongue made tiny circles over her clit and when he sucked it between his lips, she grabbed his hair and ground her pussy up to his face.

Bellamy was like some erotic picture brought to life. Her body was arched off the couch. She had one hand in his hair while she grabbed the back of the couch with the other. Luke couldn't take his eyes off of her, her eyes were glassy, her lips parted as she moaned his name over and over. He rubbed one hand down her thigh until it found her pussy hot and wet. Luke let his thumb glide down her slit until he reached her opening. He eased the tip in as he began his assault on her clit, pulling it between his teeth until she screamed over and over as her hips bucked off of the couch. Luke gently licked her pussy until the spasms stopped. He smiled as she sank into the couch with a satisfied grin on her face.

Bellamy felt like she couldn't move. It was like her muscles had turned into Jell-O. She opened her eyes to see Luke smiling at her with a devilish grin. Before she could react, he pulled her to the floor until she was sprawled on top of him. He devoured her mouth in a kiss that ignited her desire all over again. Bellamy didn't know when, but at some point he removed his pants and sheathed himself. She felt him reach between their bodies, lining up his cock with her entrance.

"Baby, I'm just gonna warn you this time is gonna be quick," Luke said, his voice coming out hoarse. The tip of his cock was right inside of her, and already he could feel the overwhelming heat of her. Luke's hands slipped down, grabbing both ass cheeks in his hands, and with one thrust he was buried deep inside of her. He loved the sound of her voice when she cried out from the pleasure. He brought his hands up to her face, stroking her cheeks as she was panting. Luke sensed something was off when she didn't start moving. "Bellamy, have you ever done it like this before?" It made his heart ache when she turned her turned her head to the side and whispered "no."

Luke pulled her face down to him, kissing her deeply. "Don't turn your head from me. Just let me guide you."

Bellamy was mortified, but when he kissed her again she managed to get out a small. "Yes."

She felt him reach down and grab her ass as he slowly started rocking her. It felt incredible that way. Bellamy swore he was deeper inside of her. She bent down, taking his lips in a kiss that she hoped would show him how much he really meant to her. Bellamy's tongue stroked his as she crushed her mouth to his. She felt him arch up into her as he continued to rock her hips back and forth. Bellamy found her own rhythm and started grinding her hips down to meet Luke's thrust. They were deep and hard, causing an ache that started deep inside of her. She started rocking herself hard against him. The pleasure built and built until Bellamy swore she was coming apart.

"Luke, oh god, I'm—I'm...!" Bellamy shrieked as she grabbed at Luke's biceps, her nails digging into his skin.

Luke took over, flipping Bellamy to her back. His thrusts began to come in a frenzied pace. Each thrust brought him closer to the brink. He slid his hands under Bellamy's rear-end, tilting her enough that he knew he was hitting the sweet spot inside of her. She was beautiful, her skin glowing from the light sheen of sweat covering her, her eyes closed as her moans became louder and louder. As she started to come around him again, she threw her head back with the expression of euphoria all over her face. Luke felt the jolt shoot straight down his spine and right up his cock as he came in violent jerks. He felt every ripple of her cunt milking the last of his orgasm from his cock. Luke collapsed on top of Bellamy, making sure he wasn't smashing her to the floor. He buried his face in her hair, trying to collect himself.

Luke pushed himself up onto his forearms. Bellamy had her eyes closed, with a soft smile on her face. He brushed the hair that was hanging in her face. "How're you doing?" Luke bent down and kissed her lips.

"I-I'm gooood," she whispered against his lips. Her breath caught in her throat as she stared into Luke's green eyes. The look he had on his face made her pull her bottom lip between her teeth. Something serious was on his mind because he was staring at her with a vehement gaze. "A-are you-are you all right?" Her voice shook.

Luke blinked his eyes and shook his head. Staring down at Bellamy made his heart flip in his chest. No one had ever made him feel that way...ever. Luke knew a part of him always had, but he'd fallen in love with her. He didn't walk into this to satisfy an urge, which was what he tried to tell himself in the beginning. Luke knew it was more that he had to see if what he was feeling when he saw her again was real or just his imagination. "Nothing's wrong, I just couldn't help it. You're so beautiful." He grinned at the sight of the blush creeping up her cheeks. He kissed her quickly on the lips then stood up. "Come on, let's go to bed. I don't think we'll feel very good if we fall asleep on the floor."

"I don't think I can get up," she groaned, which turned into a shriek as he lifted her up off of the floor, and began carrying her down the hall. Bellamy laid her head down on his shoulder, yawning so big that her jaw made a popping sound. She covered her face as she giggled.

Luke carried her into his room and tossed her onto his bed. He stood at the end of the bed smiling at her, taking in the sight of her sexy-as-sin body. Luke crawled onto the bed, pulling her up with him until they were face to face. He smiled at the sleepy grin on her face. "You sleepy, baby?" She nodded her head as she yawned, covering her mouth with the back of her hand.

The blankets were already folded down since he didn't make his bed in the morning before he left for work. Luke turned Bellamy so that her back was pulled snugly against his chest. "You know, I really should take you home. Your mom and dad might wonder where you're at." He leaned down, kissing her shoulder.

"Luke I'm an adult, but I'm pretty sure they'll just assume I'm with Travis and Brad. Let me stay." She grabbed his hand, turning it to kiss his palm. She felt him smooth her hair away from her shoulder placing a tender kiss right behind her ear and it caused a shiver to slide up her spine.

"I want you to stay, Bell." *Forever.* He wanted to say, but he didn't know where her thoughts were at yet. Luke felt Bellamy's body go lax against him, as her breathing started to slow. He smiled at the feel of her sleeping in his arms. Luke was exhausted, so he let sleep overtake him.

***

Dustin woke up at nine-thirty; he normally was an early riser, but last night he'd stayed up with his brother, talking about the incident with their sister. They both loved her equally, and she them, but Dylan's overly protective nature was always a strain between them. Dustin walked into the kitchen to find Dylan sitting at the table drinking coffee.

"Morning," Dylan said from the table. "How'd you sleep?"

"I slept all right. When did you get up?" Dustin muttered as he walked to the cupboard to get a mug down.

"About a half hour ago, I was just getting ready to call Bellamy see if I could take her to lunch, and apologize for last night."

"Yeah, probably not a bad idea, bro." Dustin watched as his brother grabbed his cell phone and dialed their sister.

"Hey, Bell, could you call me when you get this…Please."

Dustin watched him end the call and place another.

Dylan had called their mom. Bellamy hadn't come home last night and she figured that Bellamy had stayed with Brad and Travis. She told Dylan that if he apologized for whatever he did, Bellamy would forgive him because she loved her brother. She gave him Travis's number and wished him luck.

"Hello?" Travis answered, sounding like he'd just woken up.

"Travis, this is Dylan. I didn't mean to wake you, man, but I was hoping I could talk to my sister."

"Your sister? Well, she's not here," Travis whispered

"Where is she, Travis? Don't beat around the bush, either." Dylan could hear Travis whispering to someone in the background. "Travis, tell me: where is she?"

He heard Travis sigh into the phone. "We dropped her off at Luke's last night."

"Well, why in the hell is she at Luke's?" Dylan all but barked in the phone.

"Dylan, listen to me. Luke called Bellamy last night after we left the club and he wanted her to come over."

Dylan was seeing red. He made it clear to all of his friends that his sister was off-limits. He meant it when she was eighteen, and still meant it with her being twenty-four.

"All right, well—thanks, Travis." Dylan got off the phone and got up from the table. He walked into the living room slipping his shoes on and grabbing his keys.

"Dylan, this is not a good idea. Why don't you calm down first before you do something you'll regret?" Dustin pleaded with him.

"No, I'm not waiting. I wanna know what the fuck is going on." Dylan wrenched the front door open and stalked to his truck. He didn't look behind him when he yelled at Dustin. "You comin'?"

Dylan heard his brother running after him. "Yeah, yeah, I'm coming; to make sure you don't do something stupid."

Dylan grunted at that and climbed into his truck. He couldn't understand what Bellamy was doing spending the night at Luke's. She'd never been as close to Luke as they had when they were younger, granted she had a crush on him back then. If something had happened between Luke and Bellamy last night he was gonna have a serious problem. Neither brother spoke the rest of the way to Luke's.

***

Bellamy woke up to Luke kissing her shoulder. She couldn't help but smile. She wiggled her bottom closer to Luke and realized that he had an erection. Luke's hand came around her waist, pulling her to him tighter. "Good morning, beautiful," he whispered against her neck, causing goose bumps to rise up all over her skin.

"Good morning. I slept so good last night." Bellamy moaned and stretched next to him.

Luke pushed Bellamy to her back, settling himself between her legs. He smoothed her hair away from her face, leaning down to take her lips in a gentle kiss. Luke flexed his hips, pushing his erection against Bellamy's slit. He kissed her harder when she whimpered against his mouth.

Bam, Bam, Bam. They both jumped at the sound of someone pounding on the front door. *Bam, Bam, Bam.* Bellamy and Luke looked at each other and both muttered in unison. "Dylan." Luke jumped out of bed, digging a pair of flannel pants out of his drawer. He threw one of his button-up shirts at Bellamy. "Just stay here until I figure out what's going on." Luke leaned down and kissed her lips.

"Oh god, I'm sorry, Luke. I should've gone home last night. Don't worry, though, you won't have to choose between me and your friendship with Dylan. I'll call Travis to come get me."

Luke smiled at her and then kissed her again. "No, Bellamy, there won't be any choosing, all right? I was planning on talking to your brother today, anyway. I want us to keep seeing each other."

Bellamy gave him a smile that lit her whole face. "I'd like that."

"Good, now sit tight while I talk to Dylan." Luke hurried out of the room, shutting the door behind him.

When Luke flung the front door open he saw the questioning glare that Dylan was giving him. Dustin was standing behind him, shaking his head. "Mornin', boys. What's up?" Dylan didn't wait for invitation, he just pushed past Luke, hollering for Bellamy. "Dylan, what's the problem?"

Dylan stopped, frozen in place as he looked in and saw the living room. Bellamy's clothes were on the floor with her shoes and he saw the condom wrapper on top of Luke's jeans. He slowly turned to Luke. "Did. You. Touch. My. Sister?" Dylan gritted out.

Luke knew there was no point in lying, so he braced himself for the aftermath of his admission.

"Yes, I did, Dylan. I know you're pissed, but I care about your sister a lot. I didn't want you to find out this way. I was gonna find you and talk to you about her."

"So what, you want my permission? Well, guess what, you don't have it. I thought I made myself clear that I wanted none of you to touch her...ever."

No one but Luke noticed Bellamy come around the corner. She looked sexy as hell in Luke's shirt, but now was the wrong time to rub it in Dylan's face.

"Excuse me, but when did I give you permission to run my life? Again, Dylan, you can't control or decide what I do. I'm sorry you found out this way, but you know what? I. Don't. Care. I'm a grown woman who can make her own decisions. So keep throwing your little tantrums and guess what? I'll never speak to you again. I'm happy for once. I haven't been this happy in a long time, so sue me for enjoying it." Bellamy watched Dylan just stare at her. The tension in the air was so thick Bellamy almost felt like it was crushing her.

"Bell, I love you," Dylan pleaded. "I just don't want you to get hurt."

"Huh. Well, I guess you've got no faith in someone who has been like a brother to you all your life." Bellamy quickly wiped the tears that started to fall from her eyes.

"You're right. He wouldn't hurt you, at least not on purpose." He was silent for what seemed like an eternity. "Fuck! I need to get out of here." Dylan turned to Luke. "Sorry," he muttered and walked out of the door.

Dustin walked over to Bellamy, embracing her in a hug. "Don't worry, Bell, as you can see he's almost over it. Just let us get used to this."

"Yeah, sure," Bellamy said against Dustin's shoulder.

Dustin walked over to Luke. "Sorry it didn't work out the way you wanted as far as telling him, but I honest to god think he'll be cool. I'm sure I'll see ya later."

Bellamy watched her brothers pull away from the curb. Sure Luke had said that it wasn't going to be a matter of choosing, but she still felt terrible. Bellamy let Luke pull her into his arms and he just held her for what seemed like an eternity. As much as Bellamy wanted to stay with Luke forever, she knew that as soon as she told him about Rose he'd hate her for keeping something like that from him. Bellamy knew she should've tried harder to tell him she was pregnant, but she was eighteen, scared and overwhelmed. Yet with all of the conflicting emotions she was feeling, she just couldn't tell him yet.

Bellamy pulled away from Luke. "I-I should probably go home. I'm sure by now Mom and Dad are wondering where I'm at."

"Let's get dressed and I'll run you home. Are we still on for tonight?" Luke asked with a hopeful look.

"Definitely. What are we doing? I just want to know what I should wear."

"I thought we could take the boat out and grab some sandwiches and snacks to bring along." Luke pulled her into another hug. "Does that sound good?"

Bellamy stood up on her toes to plant a kiss a kiss on his lips. "That sounds wonderful." Luke kissed her again before they went back to his room to get dressed.

Chapter 9

Luke pulled out of Bellamy's driveway after dropping her off, wondering what he should do now. He decided he might as well go pay a visit to his parents. Luke was sure that when his mom heard what he was doing tonight she'd start with the inquisition. He figured now was as good a time as any. Luke wanted to go talk to Dylan, but he knew he had to give Dylan some space for now and hoped that they were still friends when all was said and done. He knew nothing was for certain with Bellamy, since she lived forty-five minutes away and they hadn't really talked about any sort of relationship, but he at least wanted to see what was there.

He pulled into the driveway of his family's home, the home he was born and raised in. The home was a huge ranch-style. It was a combination of red brick and cream-colored siding. Not only was his mom a wonderful baker, but she also was a gifted landscape artist. All along the house were different flowers: roses, ferns, honeysuckles and mountain laurel. Luke walked up the two steps leading to the front door. He checked the door, which was unlocked. Luke walked in and hollered out for his parents. He knew he needed to announce himself after the last time he stopped by and interrupted his parents enjoying each other, which just about gave Luke nightmares.

"Luke!" Lola exclaimed as she walked out of the kitchen to kiss her son on the cheek. "What are you doing here, baby?"

"I just thought I'd stop by and visit," Luke explained as he followed his mom into the kitchen. He sat down at the table as his mom placed a hot cup of coffee and a blueberry muffin in front of him. "Thanks, this looks delicious."

Lola sat across from her youngest son and smiled. "So, Luke, I just have to ask: are you and Bellamy seeing each other?" He choked on the sip of coffee he just took.

"Uh, yeah, kind of. How did you know?"

"Oh, honey, a person would have to be blind not to see the way the two of you were watching each other the other night. Of course, Ruth and I were the only ones who really noticed," his mom said as she reached across the table, grabbing his hand. "Your daddy and Charlie talked about it and we all couldn't be more thrilled."

"Mom, we're just seeing each other, don't get all starry-eyed like we're getting married or something. Plus, Dylan found out about us this morning, and right now, I don't think he's very happy with us, or at least me."

"That boy. I love him to death, but I swear his protectiveness of Bellamy is gonna drive her away.

I know Ruth is going to ask Bellamy to move back here, but if Dylan doesn't watch it he'll be the reason she doesn't," Lola said as she got up to refill Luke's coffee.

Luke was sitting at the table silently eating his muffin when his dad came in. He smiled when he watched his mom's face light up seeing her husband standing there. Luke admired his parents; he couldn't have asked for better role-models growing up. The love they had for each other was evident to anyone who knew them. When Luke was younger, they'd hit a rough patch and his dad had moved out for six months, but both of his parents were miserable. Neither of them had dated anyone while they were separated, and one night his dad had shown up crying.

Lola had sent Luke and Jason to Jason's room, where they listened from the doorway. His dad had begged their mom to forgive him for being an asshole and taking out his stress on her. They could hear their mom hesitating until their dad had promised to spend the rest of his life making up for the way he'd treated her and the boys. Jason had led Luke down the hall so they were closer to their parents to hear their mom whisper that she loved him so much and wanted him to come home. Luke remembered flying around the corner to wrap his arms around his dad's legs. Patrick had scooped up his youngest son and with his other arm wrapped around Jason's shoulders. He cried and cried.

His dad had kept his promise to make it up to his mom, even though she always insisted that he didn't need to; they just celebrated their thirty-fifth wedding anniversary.

"Mornin', Dad." Luke smiled at him from the table.

His dad walked over, patting his son on the shoulder. "Mornin', son. What brings you by?"

"Just coffee and to talk," Luke said

"Oh yeah, what did you need?" Patrick asked. He'd give him anything in the world if he asked. Patrick was so proud that Luke decided to follow in his footsteps. Even better, he loved working alongside him every day. His boys had both grown into wonderful men and he couldn't be prouder.

"He's dating Bellamy," Lola blurted out before Luke could say anything.

Patrick looked at his wife, smiled and then shook his head with a laugh. "I kind of figured that you two were, but like I told your momma over here, it's not our business. We just want you to be happy, son."

"I know, Dad We really haven't talked about what happens if and when she does go back to Savannah. She's twenty-four; I highly doubt that she's looking for something serious. Either way, we'll have fun while she's home." Luke was beginning to realize that he wanted serious with her, and if she didn't, he'd deal with it. "Can we just not talk about this anymore?" He knew how to change the subject. "So, Mom—girl or boy for Jason's kiddo-to-be?"

He smiled when his mom lit up. She loved her grandbabies to pieces and it killed her not to be near them.

"Oh, I think they're gonna be blessed with another little girl, but this one will look like Jason." She smacked her husband on the arm when he made a face. "Oh, you hush. My boys are so handsome, and of course Jason's children are beautiful. I'm sure when Luke starts giving me grandchildren they'll be just as gorgeous." She turned to look at Luke, smiling slyly.

"Mom, I hear what you're saying, but I'm a long way from having kids with anyone. So let's not jump the gun." Luke shook his head, but he knew this would happen once they all knew he was dating Bellamy. His mom practically had their wedding planned. He wondered if Bellamy was suffering through the same situation.

***

Bellamy was laying out on the deck relaxing with her mom while her dad was taking a nap in his favorite La-Z-Boy. When she got home her parents were sitting in the dining room having breakfast. They both turned when she had walked in. They both simply smiled at her and told her to sit and eat. Bellamy was thrilled that they hadn't questioned her about the night before. Now she was soaking up rays with her mom. She smiled at the sight of her mom in a bikini. Her body was still in good shape for having three children, let alone two of them at the same time.

Bellamy closed her eyes, thinking that she couldn't wait to go out with Luke. Bellamy had only brought a few dresses with her, so maybe she'd just wear her khaki skirt and a sleeveless t-shirt. She rolled over to her stomach and stretched out. Bellamy noticed that her mom had been silent for a while. She turned to look and found her mom's eyes closed and her mouth partially open. She'd fallen asleep. Bellamy smiled. How her mom did it, she wasn't sure. She ran her own business and also taught classes, but still had time for her and her brothers' activities. The woman was her role-model.

Bellamy didn't want her mom to burn, so she thought she'd wake her up. She got off of her lounger and walked over to her mom. "Mom, wake up. Come on, I don't want you getting a sunburn."

Ruth blinked her eyes and looked up at her daughter, smiling. "Hi, honey. Did I fall asleep?"

"Yes you did, Momma. I thought I better wake you. I didn't want you to get sunburned." Bellamy bent down, kissing her mom on the cheek. "I'm gonna go in and make us some lunch. should I wake Daddy?"

"Yes, darlin', wake your father up and we'll make lunch together," her mom said as she pushed herself up on the lounger.

Bellamy walked in through the sliding door, closing it behind her. She kicked off her flip-flops and padded through the kitchen to the family room where her dad was sleeping. She couldn't help but stand there looking at him. Bellamy missed him so much. It was true that she didn't come home much, and her dad was so busy with work that it made it hard for them to coordinate visits. What would he think of her if he knew that she'd gotten pregnant at eighteen? As tough as he was sometimes, he was a big teddy bear, and the baby and the secrets would break his heart. Bellamy didn't even want to know what Patrick and Lola would think of her if and when they found out. She'd have to make sure that none of this would come back and bite her mom in the ass. Bellamy and Travis had asked a lot of her mom when she drove to Savannah without telling Charlie the nature of her visit.

Ruth had been Bellamy's rock through everything, and how did Bellamy thank her mom? By making her lie to her husband and sons. She saw her dad open his eyes and she quickly tried to wipe the tears that were spilling down her cheeks.

"Bellamy? Bellamy, what is it, baby?" He grabbed Bellamy, pulling her down onto his lap like she was still a little girl.

Bellamy let her dad hold her as the tears kept coming and coming. Charlie noticed Ruth walk in looking concerned. "Honey, what happened? Why is she crying?"

"I don't know," Charlie mouthed.

Ruth knelt down in front of Bellamy rubbing her back. "Shhh… It's okay. Tell us what's wrong."

Bellamy sat up, drying her face with the back of her hands. Charlie grabbed her, hugging her tightly to his chest. He let her go so she stood up. "I-I'm sorry. I guess it just hit me that I miss living here and seeing you whenever I want. I know I've probably hurt you by not coming home more, but I promise I'll make it up to you."

Charlie watched Ruth wrap her arms around Bellamy and give her a squeeze. "Nothing would make me happier than having my baby come home more. Why don't you go lie down and rest. I'll wake you when lunch is ready."

"Okay, Momma." Ruth smiled when Bellamy leaned over to her dad, kissing him on the cheek before leaving the room.

When Ruth knew Bellamy was upstairs she came back, sitting on the arm of Charlie's chair. "What happened, Charlie? Why was she crying like that?" Ruth leaned towards her husband, when he slid his arm around her.

"I honestly don't know. I woke up and she was just standing there with tears running down her face. She wouldn't tell me what was wrong, so I just let her cry it out. I don't think it's the reason she says, though. I know she misses us, but those were different tears." Neither one of them said anything for several minutes and Ruth was lost in her thoughts.

Finally Ruth stood up. "I'm gonna get lunch started, and maybe when we sit down to eat Bellamy will tell us what's really bothering her." She walked out into the kitchen and began to wonder if Bellamy was trying to prepare herself for telling the boy who'd gotten her pregnant about their baby. Ruth understood why Bellamy didn't want anyone to know the identity of the dad. She knew Dustin and Dylan would've gone after the guy, which would've made things worse for her. Ruth shook her head, getting those thoughts out her head as she got out everything she needed to make lunch. She heard the front door opening and the voices of the twins echoing through the house.

"Mom?" Dustin hollered from the living room.

"In the kitchen!" she called back. Ruth smiled as her boys walked into the kitchen both of them coming over to kiss her cheek. "Have you boys come for lunch?"

"If there's enough. Is Bellamy around?" Dylan asked as he tucked his hands into the pockets of his shorts.

"Um, she is, but I made her go lay down. Something upset her earlier, so she went to rest for a bit."

"Mom, I think I'm the reason she's upset," Dylan sighed.

Ruth turned to look at her son. "What happened?"

He proceeded to tell his mom about the fight the night before and then this morning when he found out she was with Luke all night. She let him get it out because she could tell that he was worried that he made his sister upset.

"I think I'm gonna go talk to her," Dylan said as walked out of the kitchen.

Just as Dylan walked out, Charlie came walking in. He turned and smiled at Dustin. "Hey, son, how are ya?"

"Good, Dad, just hoping to score a free meal," Dustin said winking at his mom. His dad joined him at the table. He and Dustin started talking about work and sports while Ruth prepared lunch for everyone.

***

Bellamy was lying on her bed trying to fall asleep, but she just couldn't. Her mind was racing and she couldn't relax. Crying like that surprised her. She had so many thoughts going through her head all at once and it became too much for her. She rolled over so she was on her stomach, trying to quiet her brain. Bellamy was just about to give up when someone knocked at her door. She figured it was her mom checking on her, so she called out for her to come in. Bellamy sat up quickly when she saw Dylan walk into her room.

"Hey, Bell. Can I talk to you?" Dylan walked over and sat on the bench in front of her window.

She didn't know if she was up for his big brother lecturing again. "Um, sure." she said.

"I just wanted to tell you that I'm sorry for the way I've been acting the last couple of days." This was harder than he thought. "I know you're not a little girl anymore, and I know I shouldn't still feel guilty for something that happened almost fifteen years ago, but I can't help it. Did you know that Dad wouldn't talk to me for a week after your accident?"

Bellamy shook her head at him.

Dylan laughed with an uncomfortable edge to it. "Yeah, I couldn't take the silent treatment from him, and watching you walk around so slow and uncoordinated the first few days afterwards, it was all too much. You know me—I'm not a crier, but once I started, I couldn't stop. It was the weekend and Dustin was out. I was watching TV in the family room by myself and you came in, you were wearing that damn Backstreet Boys nightgown that

Lola got you, you climbed right into my lap and wrapped your arms around my neck and told me not to be sad because you were okay, and Dad would stop being mad soon. I felt like such a girl, my ten-year old sister holding me and whispering it was gonna be okay. I just couldn't stop crying. You got off of my lap and all of sudden Dad was there pulling me up into a hug and telling me it was just an accident and that he still loved me. I'll never forgive myself for almost killing you." He watched as Bellamy came over, sat next to him and put her head on his shoulder.

"I love you, Dylan, and I know it was an accident." Bellamy smiled against Dylan's shoulder as he wrapped his arm around her. "I'm sorry that I yelled at you this morning. I don't want you being mad at Luke, Dylan. Whatever is going on between us is just that, between us." She pulled away looking him straight in the eye.

Dylan rubbed his hand over his buzzed head. "Do you love him?"

She couldn't believe her brother just asked her that, but Bellamy decided it was probably best to be honest with him. She cleared her throat. "I always have."

"Okay," he simply said. Neither of them said anything. Dylan stood up and pulled Bellamy into a fierce hug. "If you're happy, then I'm happy."

"Thanks, Dyl. Let's go eat. I'm starving," Bellamy said as she started walking out of her room.

***

The rest of the afternoon had been fun. Bellamy and her brothers played cards out on the deck. Bellamy caught her mom and dad standing at the sliding door watching them with enormous smiles on their faces. It was rare that the three of them were together. Dylan had been stationed overseas for two years, and then he was stationed in San Diego. It wasn't until last year when he was transferred to Perris Island. Bellamy wasn't home much because of Luke, so that left Dustin the lone child.

Bellamy talked to Travis and he told her that he and Brad were going to the beach. While her mom was making dinner and the boys left, Bellamy went upstairs to get ready for her date. She had taken a shower earlier, so she just fixed her makeup and changed into her khaki tennis skirt, blue sleeveless t-shirt and her white flip-flops. Bellamy checked herself over in the mirror and decided to throw her hair up into a loose chignon. She grabbed her orange and hot pink NIKE gym sack, shoving her billfold, chapstick and sunscreen inside of it. Bellamy didn't want to be presumptuous, so she didn't grab the clothes that she had laid out. She sat on her bench, staring out the window and waiting.

***

Luke was looking forward to taking Bellamy out all day. He spent most of the early afternoon hanging out with his dad when his mom took off to go check on the bakery. They'd watched some sports, napped and raided the refrigerator. Right when Luke was gonna head home, his brother called, which meant Luke talked to his sister-in-law, nieces and nephew. Of course, with Maisy it was non-coherent babbling, but he still talked to her, laughing when she said something, and he started laughing like she was the funniest person alive. He talked to Jason for a while and could tell that his brother was really happy. But then Jason had to become a smartass.

"So Bellamy, huh?"

"Let me guess: you talked to Mom. You know how she is, we're just hanging out and she's already got us married with kids." Luke couldn't help but smile at the thought of someday being married to Bellamy seeing her belly grow round with their child and how incredibly happy they'd be. He quickly shook his head, driving those thoughts right back from where they came.

"Well, you don't have to ask how I feel about it. You know I love Bell, and someone had to protect her from you heathens." Jason laughed. "I'm serious, though, don't listen to anyone else. Just be happy." Luke cleared his throat quickly to break the Hallmark moment they were having.

"Thanks, Jason. I think. I'm heading out, so I'm gonna have you talk to Dad. Love ya, man."

"Love you too, baby brother." Luke handed the phone to his dad, waved goodbye and left. He'd run home to take a shower and change clothes. Luke threw on his cargo shorts and t-shirt. He ran his hand through his hair, checking himself in the mirror. Luke could've kicked himself because he should've planned something better than eating sandwiches on the boat, but she was still here for another week, so he'd make it up to her. He grabbed his boating shoes, which were a pair of old, beat-up Chuck Taylor's. Luke slipped a couple of condoms in his wallet and slid them into his back pocket. He wasn't expecting anything to happen, but he figured it was best to be prepared.

Luke pulled into the Carmichaels' driveway and sat for a minute. This was his first time picking Bellamy up for a date and he felt like he was in high school again. He knew her parents and loved them, but he was nervous about facing Charlie. He got out of the truck and before he reached the door, Ruth opened it, smiling widely at him.

"Hi, Luke, how are you darlin'?" she asked as she hugged him.

"I'm good. I'm just here to pick up Bell," he said as he followed her into the house. Charlie came around the corner. "Hey, Charlie."

"Hey, Luke, so where are you taking Bellamy tonight, son?"

"We're gonna go out on the boat for a while and then I guess whatever she wants to do." Luke could hear the nervousness in his own voice.

Charlie smiled and patted him on the shoulder. "Well, you two have fun." He turned towards the stairs. "Bellamy, Luke's here!"

Luke watched Charlie walk by his wife, giving her a quick peck on the cheek. He turned when he heard Bellamy come down the stairs. She looked sexy in the little outfit she was wearing. The top she wore clung to her body so snug that Luke could almost see her delectable nipples poking through her bra. She walked over to him, reaching up on her tip-toes to kiss him quickly on the lips.

"Hey, Bell. You ready to go?" he asked, smiling down at her and then grabbing her hand.

"Oh, yeah," she said. Bellamy turned, yelling bye to her dad. "Bye, Momma," she said and kissed her on the cheek.

Ruth looked on as she watched Bellamy kiss Luke quickly. She wanted to laugh when Luke stiffened at first. She knew it was probably awkward picking up Bellamy for a date for the first time, but incredibly sweet. They all had been in each other's lives for so long and she knew that Luke probably was given a hard time by Dylan, but he was here, so that counted for something.

"Bye, you two, have a good time," Ruth called out as she watched them walk out to leave. She moved closer to the door and couldn't help but watch them. Luke opened the door for Bellamy and helped her inside his truck. Ruth bit back a groan as she watched Luke ogle her daughter's behind. She turned, grateful that Charlie had gone back to finish getting dinner ready for the two of them, because if Charlie had seen that, well, who knew what he would've done.

***

Luke pulled into a parking spot at the deli to pick up snacks and sandwiches. "I'll only be a minute. Do you want to wait here?"

"Yeah, you go ahead. I'll wait," Bellamy said as she smiled at him.

He leaned in, kissing her quickly before he jumped out of the truck. Bellamy leaned back in her seat, smiling as she watched him walk into the deli. She was deliriously happy, even though she knew she didn't have the right to be. Bellamy was keeping something important from him and it was going to ruin what she thought was developing. She scanned the parking lot when she caught a glimpse of someone very familiar to her. Bellamy quickly got out of the truck, going around the back.

"Stacy!" Bellamy called after one of her oldest friends. She smiled when she watched Stacy turn and saw her. Both women screamed with delight as they ran towards each other. They hugged for several seconds until Bellamy stepped back, looking over her childhood friend. Stacy was a couple of inches taller than Bellamy. Her deep olive skin tone reminded Bellamy a lot of Travis's. Stacy's eyes and hair were a deep-golden brown color. Stacy wore her hair in a funky pixie cut. Bellamy always thought her friend was so beautiful, even when Stacy didn't have a very high opinion of herself.

"Oh, my god, Stacy, you look fantastic."

"So do you, Bell, I've missed you so much." Bellamy could see the tears in Stacy's eyes and could hear the hitch in her voice.

Bellamy grabbed Stacy, hugging her tight. "I'm so sorry about your dad. How's he doing?"

"Well, considering...he's doing well. We're hoping to bring him home in a couple of days. Bell, god, we were so scared. They honestly didn't think he was gonna make it." Bellamy's heart broke for her friend.

Stacy dried her eyes and smiled at Bellamy. "So, how does it feel to be home?"

"It actually feels good, I've had a pretty good time so far." Before she could finish she noticed Stacy look behind, her smiling. Bellamy turned her head smiling as Luke walked up.

"Hey, Stacy, how ya doin'?" When Luke walked up, Stacy hoped he hadn't noticed her crying.

"I'm doing good, Luke. When you see your mom will you thank her for me? She sent a box of goodies for us and the nurses who have been taking care of my dad and they were delicious."

Well, wasn't that something, she thought. Luke and Bellamy together, Stacy knew how much Bellamy was in love with Luke when they were in high school and it killed Stacy the way Luke had hurt Bellamy their summer before college. She stayed by Bellamy's side while she cried that whole summer. They used to be so close, but Stacy had gone to college in Chicago. Slowly they grew further and further apart, but Stacy was gonna be around for a while as her dad recovered. Stacy really wanted to reconnect with Bellamy. She never managed to find anyone that she was close to like she was with Bell.

"It's not a problem, Stacy. I know my mom and Ruth have been to your house getting it ready for him to come home, so does that mean he'll be back soon?" Luke asked.

"Yeah, I was just telling Bell that he should be home Monday. Lola and Ruth have been fantastic. They've been so good to Mom, bringing her food, books, and visiting with Dad." Stacy noticed Luke grab Bellamy's hand, lacing his fingers with hers. "Oh, god, I'm sorry, guys, you're obviously heading somewhere." She hugged Bellamy. "Call me, okay? I want to get together before you go home."

"That sounds good, Stace. Hey, why don't I take you out for lunch tomorrow?"

"Yeah, that'll be nice. My mom has been pestering me about getting out and not hanging out at the hospital all day. Here's my cell phone number," Stacy said as she grabbed a pen and paper out of her purse, scribbling her number quickly and handed it to Bellamy.

Bellamy grabbed the piece of paper with her free hand. "Good, I'll call you tomorrow. Give your mom a kiss for me."

"Oh, I will and she'll be thrilled that we're going out tomorrow. Bye, Luke; tell Lola I said 'hi'," Stacy said as they turned to walk towards Luke's truck.

"See ya, Stacy." Luke opened the door for Bellamy, closing it when she got in. He climbed in on his side.

"Wow, Stacy looks fantastic. I'm so glad I ran into her." Bellamy sighed as she looked out the window at the passing scenery. "I feel bad that we lost contact with each other. She was my best friend."

"What happened between the two of you?" Luke asked with a quick glance.

"She moved to Chicago and I moved to Savannah. A lot of stuff happened that first year and we just slowly drifted apart, but I plan to make up for it while we're both home." Bellamy almost kicked herself for opening her mouth. She didn't want Luke to ask about her first year in college because she'd have to lie and she was so tired of lying. "So whose boat is this that we're going out on today?" Bellamy said changing the subject.

"It's my dad's and it's gorgeous. He and your dad went to an auction last year when he saw it. I guess it was a repossessed boat, so he got it for a good price," Luke said as they pulled into the parking lot of the marina.

Bellamy helped Luke carry the food and drinks down to the dock. When Bellamy saw the boat she couldn't help it but stop and stare. The boat was small compared to a lot of the other boats, but it was still really nice. It was, according to the side of the boat, a Sundancer. The outside was white with a dark blue trim. Bellamy watched Luke climbed into the boat. "Here, baby, hand me the food and the cooler."

She couldn't help but smile at the endearment as she passed him the bag from the deli and then the cooler. Bellamy watched as he tucked everything in a little cubby at the front. Luke walked back over to where she stood and held out his hand to her. Bellamy placed her hand in Luke's as he helped her into the boat. "Wow, this is so beautiful." Bellamy looked around the boat taking it all in. The interior was all white. The very front of the boat looked like a spot you could lay out on, and at the back of the boat was a table with seats on both sides of it. Bellamy saw a little opening next to the steering wheel. She wasn't prepared for what she found.

"Holy cow! Uh, Luke, it's a small room. Do your parents stay out here?"

Luke smiled at the expression on Bellamy's face when she saw the cabin. He watched as she went down into it and decided to follow. Luke came up behind her, wrapping his arms around her waist and kissing the side of her neck. "Yeah, at least a couple times a month they'll take it out and sleep out here." He continued his slow assault on Bellamy's neck. She smelled incredible. It was a sort of citrusy smell that was driving him insane. Luke heard a sigh escape out of Bellamy's mouth as she leaned into him. He let his hands slide down until he touched her thighs and slowly moved his hands up under her skirt.

"Luke! You in there, boy?" Luke dropped his hands and let out a frustrated sigh.

"That's Steve, he runs the place and has the worst timing ever. I'm coming!" Luke hollered as he turned to go back up.

Bellamy smoothed out her skirt and put her hands on her cheeks, which felt flushed. She turned to go back up to find Luke talking to Steve, who was an older gentleman with a protruding belly, bald head and a deep tan. Bellamy saw him look her over and then smile.

"Well, hello, darlin'." Steve turned to Luke. "Well, who's this pretty lady?"

Luke went over and grabbed Bellamy's hand, pulling her over to Steve. "Steve, this is my girlfriend, Bellamy Carmichael. Bellamy, this is Steve Peterson, he runs the marina."

Bellamy couldn't believe Luke just referred to her as his girlfriend. She wanted to jump up and down and squeal, but instead she stuck out her hand and shook Steve's.

"Carmichael, huh? Your Charlie's girl, aren'tcha?"

"Yes, I am. It's nice to meet you," Bellamy said with a smile.

"Well, I'll let you kids get on with it then. Luke, it's all gassed up for ya. Did y'all need anything else?" Steve asked as he climbed out of the boat.

"Nope, I think we're good. Thanks for gettin' her ready." Luke went over to sit in the seat and turned the key. He loved the way the engine purred. Luke watched as Steve untied the boat for him. Bellamy walked over and sat in the seat across from him and he watched as she slipped her flip-flops off. He noticed the almost surprised look on her face when he introduced her as his girlfriend, but it felt good to say it.

Bellamy slipped on her sunglasses and watched as Luke backed the boat away from the dock. She was glad that she didn't bother with any makeup because it was humid out and she would've sweated it off already. It was a beautiful evening. The sun was a little lower in the sky, there were no clouds and the slight breeze felt wonderful against her dewy skin. The motor was purring as Luke drove the boat out onto the river, and once he was out of the no wake zone, she watched him push down on the throttle and let it go.

They cruised down the river in a comfortable silence. Bellamy took in the scenery around her:

The trees were a vibrant green, the branches hung over parts of the river and were dripping with moss. She looked up as a flock of herons flew overhead and she smiled and waved at other boaters they passed. Bellamy couldn't help but watch Luke out of the corner of her eye. He hadn't changed much in the last six years. His face had gotten leaner, his cheekbones were more defined and his eyes had tiny lines in the corner. Bellamy loved the way the sun shined off of his hair, making it look a mixture of darker blond underneath and golden blond on top. Luke must've sensed her watching him, because he gave Bellamy a devilish-grin that made her squirm in her seat.

They rode for a half-hour when Luke decided to anchor near a sandbar so they could eat and kick back. He shut the boat off and dropped the anchor. "You ready to eat, baby?" Luke asked as he stopped in front of her, holding out his hands so he could help her up. She smiled up at him as she grabbed a hold of his hands and let him pull her to her feet. Luke pulled her into a hug and just stood there holding her. He kissed the top of her head and inhaled the scent of her shampoo. The scent of gardenias was quickly becoming is favorite scent. Luke led her to the little table in the back of the boat. He set the food down in a single seat and pushed the bench seats back up to turn it into a mini-sofa, at least that's what he called it.

"Go ahead and have a seat there, Bell," Luke said as he started unloading the sandwiches and proceeded to take the seat across from her.

Maybe it was the fresh air or maybe it was just him, but Bellamy felt like being naughty when she sat down. She knew he wasn't looking at her when she slid her hands up her thighs and grabbed the sides of her panties, slowly pulling them down and leaving them on the floor by her feet. Bellamy felt herself blush when she saw him look up at her and smile. With her heart hammering in her chest, she very carefully reached out and grabbed a sandwich. She peeled backed back the paper and smiled as she took a bite. It was a good thing she had sunglasses on so Luke couldn't see that she had quickly squeezed her eyes shut, realizing what she just did. Bellamy decided to act nonchalant about it and brought her legs up to tuck them under her.

The feel of the breeze flowing up her skirt to tickle her panty-less pussy was exhilarating; maybe she was going to have to go without panties more often. She bit into her turkey on wheat, savoring the flavor of the oil and vinegar. They both were hungry because at first they didn't talk much, but she felt so comfortable in the silence.

"Are you thirsty? I bought some lemonade, if that sounds good," Luke said as he bent down to open the cooler.

"That sounds good. Thanks." She took the bottle he offered her and opened it. The mixture of tart and sweet felt so good sliding down her throat. Bellamy couldn't help it as she watched Luke's throat work as he swallowed his drink, the corded muscles in his neck gleamed from the light sheen of sweat that was covering his skin. She quickly stuck her sandwich in her mouth to quiet the moan that wanted to escape.

"How's your sandwich, Bell?" Luke asked before taking another bite of his ham and cheese.

"It's really good, thanks. So I have to ask, how do you like the construction business and working with our dads?"

Luke smiled at her. "I love it. You know we've been around it for as long as we can all remember." He took a sip of his lemonade. "Mom says that since I could crawl I was building stuff. Dad got me my first toolbox when I was five and I helped him build and repair stuff around the house all of the time. He said that I had a natural talent for it, just like your brothers. Jason was the one who always had his nose buried in books, that's probably why he became a writer. Anyway, I guess it was my calling." He laughed a little to himself like an idiot. "So I figured you'd be some famous dancer or something by now, but you're personal trainer. What made you decide to do that?"

Great, she was going to have to tell half-truths now. It was true what they say: one lie leads to another and so on and so on... "Well, my freshman year I wasn't really sure what I wanted to do. I focused on dance the first quarter, but things happened and, well, uh—I quit and just focused on my general ed classes until I decided to go into Physical Fitness. My parents weren't super thrilled with my decision, but they got over it when they knew how happy I was. I do admit that I go a little overboard with my own training sometimes, but I've learned how to design programs for people based on different factors like age, fitness level, goals and what they enjoy. It's nice to enjoy my choice of career, especially if I make a difference in someone's life for their health." Bellamy took a sip of her lemonade and hoped to god he didn't see through some of her story. She really didn't think he was ready to hear that after she lost Rose she developed an addiction to food and gained thirty pounds. She had finally had it with herself and started to realize that eating the way she was wasn't going to bring her daughter back. She began working out and watching what she ate. By that first summer she had already lost half of the weight.

"Anyway, I just really love what I do, and couldn't imagine doing anything else," Bellamy said as she finished her bottle of lemonade.

Luke could've listened to her for hours. Bellamy's southern drawl was soft and almost unnoticeable unless she was really excited, angry or turned on. This morning when Bellamy had woken up, Luke had noticed how thick her accent was when she was sleepy, too.

It made him smile to hear the enjoyment her job gave her. He always wondered why she didn't pursue dance. She was fantastic and he loved watching her move. If the night before was any indication, she was still an awesome dancer. He had to clear his thoughts of her moving against him on the dance floor or he was going to have a raging hard-on, and since they were out on the river he knew he had to control himself.

Luke watched as Bellamy pushed her sunglasses up on top of her head and smiled at him. They talked for a long time while they ate the fresh fruit he got. Bellamy told Luke about Travis and Brad, they talked about their parents, about their brothers, and just about anything and everything. Luke couldn't remember the last time he had so much fun just talking to someone. "Bellamy, you don't have to answer this, but I was just wondering have you thought about moving back here at all?" While they talked, Luke had made his way next to her turning to his side so she could lean back against him.

"Yeah, I've thought about it some. It's not that far a commute, so I could still work at the gym I'm at. Why do you ask?"

"Well, I just want to be able to see you anytime I want, and it'd be easier if you lived here." Luke kissed the top of Bellamy's head. "I don't want you to feel pressured, because I'd drive to Savannah to see you every chance I got if that's where you want to stay."

Bellamy's heart swelled at Luke's admission.

They sat for a while, neither of them saying anything. Bellamy snuggled closer to Luke as he slowly stroked up and down her arm The boat's rocking was making Bellamy drowsy until she felt Luke's hand move over to rest on her lower stomach. She tried to steady her breathing, but as his hand slid lower, her breathing became more and more shallow. Bellamy rested her head on Luke's shoulder as he started slowly kissing down her neck, the whole time his hand had slid just under her skirt.

His hands were calloused. They lightly scraped against her skin, but she wouldn't have expected anything else since he loved to work with his hands. Bellamy held her breath as his hand ventured closer to the apex between her thighs, his touch was light and gentle, barely a whisper across her skin. She heard Luke hiss in her ear when his fingers brushed her pussy and found that she wasn't wearing any panties.

"Oh, you bad little girl, I know you were wearing panties earlier, so when did you lose them, darlin'?" Luke nipped at Bellamy's ear.

Bellamy felt herself get flushed as Luke brushed his fingers across her mound. She couldn't help the whimper that escaped her lips as Luke licked and nipped at her earlobe.

"I'm waiting for your answer, Bell," Luke said as he continued his slow seduction down Bellamy's neck.

"Uh, I took them off when we sat down to eat," Bellamy whispered.

Luke grabbed Bellamy's chin and turned her to face him. He lowered his mouth to Bellamy's, gently molding their lips together. Luke could kiss her for hours; normally he wanted to get right to the good stuff, but now, kissing Bellamy, he wanted to savor every second. She was bringing out a whole other side of him that he never knew existed.

He eased Bellamy's mouth open with his lips and plunged his tongue into her welcoming mouth. He could taste the sweetness of the lemonade on her tongue. Luke's hand that was still under her skirt slid down her pussy. He could feel the juices that were already covering her. He eased one finger inside of her, swallowing the moan that escaped from Bellamy's throat. The walls of her pussy were squeezing his finger as he worked it in and out of her.

"Yeah, baby! Give it to her!" a guy shouted from a passing boat, causing Bellamy and Luke to sit up quickly. They looked at each other in shock and then burst into a fit of laughter.

"Well, that was awkward," Bellamy laughed as she wrapped her arms around Luke's neck.

Luke slipped his arms around Bellamy's back, pulling her close. "Yeah, not a moment I'd like to remember. Come on." Luke stood up, pulling Bellamy up with him.

They walked side by side until they reached the opening to the lower cabin. Bellamy walked down into it first, Luke following right behind her. Before she could turn around, Luke came up behind her, wrapping one arm around her waist and gently pulling her head to the side. Bellamy's heart started to pound against her ribs as Luke began nibbling down her neck to her shoulder. She reached behind her, stroking Luke's cock that was hard and throbbing through his shorts in slow sinuous strokes, smiling when he groaned low and deep in her ear.

"Darlin', you don't know how much I thought about fucking you today. To feel your skin so warm and soft beneath my fingers, the beautiful pink shade of your nipples and their sweet, succulent taste and the taste of that sweet, sweet honey that coats my tongue when I lick you right here." Luke let his hand slip under her skirt finding her wet, hot and so ready for him. "Are you ready for me so soon, baby?" Luke crooned in her ear.

Bellamy whimpered as he spoke in her ear, her breathing becoming labored. She tried to swallow, but her throat felt thick with arousal. Bellamy wanted to show him with action how ready she was. Bellamy turned in his arms, jumping so she could wrap her legs around his waist. She grabbed his hair, pulling his head back, attacking his mouth in a passion-filled kiss that had them both moaning against each other. As she kissed him, she felt her back hit a wall. She reached down between them to unbutton his shorts, which proved to be difficult with his cock hard and straining against the zipper. Bellamy unhooked her legs, letting them slide to the floor.

Luke broke the kiss to catch his breath for a second and then leaned in so his forehead rested against Bellamy's, both of them panting. He felt her tugging on his shorts and then slowly easing the zipper down, reaching inside to grip his cock and started stroking it gently. Luke took her lips again and he felt her clutching his shirt. He sucked her lower lip into his mouth, nipping it and then lashing it with his tongue. The sound of her whimpering made his cock throb. "Come here, baby." Luke pulled her until she was in front of a built-in sofa. He got behind her and whispered in her ear. "Get on your knees and put your hands on the back." Luke watched as she slowly did what he asked. God, if she wasn't a vision: her back slightly arched, her tan-toned legs were slightly spread and the way her hips moved as she fought to catch her breath was completely sexy. Luke grabbed a condom out of his wallet and quickly sheathed himself. He got down on his knees and grabbed her thighs, pulling them further apart. Luke groaned when she opened to him and he saw the glistening folds of her pussy. He knew he needed just a little taste.

"Um, uh, Luke, what are yo….Ah god!" Bellamy had to catch herself before she pitched forward when his tongue stroked through her pussy. She felt his hands snake up until he was holding her ass to keep her hips at the right angle for him to continue his oral assault. Bellamy felt her head spinning and the blood rushing in her ears. She felt the tingling that started in her breasts then traveled down deep in her belly until it finally reached her clit at the same moment his lips surrounded it, and when he sucked her clit between his teeth Bellamy exploded. She felt like she was floating, and before she hit the ground, Luke poised his cock right at her entrance and thrust forward. Bellamy couldn't stop the cry that escaped from her lips as he impaled her.

"Aw shit, baby, you okay?" Luke panted and let his hands rest on her hips. He couldn't help but laugh when she started wiggling back against him. "Yeah, you're okay, aren't you?"

"Please, Luke, do something," she pleaded, her voice breathless and shaky.

Luke gripped her hips and started thrusting slowly in and out of her. He could stay like this forever if she'd let him. Bellamy's hair had come loose from the chignon and he brushed his hand across her neck so he could lean forward and gently nip at her. He could tell she was close again, the way her pussy squeezed and released him. Luke's hand slid around to her front and found her clit swollen and throbbing. He gently rubbed a finger over it, loving the mewling sound that came from Bellamy's throat. "You ready to come again, baby?" She was so responsive to his touch.

"Oh god, please!" she cried.

Luke stroked it in time with his thrusts until he felt the trembles start. When she clamped down around him, he lost it and gripped her hips hard as he thrust with deep, digging strokes. He reached up and grabbed her hair, pulling her head back so he could reach her mouth, kissing her with a raging fire that had them both gasping and groaning into each other's mouths. Luke came with such force that he had to brace himself behind Bellamy to keep himself from falling over.

Neither of them moved while trying to catch their breath. When Luke regained the ability to think he slowly pulled out of Bellamy, smiling as she whimpered and then collapsed on the sofa. He quickly disposed of the condom and sat down next to Bellamy, pulling her into his lap. Luke loved the contented sigh that escaped from her lips as she snuggled closer to him.

"You doing okay, babe?" Luke asked as he kissed the top of her head.

"Oh, yeah," she mumbled as she wrapped her arms around her neck. Bellamy kissed his lips in a soft caress that caused them both to sigh. She was in heaven. Bellamy was content to stay right where she was. She looked up at the opening of the cabin and saw that the sky was starting to turn a dark blue and orange, making her aware that the sun was going down. Bellamy turned to look into Luke's eyes that seemed to have turned a darker shade of green. Her stomach did a nervous roll as his gaze turned intense as he stared at her, brushing the hair back from her face. She couldn't help but smile as he grabbed the back of her head, pulling her close so their lips were just a hair's breadth away from each other. Bellamy closed the distance, touching her lips to his softly, savoring the feel of his lips against hers.

Who would've known that the torch Bellamy had always carried for Luke would ever have been ignited the way it had. How was she ever supposed to tell him the truth and still hold on to him forever, which was what she wanted so much that it made her ache. He was such a good man. He was loyal, hard-working, loving and so smart.

Luke pulled his head back and smiled at Bellamy. Her blue-grey eyes stared back at him, he felt like he could get lost in them. Even when she was a young teen, she only had to look at him sometimes and he'd stop and stare, mesmerized by their intensity. After she moved to Savannah, Luke dated and dated. He'd had a couple of relationships that lasted for over a year, but it was the brunette sitting on his lap that had always clogged his brain. The night he made love to her and took her virginity had been on his mind all of the time that first year she was gone.

Bellamy had avoided him like the plague when she'd come home that first Christmas. She'd even gone as far as to wear an unflattering sweater to hide her body from him, but he knew what was under it since it was burned into his brain forever.

"Are you ready to head back, baby?" Luke kissed her lips. "I say we go pick up some dessert and head to my place."

Bellamy smiled at him. "That sounds great," she said as she got up from his lap. Bellamy felt like she was walking on rubber legs as she headed up to the cabin entrance. She could feel the heat of Luke's body, knowing that he was right behind her. Bellamy walked back to the little table and bent down to pick up her discarded panties. She slid them on along with her flip-flops and then walked back to the front, waiting for Luke to get the boat ready to take off again. Bellamy watched him in silence as he raised the anchor and walked back up to sit beside her in the driver's seat.

After a few minutes they hit the straightaway, pushing down on the throttle to increase his speed. He caught a quick glance of Bellamy. She wore a sweet smile as the wind whipped through her hair. Luke turned back to watch where he was going and couldn't help but smile.

On the way back to the marina they both sat in a comfortable silence, but Luke couldn't take being away from Bellamy, so he pulled her over so she was sitting in his lap.

"Do you wanna drive?" Luke asked, his lips near her ear.

Bellamy gave him a surprised look and then smiled. "Yes, please." Luke grabbed her hands, putting them on the steering wheel. Bellamy squealed when she realized that she was driving the boat. She made sure she listened intently as Luke gave her directions and cues on what to do.

When they were close to the marina, Luke put his hands on Bellamy's. "Good job, honey. I'm gonna take over now. I promise, though, before you go back, I'll bring you out again and I'll let you do it all."

Bellamy turned and kissed him. "Really? I'd love to drive it some more."

When they got back to the marina, Luke docked the boat and he and Bellamy grabbed their stuff. Luke climbed out first while Bellamy handed him the cooler and bag. He then grabbed for her and helped her off of the boat. Luke dropped the keys off in the office and met Bellamy on the sidewalk. He grabbed her hand, lacing his fingers with hers as they walked towards the parking lot.

Bellamy noticed that there were a group of about five guys standing at the back of truck across from Luke's truck laughing loudly. She happened to glance over at them and met a pair of eyes that narrowed when they saw her. Bellamy's blood ran cold when she realized it was the guy from the club the night before. She didn't even realize that she was squeezing Luke's hand until he stopped and looked at her with a worried expression.

"Baby, what is it?"

"It's n-nothing. Can we please go?" She started walking faster to the passenger door. Her insides were churning; she knew the guy recognized her. Why couldn't the lights in the parking lot be broken? Bellamy glanced nervously in his direction and saw him whispering to his friends, causing them to all turn and look at her. She looked up at Luke, who was behind her, and saw him glance in their direction. Bellamy knew he knew who the guy was when she saw his jaw clench.

"Bell, are those the guys from the club?" His voice came out in a harsh whisper.

"Y-yes. Please, let's just go. There's five of them and only one of-of you," she pleaded, grabbing his hand.

Luke could feel the anger rising in him. That asshole and his friends had grabbed and tried to assault Bellamy the night before and scared her, but she was right: he wouldn't stand a chance against them by himself. He quickly opened Bell's door and practically threw her inside the cab. Luke walked around the front and climbed in. He started up his truck and when he glanced back to pull out, he saw that they were all standing there staring after them. As Luke took off down the road, he pulled his cell phone out of his pocket, flipping it open and hit Dustin's number on his speed dial. While it rang he glanced over at Bellamy, who was staring straight ahead, her expression closed up and guarded.

"What's up, Luke? Aren't you out with Bell?" Dustin asked when he answered.

"Hey, listen: we've got a problem. We were leaving the marina and Bell saw the guys from the club. It looked like all five of them were there, so I didn't say anything, but it's freaked her out." Luke glanced over at Bellamy, seeing the single tear that slid down her cheek.

"Oh, fuck, dude. Did he say anything to her?"

"Nope, but he was staring at her and the guys he was with were all watching her, too." Luke heard Dustin talking to someone in the background and figured it was Dylan.

"Where are you now?" Dustin asked.

"We're heading back to my place. Why?"

"All right, we'll meet you there. I'm gonna call Travis and Brad, too," Dustin told Luke before he hung up.

Chapter 10

Luke closed his phone and grabbed Bellamy's hand, pulling it to his lips. He started to worry when she didn't react; she just stared blindly straight ahead. It made Luke want to turn around and pound the guy into the ground. He wasn't much of a fighter, but right now he felt like he could take them all on for scaring her. A few minutes later, he turned onto his street and saw the guys were all there already. Luke pulled into the driveway, and before he could even turn off the truck, Dustin and Dylan met him at his door while Travis and Brad went around to Bellamy.

Dylan was the first to speak. "Did you get the fucker's plate number?"

"No, they were all crowded at the back of the truck." Luke saw Zack and his brother Scott, who was a local Sherriff, walk up the sidewalk. Luke turned and saw Bellamy being hugged by Travis and Brad. They both gave him a worried look as she stood with her arms at her sides while they hugged her. He called over to Travis. "Here's my keys. Take her inside, would ya?"

"Sure, we've got her," Brad answered as they ushered her into the house.

Luke watched her as they took her inside. They were having such a good night and now all he wanted to do was kick some ass. When Zack and Scott joined them, they walked around the back to the deck. Once they all sat, everyone started talking at once. Scott, who was two years older than them, took control of the situation.

"All right, I want to know exactly what happened tonight, Luke."

Luke went through the incident from the marina and told him about the run-in with the guys the night before at the club.

"I'll look at the police report from last night when I get to the station. Does she know the guy's name?" Scott asked, pulling a notepad out of his back pocket.

"No, I don't think she knows him at all. I've never seen him," Luke said, the others all agreeing that they didn't know the guy.

"I'm sorry, guys, but without a name I can't really do anything. I'll send a patrol car to drive by the marina and see if the truck is still there, but there really isn't anything we can do unless he comes near her again. When I'm at the station I'll double check if there are any reports of other women being harassed." Scott stood up. "I will say this, though: don't leave her alone. Granted, they may not come back around because they'll know we're looking for them, but I wouldn't risk it."

The guys all said bye to him as he walked around the house to leave. None of them said anything for a long time; they were all deep in thought. Dylan was the first to break the silence.

"All right, she goes nowhere alone, and I swear, if that fuck gets anywhere near her, I'll kill him!" He growled. "Dust, I don't want Mom and Dad to know about this, either. They don't need the worry."

"I won't tell them. So how's this gonna work? You know she'll go ballistic if we follow her everywhere she goes. The girl has got the biggest stubborn streak," Dustin said.

"Don't worry, I'll stay with her as much as I can." Luke ignored the death stare that Dylan was giving him.

"I think you're right, Luke, and to be honest I'd rather she slept over here or at my place," Dustin added.

"Why not just stay at Mom and Dad's? I can always stay over there with her," Dylan added, looking right at Luke.

Just great. He was gonna act like this when they needed to protect Bell. Luke noticed Zack sitting quietly off to the side. Out of their group of friends, Zack was the most soft-spoken, but what people never realized about him was that he may be quiet, but he was always calculating and trying to find a solution to any problem they ever had. He was the problem solver of the group, and when he spoke, the others always listened.

"Listen guys," Zack began, "I know we're all concerned about Bell's safety first and foremost, but we need to handle this delicately. We don't want her to suspect what we're doing, so if we alternate, we could be around her without her thinking she's being babysat. I think she should stay here at night with Luke, which she wouldn't think anything of it if he asks her to stay here until she goes home. During the day we'll have Travis and Brad to help with that, too. If she goes out during the day by herself, we can always ask some of the guys to look out for her, too. You know, she wouldn't be suspicious if any of us just showed up where she is." Zack smiled; he looked happy with his suggestion.

"I guess that'll work. I'm gonna go check on my sister," Dylan muttered. As he stood up, the guys followed him into Luke's to check on Bellamy.

***

Bellamy had never been so freaked out in her life. The way that guy looked at her tonight had been creepy. It made her feel dirty and made her think that maybe it was her fault that the guy bothered her at all. Had she not worn the outfit maybe she would've been just another girl in the club. They wouldn't have jumped her friends, either. Bellamy felt bad that Luke was trying to comfort her, but she felt numb and ignored the sweet gesture. When Travis and Brad had brought her in the house, they sat her on the couch, sandwiching her between them, which normally made her feel safe. It didn't work this time; instead she got up and paced, wearing a path on Luke's living room floor. Bellamy could see Travis and Brad watching her, but it didn't stop the pacing. She didn't know what happened to Luke and her brothers. She knew they were there, but had no clue what they were doing. Dylan was probably plotting to lock her up in a tower somewhere so she would be "safe."

Bellamy was pulled out of her thoughts when she heard the back door open and the boys filed in. Luke, Dustin, Dylan and Zack all came walking into the living room. She saw the looks on their faces as they stood there watching her. She tried to swallow the knot that was forming in her throat thanks to the intense look Luke was giving her. Bellamy shot a quick glance at the worried expressions on her brothers' faces just waiting for the "I told you so" from Dylan, but it didn't come. Instead, she watched as Dylan walked over to her with Dustin following, both brothers enveloping her in a tender hug that brought tears to her eyes.

"Does trouble follow you, Bell?" Dylan whispered against the top of her head.

Bellamy snorted at his question as she wiped the tears falling down her cheeks. "Apparently it does." She turned to hug Dustin just as tightly as she hugged Dylan.

When she pulled away from her brothers she walked over to Luke and wrapped her arms around his waist, letting out a sigh of contentment when he wrapped his arms around her and kissed the top of her head. Bellamy felt content to stay in his arms. She felt safe, and for a brief second, felt loved. Bellamy wasn't fooling herself about his feelings for her. Sure, he cared about her, but love he did not. Only in her wildest dreams would he love her, but she knew from the start that this relationship would be going nowhere. Bellamy's heart was already involved, but she dealt with his rejection once before and she'd deal with it again.

"Well, we're gonna take off, but, Bell, you call us if you need us," Travis said as he walked over to her and pulled her into a hug.

"I will, Travis. Don't forget dinner with my parents tomorrow," Bellamy said as she kissed his cheek.

"We won't, sweetie. We'll talk to you tomorrow," Brad said, getting his hug from her.

"Hey, Travis, will you guys wait for Dustin and I outside before you take off?" Dylan asked.

Travis nodded as he and Brad walked to the door to leave. Zack came over to wrap his arm around Bell's shoulders and gave her a quick squeeze.

Bellamy always loved Zack. He was the quiet one who didn't give her a lot of grief when she was younger. Out of all the guys, she always thought that he'd be the first one to get married, but he had his heart broken by his ex-fiancée a few years ago. Ever since, he followed in Dustin's footsteps as Mr. Love 'em and Leave 'em. Like Dustin, one of these days he'd meet a girl who'd turn his life upside down.

Luke and Bellamy walked everyone to the door to say good-bye, both of her brothers hugging her once more before they left. Dylan even surprised Bellamy by giving Luke one of those half-hug half-back pats. When Luke shut the door, Bellamy watched as he turned and walked slowly over to her. A sigh escaped her lips as his hand slid up her back until he reached her neck, rubbing the tightness out of it. His touch was just right: not to firm and not to light. Bellamy felt like she could melt into a puddle right where she stood. When Luke was done, Bellamy let him lead her back into the living room. He got her settled on the couch and then sat down beside her. She couldn't resist the urge to snuggle into him.

***

Before Travis and Brad left Luke's, they waited outside for Dylan, Dustin and Zack to come out. Neither of them knew what her brothers wanted, but they figured it was about what happened. Travis heard Luke's front door open and watched as the three men walked down the steps and started to towards them. He had been so worried about meeting her brothers for the first time after hearing stories about them. He'd been pleasantly surprised when he'd met them and discovered what nice guys they were. Travis had been taken aback by the fact that he got along with them so well, but now they had to deal with this asshole who was trying to scare Bellamy and hope that it didn't escalate into anything worse, especially considering what could've happened to her the night before.

"Hey, so what's the plan?" Travis asked, smiling at Brad as he walked over to join them.

"We don't leave my sister alone." Travis gave Dylan an incredulous look. "Yeah, I know Bellamy wouldn't go for that, so that's why she won't know. Luke's gonna ask Bellamy to stay here with him while she's home, but during the day we'll all take turns watching out for her. You know, we'll just happen to show up where she's at. Zack's brother said that since we don't have a name, we can't really do anything unless he happens to approach her again, and God help me, if he approaches her when I'm there, well—let's just say it won't be pretty."

"Ditto for me, man. I'd love to get another piece of those assholes, too," Brad said.

They all agreed that in the morning, whoever heard from Bellamy first would call the others and get the plan set for the day.

Travis climbed into the driver's side of his Mustang and waited for Brad to join him. Once Brad was inside he started the car. He knew how stubborn Bellamy was and how pissed she'd be if she knew they were all gonna be playing babysitter for her. Travis couldn't help but worry about her too, not just because of the guys from the club, but because he knew she'd be over the moon to have Luke ask her to stay with him, and if she knew the real reason it'd break her heart. Travis only could hope that things would work out for Bellamy. She been through so much and he wanted nothing more than Bellamy to get the happiness she deserved.

***

Luke flipped through the channels trying to find something to watch. Bellamy had fallen asleep with her head in his lap an hour earlier and he didn't want to move her yet. He found it to be relaxing when he watched her sleep and couldn't help himself when he started running his fingers through her curls. When they had gotten settled on the couch earlier, Bellamy had taken it down and shook out her curls; they fell haphazardly past her shoulders. He looked back up at the TV and settled on watching some UFC fights. Luke wasn't sure how long he sat there, but he finally felt Bellamy start to stir. She had rolled over to her back and when she opened her eyes, she looked up at him with the most gorgeous smile gracing her face. Luke felt a tug in his chest as he looked down at her. She stole his breath with her heavy-lidded, glassy eyes and dreamy looking smile.

"Hi," Bellamy whispered.

"Hey yourself. Did you have a good nap?" Luke asked as he rubbed her stomach in a tiny circular motion.

"Mmm…Yes I did, but I'm sorry I fell asleep," Bellamy said as she arched her back to stretch. Pushing herself up, Bellamy sat up and settled in next to Luke. "What time is it?"

Luke looked at his phone. "It's 9:30. I'm hungry, do you want anything?"

Bellamy stood up to stretch and follow Luke into his kitchen. She hopped up on his counter while he rummaged through the refrigerator. A moment later he sat a carton of eggs and what looked like the fixin's for omelets. She watched as he pulled out a bowl and skillet.

"I didn't know you knew how to cook," Bellamy said from the counter with a laugh. She gave Luke her sweetest grin when he came over and kissed her.

"Do you really think my mom would've let either Jason or I out of the house if we couldn't cook for ourselves?" That was one skill that they both had to possess before she let them move out. She didn't want her boys living on take-out and TV dinners.

Bellamy giggled. "Yes, I do know your momma and she's just like mine. Dustin and Dylan both had to learn how to cook before they left home, too." Bellamy accepted the glass of juice that Luke poured for her, and watched as he cracked and whisked the eggs. When the skillet was hot enough, she watched as Luke dumped the eggs in and then threw in mushrooms, cheese, onions, green peppers and jalapeños. He definitely knew what he was doing. She enjoyed watching him cook. Bellamy sipped her juice and continued watching him flip the huge omelet in the pan. He then grabbed a loaf of bread out of the refrigerator and sat it down next to the toaster. She hopped off the counter and walked over to help, so she opened up the bread and threw a couple of slices in. Bellamy leaned against the counter watching Luke as he cooked the gigantic omelet with a precision that she knew would make his mom proud. She couldn't help the warm feeling that crept through her body when he flashed her that devilish grin of his that she loved.

Luke grabbed a plate and slid the omelet onto it as Bellamy buttered the toast she made. He grabbed the toast from her and put it on the plate and took it out to the living room. Bellamy followed behind him with two glasses of orange juice. He watched Bellamy as she sat the juice down and sat down right next to him snagging a piece of toast of his plate.

"Okay, you ready to try this?" Luke asked as he forked up a bit of the omelet.

Bellamy nodded as he brought the fork to her lips. She moaned when she tasted all of the flavors of the omelet that seemed to melt against her tongue.

"Oh, wow, that's good," she exclaimed.

They polished it off in silence. Bellamy had never had someone feed her before and it was an experience she could get used to. The way he watched her as he fed her bite after bite had her squeezing her thighs together to sate the ache that was growing there. When they finished, Bellamy grabbed the plate from Luke, kissing him quickly before she took it into the kitchen. Bellamy started rinsing the dishes and loading them into the dishwasher. The whole scene made her smile. It was domesticated and made her imagine what it would be like if they lived together. They'd make dinner together, they'd snuggle on the couch as they ate and then she'd clean up. Bellamy's heart started to ache thinking of her child and what would it have been like if she would've lived. Luke would've had her outside playing while Bellamy cleaned up. She had no doubt that he'd be a wonderful father, but she had to push those thoughts to the back of her mind or she was gonna break down and she couldn't afford to right now.

Bellamy was finally getting her emotions in check when she felt Luke wrap his arms around her waist. She smiled and leaned back into him. His body was so warm behind her and his arms felt strong as he held onto her. Bellamy looked up and in the window above the kitchen sink she saw the picture the two of them made. She looked so small with Luke's arms around her he had his cheek rested against the top of her head.

"You ready for bed, darlin'?" Luke asked.

Bellamy sighed when he kissed the top of her head. "Yeah, I'm ready." Bellamy let out a squeal when Luke scooped her up in his arms and started carrying her to the bedroom.

"Luke, what are you doing?" She laughed.

"I'm taking you to bed, baby." He wiggled his eyebrows at Bellamy and smiled when she started laughing at him.

Luke tossed her on the mattress and pounced on top of her, smothering Bellamy's laughter with his lips. Her taste was intoxicating as he brushed his tongue against her lips. They tasted sweet like the juice she had drank. Luke slid his tongue into Bellamy's mouth, stroking hers with a slow caress. Bellamy had only been home for a week, but that was all he needed to know that he was in love with her. Before she left to go back to Savannah, he was going to ask her to move in with him. Under normal circumstances, people would tell him it was too soon, but it felt right and it was the first decision he was going to make in a long time that made perfect sense.

Bellamy absorbed the heat coming from Luke's body as he kissed her with such a tender touch. She was enraptured by the assault he was unleashing on her with his lips and tongue. The hint of orange juice on his breath had her sucking on his tongue until she heard a rumble from his chest. She felt his hands slide over her breasts—dragging his thumbs across her hardened nipples.

Bellamy felt a gush of her cream coat her pussy as he teased her nipples. She let her fingers sift through his hair as he began kissing, nipping and licking down her jaw to her neck. Bellamy lifted her arms up as Luke reached down and slowly eased her shirt up and off of her body. She couldn't help the moan that escaped as he suckled her nipples through the thin satin of her bra. Round and round he drug his tongue until her breasts felt heavy and aching.

Luke wanted to take his time with Bellamy. He wanted to savor every moan and gasp that was released from her swollen lips. He undid the front clasp of bra, releasing her beautiful, perky breasts. Luke grabbed them and pushed them towards each other. With a quick swipe of his tongue he watched the peaks turn a beautiful shade of pink. He'd never get enough of the taste of her. She again had a light floral scent that had his cock aching to be freed from the confines of his shorts. Luke felt the bite of her nails digging into his scalp as he continued his onslaught.

He let his tongue trail down her stomach, circling her belly button with a quick glide of his tongue. Luke could smell her arousal the closer he got to her pussy, another scent of hers he'd never get tired of. He found the clasp on the side of her skirt and quickly undid it, sliding the skirt over her hips and down her legs. Luke tossed it behind him, not caring where it went.

"God, baby, do you even know how beautiful you are?" he asked, the words coming out as a groan as he eased her panties off of her. "Bend your legs, baby." Luke watched Bellamy lick her lips as her nervousness settled her lips into a straight line, but he couldn't help the smile that spread across his face as she eased her legs open and slid her feet up until they rested flat on the mattress. Luke could see the cream from her pussy coating her lips and it was calling to him to take a taste. He leaned down, kissing the inside of her thigh, slowly teasing as he worked his way up. Luke smiled when he heard Bellamy's groan of frustration when he almost reached her pussy and then started kissing up her other thigh. He found it to be almost fun teasing her. Luke could feel Bellamy's need vibrating through her body as he eased closer and closer to her weeping sex.

With the first swipe of his tongue against her pussy, Bellamy moaned Luke's name. She felt her body heat up with every lick. She reached down, grabbing onto his hair like it was going to keep her from flying off of the bed. Bellamy felt his hand slide up her thigh and cried out as he plunged one, then two fingers into her slick channel and began to fuck her while attacking her clit with his tongue. She felt the ache start in her belly and seemed to gain strength as it traveled down. When Luke sucked her clit between his lips, Bellamy felt herself come apart. The blood roaring in her ears blocked out any other sound. As she felt her breath and heart rate return to normal, she realized she had Luke's hair in a death grip. She looked down at Luke with his head resting on her thigh, smiling at her.

"Oh, god, I'm sorry," she exclaimed, trying to hide her embarrassment as she let go of his hair.

Luke crawled up until he was between Bellamy's legs and he was face to face with her. The blush covering Bellamy's body gave her a beautiful glow. He could tell she was tired and doing her best to hide it. As much as he'd love to make love to her, he'd be content with having her snuggle up to him. Luke could feel her eyes on him as he got off the bed to strip out of his clothes. He couldn't hide the massive erection he had, but he could ignore it. Luke could see the confusion in Bellamy's eyes as Luke got into the bed next to her and pulled the covers over them both.

"Luke?" she asked as she turned to face him.

"Baby, you're exhausted. I'm perfectly happy to wait until you've rested for a bit," Luke said and took her lips in a tender kiss. He pulled away—rolling onto his back and pulling Bellamy with him. Luke heard the sigh that escaped her lips as she settled her head on his chest. In less than a minute, he heard her breathing slow and go deeper. Luke shut off the bedside lamp and let sleep take him under.

***

Bellamy woke up with the sun streaming in from the curtains. Luke had woken her up sometime in the night. Her leg had been draped over his hip as he entered her from behind with slow, easy strokes, taking them both unhurriedly to orgasm. They had fallen back asleep, still joined together.

Bellamy rolled over to find Luke awake, watching her with a smile that made Bellamy's heart stutter. She didn't want to get up, Bellamy wanted to stay right where she was forever. Bellamy smiled at him and rubbed her hand through his wild-looking hair.

"Good morning, baby," Luke whispered as he leaned forward to place a chaste kiss on her lips. "How'd you sleep?"

"Mmm…so good. I don't wanna get up," Bellamy said as she snuggled up to him. She smiled as he stroked her hair. Bellamy wrapped her arm around his waist closing her eyes and let out contented sigh.

"Bell, there's something that I want to talk to you about." Luke tilted her chin up so he could look into her eyes. He could see her nervousness as she stared at him. Knowing Bellamy, she probably thought he was kicking her to the curb.

"W-what is it?" she asked and then began chewing on her bottom lip.

"I've been thinking, and I want you to stay here with me until you go back to Savannah. I know you're just here another week and you're gonna be helping with Dylan's party, but I want you with me at night sleeping in my bed." Luke waited for what seemed like forever for Bellamy to answer.

"Are you sure, Luke? I don't want to cause more problems between you and my brother," Bellamy said as she snuggled against him. She should be thrilled, but she didn't want Dylan to be any madder at Luke because of her.

"Sweetheart, don't worry about your brother. I talked to him last night and he was okay with it." That made her smile.

"All right, then yes, I would love to stay with you," Bellamy said as she reached up to kiss Luke.

"God, baby, I love you." Luke and Bellamy froze as soon as the words left his mouth. He meant every word, but he was waiting for the right time to tell her. Luke grabbed Bellamy's face and saw the tears threatening to spill over. "I mean it, Bell. I love you." He pushed her down, covering her lips with his, hoping to show her how serious he was.

Luke pulled back, using his thumbs to wipe away the tears that were running down Bellamy's cheeks. For a second he wasn't sure if those were happy tears or something else entirely. "Why are you crying?" Luke could hear the fear in his voice, but it quickly vanished when she smiled up at him.

"I—I love you to. I've loved you forever," Bellamy blurted out. She clenched her eyes shut.

Bellamy felt Luke's breath against her lips and slowly opened her eyes. He was smiling at her and swooped down to kiss her lips with a gentleness that had her body humming with desire.

"I know, baby," he whispered as he kissed across her face from ear to ear.

"How?" Bellamy said, her voice sounding breathless. She knew that her crush on him when she was younger was apparent to anyone that knew them. Plus, the fact that Bellamy followed him around like a lost puppy from the time she could walk until that night six years ago. When she turned sixteen and her parents finally let her start dating, Bellamy tried dating boys so she'd stop thinking about Luke, but it never worked, and in her mind back then, they couldn't even compare to him.

Luke could tell Bellamy was embarrassed about his admission, but he always knew how she felt about him when they were younger. The night they slept together when he realized that she was still a virgin, he knew that she had wanted him to be her first, and as angry as he was at first, he couldn't help but feel humbled that she chose him to be her first.

"Hey," he said as he tilted her chin up so he could kiss her lips. "Don't think about it. Just know that I love you."

Luke let out the breath he didn't know he was holding when Bellamy grabbed his face for a kiss that had his cock hardening instantly.

Bellamy groaned when Luke pulled away and he couldn't help but laugh. "Come on, if we don't get out of bed now we'll end up spending all day here. You're having lunch with Stacy today. I know you don't want to miss that."

"Yeah, you're right. When should I bring my stuff over?" Bellamy asked as she slid out of bed throwing her clothes on.

"Since we're all having dinner at your parents', I thought you could just grab your clothes then." Luke pulled his t-shirt over his head. "Do you want some breakfast?"

"Can we stop by the bakery? I want one of your mom's yummy cinnamon rolls," Bellamy said, smiling at him.

"Yeah, let me call her quick and we'll head out," Luke said as he grabbed his cell phone.

***

Bellamy smiled to herself as she stepped out of the shower. The morning with Luke had been so great. They went and ate breakfast at the bakery with Lola, whom she noticed kept giving them a funny smile. Bellamy couldn't escape the thoughts that kept running through her mind, though. She was running out of time to tell Luke about the baby. She knew the longer she waited the more angry he was possibly gonna be. Bellamy wouldn't blame him, though. She should've told him right away, but things had spiraled out of control with him so fast. She loved him so much, and she was hoping that when she told him everything that he could forgive her for not telling him sooner.

Bellamy threw on her robe and went back into her room to grab her clothes for the day. She reached into the pocket of her suitcase and pulled out a manila envelope and sat down on her bed. She gingerly reached inside and pulled all of the contents out. Bellamy's eyes started misting as she stared at the first picture: it was the first ultrasound she had done to confirm her pregnancy. She laughed to herself when she thought back to when she and Travis first saw it. Travis had told her that she looked like she was having a duck and Bellamy swore it was a bunny. Up until the moment she saw the heartbeat on the screen, she tried to tell herself that it wasn't true, that she wasn't really pregnant. But seeing and hearing the heartbeat made her own heart burst with love. She sat it aside and looked at the next ultrasound picture when she had learned that she was having a little girl. Bellamy wasn't sure who was more excited, her or Travis. He'd proposed to her that night, and as much as she loved him, she turned him down, knowing that eventually she'd tell Luke about their baby.

The next series of pictures were the ones that Travis had taken of Bellamy at various stages through her pregnancy, but her favorite and most heart-breaking photo had been one of her at thirty weeks. Her belly had really popped out by then, and Travis was kneeling in front of her, kissing her belly. Bellamy wiped the tears away because she knew it should've been Luke in those photos, not the man who had become her best friend and anchor. It was weird to think that two short weeks later, a sharp jerk in her belly and Rose was gone. Someone knocked on her door and made her jump, so she shoved the pictures under her bed. Quickly wiping her eyes, she called for whoever it was to come in.

"Hi, baby, what're you doing?" Ruth smiled as she walked into Bellamy's bedroom.

"Hi, Momma, I'm just getting ready. I'm taking Stacy out to lunch today."

"I heard. Renèe called me to tell me that and Gary is gonna be released tomorrow after lunch and she wondered if I could stop by their house to make sure everything's ready," Ruth said as she sat down next to Bellamy and leaned in to kiss her forehead. "I want you to move home, baby." Her mom was never one to beat around the bush and always got straight to the point.

Bellamy smiled at her mom, "I want to move home, too." She laughed as her mom pulled her into a hug. It felt so good to have her mom's arms around her holding her close.

"Oh, baby, you don't know how happy you've made me. We'll announce it at dinner tonight since I'm sure a certain someone will be happy to hear your news."

Bellamy's face felt flush after her mom's little statement. Would Luke be happy? Duh—he had only told her that he'd love for her to move home just the night before.

"Well, I'm gonna let you finish getting ready. If I don't see you before you leave, have fun with Stacy, and bring her back here when you're done. Renée is coming too, so she can just come here." She stood up and then leaned down to kiss Bellamy on the forehead. "I love you."

"I love you too, Momma," Bellamy said as she watched her mom walk out of her room, closing the door behind her. Bellamy quickly got dressed and then went into the bathroom to finish getting ready.

Bellamy climbed into her car, threw on her sunglasses and headed to Stacy's. She decided to take Stacy to Shooter's so they could play some pool after they ate. Bellamy wore her lime green khaki shorts and a black sleeveless t-shirt with her black flip-flops to match. When she pulled up in front of Stacy's house, she found her sitting on her front steps. She watched as Stacy strode towards her car with a long, fluid stride.

When Stacy climbed into Bellamy's car she flashed her a brilliant smile. "Hey, girlie, thanks for taking me out today." Stacy buckled her seatbelt and then turned to look at Bellamy. "So did your mom tell you my dad's coming home tomorrow?" She could hear her own excitement, but who could blame her. When Stacy's mom had called her to tell her about her dad, she had broke down, fearing she wouldn't make it in time, but thankfully when she got home, he was being settled into a room and seemed to be doing okay. That was one of the bad things about living twelve hours away. The past year she had missed them terribly and came to the decision after his heart attack to move home. Stacy was waiting to get her dad settled before she told them her plans and hoping that they'd be thrilled.

"Yeah, my mom told me. That's fantastic. Oh, and I'm supposed to bring you to my house when we're done with lunch. Everyone will be there, including your mom." Bellamy turned into the parking lot at Shooter's. It was only one, so the parking lot wasn't too crowded. Bellamy whipped into the first parking spot on the side of the building. "Is Shooter's okay?" Bellamy asked Stacy before getting out.

"Yeah, it's perfect. A beer sounds really good right now." Stacy smiled as she got out of the car. Stacy grabbed Bellamy's arm as they sauntered in ready to have some fun.

Chapter 11

After Bellamy left, Luke worked out for a while. He jumped in the shower and ended up jerking off to the images of eating Bellamy's pussy. Licking his lips, he thought of the taste of her juices. The taste was warm, musky and heaven all wrapped in one. It didn't help ease any of the aches from his cock as stepped out of the shower. One week was all it took for him to be completely addicted to her. The way she chewed on her lip when she was nervous, the way her eyes lit up as she smiled at him, and Luke loved the way she talked with her hands and the way she moaned his name when she climaxed. He meant it when he told her he'd work it out with her being almost an hour away, but inside he knew that he wanted her to move back here with him. Luke wanted her in his home—their home—and in his bed.

Luke knew he was being selfish wanting her to move home, but now that he had her he didn't want to let her go. He was just going to have to make her see that they had a future together.

He decided to check in with Dustin to see if Scott was able to find anything on the asshole that seemed to be fixated on Bellamy. Plus he knew they'd want to know that he'd asked her to stay with him until she leaves, and that she was out with Stacy today. Luke grabbed his phone off his nightstand and called Dustin.

"Hey, man, what's up?" Dustin muttered. Clearly Luke had woken him up.

"Uh, nothing. Just wondered if you've heard anything from Scott." Luke could hear Dustin whispering to someone in the background all he made out was "it was fantastic, baby." Luke could only shake his head. Leave it to Dustin to go out and find a girl after the shit with Bellamy last night.

"Sorry, man, Sasha was just leaving. I don't think we've learned anything about this guy, which pisses me off. Did you ask her to stay with you yet?" Dustin asked.

Luke was glad that Dustin really didn't seem to have a problem with his relationship with Bellamy. He knew that Dustin would help him get Dylan to get over his surprise and anger.

"Yeah, I did, and she said yes. By the way, she's out with Stacy. Bellamy was taking her out to lunch. Should one of us go to Shooter's to keep an eye on her?"

"Yeah, probably," Dustin said. "Maybe I'll give Skeeter a call and see if he was planning on going up there later."

Luke didn't like the idea of Skeeter sniffing around Bellamy, but he'd have to get over it.

Skeeter was a natural flirt, but he knew better than to touch Bellamy.

"Sounds like a plan. I think it'd be a little obvious if we all showed up. What time are you planning on heading over to your folks' place?" Luke asked as he walked into the kitchen to make some coffee.

"I don't know. I guess around five or so. Do you wanna ride with us?"

"Yeah, that sounds good. I can just ride back here with Bellamy when we're done. I'll talk to you later."

Once the coffee was done brewing, Luke grabbed a cup and headed back to his office to look over some plans that he and Dustin had been working on. He wasn't in the mood to work, but if it helped keep his mind off Bellamy and keep him from going up to Shooter's to see her, then it'd be a smart idea.

***

Bellamy finished her third glass of beer out of the pitcher they bought when she realized she was a little buzzed. She and Stacy had also ordered a small garden pizza and they demolished the entire thing. She knew she'd have to work out tomorrow or she was gonna regret it.

If Bellamy had to guess from the cheesy smile Stacy was wearing, she was feeling the same. Bellamy usually preferred wine, but beer and pizza sounded really good.

"Stace, I want you to know that I'm really sorry that we lost touch over the last few years. It's just some stuff happened that first year of school and I kind of just started to shut everyone out," Bellamy said with a frown.

Stacy smiled and reached across the table, grabbing Bellamy's hand. "Oh, Bell, you don't have to apologize. I'm no better. I got so busy with school and working that I just forgot what was important, but I've decided to move home, so we'll be closer and we can reconnect."

Bellamy broke out in a huge smile when Stacy announced that she was moving home. "Well, don't say anything to anyone yet, but I've decided to move home, too." Both girls squealed with delight. They both flew out of their booth to hug each other, only pulling away from each other when they realized people were staring at them.

"Well, hello, ladies." They both turned to find Skeeter Samuels standing behind them. Bellamy always thought he was the biggest flirt, but he was the most fun to hang around with. He'd filled out since the last time Bellamy saw him, which was three years ago at Christmas. He was the shortest out of all of the guys, standing at six foot even and seemed to have developed a well-toned body. He kept his strawberry-blond hair cut in a perfectly styled do. His eyes were light-brown and he always had a huge shit-eating grin on his face showing off his pearly whites.

"Skeeter!" Both Bellamy and Stacy squealed in unison as they wrapped their arms around him.

Bellamy stepped back, giving him the once over. "Wow, you look great. How are you?"

The girls sat back down and Skeeter slid in next to Bellamy. "I'm doing well, I've been managing The Waterfront for the past three years. I heard you and Luke were there for lunch earlier this week, but I missed you guys." Skeeter turned to Stacy. "You're looking good, girl. How's your dad?"

"I'm good, and he's doing well, too. We're bringing him home tomorrow." Stacy took a sip of her beer. "I think we're gonna play some pool, do you wanna play with us?" Stacy asked as she grabbed the pitcher and Bellamy grabbed their glasses.

"You guys go and start without me. I'm gonna sit at the bar and finish watching the ballgame."

Bellamy and Stacy got settled at one of the pool tables in the back corner. Bellamy glanced around and realized that they were the only women in the entire place. She turned to see Stacy putting quarters into the pool table and went to grab a couple of cue sticks.

"So Skeeter got kind of hot," Stacy said as she came over to get a stick from Bellamy.

Bellamy turned towards the bar to look at Skeeter. She had to agree, but he didn't hold a candle to Luke. "Yeah, I guess so," Bellamy said as she picked up her beer. "So, Stace, are you seeing anyone?" Bellamy sat down on one of the stools at their table.

"No. I was seeing someone up until six months ago."

"What happened?" Bellamy asked.

Stacy shrugged her shoulders. "He wanted to take the next step, and I wasn't ready to make that kind of commitment to someone. I may never be ready."

"Really? Did he propose to you?"

"Yeah, he did. His name's Brian. Don't get me wrong, I truly loved him, but I'm only twenty-five. Anyway, that's what I got for dating someone older than me," Stacy said, hoping that the heartbreak didn't show in her eyes.

"How old is Brian?" Bellamy asked.

"He's thirty-nine." She saw the surprise in Bellamy's eyes. "I know, I know, I never even told my parents how old he really was. Luckily, he looks much younger, and when my parents met him they didn't notice, but enough about me and my train wreck of a love life. I really want to know is exactly what's going on with you and Luke."

Bellamy gave Stacy a recap of the events that happened with Luke. she decided not to tell Stacy about the guy who'd attacked her, Travis, and Brad. Bellamy didn't think Stacy would need that worry along with everything else. She told Stacy that Luke had told her he loved her and had asked Bellamy to stay with him while she was home. It felt good to talk about all of the stuff about Luke with someone who knew how she had always felt about him.

***

Skeeter sat at the bar watching the game and the girls. He'd been shocked to hear about what had happened to Bellamy. Dustin had called him to ask if he'd go to Shooter's to keep an eye on her, but he wasn't supposed to let her know what he was doing. Skeeter dug his cell phone out of his pocket and dialed up Luke.

"Hey, Skeeter, what's up?" Luke asked.

"Hey, I just wanted to let you know that I'm at the bar keeping an eye on your girl." Skeeter turned to look at the girls. "They're playing some pool right now."

"Okay. Call me or Dustin right away if you sense something's off. Keep an eye out for a guy who's about six foot four or five. He's built like a linebacker with dark-brown hair and a goatee," Luke said. He hoped that the guy wouldn't show up there when there was only Skeeter to watch out for her.

"Holy fuck, dude! What am I supposed to do if he shows up? I can't take a guy on that's built like a mountain," Skeeter hissed at Luke.

"Relax, man. If he shows up, you get her the hell out of there. I think she'll be fine, but just make sure she's okay."

"All right, I'll keep an eye on her. Oh, but before I forget, they may need a ride home. They were getting all giggly when I got here," Skeeter laughed into his phone.

Skeeter could hear Luke groan into the phone and then Luke was laughing. "Well, don't let them get too giggly, and if Bell's in no condition to drive, just call me and one of us will come get them unless you want to come to Bellamy's parents' tonight. We're having a big cookout."

"Thanks for the invite, but I promised to go have dinner with Valerie and Jim tonight," Skeeter said as he turned to look at the girls who were, from the looks of it, polishing off their pitcher.

"Okay, well, tell your sister 'hi' for me and thanks again for keeping an eye on Bellamy."

"No problem. I'll call you when I'm getting ready to leave if they need a ride." Skeeter said bye to Luke, closed his phone and then watched as some guy came walking over to Bellamy and Stacy. He narrowed his eyes at the guy, but let out a sigh when he realized the guy was tall and skinny and talking to Stacy.

***

Bellamy watched as a guy approached her and Stacy. He was tall like her brothers, with dark-brown hair that he wore in a faux-hawk. He had tattoos on both of his exposed forearms. His body was long and lean. Bellamy watched as he stopped next to Stacy.

"Hey, sweetness, do you mind if I play a game with you ladies?" he asked.

"Uh, sure. I'm Stacy, by the way, and this is Bellamy," Stacy said, holding out her hand.

"Well, Stacy, it's very nice to meet you." He held her hand for several seconds; Stacy could've swore that she felt sparks when he grabbed her hand. His voice flowed through her like honey. Stacy couldn't remember anyone, except maybe Brian, who affected her so much just by the sound of their voice. She could tell this guy was from the south because he had that slow southern drawl that so many guys they grew up with had.

"My name is Mark, by the way," he said with a lopsided grin.

"Well, Mark, it's a pleasure to meet you," Stacy said, letting the words flow off of her tongue. "So are you here for the Fourth of July festivities?"

"Yeah, some buddies and I came down from Charleston for the week. I take it you girls live here?" Mark asked.

"Actually, I'm moving back here from Chicago and Bellamy is moving back from Savannah. We both grew up here," Stacy said, looking at Bellamy with a huge smile. "Shall we play a game of pool?"

"Definitely," Mark said as he walked over to shake Bellamy's hand. "Hi, Bellamy, it's nice to meet you."

"You too, Mark," Bellamy said as she grabbed his hand to shake it. When he let go she grabbed the empty pitcher. "Would you like to share our pitcher with us?"

"Sure, thanks." Mark pulled out his wallet and handed Bellamy a twenty. "It's on me."

"Thanks," Bellamy said as she walked past him to the bar. She smiled at Skeeter, who was watching her as she walked up. Bellamy placed the pitcher on the bar and asked the bartender for another.

"Hey, Skeeter—come play pool with us?" Bellamy asked.

"Who's the guy talking to Stacy?" Skeeter asked, looking towards the pool tables.

"Some guy named Mark. I guess he's down here from Charleston for all of the festivities this week. I think he interested in Stacy," Bellamy said as she smiled towards them. Mark was whispering into Stacy's ear and she had a huge grin on her face. Bellamy turned back towards Skeeter who had a huge scowl on his face. Interesting, Bellamy thought. She paid for the pitcher and grabbed Skeeter's hand. "Come on, let's go," she said, dragging him back to the pool tables. Bellamy introduced him to Mark and they began playing.

***

Ruth was grateful that Patrick took Charlie fishing so she could get things ready for the cookout without any distractions. She was expecting Lola anytime to help prepare all of the side dishes. Ruth put the groceries away, enjoying the quiet of the house. She was so happy that her little girl was moving home. In a year she'd have all of her children home and she couldn't wait. From the looks of it, Bellamy was probably going to be the first to get married. Ruth knew she was jumping the gun, but she saw the look in her daughter's eyes whenever she was with Luke or his name was mentioned. Maybe in a few years she would give them a grandchild. After Bellamy lost Rose, Ruth did a lot of research of cord accidents and she knew it was highly unlikely that it'd happen again, but she knew that it would always be in the back of Bellamy's mind.

Ruth didn't know if Bellamy had told the father yet, but she was hoping that it wouldn't cause problems between Bellamy and Luke. She had no idea who it could be. Bellamy had dated a lot in high school, but it was never anything serious. During every summer she was always tagging along with her brothers so she could be closer to Luke. Everyone knew Bellamy had feelings for him, but the boys all assumed it was just a school-girl crush, but Ruth knew better. She sat at the dining room table racking her brain trying to figure out who it possibly could be.

"Oh no!" she whispered to herself. "Luke's the father." It made perfect sense. That summer before Bellamy left for school everything was fine, but all of a sudden Bellamy quit leaving the house and stayed in her room crying a lot. Ruth and Charlie always thought it was her just scared to go away to school, but now she knew the truth, or at least she thought she did. Things were beginning to make sense. They had a cookout for Bellamy before she left for school and they had had everyone over. She wouldn't talk to anyone. Bellamy and Luke seemed to avoid each other the whole evening, which no one seemed to notice at the time.

Ruth still wasn't sure how Bellamy was able to keep her pregnancy from them for as long as she did. Ruth closed her eyes, remembering when Travis had called her in a panic asking her to come to the hospital in Savannah, but not to tell anyone where she was going. The whole drive there she thought Bellamy had been attacked or in an accident. She didn't expect to walk onto the Labor & Delivery floor and see her baby girl lying there crying hysterically because her baby was gone and she was going to have to deliver her. Ruth had so many questions, but instead of asking them she just held her daughter and rocked her as she cried. She stayed with Bellamy and Travis until Bellamy was settled at home, and Bellamy was set up with therapy.

The first few weeks that Ruth had been home, she had nightmares and bouts of insomnia, but she couldn't tell Charlie why because Bellamy made her swear that she would never tell him or her brothers. How could she not have known that it was Luke's baby? What was gonna happen between them once Luke learned the truth?

"Ruth!" Ruth snapped her head up to see Lola walking into the kitchen. "There you are, didn't you hear me knocking?"

She stood up and walked into the kitchen. "Sorry, Lola, I was just lost in thought. You ready to start cooking?" Ruth asked as she gave Lola a quick hug and they began to go over the menu with her.

***

Bellamy racked up the balls for the third rematch. She and Skeeter were partners while Stacy and Mark were paired up. The four of them finished off their third pitcher and Bellamy couldn't stop laughing. Her gaze kept landing on Stacy, who was flirting shamelessly with Mark, who was dishing it out as well as he was getting it. Skeeter was even beginning to loosen up and stopped shooting daggers with his eyes at Mark. Miss Stacy Hutchins had two good-looking men battling for her attention. Bellamy watched as Mark walked by and winked at her. She watched as he took off towards the bathroom. Bellamy turned back to hear Skeeter and Stacy arguing about who was going to break. She walked around the pool table and got in between them and proceeded to break the balls while they argued.

"Bell, what are you doing?" Skeeter asked.

"Uh, what does it look like I'm doing?" Bellamy retorted with smirk.

Stacy rolled her eyes and walked over to get a drink of her beer. Bellamy's brothers and their friends never paid any attention to her when they were younger, so she didn't know where Skeeter's hostility was coming from. Skeeter was fine until Mark came over and joined them, but she wasn't about to let Skeeter ruin her afternoon. She came up next to Bellamy and lined up her shot and scratched.

"Okay, that sucked. What happened to Mark?" Stacy asked with a frown.

"I saw him walk towards the bathrooms," Bellamy said and then smiled as Mark approached holding a small tray with four shots on it. "Here he is."

"Hey, guys, I thought we could all use a shot." He handed Skeeter and Stacy two shot glasses with clear liquid in them, while he handed Bellamy a pink one; his was the color of light caramel.

Bellamy picked up her glass and sniffed it. "What is this, Mark? It smells yummy."

"Stacy said you'd probably like something fruity. It's a cherry pie. Cherry pucker and vanilla schnapps," Mark said as he flashed Bellamy his dimples

"Okay then. Cheers guys," Bellamy said right before she tossed back the shot. The only thing that kept going through her mind was that it tasted nothing like cherry pie. She watched Stacy, Mark and Skeeter toss back theirs.

A half hour later Bellamy handed over her cue stick to Skeeter. "Here, Skeeeeter, your turn," Bellamy said with a laugh. She leaned back against wall, trying to decide if she should call Luke to come get her and Stacy since she was beginning to feel like she was in no condition to drive. Bellamy looked up to find Mark staring at her. She didn't know why, but it made her feel a little uncomfortable. Bellamy let out the breath that she was holding as Skeeter came to stand by her.

"Hey little girl, you okay?" Skeeter asked.

"Yeah, but I think I'm drunk," Bellamy whispered, or least she thought she was whispering since Stacy, who was standing on the other side of the pool table, started to chuckle. Bellamy shot her a look and then turned to Skeeter. "I-I think I sh-should call Luke to pick us up."

"Don't worry about it, sweetie, I'll call him. I'd take you myself, but I'm having dinner at Valerie's."

"Aw...How shis she?" Bellamy asked. She was surprised she was starting to slur.

"Um, she's good. She and her husband are expecting their first baby in a couple of months." Bellamy started slumping against the wall. "Bellamy, I'm gonna call Luke, okay?" Skeeter dug his cell phone out of his pocket and walked out of the bar.

"Where did he go?" Stacy asked.

"Luke…our ride home," Bellamy said, leaning heavily against the wall.

"I can give you ladies a ride home," Mark said, coming up to stand next to Stacy.

Stacy smiled at him. "Maybe some other time. Thanks, though."

***

Skeeter stood outside of Shooter's waiting for Luke to pick up, but it went to his voicemail. "Hey, Luke, it's Skeeter. You need to call me back—your girlfriend is smashed. Call me back." He hung up and called Dustin.

"What's up, Skeeter? You still at Shooter's?" Dustin asked.

"Yeah, I'm still here. Where's Luke? I tried to call him, but it went to voicemail."

"Luke's right here. Dylan and I came over to hang out. What's going on?" Dustin asked.

"Bellamy is hammered. You guys need to come get her and Stacy," Skeeter said. He could hear Dustin talking away from the phone he knew he was relaying the message to the guys.

"We're on our way," Dustin said, his voice sounding amused.

Skeeter walked around the side of the bar to call his sister to tell her he was gonna be late. When that was done, he walked back towards the entrance and saw the guys climb out of Dustin's truck. They said their hellos and walked inside.

"Luuukkee!" Bellamy squealed as she saw him walk into the bar. When he was right in front of her she threw her arms around his neck, and planted a loud-smacking kiss on his lips.

"Hey, baby. Are you okay?" Luke asked, his voice laced with concern.

"I-I'm d-d-drunk. Sshh…" Bellamy said with a giggle.

Luke looked at Stacy, who just shrugged her shoulders and grabbed Bellamy's purse. He scooped up Bellamy in his arms and started walking towards the doors. Luke smiled when she snuggled into him. He turned to see Dustin and Dylan questioning Stacy and Skeeter about Bellamy's condition. Outside they all said bye to Skeeter and they piled into Dustin's truck. Stacy was sitting up front with Dustin and Bellamy was sandwiched between Dylan and Luke in the back.

Luke gave Dylan a worried look over Bellamy's head. They watched as she stared straight ahead and her breathing started to slow. Luke grabbed her face and tilted it up to look at her. "Baby…are you okay?"

Bellamy only grumbled at him and slumped against him. "Jesus, look at her, Dylan… she's as white as a ghost. Stacy, how much did she drink?" Luke asked. He was starting to panic.

"Between the four of us we had three pitchers, but Bellamy didn't drink that much from the last one. She did do a shot though, but it wasn't anything heavy just some fruity stuff. I feel fine;

well, maybe I'm a little buzzed," Stacy said looking at her friend closely.

"What do you mean the four of you?" Dustin asked, glaring at Stacy.

"Well, Skeeter joined us, and then we met Mark, who's in town with some friends. He bought the shots for us." Dustin saw her brow furrow. "You know, it was a little strange that he'd be in a bar alone when he came down with his friends. Oh, god. Her shot was different than ours! I told Mark to give her something fruity. You know what else? After he offered to give us a ride, he high-tailed it out of there." Stacy leaned over the seat and pulled Bellamy forward. "Bellamy!" She lightly slapped her cheek. "Come on, sweetie, wake up. Oh, Christ! Dustin, we need to get her to the hospital. Her lips are turning blue!"

As Dustin raced them towards the hospital, he could hear everyone's panicked sounding voices. When Dustin heard a gurgle from Bellamy, Luke shouted at him. "Hurry the fuck up!" And then Dustin heard the awful sound of Bellamy vomiting and coughing. He watched out of the corner of his eye as Stacy climbed in the backseat, sitting on Dylan's lap.

"I've got her hair, Luke, just make sure she doesn't start to choke," Dustin heard her say from the backseat.

Luke rubbed her back as the retching came and went. He carefully lifted her face to look at her; her eyes were glassy and unfocused. "Come on, baby, look at me," Luke pleaded. His heart was beating so fast he couldn't think. All he knew was he should have been with her today and now he felt like he'd failed her. Bellamy slowly turned her head to look at him. The look she gave him was one where he didn't even think she knew who he was. "Dustin, how much longer? She really doesn't look good," Luke asked, holding Bellamy tightly to his chest.

"Luke," Bellamy could only manage a whisper.

"What is it, baby?" he asked, kissing her forehead.

"I-I h-have t-to t-t-tell you about our ba-baby." Before Bellamy could finish, she hurled herself forward and started gagging and then fell eerily silent.

"Oh, God, is she dead?" Stacy cried.

Dustin glanced back. "Get ready to run with her, dammit!"

Stacy climbed back up front with Dustin while Dylan helped get Bellamy into Luke's lap. Her breathing had become too shallow and as soon as they stopped Dylan and Luke flew out of the truck Luke cradling her to his body. "Dammit, baby, hold on!"

When they reached the ER doors Dylan yelled for some help.

***

Ruth, Lola and Renée were putting the final touches on the side dishes when the phone rang. Ruth wiped her hands on a towel and grabbed the phone. "Hello."

"Mom, I need you and Dad to come to the hospital right now!" She could hear the panic in Dylan's voice.

"Oh god, what is it?" Ruth didn't even notice Lola and Renèe standing next to her.

"Something's wrong with Bellamy, they think someone drugged her. Please, just get here." Dylan disconnected before she could respond.

"Ruth, what is it?" Lola asked.

"B-Bellamy…They took her to the—to the hospital, they think someone d-drugged her." Ruth started scrambling around looking for her purse, and before she knew it, Charlie and Patrick came into the house; Lola was telling them about the call.

Charlie grabbed Ruth. "Honey, you've got to calm down, we won't know anything unless we get there okay." He threw the keys to the Charger to Patrick as they all rushed out of the house.

Everyone was quiet all the way to the hospital, none of them knowing for sure what they were going to walk in to. Ruth closed her eyes and silently prayed the entire way there that her baby would be okay. She felt Lola and Renée grab both of her hands as they all sat together in the backseat. Before she knew it, Patrick whipped the car into the hospital parking lot, all of them jumping out and running towards the emergency room entrance.

Charlie made it to the desk first. "Ma'am, my daughter Bellamy Carmichael was brought in. Can we please go back to her?"

The young woman looked up at Charlie through her horn-rimmed glasses. "Let me check for you, sir." She quickly got up and stepped through the door in back when they heard yelling.

"Please, just let me stay with her, dammit! Dylan, get your fucking hands off of me!"

"Oh god, is that Luke?" Lola asked and went around the desk and went through the door the others rushing in behind her. Lola couldn't help the cry that left her. Both Dylan and Dustin were trying to drag Luke away from a doorway and Stacy was leaning against the wall crying.

"Luke!" Lola cried.

Luke, Dustin, Dylan and Stacy all turned to see their parents standing there. Stacy sobbed and ran to her mom while Luke turned back to the room, trying to throw Dustin off of him as he tried to get to Bellamy.

"Son, you need to step back before we remove you from the premises," a middle aged man in a uniform said. "We'll call the police if you don't step back." The man looked at Luke, then through the doorway and let out a sigh. "Just let them help her."

Luke finally let Dylan and Dustin lead him away where they were greeted by their parents. Luke collapsed into his mom and dad and didn't even try to hide the sobs that he was unleashing. He felt his mom kiss the top of his head.

"What happened?" his mom asked, her voice shaking with every word.

Luke could only shake his head. He felt his dad wrap an arm around him as they both led him out into the waiting room. They settled down on both sides of him as he covered his face with his hands and began to pray.

***

Charlie hugged Ruth to his chest as they stood there waiting to hear what happened. He couldn't stand not knowing what was going on, so he led Ruth towards the door. When they looked through the doorway, Ruth let out a sob. Bellamy was strapped to a table with a nurse sticking an IV in her arm, while another one held a mask over her face giving her oxygen. Charlie could barely see her, but when he caught a glimpse of her face he could see how pale she was. They listened as a man shouted out "tox screen and gastric lavage." When the man turned and saw Charlie standing there with Ruth, he called one of the nurses over and whispered in her ear. She quickly walked over to them.

"We're gonna need you to go out to the waiting room. The doctor will be out as soon as he can," the young nurse said with a sad smile.

"Miss, can we please see her quickly?" Charlie asked with desperation.

The doctor nodded from the bedside. "You need to make it quick…okay?"

Charlie and Ruth rushed into the room to Bellamy's side. Ruth brushed Bellamy's hair away from her face. "We're here, baby…we'll be back soon." She quickly kissed her daughter's forehead and made room for Charlie. Ruth watched as he leaned down, kissed her forehead, and whispered something in her ear.

They met Dylan and Dustin out in the hall. Ruth felt the strength of her sons' embrace as they walked out to the waiting room. Ruth saw Luke sitting between Lola and Patrick. He looked so lost it broke her heart. Stacy and Renée were sitting in the corner; Renée had her arms wrapped around her daughter, trying to quiet her sobs. Ruth approached them, and when Stacy saw her approach, she jumped up and ran to her, wrapping her arms around her.

"I-I'm s-s-so sorry," Stacy cried.

Ruth hugged her tight. "Sweetheart, it's not your fault. You didn't do it."

"B-but he-he was flirting me, and I-I couldn't s-see what-what he was try-trying to do," Stacy choked out.

"Oh, honey, please don't blame yourself. I wish I knew why someone would try to hurt my baby like this..." They were interrupted by Dustin when he motioned to the ER door. Two officers walked in, one of them was Zack's brother Scott.

"Mom, I'll talk to Scott, but you might want to call Travis and Brad. They'll want to be here," Dustin said as he kissed his mom on top of her head.

"I'll call Travis right now. Take Stacy with you, she'll be able to give them a description." Ruth grabbed her phone and watched as Dustin put an arm around Stacy's shoulders as they walked over to Scott.

***

Luke sat there. The only thing that kept running through his head was that he couldn't lose her. He knew it was the guy from the bar, it had to be.

271

Earlier Scott and another officer spoke to Stacy, who was able to give them a good description of "Mark." Travis and Brad showed up shortly after Ruth had called them, and now everyone sat in silence as they waited to hear how Bellamy was. Luke couldn't take the waiting. He got up and walked out the ER doors to get some fresh air. He found a bench right outside of the doors and sat down. The air was so thick with humidity that anyone who wasn't used to it would have trouble breathing, but to Luke it was a comfort. He heard the whoosh of the doors and watched as Charlie came out and sat down next to him.

"How you holding up, son?" Charlie asked, staring out into the parking lot.

Luke cleared his throat. "I'm sick of waiting. How long is it gonna take for the doctor to let us know if she's okay?" Luke scrubbed his face with his hands and sighed.

"I honestly don't know. It's already been a...hour." Charlie cleared his throat when he felt his voice start to crack. He was trying to keep it together for Ruth, but with each passing minute he felt more and more like he was going to lose it. Charlie felt helpless; that was his baby girl in there and it was completely out of his hands.

They sat in silence for what seemed like an eternity when Lola ran out to where they sat. "The doctor just came out, and he wants to talk to us." Charlie and Luke followed her back into the waiting room where the doctor was pulling a chair towards Ruth and then sat down.

"Mrs. Carmichael, I'm Dr. Klauer and I've been the one treating Bellamy. When she was brought in she was unconscious and we learned that she may have been slipped something in her drink. We ran a toxicology screen, which showed that she ingested a large amount of Benzodiazepines. Whichever drug she was given is primarily used for a sedative, anxiety and seizures. My guess is someone slipped her Rohypnol, or commonly called a roofie."

Ruth gasped. "I-isn't that the date-rape drug?"

Charlie put his arm around Ruth. "Please, continue doctor."

"Yes, you're right. It is one of the most frequently used date-rape drugs. On a person Bellamy's size it can cause a more severe reaction, and factoring in the alcohol she drank prior to ingesting the drug, only intensified the effects. We gave her a drug called Romazicon through her IV, and what it'll do is bind to Benzos and help stop the depressant effects. I know when she was brought in, the gentlemen with her said she vomited, so she may have gotten rid of some of the drug herself. Now, we did pump her stomach because we wanted to make sure it was completely cleaned out. We're gonna keep her here overnight and monitor her oxygen levels and keep her hydrated with fluids. She'll probably be out for the next several hours. I do want to warn you that she'll probably have no recollection about what happened after the drugs started to make their way through her bloodstream, but I assure you its normal. We've transferred her to the medical floor and once she's situated, she can have visitors, but I want them to be kept to a minimum. Do you have any other questions?" Dr. Klauer asked as he stood up.

Charlie stuck his hand out to shake Dr. Klauer's. "No, sir, we thank you for what you've done for our baby girl."

"You're welcome. I'll have one of the nurses come get you when she's settled in her room. You folks take care."

They all said thank you to the doctor and watched as he walked back into the ER. Luke let out the breath he felt like he was holding while the doctor was talking to them. He watched his mom and dad hug Ruth and Charlie; the moms were both crying again. Dustin and Dylan had their arms wrapped around Stacy, who had finally stopped crying. Luke turned away, staring out the window, letting the relief settle through his body.

Luke felt a hand touch his arm. He turned to see Ruth smiling up at him. She threw her arms around him, hugging Luke so tight he had to fight for a breath. Ruth pulled away and then grabbed his face with both hands, kissing his forehead. Luke tried to fight the tears that were trying to spill over, but one look at Ruth's face, which was so similar to Bellamy's, made him crack.

"Oh, honey, she's gonna be fine," Ruth said as she wrapped her arms around him again.

Luke cleared his throat. "I know, I've just never been that scared in my entire life." Luke felt Charlie wrap an arm around his shoulders and gave him a reassuring smile.

While they waited to see Bellamy, Dustin took off to clean out his truck, taking Stacy with him.

Dylan sat in the corner with Travis and Brad. Ruth, Lola and Renèe went to the cafeteria to get everyone coffee, and Charlie and Patrick went to sit outside, leaving Luke to pace restlessly, waiting to see Bellamy. He was about to go join his dad and Charlie outside when a nurse came out.

"Are you with Bellamy Carmichael?"

"Yes, ma'am. I'm her boyfriend."

"Well, they've got her all settled in her room, so you can go see her now. She's in room 324, just take the elevator to the third floor. The nurse's station is to your left and they'll show you to her room." She smiled at him and then walked back through the ER doors.

Luke walked over to Dylan. "They've moved your sister to her room, it's 324. Will you wait for the moms and let my dad and yours know, too? I'm going up now."

"Yeah, go ahead. We'll all be up shortly."

Luke could've sworn that Travis wanted to go with him, but he wanted a few minutes alone with her and he didn't give a damn if it pissed Travis off. He saw Brad whisper into Travis's ear and he just nodded and stood back. Luke turned and walked towards the elevators, anxious to see Bellamy. Once he was on the third floor, he went to the nurse's station and was led to Bellamy's room. As he approached the door, a nurse stepped out into the hall.

"Is it okay if I go in and see her?" Luke asked.

"Oh, sure. She's sleeping, so let her rest." The nurse walked off down the hall.

Luke pushed open Bellamy's door and walked slowly into the room; he hated hospitals and he hated the smells. It was far too medicinal for him. His breath caught in his throat when he came around the corner and saw Bellamy lying in the bed. She looked so small and fragile; the lights above her head glowed and made her skin look even paler then it was. Bellamy had an IV sticking out of one hand, a clip looking thing on her middle finger and a tube that was around her head going into her nose. Luke quietly pulled a chair next to the bed and hesitantly reached out and grabbed Bellamy's hand. He leaned forward, listening to her soft breathing. Every inhale and exhale made him happy. Luke knew if he found the guy that did this to her, he'd kill him, and he honestly didn't care about the consequences. He reached up with his other hand and gently rubbed his hand over her head.

"Bell, I'm here, and I love you so damn much. I promise we'll make that bastard pay for what he did to you." Luke kissed Bellamy's hand and continued to hold it. There was no way he was gonna leave her room until she was awake.

Chapter 12

Stacy and Dustin worked in silence as they cleaned up the mess in his truck. Stacy was too emotionally drained to speak. She also knew Dustin was stewing in silence about his sister. She was always envious of Bellamy growing up. Stacy had been an only child, and always wished that she had brothers or sisters of her own. Stacy's mom had hemorrhaged right after having her and ended up having a hysterectomy. Luckily, Stacy spent so much time with Bellamy when they were younger that Bellamy's brothers became her pseudo-brothers. Stacy was so happy that she and Bellamy were both moving home, but now she just wanted her friend to be okay. How could she be so blind? Oh, she knew, Mark, if that was his name, all he had to do was flirt with her and she was practically humping his leg. Stacy couldn't help that tears that started to flow again.

"Stacy?" Dustin came up behind her, enveloping her with his warmth as he held her in the parking lot of the car wash.

"I-I'm sorry, but I can't help but feel like this is my fault. A guy shows me some attention and I can't see that he's trying to hurt my friend. God, I'm an idiot!" Stacy cried.

"You're not an idiot, Stacy. There's been this guy who has been creeping around Bellamy and we think he's behind what happened today. We should've been watching her better, but she would've had a fit if we crowded her, so if it's anybody's fault, then it's mine and Dylan's. We should've just stuck to her like glue."

"Why didn't she tell me what was going on? I would've been more watchful," Stacy asked.

"I don't know. Maybe she didn't want you to worry."

"Yeah, maybe you're right. Do you mind running me by my parents' house? I want to take a quick shower and change my clothes before we head back to the hospital."

"We can do that," Dustin said as he opened the door to his truck and helped Stacy inside.

They rode in a comfortable silence all the way to Stacy's parents' house. Once inside, Stacy told Dustin she'd be back in a few minutes. She ran up the stairs to her bedroom and pulled a simple knit dress out of her suitcase, along with some clean panties. Stacy hurried into the bathroom and welcomed the heat from the shower as the water ran all over her body. She quickly washed and rinsed herself off. Stacy got out and dried off, taking time to quickly moisturize her body. Satisfied, she got dressed and just ran her fingers through her hair she threw on a pair of flip-flops and went back downstairs so they could head back to the hospital.

Dustin wasn't prepared when Stacy came down the stairs. She'd always just been Bellamy's best friend, but when he saw her in the little dress she was wearing and the fact that it hugged an extremely sexy, curvy body, it reminded him that she was a grown woman now. He could tell she wasn't wearing a bra, but her breasts appeared to be high and firm. Her skin tone gave her a hint of a tan, and her long legs seemed to call to him like a beacon. Jesus, he was fucked up. His sister could've died today and all he could think about was how gorgeous Stacy got.

Stacy hurried past Dustin and went into the kitchen. She heard his footsteps following her. She went to the refrigerator and grabbed the pitcher of tea, took it to the counter and pulled two glasses down. "Did you want a glass, too?"

"Yeah, thanks," Dustin said as he took the glass she offered him. He slammed it back in two gulps. Before he could ask, Stacy refilled it. Dustin watched her as she went to the pantry and grabbed a bottle of Ibuprofen. He watched as she shook out three tablets, threw them into her mouth and then washed them down with some tea. Dustin could tell she was still upset because she was flitting around the kitchen on autopilot. He couldn't take it anymore, so he stood in front of her, blocking her way.

"Stacy! You need to calm down. All of this pacing isn't helping anything."

Stacy stared into Dustin's blue eyes and felt like she was being sucked into some sort of vortex. His dark-brown hair was sticking straight up on top and he had the start of a five o'clock shadow dusting his face. When had she ever really looked at him? Not since she was a small girl. God, he was big; he towered over her. His body was that of a swimmer, long and lean. He stared down at her with a questioning look.

"What did you say?" Stacy asked her voice no more than a whisper.

"I said you need to stop pacing. It's not going to change anything," Dustin said as he rested his hands on her bare shoulders.

"Don't you think I know that? I-I just can't help it. Her lips turned blue right before my eyes, Dustin. I swear I thought she was dead! So you'll have to excuse me while I try to burn off this nervous energy." Stacy backed away from Dustin and tried to go around him. "Geez, will you just move out of my way?"

Dustin didn't think, he just acted grabbing Stacy by the shoulders and hauling her up against his body. He grabbed her face tilting it up to reach her lips. The first contact of her lips to his caused Dustin to groan. Stacy's lips tasted like the tea they had drank. Dustin's tongue slid across Stacy's lips until she parted them slowly, inviting Dustin's tongue into her hot, welcoming mouth.

Stacy didn't know what happened, but she couldn't help but suck on Dustin's tongue as he tickled the inside of her mouth with his. His lips were soft and pliant against hers. She felt his hands slide down her back until he cupped her bottom and then lifted her. Stacy wrapped her legs around his waist, never breaking the kiss. She could feel his cock already straining against the front of his shorts. Stacy gasped as he laid her on the kitchen table and began kissing down her neck. She moaned with every nip of his teeth down her shoulder and then to the tops of her breasts. Stacy felt Dustin tug the front of her dress down until her breasts were free. The cool air from the air conditioner caused her nipples to harden instantly.

"Jesus, Stacy, you're beautiful." Dustin took the tip of his tongue and circled the mauve-colored tip. He smiled against her breast as he felt her writhing beneath him. The only sound in the kitchen was his panting and her soft moans as he sucked the nipple. Dustin kept working both nipples until both peaks were red and swollen. He felt Stacy grab his head, pulling him up until their lips met in a frenzy, licking and biting at each other. Dustin's cock throbbed beneath his shorts, it was begging to get out.

Stacy couldn't take it, so she reached down and quickly unfastened his shorts, sliding her hand inside. She gasped when she found his cock, thick, hard, and ready for her. Stacy worked his shorts and boxers past his hips, with their lips still fused together. She cried out when she felt Dustin pull her panties down and off. Stacy watched as he grabbed his wallet and pulled out a condom. He quickly sheathed himself with the latex and then he came back to Stacy's mouth, kissing her so hard that it stole her breath.

Dustin kept kissing her as he reached down and found her pussy, swollen and wet for him. He could feel her grinding her hips up against his hand. Dustin smiled when she protested, but it became a sigh as he lined up his cock. She was so hot; even with the latex between them, he could feel the heat. Dustin bent his head down and took a nipple in his mouth as he thrust inside her. She was so fucking tight he had to stop moving before he embarrassed himself. He groaned when Stacy wrapped her legs around him and thrust up so he was embedded deep in her pussy.

"Shit, baby. Slow down or this is gonna be done before I make you feel good."

Stacy smiled up at him and then reached between both of their bodies. She slowly started circling her clit with her middle finger. "Please just start fucking me, Dustin."

Dustin groaned and then pulled her closer to the edge and put her legs over his shoulders and started fucking her with relentless strokes. He loved the way her breasts jiggled with each thrust; he could tell she was getting close. Her eyes were shut and she was biting her lip. Dustin felt the pulses start around him and nailed her with hard strokes that had them both crying out.

"Oh god, Dustin! Now….Now!" He felt her go liquid around him and then he screwed his eyes shut. Dustin leaned forward, biting her shoulder as he started to come.

Dustin was coming so hard that he started to see stars. When it stopped he had his face buried in Stacy's neck, her arms wrapped around his. Neither of them spoke; he could feel her heart beating against her ribs. Dustin didn't know how long they stayed like that, but his phone ringing seemed to snap them both out of the trance that they were in. With a groan he pulled out of Stacy, who quickly sat up and straightened her dress. Dustin pulled up his shorts and grabbed his cell phone out of the pocket.

"Hey, Dylan. What's up?" Dustin watched Stacy slide of the table and pick her panties off the floor and disappeared around the corner.

"I just wanted to tell you that they've moved Bellamy to a room. Luke's already up with her, but we're heading up now."

"Okay, I'll be there in ten minutes. What room is she in?" Dustin looked up to find Stacy walking back into the kitchen and grab a glass of water.

"She's in room 324. We'll see ya in bit."

Dustin put his phone back in his pocket and turned to Stacy. "They moved Bellamy to a room, I'm just gonna use your bathroom and then we can head back."

Stacy turned to Dustin. "Okay, sounds like a plan," she said with a smile.

Dustin ran up to the bathroom, got rid of the condom, and splashed some cold water on his face. He looked at himself in the mirror, he had no idea what had possessed him to fuck Stacy, and on her family's kitchen table, no less. Dustin never made apologies for his sexual exploits, but this was different—she was different. He wasn't even going to take the time to think about that one, at least not now. When he finally had his shit together he went back downstairs and found Stacy throwing a cardigan on over her dress.

"Aren't you gonna be hot with that on?"

"Probably, but it's better than trying to explain the bite mark on my shoulder," Stacy said.

"Shit, I'm sorry," Dustin said as he held the front door open for her.

"Don't worry about it, Dustin. It's not a big deal." Stacy quickly locked up the house and followed Dustin to his truck.

Stacy sat in a comfortable silence as they headed back towards the hospital. Dustin, on the other hand, seemed to be a little nervous. She could understand that; she was, after all, his baby sister's friend, but she wasn't gonna let it bother her. Stacy had spent the last few years always worried about what Brian thought about everything she did, but not anymore. No man was ever going to have that power over her. Did that mean she didn't want to sleep with Dustin again? Hell no! It was amazing, but she wasn't gonna sit at home and wait for him to call. If he didn't, then oh well. She'd deal with it.

***

Through the course of the night everyone took turns sitting with Bellamy and Luke. Luke was grateful to everyone for letting him stay constantly by her side. The nurse taking care of Bellamy came in throughout the night checking her vitals, which she said were stable and strong. She was kind enough to bring Luke a blanket and pillow. He couldn't sleep, but he was able to get comfortable in a chair that he had right next to Bellamy's bed. His dad had taken Stacy and Renèe home because Stacy was clearly exhausted and dead on her feet, telling Luke she'd be back in the morning.

Around three, Ruth fell asleep in the recliner that Luke had insisted she rest in. He started pacing the room, thinking about what Bellamy said in the truck on the way to the hospital. She said that she needed to tell him about their baby, but what baby? He knew that they had been safe when they'd had sex, so what was she talking about? Luke continued to pace when it dawned on him that they hadn't used protection the night he took her virginity, but had he gotten her pregnant she would've told him. Before he could think about it further, moaning from the bed brought his attention back to Bellamy. Luke rushed to her side as Ruth flew up from the chair.

"Baby? I'm here, sweetheart," Ruth cried.

"M-momma? Luke? Wh-what happened?" Bellamy asked, her voice coming out as a soft croak.

"Bell, thank god, you had us so scared," Luke said as he sat down on the bed next to her.

Bellamy had no clue how she ended up in the hospital, the only thing she remembered was being at Shooter's with Stacy and then nothing. Her head hurt and she was sick to her stomach. "Did I have alcohol poisoning? I swear I didn't drink that much. Where's Stacy?" She was quickly becoming agitated.

"Baby, just settle down, we'll tell you everything in the morning. Why don't you go back to sleep."

Ruth tried to encourage her daughter to get some rest, but Bellamy was getting more and more upset.

"I don't want to sleep, I want to know what happened to me. I want to know why my head hurts and why I feel sick," Bellamy said as she started to cry. She lifted her hand to her mouth and realized she was trembling. "What's wrong with me?" Bellamy quickly tried crawling out of the bed.

Luke climbed up behind Bellamy and wrapped his arms around her waist while her mom pushed the emergency button on the wall. "Shhh...baby, you need to relax," Luke said against her ear. She kept fighting him, trying to get up, Ruth climbed on the bed in front of her and grabbed Bellamy's face whispering to her. Several nurses came into the room and surrounded the bed. They all spoke in hushed tones, trying to get Bellamy to relax, but it wasn't helping. Luke heard one of the nurses tell Ruth that they had an order from the doctor for a shot to help calm Bellamy if she woke up agitated. Luke watched her disappear out of the room. It was killing Luke to watch Bellamy struggle against him, but from the look on Ruth's face, he knew that it was devastating her as well. He kept watching the door, waiting for the nurse to come back, but it was Charlie and her brothers who appeared in the doorway first. They all wore the same horrified expression.

"P-please l-let me go. Why don't I remember anything?" Bellamy cried.

Charlie came over and got right in front of Bellamy's face. "Honey, settle down. You're killing me, darlin'."

Luke held tighter as Bellamy tried wiggling out of his hold, he watched as she reached for her IV, but luckily Charlie grabbed her arm to stop her from yanking it out. He let out a sigh of relief as the nurse rushed into the room with a syringe. Dustin and Dylan came over to help hold Bellamy while the nurse attached the syringe to her IV.

"Bellamy, this medicine is gonna burn for a second, but then you'll feel better," the nurse said as she depressed the plunger.

"Ouch! It hurts. S-stop h-hurting me!" Bellamy hollered as they continued to hold her, but thankfully, within thirty seconds she started slumping back against Luke.

It didn't take much longer after that until she was asleep. Luke carefully eased her back down to the pillow and situated himself next to her. He watched Charlie hug Ruth to his chest as she cried.

"I spoke to one of the nurses and she told me that the medicine they gave her to counteract the drug she was slipped can sometimes cause a person to become agitated," Dustin said from beside the bed. "She said that the fact Bellamy can't remember anything also probably triggered her reaction."

Luke just nodded his head as he draped an arm across Bellamy's stomach. He was exhausted, and before he could sit up he fell fast asleep.

***

Luke woke up to sunlight streaming in through the window. He felt stiff from sleeping on the edge of Bellamy's hospital bed. He turned his head to see

Bellamy smiling at him. He sighed when she reached over and rubbed a hand down his stubbly cheek. "Good morning. How are you feeling?" Luke asked as he leaned forward and kissed her forehead.

"I'm okay, just tired. Did I freak you out last night?" Bellamy asked as she grabbed his hand, kissing it.

"You didn't freak me out. I was just worried about you." Luke turned when he heard someone clear their throat: Dylan.

Luke sat up in the bed and helped up, Bellamy who leaned against him. He smiled and kissed the top of her head. Dustin and Dylan were stretched out in a couple of chairs at the end of the bed.

"Where are Mom and Dad?" Bellamy asked, her voice sounding groggy.

"Dad took Mom to get something to eat. They should be back in a little bit," Dylan said as he got up to hug his sister. Dustin followed. They were interrupted by the nurse coming to check on Bellamy. The three men excused themselves so the nurse could help Bellamy get up and use the restroom.

Once they were in the hall, Luke stretched his stiff muscles and groaned. The hospital bed wasn't the most comfortable thing to sleep in, but being near Bellamy and knowing she was gonna be okay made it worthwhile. Luke poked his head back in Bellamy's room; she must've been getting in the shower because he heard the water running, so he shut the door.

"Have you heard from Scott if they found the fucker yet?" Luke asked.

"I talked to him on my way back here this morning, but they haven't found the guy yet. They're looking, so I hope they find him before anything else happens to her. We need to come up with a new plan because the one from before didn't help, I just keep thinking about what could've happened to her and Stacy if Skeeter hadn't been there and called us when he did." Luke could tell Dylan was getting angry by the way he kept clenching his jaw. He quickly quit talking when he saw people coming down the hall.

Luke looked up and saw Charlie and Ruth walking towards them. Poor Ruth looked exhausted. Her always bright eyes were dull and puffy from crying the night before. Charlie didn't look much better, granted he slept very little out in the family room.

"Why are you out here? How's Bellamy?" Ruth asked, her voice sounding anxious.

"Mom, it's okay. The nurse came in to help Bellamy into the bathroom. We stepped out to give them some privacy," Dustin said as he walked over to give his mom a hug.

"How was she when she woke up?" she asked, looking at Luke.

"She seemed better. She said she was tired and asked if she freaked us out," Luke said with a laugh.

Ruth smiled and kissed Luke on the cheek as she went into the room, shutting the door behind her. "Bellamy," Ruth called out as she moved further into the room.

The nurse poked her head out of the bathroom. "Hi, ma'am, she's just getting out of the shower. Thank you for bringing some of her stuff from home." The young nurse smiled at Ruth and then turned back to Bellamy. "Since your mom is here, I'm gonna step out. Holler if you need anything."

"Okay. Thanks, Bridget," Bellamy called out from the bathroom.

Ruth watched the nurse leave the room, and turned back as Bellamy walked out of the bathroom. Ruth thought Bellamy still looked a little pale, but she could tell the color was coming back into her cheeks. She wrapped her arms around her daughter and hugged her tight. The last time Bellamy was in the hospital was when she had lost the baby. Ruth wondered if maybe being in the hospital again brought back some of those painful memories. Ruth walked her over to the bed and sat her down. She grabbed the overnight night bag they had sent Travis to get the night before and pulled out the hair dryer and a brush. Ruth got everything situated, then sat behind Bellamy and started brushing and drying her hair.

It brought back wonderful memories for Ruth. It was always such a treat when Bellamy would let her brush her hair and they'd have their girl talk. They sat in silence as Ruth brushed out all of Bellamy's curls until her hair was shiny and soft. When she shut the hair dryer off, she kissed the back of Bellamy's head and hugged her to her chest. They sat there for a long time saying nothing, but Ruth knew the question was coming.

"Mom, what happened to me last night? How'd I end up here?"

"Well, sweetie, someone slipped something in your drink yesterday. We don't know why, but if Skeeter and Stacy hadn't been with you, he may have tried to hurt you." Ruth wiped the tear that slid down her cheek with the back of her hand.

Bellamy was trying so hard to remember. She'd taken Stacy to Shooter's to eat and then they went to play pool. Bits and pieces started coming back. "M-Mark. It was Mark, wasn't it?" Bellamy's voice cracked when she asked.

"Yes, baby, it was Mark, but they're looking for him. We won't let him hurt you."

The door to her room opened as she saw everyone come in. Her dad, brothers, and Luke all walked silently into the room. She stood up and walked over to her dad and wrapped her arms around him. It felt good to have his arms wrapped protectively around her. A knock on the door had everyone turning to see an older woman in a white coat walk in.

"Hi there, I'm Dr. Murphy. How are you feeling, Bellamy?"

"Better. I'm just really tired, but my headache's gone," Bellamy said as she sat down on the bed.

"Good, I'm glad. I'm just gonna check you over and then we'll probably let you go home. We're gonna send you home with something to help calm you down if you start getting upset again. It's totally normal, especially when you're missing a chunk of time." Dr. Murphy turned to her family. "If you give us a few minutes, we can get her out of here within the hour."

Bellamy watched as everyone left the room and then turned her attention back to the doctor. Dr. Murphy talked to her for a few minutes about the drug that they suspected she had been given and about being careful when she was out and not to take drinks from people she didn't know. She gave Bellamy a quick exam and left to get her discharge instructions together. Bellamy smiled when Luke came walking back in alone. He sat down next to her and wrapped his arms around her.

"We're gonna find him, Bell. I promise."

"Okay." Bellamy couldn't say anything else because she was already close to losing it again, and she had already probably scared him off with her hysterics during the night. She was just glad some of it was still hazy so she didn't have to feel like a total fool.

***

By early afternoon Bellamy was home and being babied by her mom and Lola. She hated to admit she enjoyed the care they were giving her. Bellamy was snuggled up on the couch with Luke, she napped on and off for a while with her head in his lap. Ruth had informed Bellamy and Luke that everyone was gonna come over to have dinner. Bellamy kept getting the feeling that something was off with Luke; sometimes she'd catch him studying her, but she had no idea why.

Dustin and Dylan were sprawled out in the family room with them, and thankfully Dylan didn't make any comments towards Luke. Maybe he had finally accepted that Luke and Bellamy were going to be together, but it would end as soon as she told him about Rose. She had every intention on telling him when she was staying at his place, but she probably wasn't going to be going anywhere. Her dad had been furious earlier when the men told him about what happened this weekend, he had gotten on the phone trying to find out if they had caught him yet. Luckily Patrick had shown up with Lola and Charlie took off with Patrick for a drive to cool off.

Stacy arrived later in the afternoon. She walked into the family room and smiled when she saw Bellamy snuggled against Luke. She was looking so much better from when Stacy had seen her the night before. She wanted to be at the hospital, but her dad was discharged so she helped her mom get him home and settled. Stacy wasn't even gonna come see Bellamy today, knowing Bellamy would understand, but her mom and dad wouldn't hear of it. They both insisted they were fine. She happened to glance over and saw Dustin sprawled out on the love seat. Stacy sucked in a breath when Dustin lifted his head and saw her standing at the top of the stairs. He didn't try to hide the way he gave her the once over, and it had her nipples hardening immediately. Stacy quickly looked away from him and walked down into the room towards Bellamy, who glanced up and saw her as she approached.

"Stacy! I'm so glad you're here. How's your dad?" Bellamy asked as she wrapped her arms around her friend.

Stacy couldn't help but smile. Leave it to Bellamy to worry about Stacy's dad when the night before she'd been lying in a hospital unconscious. "He's good. I was gonna stay home and help Mom, but he's been up and around, so they told me to get out," Stacy said with a laugh.

Bellamy led her over to the couch, and while the girls got into a lengthy conversation, the guys headed outside with a six pack of beer.

***

Everyone was sitting out on the deck after eating dinner. It made Luke thankful to be surrounded by family, even if some of that family was non-blood related. He still planned on taking Bellamy back to his place. He wanted her in his bed, but he also wanted to ask her about the "baby" she'd mentioned in the truck the night before. Luke just kept hoping that it was just the drug. He knew Bellamy would never have kept something like that from him.

He glanced over at Bellamy, who was curled up on a bench with his mom. Luke couldn't help but smile at the sight of them. His mom had always loved Bellamy. When Luke would spend the night with Dustin and Dylan, Bellamy would sleep over at his parents' house so she could get away from their tormenting and his mom could fuss over her. Luke noticed Bellamy stifling a yawn; she looked exhausted and was trying her hardest not to let anyone know. He got up and walked over until he was standing right in front of her, lowering himself to his haunches.

"Hey, why don't we take off. You look tired darlin'."

Bellamy looked surprised by Luke. "O-okay, I'll go throw my stuff into my suitcase."

As soon as she started to stand up Luke gently pushed her back down to the bench. "Nope, you stay right here with Mom. I'll be right back."

"Okay, thank you."

Luke leaned forward to kiss Bellamy quickly before he ran into the house and up the stairs to her bedroom. Grabbing her suitcase and throwing on her bed Luke quickly opened it and started throwing her clothes into it. When he got everything packed he noticed a picture sticking out from under the dust ruffle on Bellamy's bed. He bent down and grabbed the piece of paper and looked at the writing on it. It said: *Bellamy, Travis and baby bump January 2005.* Luke flipped the picture over and quickly fell back onto his ass. It was a picture of Bellamy very obviously pregnant. Travis was down on his knees kissing her belly and smiling. "Fuck!" Luke muttered to himself. He flipped the dust ruffle up and pulled out the rest of the pictures and some papers that were under her bed.

Luke was in shock as he flipped through pictures of Bellamy. Her belly was smaller in most of the other pictures. He looked at what he assumed were ultrasound pictures. The first one he couldn't tell what he was looking at, but the second one had him lower his head into his hands. It was clearly a little

295

face looking at him and in the corner it said, "it's a girl." Luke unfolded a piece of paper and read the words,

Certificate of Birth Resulting in Stillbirth.
Rose Carter Carmichael; February 11th 2005.
6:05pm
  Mother: Bellamy Ann Carmichael; Savannah, GA.
Father: Luke Allen Carter
Gestational Age: 32weeks 2days
Weight and Length: 3.70 pounds/ 15.5 inches
Cause of Stillbirth: Cord Accident
Jane Flowers, MD. OB/GYN attending

Luke stared at the paper in his hand and felt like he couldn't breathe. They had a daughter; he was a dad. How could Bellamy keep something like that from him? Luke would've been there for her. Bellamy chose to keep him from knowing about her pregnancy, but why? It explained why she avoided him like the plague until now, but who else knew about it? Didn't they think he had a right to know? Luke grabbed the papers and pictures and stormed out of Bellamy's room with his thoughts racing.

Bellamy was sitting with her mom, Lola and Stacy talking. She kept looking towards the sliding doors waiting for Luke. She didn't know what was keeping him, but then he was pulling the door open and he looked really mad. He walked right over to her and held out his hand, when she looked down she felt all the blood rush from her head. "Oh god. Luke, I can explain," Bellamy said, standing up.

"Oh really? Then explain to me why you never told me that I'd gotten you pregnant and that she was stillborn," Luke seethed. Neither he nor Bellamy noticed everyone had stopped talking. "Why, Bellamy? What did I ever do to you that would make you think I wouldn't have been there for you and our baby?"

Bellamy couldn't help it when the tears started to flow. "I-I didn't realize I was pregnant until I was already away at school. I tried to call you, but I'd always chicken out. Luke, you made it very clear that night that what happened between us was a mistake. How was I supposed to know how you were gonna react? I was eighteen and scared to death."

"Well, it's been six years. When were you gonna tell me? Was this all some twisted game for you? I rejected you back then, so now it's your turn to get me to fall in love with you and then drop this bomb on me?" Luke scrubbed his hands over his face. "I need to get the fuck out of here."

"Please, Luke, wait!" Bellamy cried.

Luke turned to see his dad and Charlie holding Dylan back, and his mom was crying along with Ruth. He pointed at Dylan. "You wanna punch me, asshole? Well, go ahead, because I probably wouldn't even feel it." He quickly turned and went down the steps, walking around the side of the house to the front.

"Luke! Please don't go! Just please let me explain." Bellamy ran after Luke, she grabbed his arm, but he jerked it away.

"Don't fuckin' touch me, Bellamy. I need to be alone right now."

Bellamy stood there, watching him climb into his truck and pull out of the driveway. She couldn't help but feel an eerie sense of déjà vu. It was almost six years ago that the very same thing happened between them.

Chapter 13

Everyone sat on the deck in silence. Ruth wiped the tears from her face and stood up. Should she go after Bellamy? It killed her to see her baby girl so upset. She felt Charlie wrap his arms around her from behind. She leaned into his warm embrace and shuddered. What was he going to say when she told him that she knew about the pregnancy?

"Ruth, did you know about Bellamy?" Charlie asked, turning her in his arms.

Ruth looked into his eyes and nodded. "Y-yes, I d-did. Travis called me and asked me to come to the hospital in Savannah. He said Bellamy needed me, but not to tell anyone where I was going. I-I remember driving there like a bat out of hell. I thought maybe Bellamy had been attacked or had an accident." She wiped her eyes. "When I got there, they sent me up to labor and delivery. I was confused and didn't understand what she'd be doing there. I-I walked into her room and there was our baby lying there, hysterical. Travis told me what had happened to the baby. The cord had wrapped around-around h-her neck and it killed her. I swear,

I didn't know it was Luke's baby. She wouldn't tell me whose baby it was, and then she begged me not to tell anyone. I knew if I betrayed her she'd never tell me anything ever again. I'm s-s-so sorry." Ruth sobbed against Charlie's chest.

Charlie couldn't say anything. It was clear that it had killed Ruth to keep something like that from him. He was worried about Bellamy, and even Luke. Charlie hated to think of his baby girl dealing with something that heartbreaking all alone. It made sense why she always avoided coming home. She did come home, but she only stayed a short time.

"Charlie? Do you want us to go after Bellamy?" Travis asked, standing with Brad and Stacy.

"I don't know, Travis. Maybe we should let her be."

"Dad, I don't think that's a good idea right now. We have no idea if the guy from the club is gonna try to make contact with her again," Dylan said.

"I'll go talk to her," Lola said quietly. Charlie watched as she started walking towards the steps.

***

Lola found Bellamy sitting at the end of the driveway staring straight ahead. Her heart broke for Luke and Bellamy. The hurt would always live inside Bellamy, but it was all fresh and new for Luke. Lola would go see her son later to make sure he was okay, but first she wanted to let Bellamy know that she loved her and share her story.

"Hi," Lola said as she sat down on the ground next to Bellamy and wrapped her arms around her when Bellamy started to sob. She held Bellamy for a long time, letting her get her tears out.

"Lola?" Bellamy whispered.

"Yes, darlin'."

"I'm so sorry I hurt Luke. I wanted to tell him over and over. I tried, but I always chickened out. Do you hate me?"

"God no! Sweetheart, I love you so much. Don't ever forget how special you are to me. Am I happy that you never told us? No, but you were just a baby yourself." Lola kissed Bellamy on top of her head. "Bellamy, I want to tell you something that a lot of people don't know. When Luke was a year old, I got pregnant. Patrick and I were surprised since we weren't planning on any more children. Well, we wanted to wait until after the first trimester to tell everyone, because I had problems with my pregnancy with him. Your mom and I had the boys at the park for the afternoon and I started cramping really bad, and by the time she got me to the hospital, I had already lost the baby. It was just mother nature's way of telling me something wasn't right, but it still hurt." Lola tucked a piece of Bellamy's hair behind her ear. "I guess what I wanted to say was that you're not alone. Unfortunately, women lose babies all of the time. As far as Luke is concerned, give him time, sweetheart. I know he loves you, Bellamy. Just give him a chance to deal with this and just love him." Lola knew she was rambling, but she wanted Bellamy know that she wasn't alone. She could only hope this whole revelation wouldn't come between Bellamy and Luke.

Bellamy stood up with Lola and wrapped her arms around her, hugging her tight. They walked hand in hand around the side of the house when Bellamy stopped cold. "Um, I don't want to face anyone right now. I think I'm gonna head in through the front and go to my room. Please tell them not to worry, okay?"

"Sure, honey. You get some rest and we'll talk later. Remember: if you need me, all you have to do is call," Lola said as she leaned forward to kiss Bellamy's cheek.

Bellamy watched Lola walk around to the back of the house. She turned and ran to the front door. She had to talk to Luke, Bellamy had to make him understand and hope that he could find it in his heart to forgive her. She ran into the living room and found her purse. She picked it up along with her keys and hurried back out the front door. "Dammit," she muttered. Dustin's truck was parked right behind her car. Bellamy knew it was stupid, but she was going to have to hoof it. She walked along the tree-lined street. Bellamy was hit with memories of her childhood when she and Stacy would ride their bikes all over town. This was a great place to raise a family. Most everyone knew each other one way or another.

Bellamy started feeling the butterflies flitting around in her stomach the closer she got to Luke's. After what seemed like forever she finally reached Luke's street. The last half of her walk, she kept going over what she wanted to say to him, but it was useless if he wouldn't see her. Bellamy was finally in front of his house. She knew he was home because his truck was in the driveway. Although the house was dark she could see his TV was on. Bellamy took a deep breath and walked up his steps to his front door.

***

Travis and Brad were getting ready to leave, but they wanted to check on Bellamy before they left. When Lola came back after going to find Bellamy she told everyone that Bellamy was going up to her room and didn't want anyone to worry about her. Travis couldn't leave without knowing if she was okay or not, so he and Brad went up to her room. They knocked on her door, but heard nothing. They waited a minute and then Travis slowly pushed her door open. Brad walked in first, but it was obvious that she wasn't in there. Travis poked his head into her bathroom and found it empty.

"Where do you think she is?" Brad asked as he walked out into the hall.

"I don't know, maybe she's outside. Let's go look out front before we let the family know we can't find her," Travis said as he led the way out of the front door.

As soon as Travis stepped outside he knew she was gone, his only guess was that she took off after Luke. He was tempted to go over there to make sure Luke didn't do anything to hurt Bellamy anymore than she was already hurting. Travis saw the look on Bellamy's face when Luke had come to her with the pictures, and it broke his heart. Luke had to understand why she did what she did. Yes, she made a mistake in waiting so long, but it was so painful for her. Now that they were together, Travis knew Bellamy was afraid of losing Luke for good. She may have said she wasn't going to let her heart get involved, but it was obvious that Luke had her heart.

"So should we go out and tell them she's gone?" Brad asked as they walked back into the house.

"Yeah we better," Travis said as they walked out back.

***

Luke sat staring blindly at the TV. He couldn't get the look of Bellamy's face as he pulled out of the driveway out of his head. She was crying so hard when he left. If he didn't get out of there he was afraid he'd have said something that he would've regretted. Luke knew he was going to have to hear Bellamy out, but he was so mad. Maybe not totally at her, because she didn't get pregnant by herself. He was mad at himself for not realizing why she always avoided him. That Christmas when she had worn that oversized sweater, he had thought it was to hide her body from him, but in a way it was. She was hiding her pregnant belly from everyone. If only he hadn't brought Jessica home with him that Christmas. Then Bellamy probably would've told him about the baby. Truth was he'd liked Jessica, but he'd only brought her that Christmas because he'd known Bellamy was coming and he'd needed a reason to stay away from her.

When he had gotten home, Luke cracked open a beer and sat on his couch, staring at the picture of Bellamy heavily pregnant with their daughter. She looked so young and when he had stared at the picture more closely, he saw how thin she was except for her belly. Luke wondered if it was the stress of being pregnant so young and away from home, or was it that she had been sick. He was torturing himself looking at the pictures over and over. All he kept asking himself was why didn't she tell him?

A knock on the door pulled him out of his thoughts. He had no idea who it was. Maybe it was his mom and dad checking on him. Hell, maybe it was Dylan and Dustin coming to kick his ass for getting their baby sister pregnant when she was only eighteen. Luke stood up and put the pictures on the coffee table. Walking slowly to the door, he braced himself for whoever was on the other side. Luke pulled the door open and found Bellamy standing on the other side.

She looked so small and fragile when he saw her standing there. Her eyes were swollen and red from crying. Neither of them spoke as he pushed open the screen door and let her in the house.

Bellamy walked into Luke's living room and saw the pictures on his coffee table. She picked up the one of Travis kissing her belly, and studied it closely. Bellamy heard Luke walk up behind her. She didn't look up from the picture. "I threw up on myself in my English class."

"What?" Luke responded.

"My first week of classes I didn't feel well, but I thought it was my nerves. I was sitting through my English class when my mouth started watering so bad, and all of a sudden I threw up on myself. I was mortified, so my teacher sent me back to my dorm. It was terrible. I had to stop twice to throw up in the bushes. After getting sick several times over the next week, I finally went to the clinic on campus. It sounds so cliché, but I thought I had some weird stomach flu." Bellamy wiped a tear that was sliding down her cheek, and kept staring at the picture. "When they told me I was pregnant, I freaked out. I ran out of the clinic, and that's when I met Travis. He must've been walking by and heard me crying. Anyway, after that we became inseparable. Travis was a junior and lived off campus, so he asked me to move in with him. He told me right off the bat that he was gay and that he wasn't trying to get it my pants." Bellamy let out a watery laugh.

"We got extremely close really fast. He would hold my hair for me when I was getting sick a lot. He held my hand when I tried calling you to tell you about the baby. He would even lecture me when I chickened out and hung up. We fought a lot at first because I didn't even want to tell my parents. I know they would've been there for me and I know you would've, too. I never doubted for one minute that I wanted the baby. I went and got the medical card and found a good doctor. I had a good pregnancy."

Bellamy finally got the courage to look Luke in the eye, and found him watching her with a strange intensity. "Week by week went by and I knew I was running out of time to tell you, my parents, too. After Christmas, I really started to show, so I knew I couldn't come home anymore because I couldn't hide my belly. Travis told me I was taking the easy way out by not telling anyone. He even offered to marry me and raise her as his own, but I couldn't do that to him, and I knew once you knew, you'd want to be a part of her life. I remember the morning I lost her. I wasn't feeling well when I woke up. I stayed home instead of going to class, thinking all I needed was some rest. Travis came in to check on me before he left for his lab."

"He came in and crawled into bed with me and put his h-hand on my stomach. She was really active for some reason, because she usually didn't really start moving around until the afternoon. All of a s-sudden we felt a jerk and then—nothing. I-I started to panic, so we called my doctor and she told me to get to the hospital. They brought me into the birthing unit and couldn't find her heartbeat when they hooked me up to the monitors. Somehow she got her cord wrapped around her-her neck and it-it-it killed her." Bellamy felt her legs give out. Before she hit the floor Luke had his arms around her and started rocking her while she sobbed.

Luke wasn't sure how long they sat there. He felt tears running down his own face. They were tears for the pain Bellamy was still living with and for the loss of his little girl he'd never know. He didn't even want to go there, but would there have been a different outcome if he'd been there with her? Luke knew it probably wouldn't, and it wasn't going to help neither he nor Bellamy to think about the what-ifs. All he did was hold her close and let her get it out.

He knew Bellamy stopped crying because her breathing had slowed, and her body was no longer trembling. Luke looked down and saw that Bellamy was asleep. Even with her tear-stained face she was breathtaking to him. Luke closed his eyes. *What a mess*. He wanted to be mad at her, but hadn't she suffered enough? He'd let her sleep for now, but they were gonna have to talk. Luke had still so many questions that he wanted answered. A knock at his door pulled him out of his thoughts. He lifted Bellamy, laid her down on the couch, and stood up.

As he walked to the door, he saw his mom and dad through the window. "Oh, great," Luke muttered to himself as he went to open the door.

His mom threw herself at him as soon as he got the door open. "Oh, honey, please tell me you know where Bellamy is. We can't find her anywhere."

"It's okay, Mom she's here. Bellamy showed up a little while ago. She fell asleep on the couch," Luke said as he stayed on the porch with his parents. He watched his dad pull out his cell phone and told who he figured was Ruth not to worry, that Bellamy was with Luke.

"Luke, Ruth wants to know if she should come get Bellamy," his dad said, still holding his phone to his ear.

"No, Dad, tell Ruth that I'll bring Bellamy back tomorrow."

Luke watched as his dad relayed the message to Ruth. He turned his head to see his mom watching him with caring eyes. Luke couldn't control it as he walked into his mom's open arms and the tears started to fall. He felt his mom's grip tighten around him. "What am I supposed to do, Mom?"

"Oh, my sweet boy, just remember that she needs you and you need her. You both have lost something so precious. I know it's hard for you right now, but just imagine what Bellamy went through. She carried that little girl in her body and then had to deliver her, knowing she wasn't alive. Bellamy knows that she hurt you, sweetheart, but I don't think she meant to. She was young and scared. I was the same age that she was when I got pregnant with your brother." She let out a light-hearted laugh at her son's face. "Shocking, huh? Luckily, your dad knew before my parents could send me away to stay with my grandparents. It was hard. I was so scared, but we were together from the start. I don't know the whole story about what happened between the two of you, but if you truly love each other, this will bring you closer together." Lola grabbed her son's face, bringing it down to hers to kiss his forehead. "I love you, my sweet baby boy."

"I love you too, Mom." His dad walked over to them and pulled Luke into a bear hug. "I love you too, Dad. I'm sorry if I've disappointed you."

Luke felt his dad's arms tighten around him. "Son, you've never disappointed me. You and your brother, aside from your momma, are the best things that have ever happened to me. We'll leave you two alone, but call us if you or Bellamy needs anything. We love you both, okay?"

"Yeah, okay, Dad." His mom kissed him one more time before his dad led her down the steps to their car. Luke stood there watching them pull out and then drive away.

Luke wasn't sure how long he stood out there, but the sun had finally set and the only light coming from inside his house was the light from the TV. Luke walked back inside and locked the front door behind him. His heart stopped when he came around the corner. Bellamy was curled up in the fetal position on his couch. She was still asleep, which was a good thing since she hadn't even been home from the hospital for twenty-four hours yet. Luke walked around the couch until he was standing by her head. He crouched down, rubbing his hand over her hair. Luke watched as her eyelids started fluttering open.

***

Bellamy opened her eyes to see Luke staring at her as he was rubbing a hand through her hair. She couldn't help the endless supply of tears that started to fall again. Bellamy felt like she was the biggest idiot. Because of her stupid selfish actions she'd probably lost the best thing that had ever happened to her. Sure she didn't know if Luke was lost to her, but she didn't blame him if he didn't want her any longer. Bellamy knew if she had the chance to do it over again she would've told him about the baby as soon as she had discovered she was pregnant. Would it have made for a different outcome? Would they be raising their little girl together? It wasn't going to help her right now to think of those things.

"I'm s-s-so sorry, Luke, please for-forgive me," she cried, grabbing the front of his shirt. Bellamy felt Luke's arms wrap around her, holding her tightly against his chest. He was murmuring words against the top of her head, but she couldn't hear him over her tears. Bellamy lifted her head until she and Luke were eye to eye.

Luke stared at her for a moment then lowered his lips to hers. He knew he was putting everything he was feeling into that kiss. He wondered if she could feel his anger, his love and his frustration towards her. He was surprised she didn't pull away from him. He knew she could feel the magnetic pull that was between them. Even with everything that had happened in the past twenty-four hours, he still ached for her.

Luke felt too much staring into Bellamy's eyes; maybe that was why he had to kiss her, but deep down he knew it was because he loved her and wanted her forever. He wanted to someday give her more children, not to replace the one they lost, but because he knew they'd make beautiful babies together and she'd make an amazing mother.

Luke knew he still needed more from Bellamy regarding their daughter, but right at that moment he needed Bellamy in the most primal way. As he kissed her, Luke slid his hand down Bellamy's stomach until he reached the elastic of her shorts. He slipped his fingers under it and gently started to work them down her legs until they reached her feet. Once Luke got them off, he threw them on the floor next to the couch.

Luke felt Bellamy sigh against his lips as he cupped her mound. He eased a finger into her slowly, and relished the feeling of her sheath around him. Bellamy was already so wet for him. Luke loved how responsive she was to his touch. He moved his finger in and out of her until she was moaning and panting against his lips. Luke added another finger and continued fucking her with his fingers. He could feel Bellamy's hips thrusting against his fingers, and so he started rubbing her clit with his thumb. It didn't take long before Bellamy flew into an orgasm that had her crying out into Luke's mouth. He slowed his ministrations as her climax started to fade and Bellamy's body went lax against him.

Neither Bellamy nor Luke moved, as she tried to catch her breath. Bellamy felt drained, mentally and physically. as Luke leaned over her with his forehead resting against hers. She was scared to open her eyes and look into Luke's. Bellamy knew she had a lot of explaining to do and a lot to ask forgiveness for.

Bellamy let her eyes open slowly, watching Luke between her lashes. The look on his face broke her heart. His eyes were so full of pain, pain that she willingly caused. Bellamy reached up hesitantly, touching his cheek with gentle fingers. He pulled back so they could see each other more clearly and covered her hand with his. Bellamy opened her mouth to speak, but he put a finger over her lips and shook his head. She could only nod as she stared at him. The tears started streaming down her face again. Bellamy watched as Luke got up, grabbed her panties and shorts, slipping them back on her. When he held out a hand to her, she slowly reached for it and let him help her to her feet.

The silence was deafening as he led her back to his bedroom. Bellamy climbed into his bed when he pulled back the covers for her. Once she was settled, Luke bent down and kissed her gently on her forehead, then her lips, and walked out of the bedroom, shutting the door behind him. Bellamy was confused by what just happened, but fatigue overtook her and she fell asleep.

***

Luke walked silently down the hall into the kitchen, grabbing a beer before he went out to sit on his deck. He leaned back in his chair, listening to the sound of thunder that was rumbling in the distance. Luke took a generous drink from the bottle in his hand and closed his eyes. He knew his mom was right. Luke knew that Bellamy had already had a lot of time to deal with the loss, but to him, it was all still fresh and new.

The only proof he had of his daughter were in pictures. He never got to feel her moving around in Bellamy's belly, he never got to hear her heartbeat or got to watch Bellamy's belly as their baby grew and grew. A part of him was so angry at her, but he did understand her not telling him right away. It was obvious that after all of this time, she was ready and willing to talk to him about it, but why did she wait six years? He wondered if they hadn't gotten involved if she would've told him at all.

Luke had a lot of questions for Bellamy, but he wasn't ready to ask them. He wanted to know where Rose was now. Did she get cremated? Did she have her buried? Luke wanted to be able to go see where his daughter was memorialized. He rubbed a hand roughly over his face and took a huge swig of his beer, trying to loosen the knot that seemed to be lodged in his throat. Luke put down his empty bottle and leaned back in his chair, closing his eyes.

***

Luke walked down the hall, following the sound of a baby crying. No matter which door he looked in, there was no baby. He went through the kitchen and dining room first, but couldn't find the crying baby. He walked into the living room to find Bellamy asleep on the couch. He walked over and gently nudged her to wake her up. Luke was shocked when she rolled over and he saw her swollen belly. She smiled sleepily at him. "Luke, why do you look surprised to see me like this? It's your fault, you know. I'm not the one who forgot the condom."

Luke stood back as Bellamy got up off of the couch and walked past him when the crying started again. "Bell, don't you hear the crying? I can't find the baby." Bellamy turned, looking at him with confusion written on her face.

"Luke, what are you talking about? I don't hear any crying," Bellamy said as she walked out of the front door.

He watched Bellamy walk out of the house and then the crying started again. "Goddammit!" Luke yelled as he started searching the house again. He checked the hall closet, the bathroom, his office, and when he went to check his bedroom he noticed a door that seemed to have appeared out of nowhere in the corner. As he gently opened the door, the crying got louder. The room was huge. It was obvious it was a nursery. The walls were painted a deep shade of pink with white trim. The furniture was all white and decorated with pink fabric. Luke found the crib hidden in the corner. Just like the rest of the room, the crib was white and was topped by a pink canopy. The closer he got to the crib, the louder the cries got. When he was finally standing right next to it, the cries stopped. Luke looked over the side of the crib and couldn't understand why it was empty. He knew he heard her cry, so where was she? "Baby?" Luke called out.

"Luke?" He heard a voice call out. "Luke, wake up." He couldn't understand what was happening.

"I can't. I've got to find her," he called out.

"Luke, please wake up," the voice called again and now the house was shaking.

***

Luke jerked awake and found Bellamy leaning over him. "Luke, you fell asleep and it's started to rain. Why don't you come inside and come to bed."

He shook his head, trying to clear the cobwebs that seemed to be clouding his mind. Luke followed Bellamy into the house. "What was it about?" Bellamy asked.

"What was what about?" Luke didn't want to talk about what he was dreaming about.

"Come on, I know you were having a bad dream. You were talking, but I couldn't tell what you were saying. Were you dreaming about her? I did a lot that first year," Bellamy said to him softly.

"It was nothing. Let's just go back to sleep." Luke quickly pulled off his shirt and jeans and climbed into bed. He pulled Bellamy to his side so he could snuggle her. It didn't take long before he succumbed to sleep.

***

Bellamy wasn't sure what time it was when she woke up. From the bed she could see out of the window and the sky was gray. The rain falling lightly created a light patter against the window. She rubbed at her eyes, which felt puffy and raw, trying to get the sleep out of them. When Bellamy rolled over she found Luke showered and dressed, sitting on the end of his bed watching her. The look on his face made her feel very nervous and uncertain. She gave him a small smile and sat up.

They hadn't really talked at all since yesterday, and she was extremely nervous. Bellamy watched as he stood up, turning his back to her.

"Bell, can you get up? I'm gonna run you home. I've got stuff to do today." She cringed at his flat tone.

"Y-yes, s-s-sorry." Bellamy hated that she sounded so vulnerable, but that was how he made her feel. She scrambled out of his bed and made a quick trip to the bathroom. When Bellamy came out she found Luke standing in his living room. He had one of the pictures of Bellamy clutched in his hand. She watched as he dropped it back onto the table and turned towards her. Bellamy followed him silently out of the front door. Neither of them said anything as they climbed into his truck. She knew it was her fault, all of it. Luke was never gonna forgive her for anything that had happened. Bellamy could see that now.

They pulled into her parents' driveway a few minutes later. Bellamy sat there for a few minutes, trying to come up with the right words to convey how sorry she was for everything. She opened her mouth to speak, but Luke stopped her.

"Please, Bellamy, not right now. I need some time to think. I'll let you know when I'm ready to talk." Luke's voice sounded so full of pain that it broke her heart.

"O-okay, if that's what you want," she said. Bellamy opened the door and jumped out of his truck as fast as she could. She didn't want him to see the tears that were starting to fill her eyes again. Bellamy didn't notice her brothers had just walked out of the house and were standing at the bottom of the stairs. Quickly moving past them, she was barely aware of Dylan's voice behind her asking her to stop. She didn't let out her grief until she was safely in the house.

***

Luke watched Bellamy jump out of his truck, run right past her brothers and slammed through her front door. He watched her brothers watch her and then turn towards him. Luke was expecting to see murder in their eyes when they looked at him. Instead he saw regret and pain. They made their way to his truck, so he cautiously rolled down his window.

Dylan was the first to speak to him. "You doing all right?"

Luke was surprised by Dylan's question and apparently Dustin was too by the raised eyebrows in Dylan's direction. "Nope. I'm doing shitty, to be honest," he muttered.

"Listen, man, I can't even begin to imagine what you're going through right now, but just know we're here for you," Dustin said as he leaned against the door.

Luke looked down at his lap and muttered. "Thanks. I appreciate that."

Dustin and Dylan backed away from his truck and gave him a salute as Luke began pulling out of the driveway.

Once on the road, he decided he was just going to drive. He ended up going up to Hilton's Head to think. He needed someone to talk to. Someone who'd give it to him straight always.

"Hello?"

"Jase, it's me." Luke's voice cracked at the end.

"Luke, what is it?" Jason asked urgently on the other end of the phone. Luke had clearly scared his brother.

"Shit, I'm sorry, Jase. Everything's fine. I-I ju-just needed to talk to you." Luke finally couldn't help it and broke down.

"Jesus, Luke, what is it? I'm here for you, bro," Jason whispered to him.

Luke told him everything. Over the next half hour Luke poured out his heart to his brother. He told Jason about the baby, about Bellamy and about what this was doing to him. Jason never interrupted. He just listened as Luke broke down over the phone.

Luke listened as Jason started talking to him. He understood why Luke would be upset, but could understand Bellamy, too. To be eighteen and carry such a heavy burden. He listened as his brother told him he didn't even want to think about that happening to either of one of his girls. He said that he'd never understand why Bellamy kept it all from Luke, but not everyone always made the best decisions when they were that age, either.

"I'm so sorry, brother. It sounds like you've got a lot to think about. Do you love her?" Luke didn't say anything at first.

He wasn't surprised by Jason's question. "I love her more than anything. I think that's why it's making this so much more painful. How do I get past the lies? How do I forgive her for making me miss those little things from her pregnancy? She's had six years to deal and cope with this. I haven't even had twenty-four hours."

"I wish I could give you a simple answer, but I don't think there is one for this. I think you should take some time to think and do what you need to do to cope with this. Maybe you could talk to her friend Travis. He was there through the whole thing, you said. He might be able to help you understand her thinking," his brother offered.

"Yeah, maybe you're right. Thanks for the talk. I love you, man."

"I love you too, Luke. Just remember what I said, and don't forget you can call me anytime."

Luke said bye and then stuffed his phone in his pocket. He knew the call he had to make, but he needed a walk first to clear his head.

***

Bellamy rolled to her stomach, balled up the washcloth that her mom had brought up earlier to put over her eyes and threw it on the floor next to the bed. When she had come into the house earlier, both of her parents greeted her in the hallway. Her dad was the first to reach her when she collapsed on the floor sobbing. He held her to his chest as her body shuddered over and over. Bellamy felt the strength of her parents' love for her as they both hugged her tightly. When the tears stopped, Charlie had carried Bellamy upstairs and laid her down on her bed. Ruth had come in with a cool washcloth and draped it over her eyes.

She expected questions, especially from her dad since he never knew about the baby. Instead she got their love and quiet understanding. Both of her parents sat down beside her on the bed, never saying a word. Before long Bellamy heard the door open and knew it was her brothers. She heard one of them whisper to her dad while the other came over and kissed her on the forehead. After several long minutes they all got up and left the room. Her mom had promised to be back in a while with some soup for her.

Bellamy looked at the clock and saw that it was after two. She snuggled under the blanket her mom had laid on her and fell back into a deep exhausted sleep.

***

Charlie was sitting out on the deck looking deep in thought when Ruth came out to check on him. He started when she came up to him. Charlie gave her a small smile and then held his hand out to her. She yelped when Charlie grabbed her hand and pulled her into his lap. Neither one said anything as they sat there until finally Charlie spoke.

"To see my daughter like that broke my heart, Ruth. How could something like that have happened right under our noses?" He rubbed a hand down his face. "I mean, I knew she always followed him around everywhere, but to love him at that age and then to deal with the aftereffects all by herself." Charlie paused. "I know if I would've found out back then Luke would've been a dead man."

Ruth sighed and leaned into him. "Oh, honey, you wouldn't have gotten the chance to kill him. Dylan would've done it first." They both let out a little laugh. "I'm so worried about her. She's been through so much since she's been home. I'm afraid if things are finished with Luke she'll never come back."

"I'm worried too, honey, I have to believe that it'll work out between the two of them. I love that boy, but it's gonna be real hard to work alongside of him if Luke hurts her any worse than she already is. Speaking of work, I should probably call the guys with an update on Bell. I'm going back to work tomorrow. Patrick said things have been running smoothly today, but I don't want him feeling stuck with everything." He looked at Ruth as she stood up. "I know that's not how he'd feel, but really I need to just keep my mind on something else." He stood up and kissed Ruth on the forehead before he headed into the house.

Ruth stood there for a moment staring at the house, finally shaking her head. "What a mess."

***

Luke started heading back to his truck after walking for over an hour. He hadn't realized how far he walked until he was several miles down the beach. It was busy this time a year, but with the earlier rain and slightly chilly temps, there were barely a soul around. He stood on the shore watching the water. Normally it'd calm him, but today he was far from calm. All he could think of was Rose. He wondered who she would've looked like. Luke imagined her looking like a mini-version of Bellamy. No doubt she would've been a beauty like her mother. Luke didn't have a lot of experience with kids since he didn't see his nieces and nephew often, but he knew he would've been a good dad.

When he made it back to his truck, Luke pulled out his phone to call Travis. He'd gotten Travis's number from Dustin earlier. Luke hoped that in talking to Travis he'd have a better understanding about what Bellamy went through.

"Hello?" the male voice asked.

"Uh, hi, is this Travis?" Luke was suddenly nervous.

"No, this is Brad. Who's this?"

"Hey, Brad, it's Luke. Can I talk to Travis?" Luke asked. He could hear Brad talking to Travis in the background.

"Hi, Luke. Whatcha need?" Travis asked, his voice sounding tense.

"Travis, I really need your help. Will you help me?" Luke pleaded.

Chapter 14

Travis closed his cell phone, sighing heavily as he stood up. He grabbed some clean clothes and walked into the bathroom to shower. Travis had no clue what he was going to say to Luke when they met up in an hour. He was going to tell him no, that he needed to talk to Bellamy, but he could hear it in Luke's voice how much he was hurting. He knew Brad was standing in the doorway of the bathroom watching him and wanting to know what Luke said.

"I think he wants to know about Rose," Travis said as he stepped into the shower.

"I figured as much. He sounded terrible on the phone. I really feel for the guy. I'm sure that's not the way Bellamy wanted Luke to find out."

"No, it's not. I love her so much, but if she would've just told him at the very beginning they both wouldn't be hurting now. I tried—oh how I tried to get her to try harder when it came to telling him she was pregnant, but she was just so scared to do it. She was convinced that everyone would hate her, especially Luke." Travis and Brad were both quiet for a couple of minutes until Travis spoke up again.

"What do I tell him, Brad? Do I tell him everything? Did you know I've got a picture of Rose?" The last part was nothing more than a whisper.

"You never told me you have a picture. Does Bellamy know?" Brad asked.

"No, she doesn't. She knew they were willing to take pictures of her, but Bellamy told me to tell them no. I went out to the nurse's station and I don't know why, but I told them yes." Travis felt a lump grow in his throat. "Um, I only kept the one of her face. Babies who die in-utero can sometimes look heavily bruised if they're not delivered very quickly, but Bellamy had her within a couple of hours. She was perfect and so beautiful. She looked like she was just sleeping." Travis shut off the water, grabbed a towel and stepped out of the shower. He tried to wipe away the tears before Brad saw them. Travis didn't like Brad to see him cry because it made him feel weak. He didn't even notice Brad standing directly in front of him. Travis felt Brad's strength when he wrapped his arms around Travis.

Neither of them said anything as they stood in the bathroom. Finally Brad leaned back and smiled at Travis before he took his lips in a gentle but firm kiss that had Travis sighing.

"I'm gonna go check on Bellamy while you meet with Luke. Call me later if you need to," Brad said as he kissed him again and then turned and walked out.

Travis finished getting ready and headed out to Luke's.

***

Luke hadn't been home more than a few minutes when a knock sounded at his door. He knew it was probably Travis, but a small part of him was hoping it was Bellamy.

Luke opened the door to see Travis standing there. He pushed the screen door open. "Thanks for coming." Luke led Travis into the living room. "Do you want a beer?" Luke asked as he walked into the kitchen.

"Yeah, sure," Travis replied as he sat down on the couch.

Luke returned to the living room and handed Travis one of the beers. Neither of them spoke as they drank their beers down.

It was Travis who broke the silence first. "I know you want answers, and I'm more than happy to do it. I know you're hurting, but believe it when I say I always believed Bellamy made a mistake keeping her pregnancy from you. She's very stubborn." They both laughed, both of them knowing how true that was.

"I guess I'll start from my beginning. I found Bellamy near the college clinic bawling her eyes out. There was just something about her that drew me to her. Long story short, we went for coffee and she told me everything. In the middle of our talk she got sick, so I took her back to my place. I had an apartment near the campus and helped her clean up." He took a deep breath and looked Luke right in the eyes. "I was sitting right next to her the first time she tried to call you about the baby. We'd been living together for a couple of weeks by then and I'd been pushing her towards it."

"When she called, she looked panicked when there seemed to be a party going on in the background. I nodded at her to ask for you, but when she did, the girl who answered the phone, in Bell's words, started purring, 'Luke, baby, there's some little girl on the phone.' She didn't even wait for you to get to the phone… she just hung it up and cried in my arms." Travis noticed Luke's cheeks turning pink, like maybe he was embarrassed. "Man, I'm not telling you this to make you feel bad at all. Bellamy was crying because she said that she'd ruin your life if you knew about the baby. She said that you'd never want to be with her and she didn't want the reason to be because she'd gotten pregnant. She was a kid herself, you knew her back then. She was the baby with two older brothers and lots of people around her to baby her and take care of her. She was away from home and all alone.

Before her first doctor appointment she went and got the medical card so she and the baby would be covered. You should've seen it when we went to her first visit. The bitch receptionist looked at Bellamy's medical card and how young she looked and treated her like she was trash. I'd had it with the girl's attitude towards Bellamy, so I went up to the counter and told her that if she didn't treat my fucking fiancée better, then I'd speak to her manager. After that she got the picture and left her alone. Of course, I went to every appointment pretending to be the devoted fiancé." Travis shook his head.

"Sorry, I get a little worked up and lose track of what I'm saying. But the first time she saw the little fluttering on the screen she fell in love and to be honest, I did, too. Anyway, things went well. She quit dancing because she was sick a lot. We argued all of the time about her calling you and even about telling her parents. It was easy at first for her to hide it because she didn't really start to show until the end of November. Nobody noticed her growing belly or boobs because she was always in sweaters and sweatshirts. She went home with me for Thanksgiving, so she didn't have to face her family, but of course that caused problems since Ruth was upset. Bellamy told me that she heard from her mom that you were involved with someone and it was getting kind of serious, so of course she had another reason not to say anything to you or anyone else."

"Travis, can I ask you a question, and trust me, I'm not trying to be a dick, but it's just something I need to know. Was Bellamy sure that I was the father?" Luke looked pale when he asked.

Travis had the urge to punch Luke in the face, but the guy was entitled to some answers. "You're the only guy Bellamy has ever slept with." Travis noticed Luke's look of confusion. "She dated some, especially the last couple of years, but she's never slept with anyone else."

"Travis, how can you be certain that she didn't? It's not like it's any of my business, but come on, man; six years without anyone?" Luke wanted to believe that he was the only man Bellamy had ever been with, but a part of him doubted it. Bellamy was a gorgeous girl: how could some guy not snatch her up? Thankfully, though, no one ever did. Even though things were a mess right now, he still loved her. Luke knew he needed to hear all of this, but it still didn't make it any less painful.

"Luke, you have to realize that after Bellamy lost Rose, she shut down. She went to class, went to work and came home: that was it. It's hard to believe by looking at her now, but she started eating all of the time. The girl gained thirty pounds in a very short period of time. Her therapist, Maggie, said that it was a comfort thing. Some people starve themselves when they get depressed and some gorge themselves. She was at school away from everyone. Her mom was there for a while, but after a couple of weeks, Bellamy made her leave.

"She saw Maggie three times a week over two years. In that time she lost all her baby weight and was almost done with school. I'd set her up on a couple of dates, but they didn't go great. She didn't mope around waiting for you, but she was afraid to be intimate with anyone. Bellamy dated a guy she worked with for a couple of months and she'd decided that she was going to sleep with him, but they didn't get beyond…Um, do you really want to hear this?" Travis asked, embarrassed that he almost started talking about her sex attempt in front of Luke.

Luke cleared his throat. "Yeah, could you skip the details."

"Sorry, man, I didn't even think. Anyway, let's just say that she got to a point and would freak out. The guy was an asshole and didn't want to take no for an answer and she freaked out. Mason had called me from her phone and told me to come get her. When I got there she was standing in his driveway crying. I took her home and got her to open up about what happened. She said the whole time she wanted to do it, but she just couldn't go through with it. Of course, Mason never called her again and even quit his job. It happened a few other times, but each time it wasn't as bad as the first. I was beginning to think she was getting better, but she just sort of gave up and threw herself into her work. Maggie thought that maybe it was the guilt and keeping such an important secret from you, her first and only lover. I think that's why she was ready to tell you now, after all of this time, because she had told me that she was ready to really try dating and working through her sexual hang-ups. Obviously she, um—worked those out.

"I know this is a lot to take in, but if you have questions you want to ask me, I'll answer them the best I can," Travis said, rubbing a hand through his hair.

Luke wasn't sure what to ask first. He had a lot to take in and to think about, but there was one thing he desperately needed to know. "Where is Rose now? Was she buried?"

"Bellamy had her cremated. She's in an urn in Bellamy's room in Savannah." Luke noticed Travis looking like he was struggling with something. "I have something to show you, but you have to promise not to tell Bellamy—well, maybe when you think she's ready. Uh, would you like to see a picture of your daughter?" Travis asked as he pulled his wallet out of his back pocket.

Luke was speechless when Travis asked him if he wanted to see a picture of his daughter. "Why can't Bellamy know?"

"They offered to take Rose's picture for a keepsake while Bell was in the hospital, but she'd said no. I knew she'd someday regret not having it, so I told them yes." Luke could see Travis's fingers trembling as he handed him the picture.

Luke took the picture. He didn't look at it first. He wasn't sure what to expect and it scared the shit out of him. His heart pounded in his chest as he looked down at the face of his daughter. He sucked in a breath when he saw the beauty that she was. Luke would've sworn she was just sleeping. She was swaddled in a pink blanket and all he could see was her head.

Luke could see the light bruising around her neck. She had the most perfect lips, and her nose was slightly turned up like Bellamy's. She had just a fair hint of dark hair on her head and tiny little ears. Luke felt a lump form in his throat as he continued to stare at the photo. His heart ached for what he and Bellamy had lost. He couldn't imagine what it had been like for Bellamy to deal with all of that. Luke was grateful to Travis for being with Bellamy through it all.

Luke quickly swiped at the tear that escaped and rolled down his cheek. He cleared his throat before speaking. "What was it like when Bellamy had her?"

"Um, well, after we got to the hospital and they found that Rose had died, Bellamy had to have labs done and an IV started. When they told her that she'd have to deliver Rose, Bellamy became hysterical. The nurses were great as they tried to calm her down. While they were waiting for orders to start inducing her, I called Ruth. I hated being so cryptic when I called her, but Bellamy didn't want anyone to know what was going on. God, Luke, when Ruth got there it was awful. They were talking about possibly sedating Bellamy because she wouldn't stop crying hysterically. Ruth was perfect, though; she didn't ask any questions, she just crawled into bed with Bellamy as she cried, and after a while Ruth was able to get Bellamy settled down. Once they got everything going they said it could either happen quickly or could take over 24 hours. Luckily it happened rather fast. Within a couple intense hours, Bellamy delivered her." Luke could hear the emotion in Travis' voice as he continued.

"At first, Bellamy wouldn't look at her, but the doctor and nurses said that it'd help with the grieving process. It took a little convincing, but they finally talked her into holding her. They wrapped Rose in a blanket and put her Bellamy's arms. Bellamy kissed the top of her head and laid with her in her arms for forever. Well, until they were ready to take her. Ruth got the chance to hold her for a second before they took her away, too." Travis kept it to himself that he got to hold her as well. There was no reason to rub it in Luke's face that Travis got to hold Luke's daughter. "Anyway, it was rough."

The silence was deafening as Luke sat there trying to process everything that Travis had told him. He could tell that the whole experience affected Travis, but he was so grateful to him for being so good to Bellamy. Luke knew he still had a lot to think about before he talked to Bellamy again. He had to decide if they had a future, even though a part of him felt betrayed by the secrets she kept from him. At least now he knew the story and the reason things transpired the way they had. Was he ready to forgive Bellamy? No, but he was getting close. Luke just needed a little more time.

"I want you to keep the picture of Rose." Travis noticed the relief written all over Luke's face. Travis figured Luke would think that he wanted it back. "I just want you to promise me that when she's ready, you'll share it with Bellamy." Travis got to his feet, needing some air.

Luke watched as Travis stood up. Luke tucked Rose's picture into his wallet and got up as well. He led Travis to the door putting a hand on his shoulder to halt him. "Thanks a lot, Travis. You didn't have to come over and tell me everything, but I mean it when I say thanks. Thanks for being such a good friend to Bellamy when she needed you. She's lucky to have you in her life."

Travis nodded, "You're welcome, and you know what? I'm the lucky one. She's one of a kind. Whatever you decide to do, just know that she loves you and if she could, she'd do it all differently."

Luke watched Travis turn, head down the porch, and start to walk down the street. Bellamy was lucky to have found such a good friend and it made Luke happy to know that she wasn't alone when she went through everything. Now he had things to think about and a decision to make. He closed the door and walked silently back into the living room.

Chapter 15

The past two days had gone by surprisingly fast for Bellamy. After Wednesday morning when Luke dropped her off at home she'd merely existed. Brad had informed her that afternoon that Luke had called and wanted to meet with Travis. Bellamy knew why and she was okay with Travis talking to Luke about everything. She figured if he didn't want to talk to her, why not the person who was with her throughout it all.

Bellamy saw Luke Thursday morning for the first time when he stopped by the bakery to see his mom. Bellamy had been recruited by Lola to help with all of the desserts for Dylan's party and for the shop. Bellamy had been so worried how Lola was going to treat her when she'd shown up that morning to get started. She was relieved when she walked into the shop and was embraced in a bear-hug by Lola and a kiss to her forehead. Bellamy had been in the back finishing putting sprinkles on the frosted cookies she helped make. She'd looked like a mess. Her hair had been piled on top of her head and covered with a hairnet. Bellamy's apron had been splattered by several different colored frostings. She had grabbed the tray and carried them out front and had almost dropped them when she saw Luke standing at the counter talking quietly to his mom.

Bellamy's plan had been to quickly retreat into the kitchen, but Lola had spotted her and smiled a sympathetic smile. Of course Luke noticed his mom's shift in attention and turned to face Bellamy. She could see the muscle in his jaw twitch, like maybe he was trying to stop himself from talking to her. Then he turned back to his mom, kissed her cheek and high-tailed it out of there. Bellamy tried to swallow the lump that seemed to have lodged itself in her throat. Lola started to speak, but Bellamy had cut her off and quickly escaped to the bathroom. Once she closed and had locked the door behind her she splashed water in her face. She looked up and examined herself in the mirror. Bellamy looked tired and her bags under her eyes were so dark they stood out against the slight paleness of her face.

She still didn't feel a hundred percent after the ordeal from Sunday, and the stress of the last few days wasn't helping, either. Bellamy could tell by the way her clothes fit that she'd even lost some weight, which wasn't a good thing, but her appetite had become non-existent. She tried to force herself to eat, but at times she'd almost become physically ill, so she gave up.

After the Luke incident, Bellamy hadn't seen him at all. She'd overheard Dylan that night talking to their father about how Luke was doing. Both of them incredulous about the whole situation and both men voiced their disbelief of what Bellamy had gone through virtually alone.

After she finished the jobs that Lola had given her she went back to her parents' to take a nap. She had woken several hours later to her dad knocking on her door. Bellamy smiled weakly as he came and sat down next to her on her bed. They both sat silently for what seemed like forever.

***

Charlie walked into the house knowing that Ruth wasn't home yet. He wanted a chance to talk to his baby-girl alone. Charlie had been beyond shocked to learn about Bellamy and Luke. He knew that if he would've known what happened back then he sure as shit would've had to have beat that boy's ass. Now all he wanted to do was to fix things.

Bellamy had been almost non-existent the last couple of days since Luke had dropped her off. She'd left the house to help Ruth at the studio and Lola at the bakery. She'd come home and kept to herself in her room. Dinner the night before had been quiet and strained. The boys had both come and Charlie could see the questions in their eyes as they watched their baby sister push her food around her plate, and then quietly excuse herself from the table.

"Dad, she looks like a ghost," Dylan had said to him.

They all could see how tired she looked, and even in two days she looked thinner. Charlie had spoken to Patrick about Luke, too. He hadn't shown up back to work since the week before, and Patrick said that he and Lola hadn't heard from him, either. They knew he was okay because he'd called Jason the day he brought Bellamy home, and he just needed time to figure things out.

Now as Charlie stared down at his little girl, he didn't know what to say. He knew it was six years too late for a lecture; it wasn't like she wasn't already hurting enough. Charlie reached a hand out to smooth the hair that was hanging in Bellamy's face back behind her ear. "How'ya feeling, sweetheart?"

Charlie watched as Bellamy moved to put her head on his lap like when she was a little girl. He rubbed a hand over her hair while he waited for her answer.

"I'm okay, Daddy. Just really tired. I didn't realize it would take so much time to get my strength back."

Bellamy knew that wasn't the only reason for how she was feeling, but she was too scared to have the conversation she knew was coming with her dad at that moment. He had to be so disappointed in her. He'd had the sex talk along with her mom on her fifteenth birthday when they realized boys were starting to pay attention to her. They drilled it into Bellamy's head that if she wasn't going to wait until she was married that she just be safe about it. Because of her, her mom had lied to her dad and brothers. She knew things had been weird in the house since she came home the day before.

"D-daddy, I'm so, so sorry. I never meant for any of this to happen. I know you're disappointed in me and upset with Mom, but please don't be mad at her. I begged and begged for her not to tell anyone about the baby."

Charlie looked down at his daughter as she poured her heart out to him. Yes, he was mad at his wife, because even though she promised Bellamy to keep her secret, she should've at least told him. He should've been there for his baby girl. Bellamy had been such a wonderful surprise. After the boys they were done; they were shocked when Ruth had gotten pregnant again. He'd never forget the look on Ruth's face when the doctor held up a squawking, pink little girl. Bellamy was such a loved child, and although they all spoiled her, she never acted like it. Sometimes Charlie thought that maybe his and his sons' overprotectiveness had caused Bellamy to be a bit sheltered, but as she headed into the teen years he knew she'd been coming into her own. Charlie, Ruth, Lola and Patrick would always get a chuckle out of the way she'd follow Luke around like a little lost puppy.

He'd never said anything to anyone when he saw that when Bellamy turned fifteen and she started getting more flirtatious with Luke, but Luke had never seemed to notice. Not until Bellamy turned sixteen and Dustin and Luke had come home that summer from school. He remembered all too well when they had the Carters over for a cookout, and Luke caught sight of Bellamy for the first time in over six months. The look on that boy's face when Bellamy stepped out of the house in a too-damn-short sundress was Luke's one way ticket to throttle town. Charlie knew his daughter was a beauty like her mother, but it still killed him to see her growing up and knowing that boys were starting to notice her.

That summer when she'd turned eighteen, he should've just locked her in her room, especially when she was constantly tagging along with her brothers when they'd all go out. He knew the boys had watched her like a hawk, but obviously not enough since they were all dealing with the fallout.

"Baby-girl, I might be disappointed, but it's only because I wish you would've been honest with us from the beginning, sweetheart. All of this doesn't make me love you any less than I do. As far as being mad at your momma, well, I just think that if she would've told me, we both could've been there for you." He smiled when he heard Bellamy's breathing start to slow down, and knew she had fallen back to sleep.

Charlie eased off of her bed and walked out of her bedroom, shutting the door quietly behind him. He was surprised to see Ruth standing in the hallway, her eyes glistening with unshed tears. Charlie hated to see his wife cry. Even after all of these years it broke his heart. He reached out and pulled her against him taking her lips in a kiss hoping that it would express that he stilled loved her with all of his heart and soul.

Ruth slid her arms over his shoulders as he felt her hold on tighter. He blindly backed her towards their bedroom and once inside, shut the door with the practice of a man who had many a time slipped quietly into the bedroom with his wife. As he lowered them both to the bed, he was going to show her how much he loved her, and how no matter how mad he was, that she was his forever.

Chapter 16

Bellamy woke up at five o'clock when she heard an incessant pounding on her bedroom door. She hadn't even sat up when the door opened. Bellamy frowned when she saw Dustin, Dylan, Stacy, Brad and Travis all file into her room. "Wh-what's going on?"

Dylan, who for the most part had remained silent about everything, shocked her when he spoke first. "Little sister of mine, we've come to kidnap you and take you out for dinner, maybe a movie."

Bellamy looked at all of their expectant faces. "Um, that's really sweet of you, but I think I'm just gonna go back to bed." She quickly laid back down and threw the blanket over her head, and just as quick it disappeared. "Damn you, Dylan, let me go to bed!" Bellamy shouted.

Dylan sat down next to her. "Honey, you can't mope around here for the rest of your visit." She turned towards him and she saw the smile he only ever used on her. "I know you're hurting, but sitting here is not going to help because all you're gonna do is think about everything that's happened.

Listen: I know I'm overprotective and pushy with you, but please, Bell, come out with us tonight." She didn't want to hear what he was gonna say next. "Bell, you know I leave in five days, and—well—I just want to spend some time with you before I leave. You never know what could happen and I have to know you're okay before I go."

Bellamy knew he was right, and she hated to think that her brother could leave and never come home. Sitting around moping wasn't going to help keep her mind off Luke, and since she didn't know if he'd be coming around anytime soon, she decided that spending time with her friends and family was the perfect cure for her depression.

She smiled at Dylan, sat up, and threw her arms around his neck, hugging him tightly. "I love you, Dylan, so much. Even if you think you're the boss of me." That earned a chuckle from everyone.

"Let me take a shower and I'll meet y'all downstairs." Bellamy watched as they all filed out of her room, except for Stacy.

Stacy shut the door after all the guys left and walked over to sit down next to Bellamy. They hadn't seen each other since the night that Luke and everyone else found out about the baby. She knew when it happened because she knew about Bellamy's plan to make him see that she was a woman. After their night together, Stacy had stayed by Bellamy's side when she'd cried over Luke's reaction to her being a virgin. It devastated Bellamy then, and she couldn't imagine what Bellamy must be feeling now. Especially since it was very obvious that Luke loved Bellamy as much as she loved him.

She just knew they had to work through this, and if she believed in soul-mates, Stacy knew that Luke was Bellamy's.

"You look like shit, Bell."

Bellamy couldn't help but laugh. "Gee, thanks," she said with a smile, and Bellamy was so glad to have her best friend back in her life. "I know I look terrible, but I haven't been sleeping real well and the thought of food has been making my stomach turn." Right on cue her stomach growled loudly. With a laugh Bellamy stood up. "Okay, that's my cue to jump in the shower. I'll see y'all downstairs." Bellamy smiled at Stacy as she stood up, but it turned into a frown when she noticed a bruise on her shoulder that was sticking out of her sleeve.

"Stacy, what the hell is this?" Bellamy quickly pulled up the shirtsleeve to see the bruise and as she peered closer she realized it was a bite mark.

Stacy looked down and immediately jumped up, backing away from Bellamy. "Hmm…I don't know how that got there," she said as she quickly escaped Bellamy's room. Stacy leaned against the wall and sighed. "I should've worn long-sleeves," she murmured to herself as she went downstairs.

A half hour later, Bellamy joined the group, who were all standing around the dining room. They all heard her enter and greeted her with relieved smiles. She looked around the room. "Where are Mom and Dad?" Bellamy asked.

"Right here, baby."

Bellamy turned around to see her parents walk into the dining room with their arms wrapped around each other. They both had that sleepy look and it seemed like all had been forgiven.

"Mom, we're taking Bell out for a while. She needs to get out of the damn house," Dylan said as he stepped forward, wrapping his arm around Bellamy's shoulders.

"Well, that's a good idea, baby. Y'all have fun and take care of your sister." Ruth made the rounds hugging and kissing everyone as they started to leave.

Bellamy was the last one out of the house. She turned and ran to her dad and threw her arms around his neck, squeezing him tight. "I love you, Daddy." Bellamy kissed him quick and then threw her arms around her mom. "I love you too Momma."

"We love you too, baby. Have fun," they said in unison as she ran out the door and towards Dustin's truck. Stacy was riding with Travis and Brad and would meet them at the bar.

Once Bellamy was settled in the middle of her brothers, she let out a sigh of contentment. She always felt safe with them, and even though they were protective of her, she still loved them.

After they pulled out of the driveway, Dustin wrapped his arm around Bellamy's shoulders giving her a squeeze. "How you holding up, squirt?"

Bellamy laid her head on Dustin's shoulder, "I'm okay. I miss him, but I think he hates me now," her voice catching at the end. She couldn't cry; no, she wouldn't cry. She'd cried more in the last week then she had in a long time. There had to come a point when the tears dried up, but Bellamy was beginning to think that it was never going to happen.

Dylan grabbed Bellamy's hand and gave it a squeeze, "Bell, you know he doesn't hate you. He just needs time to deal with everything. He had a huge bombshell dropped on him, so he's just gonna need some time. I know I haven't been a big supporter of the two of you together, but he loves you. He'll come around when he's ready."

They were silent the rest of the drive to Shooter's, which Bellamy wasn't thrilled to be going to, but she had enough people around to protect her this time.

They pulled into the first parking spot they found, with Travis pulling in right next to them. Everyone climbed out of the vehicles. Dustin turned to Travis. "Hey, man, when you gonna let me drive that sweet car of yours?"

"How about never, dude. I've heard horror stories about your driving abilities. That car is my baby," Travis said with a smirk.

The mood was light while everyone sat and enjoyed their pizza and beer. The only one who wasn't drinking was Bellamy. She just couldn't stomach the idea of touching alcohol, especially after the last time. Her stomach was still bothering her as well, so she didn't want to chance it. She looked around their crowded booth and smiled. At that moment she felt blessed to have so many people she cared about. It just made it worse the one person who should be there with them was Luke and he was alone.

Bellamy looked across the table at Stacy and smiled until she saw that bruise again. "Stacy, where did that bite mark come from?" She watched as Stacy's face turned beet-red. Bellamy only said something because the guys were all involved in some in-depth conversation about baseball, but Dylan happened to hear her since he was sitting next to Stacy.

"Bell, please just drop it. It's not what you think," Stacy said, her eyes pleading with Bellamy to drop it.

"What's she talking about, Stacy? Did someone hurt you?" Dylan asked. His voice had gotten that deep-growly sound it gets when he's upset.

By then the others were looking in her direction. Bellamy noticed Dustin's eyes go wide and then drop to his lap…interesting. She turned backed to Stacy and cleared her throat. "Oh, wait, is that from Sunday when we were horsing around? I thought maybe I bit you. I'm so sorry, sweetie, I didn't think I got you that bad," She gave Stacy a smile.

"Yeah, that's from you. I didn't say anything because, uh—I didn't think you'd remember."

Dylan looked at both girls and shook his head, at least he bought it. Bellamy was going to have to have a serious talk with Stacy to find out exactly why Dustin had bit Stacy on the shoulder, but on the other hand, it really wasn't her business unless Stacy wanted her to know.

***

Luke pulled up outside of Shooter's and sat in his car staring at the sight before him. Bellamy was sitting against the window wearing that smile that made his heart ache. She was smiling at Stacy across the table, but even from where he was sitting he could tell it didn't reach her eyes. He'd stopped by her parents' home, and Ruth had told him where he could find her.

The past few days had been tough for Luke, but he was finally starting to see things a little clearer. The first night after Travis had left, Luke wallowed in self-pity and Jack Daniels. He mourned the loss of their baby as he drank straight from the bottle until the picture in his hand became blurry. Luke knew that drinking wasn't going to help, but he needed something to ease the pain in his heart. It's true what they say, though: that after the alcohol wears off, the problems are still there. So he woke up Thursday with a hellacious hangover. He'd seen his mom that morning and while she gave him a pep-talk, Bellamy came through the swinging doors, and because he didn't want her to see him in such a mess, he quickly kissed his mom and left.

After he had gotten home, he showered and shaved and felt somewhat better. He knew that they were gonna have to have a talk, but more than anything he just wanted to hold her in his arms again. Luke wanted forever with her. He wanted to marry her and fill their home with as many children they were to be blessed with.

Luke climbed out of his truck and walked steadily to the front door. The night air was humid and filled with the scent of honeysuckle. As he pulled the door open, he was welcomed by the sound of the jukebox and the laughter of many of the patrons. Luke turned towards Bellamy's table and stopped just to watch them. Dustin was talking to Brad as they both kept turning towards one of the flat-screens, while Travis and Dylan talked over by the bar.

"L-Luke?" He turned to see Bellamy standing a few feet away from him. Her eyes filled with questions. Luke took a deep breath and knew it was now or never.

***

Bellamy and Stacy excused themselves to head to the restrooms. Once inside, Bellamy couldn't help herself. "So is that bite mark courtesy of Dustin?" She watched the blush that quickly crept up Stacy's neck until her cheeks had a dark tinge of pink. Bellamy already knew the answer, but she just couldn't wrap her head around how it happened. She'd never known Stacy to be interested in her brother at all, but stranger things had happened. Bellamy just hoped that Stacy knew the score when it came to Dustin. He never treated the women in his life bad, but he never kept them around either.

Stacy cleared her throat and stared down at the floor nervously. "Uh, yes," she croaked. "It just sort of happened." She looked up. "Are you mad?"

"Why would I be mad, Stacy? I just don't want to see you get hurt, that's all. He's my brother and I love him dearly, but he's not one to stick around long."

Stacy started to laugh. "I'm sorry, I don't mean to laugh. It's just I'm not looking to get involved with anyone anytime soon. I know how your brother is, so you don't have to worry because it's never going to happen again." Stacy wasn't even the slightest bit interested in getting into another relationship, especially after Brian. Maybe he was right—maybe she wasn't built to hold on to someone long-term.

Bellamy smiled at Stacy because she could see it in her eyes that Stacy was telling her the truth. She didn't see any sort of twinkle in Stacy's eyes. Bellamy would hate to see her get her hopes up and then have to watch Dustin lose interest and move on to the next girl.

"Bell, I hate to bring this up, but have you guys heard if they caught the guys that attacked you Friday night?" Stacy hadn't heard anything mentioned so maybe it was done and over with.

"N-no I haven't. I guess with everything else that's happened I haven't even thought about it." It still shook her to her core that she'd come close to being seriously hurt, but the look on Stacy's face showed Bellamy that Stacy felt awful for bringing it up. She grabbed Stacy in a big hug. "Don't you dare feel bad for asking me about it. It was bound to come up again." Bellamy pulled away smiling. She was surprised by her calm demeanor.

Bellamy followed Stacy out of the bathroom and back to the table when she froze. Luke was in the bar looking around. She didn't know what to do, should she turn around and run back to the bathroom or should she just face the music and see what he wanted? Bellamy decided on the latter. Stacy gave her an encouraging smile and quickly walked back to their table, leaving Bellamy alone.

"Luke?" Bellamy said. She stood there immobile as he turned around to face her. He looked tired and worn out and she knew it was because of her, and she hated herself for it. Luke walked towards her slowly, his face showed no emotion.

"Hey, Bell. Can we go somewhere and talk?"

"Sure." Bellamy walked over to the table and was met with curious glances from everyone. She quickly said goodbye to everyone and met Luke by the front door.

As they stepped out into the humid air, Bellamy felt her nerves take over. Neither one of them spoke as he helped her into his truck. Bellamy snuck glances at Luke as he silently drove them. She had no clue where he was taking her, since they were going the opposite direction of either one of their homes. All she knew was that she was scared of what he was gonna say.

Bellamy stared out the passenger window and noticed that they were heading towards the Bartlett Plantation. Luke pulled into the long driveway and pulled his truck next to the house.

"Are we going to be disturbing the owners by being here?" Bellamy asked, looking at Luke.

"Nah, they're down in Florida. I don't think they'll be back until we've finished," Luke said as he climbed out of the truck. He came around to help Bellamy out and then took her hand as he led her around to the back.

Bellamy watched Luke out of the corner of her eye. She just couldn't tell what was going on in his head. When they reached the back, Bellamy was confused. There really wasn't anything to see. All of the shrubbery was overgrown or dying, the grass was knee deep in spots and the dumpster they had delivered was set up right in the back.

Towards the back of the field were several trees lining the property. As Bellamy walked alongside Luke, she noticed an opening between two of the larger trees. Next to one of the trees was a bench. Bellamy felt Luke's hand at the small of her back as he led her over to sit down. She swallowed nervously as he sat down next to her. Bellamy twisted her hands together in her lap as nervous energy ran through her body. She was shocked when Luke grabbed her left hand, threading his fingers with hers and held it in his lap.

The wait was killing her. Bellamy didn't know what he was waiting for. If he was going to break things off with her, she wanted to get it over with. It was starting to drive her mad.

Chapter 17

Luke rubbed his thumb gently over Bellamy's wrist. He could feel the frantic beat of her pulse. Luke knew that she must be thinking the worst. He knew that she was beating herself up more than he ever could for what she did. The more and more he thought about it, Luke knew that her age and the circumstances revolving around Rose's conception were the major factors in how everything played out.

He brought her to the Bartlett plantation because he wanted to be somewhere he knew no one would bother them. All day he kept playing the conversation they were about to have over and over in his head, and no matter which way he worded it, the results were still the same. He loved this woman so much and wanted to try to get past the secrets and lies. Luke could feel his wallet in his back pocket and was comforted with the fact that their daughter's picture was nestled in there and when the time was right he'd share it with Bellamy. They'd be able to mourn her together and get some closure.

Luke took a deep breath and turned to face her. It took him a minute to compose himself, she was just so damn beautiful to him. Even when she was an annoying little brat, she had a pull over him that he could never explain.

"Please look at me, Bell," he said as he reached over and tilted her head up so he could look into her eyes. "Thank you. I had this whole speech prepared, but it all flew out of my head the minute I looked into your eyes." He couldn't help but smile at the light blush that stained her cheeks.

"Baby, first I want to say that I'm sorry that I was so horrible to you the night we slept together the first time. I was mad at myself because I knew I crossed a line that could damage my friendship with your brothers, but when it came to you, I was always weak. You've had this power over me ever since you were little. Sleeping with you that first time was something I never expected to happen and I got freaked out because it made me feel too much. It humbled me that you wanted me to be your first." Luke rubbed a hand through his hair. "I know that if you would've come right out and asked me to be your first I would've told you no way."

Luke watched as Bellamy gave him a small smile. He had a feeling she knew that's exactly what would've happened. He couldn't help but reach out and tuck a stray curl that had fallen from her messy bun back behind her ear. Luke savored the feeling as Bellamy leaned slightly into his hand. He slowly rubbed his thumb over her cheek savoring the feel of her soft skin.

"I'm sorry that the way I treated you caused you to believe that you couldn't come to me when you found out you were pregnant. I just wish you would've had faith in me and your family to tell us."

Luke hated to see the tears welling up in Bellamy's eyes. As one tear escaped, Luke wiped it away with the pad of his thumb. "Baby, please don't cry."

Bellamy was tired of crying. Ever since she came home it seemed like that's all she did. Why was he being so sweet to her? Bellamy didn't deserve it. She knew she deserved his anger. She stared down at their entwined hands and took a deep breath.

"I know" she whispered. "I can't undo what I did, I'll never be able to forgive myself for hurting everyone the way I have." Bellamy felt the scalding tears slide down her face as she looked up into his eyes. "Worst of all, I'll never forgive myself for hurting you." She pulled her hand away from his and buried her face in her hands as sobs racked her body.

Bellamy felt Luke wrap his arms around her and lift her onto his lap. She couldn't help but snuggle into him as she cried. Time was lost to her as he held her. Bellamy took comfort in his strength and warmth. She wasn't sure how long they stayed like that, but before long the sun escaped behind the tall trees and they were encased in the shadows.

"Bell," Luke said as he cupped her face in his hands and pulled her up until he could see her red-rimmed eyes. "Baby, I love you no matter what, okay? Please believe that."

Bellamy couldn't help but feel hope bloom, that things were going to be okay. She reached up to gently stroke his cheek until he lowered his lips to take hers in a tender kiss. Bellamy's heart sped up as she felt his tongue tease her lips, causing her to open to him. She slanted her head to the side to allow him better access to her mouth. Luke must've been pleased because she could feel and hear his groan. Bellamy felt his hands slide down her back until they started making their way back up under her shirt. The familiar feeling of his calloused fingers against her skin caused her to shiver.

Luke couldn't get enough of her, but he knew they had to finish their talk. He kissed her one more time and as he started to pull away, he heard a twig snap and watched in horror as Bellamy was ripped off his lap. Before he could even get up off the bench, he suddenly felt like he was being electrocuted. Luke's body seized up and he fell to the ground. He could hear Bellamy screaming his name, but he couldn't move to help her. Luke tried to fight it, but he couldn't. His mind started going blank and all of the noise around him started to fade away.

***

Bellamy fought against the arms holding her as she watched Luke fall to the ground. "Stop, please! You're hurting him," she cried.

Bellamy looked up into the black and blue eyes of the man who attacked Brad, Travis and herself outside the club and froze. How did they find them?

356

She began to fight furiously against the man holding her as she watched the big man walk over and kick Luke right in the side. Bellamy screamed in horror as they tased Luke again, each man taking a shot at kicking him.

She still hadn't seen the guy holding her yet, but Bellamy got her chance when she was shoved towards the big guy and he walked over to kick Luke right in the same spot the others had. When he turned, Bellamy felt the blood drain from her face. Mark walked towards her with a grin on his face that made Bellamy sick to her stomach. "Luke! Please get up," she cried as the big guy grabbed her and they started heading back from where they came.

"Shut up, you slutty bitch! That was just part of your payback for what you did to my face." He started to chuckle. "You'll get the rest of your payback later." With that he leaned down and nipped her earlobe.

Bellamy cried out and tried to get away from him, but he wrapped an arm around her waist and pulled her up tighter against his body. Her thoughts kept going back to Luke. Was he okay? Was he coming to save her? Bellamy quietly cried as they walked up on a truck and a sports car. She knew what she had to do: she had to fight as hard as she could to try to escape. Bellamy needed to find help for Luke. He was all that mattered. Channeling the little girl who was taught how to defend herself by her overprotective big brothers, Bellamy took a deep breath and slammed her heel right into his shin. He grunted and before he could react, she elbowed him in the gut. He dropped her and Bellamy tried to get away, but felt a jolt before she cried out in pain and collapsed to the ground.

***

Mark watched as Pete took the taser to Bellamy. Working undercover was what he loved, but sometimes it wore at him. He'd been working his way into Jake Webb's inner circle for the past six months. Jake was the son of the District Attorney up in Charleston. He was a suspected drug supplier who occasionally liked to dabble in sexual assaults. Jake had pretty much followed the same pattern as he had before, but Bellamy became an obsession to him. Probably because she's the first one to ever get away before he could hurt her.

Sometimes when he was undercover he had to do things that he wasn't proud of, things that sometimes gave him nightmares. But he had to put that all aside because sometimes you had to do what you could to get the job done. He didn't want to drug her that day at the bar, but one of Jake's cronies, a guy they called Tigger, was sitting at the bar watching the whole time to make sure he did it.

Mark would never forget walking into Shooter's and seeing Stacy for the first time. That girl was a dream. Her tall, tanned body and the curves that were in all the right spots. Just thinking about her made his hand tingle from where they touched before. What he wouldn't give for just a couple of hours with her. Before his thoughts could go any further, Jake was calling to him.

"Mark, get your fuckin' head out of your ass. Open the trunk, we're gonna throw her in there," Jake hollered as he picked Bellamy off of the ground like she weighed nothing.

Mark went over, popped the trunk open, and watched as Jake callously tossed Bellamy inside. God, that fucker was cruel. He hated that he had to wait until they got to their destination before he called in the cavalry. They were waiting for his signal and then they'd come in. Luckily they agreed that if they hadn't heard from him by 10 p.m. they'd come anyway, but that was still hours away and a lot could happen. "Please, let this work," he said to himself. Mark looked down at Bellamy in the trunk and quickly closed it.

"All right, boys, let's hit it," Jake hollered and jumped into his truck.

Chapter 18

Dustin sat quietly observing Stacy as she played a game of pool with his brother. He felt his groin tighten as he thought about the other day in her parents' kitchen. Ever since that day he hadn't been able to stop thinking about her. The way she smelled, the way she came undone in his arms and the way her lips seem to fit his so perfectly. He held in a groan as she leaned over the table to take a shot, giving him a great view of her gorgeous heart-shaped ass.

Dustin's cell phone rang and brought him out of his musings. He saw it was Luke. He smiled thinking maybe he and Bell had patched things up. "Hey, ma—" Dustin couldn't even finish before Luke's panicked voice came over the phone.

"D-Dustin—" Luke groaned into the phone.

"Luke, what is it?' Dustin knew something was wrong.

"They tased me a-a c-couple o-of t-t-times. T-th-they ki-kicked me. I-I think I-I have r-ribs broken."

"Who's they? What are you talking about?" Dustin voice rose catching his brother's attention.

"The guys fr-from the-the cl-club. They t-t-took her, I-I c-couldn't stop them."

Dustin could hear Luke breathing shallow into the phone. "Where are you, Luke?"

"Behind-behind the Bartlett place."

"Dylan, call an ambulance and get them to the Bartlett place. Stacy, call the Sherriff's station and tell them those guys from the weekend found Bellamy and Luke." Dustin took a deep breath. "They took my fucking sister." He watched his brother and Stacy whip out their phones and start dialing. "Travis, you better call my parents. Have everyone meet us there."

"Luke, buddy, hang on, bro, we're coming and we're gonna get her back."

"P-please hurry," he heard Luke mutter before the line went dead.

Dustin called Luke's parents as they all took off for the Bartlett Plantation. The whole drive there he silently prayed that they'd find his sister and fast.

***

Luke laid there on the hard ground, struggling for every breath he took. He'd just started coming around when the sound of Bellamy screaming had him trying to get up, but his body wasn't letting him. Luke held a hand to his ribs, knowing at least a couple were broken. Tears leaked out of his eyes because he couldn't move, he couldn't get to her and it was killing him. He could hear car engines start up, then nothing, Luke knew she was gone. "I'm sorry, baby," he whispered over and over again. If they hurt her, he'd kill every last one of them.

Luke wasn't sure how long he laid there until he heard vehicles and then sirens. Someone was yelling his name and then he heard the pounding footsteps. He opened his eyes to see the two men that were like brothers stop on both sides of him. "I-I'm s-sorry," Luke said as he quickly tried to wipe the tears from his eyes.

Dylan was the first to speak. "Nothing to be sorry for, brother. It looks like they did a number on you. I'm gonna pull up your shirt and take a look, okay?"

Dylan could see the paramedics heading towards them, but quickly pulled up Luke's shirt to assess the situation. He could see the bruising already starting and there was a spot that almost looked swollen. Dylan put Luke's shirt down and moved away as the paramedics came up to them. Luke was able to tell them for the most part what happened. Dylan watched as they looked Luke over before they got him on the gurney.

He, Dustin, Travis and Brad helped the paramedics get Luke back to the front where the ambulance was waiting, trying hard not to jostle him because of the pain he was in. When they rounded the corner he saw his parents and Luke's flying into the driveway, followed seconds later by several patrol cars. Luke's mom and dad were quickly by their son's side.

"Oh god, baby, what happened?" Lola cried, kissing her son's forehead.

"They got me I think with a-with a taser. I-I couldn't stop them from-from taking her."

Lola looked into her son's pain-filled eyes and it broke her heart. She gently brushed a hand over his head and leaned down to place a kiss on his forehead. "Baby, if you could've, you would've stopped them. They're gonna find her and bring Bellamy back to you." Even as she said it she wasn't sure if she believed her own words. No one knew what kind of car they had taken her away in or even the names of the men, except Mark, the man who had drugged Bellamy.

Patrick grabbed his son's hand. "You hang in there, son. Your momma is gonna ride with you to the hospital. I'm gonna help them find Bellamy, you hear me? We're gonna get her back." He gave his hand a squeeze as Ruth and Charlie came over before they loaded him in the ambulance.

"Oh god, Luke!" Ruth cried as she leaned down to kiss his cheek.

"I'm-I'm sorry I couldn't stop them, Ruth. Th-they took her before I knew what was happening." He was becoming short of breath. So the paramedics lifted him into the back of the ambulance and quickly put an oxygen mask on him.

They helped Lola into the back where they settled her on a bench right beside her son. She cradled his hand in between hers and as she looked out of the back she saw the faces of her family. Not family by blood, but family of the heart as they all stood there watching the ambulance start to pull away. Lola offered up a small prayer that they found Bellamy and that she was unharmed.

***

Stacy watched Dylan and his dad talk to Scott and the other officers. From the looks of it, it was an intense conversation. Hopefully they had some leads and would find Bellamy soon. Stacy turned and noticed Brad was comforting Travis off to the side. The poor guy looked like a mess. She was watching them so intently that she didn't notice Dustin coming and sitting down next to her until she felt his thigh brush hers.

"Uh, hey," she said. "So do they have any leads?"

Dustin ran his fingers through his hair. "Well, Scott said they've put out a bulletin with Bell's picture and they're hoping someone spotted her. They also put one out using the description that you gave them of Mark. I'm trying to stay optimistic that they'll find her soon."

"What if she gets hurt before they find her, Dustin? You can't tell me they're making any progress when they don't have any idea what kind of car she's in or who the other guys were. What if they find her and it's too late?" She put her head in her hands and couldn't help the tears that started to fall. Stacy felt Dustin's arms wrap around her and he just let her cry it out. It just didn't seem fair. Why were these bad things happening to Bellamy? She was one of the sweetest people that Stacy had ever met. Stacy dried her tears and sat up when she saw Dylan walking towards them. "What's going on, Dylan?" she asked as she and Dustin stood up.

"We're gonna head to the hospital and wait there. Scott said someone will be by to keep us informed about what's going on. I want to make sure Luke's doing okay, too. He doesn't need to be blaming himself when those pussies tased him in the first place."

They all started heading to the hospital where they'd hold a vigil until the authorities brought Bellamy back safe to them.

***

Bellamy came to while she was in the trunk. Her first thought was of Luke, and if he was able to get help. She'd never forget what it was like to watch him fall to the ground and seeing each of those bastards kick him. This was like being in some fucked up nightmare. One that she realized she may never wake up from, but she had to try and get away because she knew that whatever "punishment" the big guy, Jake, had for her wasn't going to be pretty. She'd go down swinging if she had to, but Bellamy was definitely not going to make it easy on them.

Bellamy panicked when she felt the car slow down. She knew it wouldn't be long before the car stopped. Bellamy felt around for anything to use as a weapon. She remembered from when her dad taught her how to change a tire that there was usually a lug wrench in the wheel well. Bellamy slid her hand around until she felt a little lever. She scooted as far as she could go and quickly pulled it up. Using only touch she felt around and found the lug wrench. Bellamy quickly pulled it out and laid the covering back down.

She had wanted to cry with relief that she'd found it, but Bellamy knew she would have only one chance, so she had to get herself calmed down. Bellamy felt the car slowly come to a stop and felt her heart start to beat rapidly in her chest. She heard the voices get closer as she held her weapon behind her back and get as close to the front as she could.

Chapter 19

Luke winced in pain as the radiologist positioned him on the table to take x-rays of his ribs. He wasn't sure how much longer it was gonna take, but Luke needed out of there so he could help find Bellamy. Luke was so scared for her, and he was growing more and more agitated. He'd already yelled at a poor nurse who was only trying to take his vitals. Didn't they understand that the love of his life was in danger and he needed to be out there helping?

After the x-ray they wheeled him back to the exam room where everyone was waiting for him. The ER staff had balked at letting everyone in the room at first, but when Scott and some of his fellow officers showed up, they moved Luke to a bigger room to accommodate everyone.

A nurse walked in after they got him settled back on the bed and wanted to give him something for the pain. Luke flat out refused to let her do it.

"Son, you're in too much pain to be so stubborn," his dad said with a frown.

"I know, Dad, but I need to stay clear-headed. What if when they find her and she needs me?"

Everyone grew quiet at Luke's question. He knew they were trying to be supportive but the silence was unnerving. Luke watched as Ruth came over and sat down next to his mom. She reached for his hand and squeezed it.

"Sweetheart, you know that you'll be more capable of helping if you have something for the pain. I promise you we'll wake you up if you fall asleep. You know Bellamy wouldn't want you to be in pain." Ruth gave him a gentle smile, but Luke could see the tears in her eyes.

"All right, I'll take it," Luke said as he watched the nurse inject the clear liquid into his IV. He felt it burn as it made its way into his bloodstream and then he started to feel drowsy.

"Just rest, baby," he vaguely heard his mom say as his eyelids drifted shut.

***

Dustin and Dylan sat with their dad as they talked to one of the sheriffs. Dustin could tell this was taking a toll on their dad. He looked tired and worn out. He watched Stacy walk by with a cup of coffee and head out of the automatic doors. Dustin wasn't sure why, but he got up and followed her out. He found her sitting on the steps, staring blindly at the street. When he walked up on her she started.

"I'm sorry, I didn't mean to scare you," Dustin said as he sat down next to her.

"It's okay. I think we're all a little on edge right now. I checked on Luke before I came out here and he was sleeping. What the fuck happened, Dustin? Why her? What did she ever do to ask for this? I keep thinking this is some twisted nightmare, but I can't wake up." Stacy looked down as Dustin started holding her hand. He felt her give it a squeeze and him a small smile. It was nice to have such a large group of people to be close to and who were there to support one another.

Dustin couldn't answer her. He wasn't sure how long they sat there holding hands, but he'd never felt more comfortable. Dustin tucked her into his side as they sat there in a comfortable silence. There was none of the mindless chatter that he usually dealt with, with some of the girls he'd taken out. She was so different: her olive skin tone, her dark hair and eyes gave her an almost exotic look. Stacy was tall and had curves that made his mouth water, but his favorite were her legs. They were long and shapely and felt right hugging his hips. God, what was he doing lusting after her as they were waiting to find out about his sister? Maybe he just needed to take a break from women for a while.

Dustin started to stand, dragging Stacy with him. "Come on, let's see if anyone knows anything yet." She nodded her head and walked alongside him back inside.

***

Mark got out of the passenger side of the truck and followed Jake to the back of Pete's Camaro. He checked his watch and knew he had to wait for Jake's supplier to show up before he called for backup. Mark could feel the adrenaline starting to pump through his veins. He always got like this before the finale of an assignment. This one had lasted longer than he wanted it to, but Jake was one paranoid fucker. Always suspicious of everyone's motives, even his closest friends.

"So what're we gonna do with her, Jake?" Mark asked casually.

The smirk on Jake's face made his skin crawl.

"Well, Marky boy, my supplier will be meeting up with us in about thirty minutes, so my little treat will have to wait, but let's just say this: that bitch won't be walking right when I'm done with her tight little body."

The rest of Jake's boys started laughing, so he knew to keep up appearances and joined in. They all wanted to know if they were gonna get a turn with her and Jake simply told them that when he had his fill, they could do whatever they wanted. They all jockeyed for position on who was going to get to go first after Jake. Mark had a feeling that he was gonna have to pull some shit out of his ass if he was gonna keep Bellamy safe until the backup arrived. He watched as Pete stuck the key in the lock and it was like everything went in slow motion.

The lid popped open and then Pete hit the ground. Bellamy was crouched down in the trunk swinging a lug wrench. He could see her eyes went wild as she swung at John, catching him on his arm.

"Stupid bitch!" John shouted and grabbed for her. She swung again and caught the side of his face. By then everyone else seemed to have caught on to what was happening. Jake marched over and caught the lug wrench as she swung it at him.

"You're gonna get it now, little girl." He pulled Bellamy, along with the lug wrench, out of the trunk. She struggled against his hold until she slipped free and took off in a sprint.

Mark knew Jake wasn't as fast as he was strong, so he wasn't surprised when Jake made him run after her. "Get her, you prick." He had no choice but to take off after her. Mark could tell she was physically fit because he could see the muscles in her legs as she sprinted down the drive. He was gaining on her and he could hear her panicked cry. Mark dove for her, wrapping his arms around her and then quickly turned so he would take the brunt of the fall.

Bellamy felt her heart beat a rapid staccato in her chest. The fight or flight kicked in and she started kicking her legs and swinging her arms. She could hear the grunts from the impact by her captor.

"Let me go, you son of a bitch!" Bellamy screamed as she fought harder. She heard the footfalls of the others and couldn't help the cry that left her lips. "P-please l-l-let me g-go," she stammered, her voice laced with fear.

"Sorry, sweetheart, I just can't do that," he said as he hauled her up and kept her back to his front.

Bellamy shuddered as she watched Jake stalk towards her. She wasn't sure why, but she sought shelter against the man holding her. Jake's eyes were cold blue orbs that made her skin crawl. He stopped right in front of her, smiled, and before she could duck, smacked her across the face twice. He never stopped smiling as she rubbed a hand across her mouth. She pulled her hand away and noticed blood. She brought her other hand up to hold her cheek that started throbbing immediately. Bellamy gasped in pain as he grasped her arm in a hold so tight it brought tears to her eyes. She didn't think she just reacted when she turned and spit in his face. Bellamy flinched as he pulled her tight against his body and roughly grabbed her face.

"You are gonna be so sorry you did that, little bitch!" he spat.

Bellamy fought against his hold as he leaned down and licked the blood right from her lips. She fought the urge not to vomit all over him. He started dragging her towards the house, ignoring her pleas and cries for him to stop. She knew it fell on deaf ears because he was barking orders at his men. They followed the men inside a beach house that looked like a bachelor pad. She could see empty beer cans, overflowing ash trays, which included joints and cigarettes and empty fast food containers littering countertops, and random bits of trash everywhere but in the garbage can. The smell was enough to make her gag. He pulled her down a long hall, and when he reached the last door, he opened it and shoved her inside.

Bellamy ran to the furthest corner of the room and cowered against the wall.

"You're lucky I've got business to take care of, otherwise we'd get to your punishment now. You never know, though; maybe my friend will join me for our own private punishment session." She watched as he licked his lips. He smirked at her and then left the room, shutting the door firmly behind him.

Bellamy felt her body trembling as she slid down the wall and started rocking herself back and forth. "Please, someone help me," she whispered over and over again as the tears ran down her face.

***

Mark was waiting in the kitchen for Jake to come back. He couldn't do anything until Jake's supplier got there, and then it'd be time to take that piece of shit down. Mark heard a door slam and then Jake was stalking down the hall toward him.

"Mark, I need you to go guard that little bitch. If she gets away, I'll fuck you up. Is that understood?" he said, getting right in Mark's face.

"Yeah, man, I got it," Mark said and turned to head down to the room Jake pointed to.

"Oh and one more thing, Mark: you touch her except for restraining her before I get there, you'll be so fucking sorry." He watched Jake lean down, snorting a thick line of cocaine up his nose. Mark knew that Jake was a big user of his own supply and was surprised he'd been able to keep it together this long. He'd seen it before when dealers and suppliers got into their own stash a little too much and started making lots of mistakes.

When he reached the bedroom, he opened the door slowly and found the room empty. He knew she couldn't have gotten away because there were bars on the windows and Jake had stayed in view of the hallway. He checked the closet, but came up empty. Mark listened closely when he thought he heard whimpering by the bed. He walked around to the side by the wall and saw Bellamy tucked in a little ball. It was obvious she was trying to make herself as small as possible.

"Bellamy, I need you to be quiet and listen to me. I'm not going to hurt you. I can't tell you why, but you're going to have to trust me and do what I say."

Bellamy couldn't believe she was alone with Mark. He scared her, especially since she knew he was the man who drugged her. Her heart was beating against her ribs so hard she was sure he could hear it. The nerve of him asking her to trust him. Like that would happen. Bellamy shuddered as he got closer to her and got down on his haunches so they were eye to eye.

"Why should I trust you?" she whispered. "You dr-drugged me and I ended up-up in the hospital because of you."

She watched him stand up and pace back and forth. Bellamy would never ever trust that man after what he did to her. She stayed down on the floor against the wall willing Mark to just disappear.

Bellamy let her thoughts drift to Luke. She wanted to be with him so bad and see if he was all right. Things seemed to be heading in a positive direction. Bellamy wanted to make things right and just love him forever if he'd have her. When she got out of this mess, which she was, she was going to bring him with her to Savannah and take him to Rebecca's garden. It was a beautiful spot near the hospital where families that had lost babies could have plaques made in remembrance. And it was where she had a plaque made for their daughter. She'd tell him how every Sunday morning she'd go there and place a pink rose next to the plaque with their daughter's name. Bellamy would even bring Rose's urn back to Beaufort so Luke could have their daughter near him.

She had to get out of this. There was no other way about it.

Bellamy heard pounding coming from outside and knew it must've been the "friend" that Jake was taunting her with. She tried to hold in the whimper that left her lips as she sunk further into the corner.

Bellamy watched as Mark's pacing became faster until he stopped by the door and put his ear against it. She didn't know what he was listening for, but she wasn't about to ask him. Her heart was hammering away in her chest and her eyes were filling with more tears. She was starting to think that this wasn't going to end well. Bellamy had wanted to be positive, but it was obvious that if Jake and his friend came through the door she was dead. She watched as Mark pulled his cell phone out of his pocket. He hit a couple of buttons, put it back in his pocket and pulled out a gun that was strapped under his pant leg and tucked it into the back of his jeans.

Mark turned to her. "Bellamy, get down on the floor, and no matter what, do not leave this room." She watched him open the door slowly had head out into the hall. The only sound was the soft click of the door shutting behind him. She laid down flat on the floor and managed to wiggle herself under the bed.

Bellamy's breath was leaving her in shallow puffs. She tried to listen for any sounds, but couldn't hear anything. With her eyes closed, Bellamy said a little prayer to keep her safe through whatever was happening. She also said a little prayer that Luke was all right and that she'd see him again and tell him she loved him.

***

Luke was beyond pissed. The damn ER doctor wouldn't let him go yet. He was still in a lot of pain, and until they had it under control, he wasn't going anywhere. The shot the nurse had given him a little while before knocked him out, but not for long. Every time someone in the room would talk he'd wake up. Luke was grateful that they didn't admit him because he would've had to sign himself out AMA. Scott had stopped by a few minutes before and told them that they still had nothing. The Crime Scene Techs were still at the Bartlett Plantation going through the grounds trying to gather evidence.

He could see the look of helplessness on everyone's faces as they all sat in Luke's room. All he wanted was to hold her again. He knew the longer she was missing the harder it would be to find her.

Luke felt his mom grab his hand and give it a squeeze. "How're you holding up, baby?" she asked gently.

"I'm okay."

Luke tried to get comfortable on the cot he was laying on, but no matter how he moved, the pain was unbearable. They were still waiting for the radiologist to read his X-rays and let them know the damage. He knew he had to have at least one broken rib because he couldn't take a deep breath without it hurting like a son of a bitch.

Luke glanced across the room at Dustin, Dylan, and their dad. He couldn't help but feel guilty. Bellamy was with him; he should've protected her. If they hadn't got him with the damn taser he would've been able to at least fight them off enough for her to get away. That thought alone was killing him. What kind of man was he that he couldn't protect the woman he loved? They should've just killed him because if anything happens to her and she doesn't come home, then Luke might as well be dead.

"Luke, I know what you're thinking right now and you better knock that shit off," Dylan said as he walked over to stand by the foot of Luke's bed.

Luke took the deepest breath he could. "You don't know what I'm thinking, asshole!" he growled.

"I may be an asshole, but you aren't to blame for this. Do you really think anyone blames you for Bellamy being taken? Dude, you've got burns on your neck from where they got you with the Taser. We're all grateful that your alive and not in a fucking body bag down in the morgue. They could've taken any of us down the way they did to you." Luke met Dylan's eyes when he grabbed

Luke's hand. "We all know that you would've done everything in your power to protect her if you could. She would be pissed if she knew you were sitting here blaming yourself. We're gonna get her back, bro. We are."

Luke closed his eyes, taking in Dylan's words. He knew Dylan was right, but he couldn't help but feel some guilt. Luke opened his eyes just in time to see Scott come racing in the room.

"I just heard from my Captain. Apparently the guys who took Bellamy were under a heavy investigation. There was someone on the inside and knew about Bellamy, so she's been safe. Someone should be bringing her here shortly."

With that everyone started to cheer. Luke watched Bellamy's parents embrace as happy tears ran down both of their faces. His mom and dad both came over, hugging him gently. Even Dylan and Dustin hugged it out. Stacy came over to Luke and grabbed his hand and brought it to her lips for a quick kiss. He watched her as she hugged the others and stepped out into the hall, probably to call her folks.

Luke grit his teeth through the pain as he pushed himself up because there was no way he was going to greet his girl lying flat on his back. Dylan rushed over to help him sit all of the way up.

"Dude, what are you doing?"

"I don't want Bell seeing me lying flat in bed when they bring her back," Luke said as he tried to breathe through the pain. Everyone seemed to understand his reasoning, so his mom and Ruth situated pillows so he could rest back against the wall while they all waited. He just hoped she didn't have to endure much while those bastards had her.

***

Dustin walked out of the room and spotted Stacy talking on her phone.

"Yeah, Mom, she'll be here soon. I will, and tell Daddy I love him." He watched her slide her phone back into her pocket. Dustin leaned casually against the wall while he waited for Stacy to notice him. He watched her turn and gave him the most breathtaking smile. She came right over to him and threw her arms around his neck. "This is such great news, Dustin. I can't wait to see her."

Before he could answer her, Stacy placed a chaste kiss on his lips, but as she pulled away, Dustin grabbed her by her waist and pulled her to him. He smiled at her surprised look and then crushed his mouth to hers. She tasted of coffee and a flavor that was uniquely hers. At her moan he thrust his tongue into her mouth, her tongue twining with his. Dustin really couldn't get enough of this woman. He could feel her hands slide up into his hair, tugging gently on the strands. They were lost in each other and didn't stop until someone cleared their throat…his dad.

Stacy jumped back so fast she almost fell on her ass. "Oh my gosh, Charlie. I-I was just telling Dustin how happy I am about Bell." Dustin tried to hide the smile that spread across his face. He could tell his dad was clearly amused by the whole thing.

But being the good guy that he was, he changed the subject.

"Are you gonna stick around, honey, and wait with us? I know Bell will want to see you."

"Uh, um, sure. I'd like that," Stacy said, and then as quick as her feet would carry her, she ran back into the room.

Dustin turned towards his dad, who was eyeing Dustin like he was up to no good.

"Son, what was that?" his dad asked.

"I don't know what you're talking about," Dustin tried to feign ignorance.

"Oh really. Since when do you have your tongue shoved down Stacy's throat? I didn't know you two were an item."

An item? He didn't know where his dad even came up with that stuff half of the time. Just thinking about them being an item did get his pulse racing in a good way. Surprisingly, it didn't scare him at all, and Dustin wondered if he could convince her to go out with him on a real date. Maybe dinner, a movie or whatever. But it was best to just change the subject for now.

He turned to his dad. "Do you really think that whoever was on the inside kept her safe?"

"I don't know, son, but we'll find out soon enough."

Chapter 20

Bellamy didn't know how much time had passed. She could hear loud talking going on outside the door. It scared her, so she slid back further under the bed. Out of nowhere she heard a loud crash, sirens, and lots shouting. Bellamy's heart was pounding in her chest. Was it the police to come rescue her? She wanted to run out to let them know she was there, but Mark's words kept replaying in her head. He asked her to, no matter what, stay where she was. Bellamy had no reason at all to trust him, but a small part of her felt like she should.

She felt like she was arguing with herself about what to do, but the gunshot that rang out made her decision for her. Bellamy threw her hands over her mouth to stop the scream that threatened to escape. She could feel her body shuddering as the shouting outside of the door got louder.

Suddenly the door flew open and heavy footsteps entered the room. Bellamy wasn't sure who it was until she heard that voice.

"Where are you, you little bitch!" Jake gritted out.

Bellamy tried to curl herself into a tiny ball, hoping it would make her invisible. She could hear his heavy breathing and then the thump as he dropped to the floor right by her legs. Bellamy couldn't help the squeak that left her lips.

Jake smiled at her and quickly grabbed her and pulled her out from under the bed. He hauled her against his body. "You thought you could really hide from me, bitch? You're my ticket out of here." He wrapped his arm around her neck and pulled her body tight against his front. "You're my shield, baby, and then you and I are gonna ride off into the sunset."

Bellamy fought against his hold as he pushed her into the hall. She could see men in black everywhere, all of them armed. Jake slowly started walking her down the hall, and he pressed something hard and cold against her temple. Bellamy knew it had to be a gun. Her brain was telling her to run, but her body was paralyzed with fear.

He walked them slowly to the end of the hall when she noticed several men being led out in handcuffs; one had blood running down his arm. It took a second for any of them to notice they were standing right there. Several men turned on them at once. Their guns trained on them.

"Please let me go." She couldn't control the shaking in her voice.

Bellamy watched the officer speak into a little microphone and then he looked directly at them.

"Son, why don't you let her go so we can get her home to her family and then you and I can talk," the man told Jake.

Bellamy felt his grip tighten on her. "Are you kidding me? The moment I let her go y'all will pounce on me, and that's not gonna happen. This bitch and I are getting out of here. You try to stop us and I'll put a bullet right into her pretty little skull. So y'all can move out of my way so we can leave."

She watched the men slowly back away and couldn't help it as she started to cry again. "Please let me go. I don't want to leave with you." Bellamy couldn't help the hopelessness that she was feeling. If he got her outside she'd never see her family again. She'd never see her friends again, and worst of all, she'd never see Luke.

Bellamy saw someone out of the corner of her eye with a gun trained on Jake. She didn't think Jake noticed because they were making their way slowly to the door. She mustered up some courage and reached up and slowly rubbed his arm. She prayed that it would distract him enough that the man she couldn't clearly see could take Jake down. Bellamy didn't think it was going to work until he halted and quit digging the end of the gun in her head. "Oh, baby, I see you've changed your mind about fighting me. That's real good, because the only place I want you fighting me is in bed." She felt him lean down and kiss her cheek. It took all the strength that she had not to shudder from his lips touching her face and give him a small smile.

"All right, gentleman, it's been fun, but as you can see this little peach has decided she's coming with me willingly, so we'll just be on our way now. " He loosened his grip enough that she was able to bring down her hand that she curled into a fist and hit him right in the balls.

After that everything happened in slow motion. The man that she could see out of the corner of her eye charged Jake as he howled, holding himself where Bellamy hit him, and knocked the gun from his hand. Two of the men in black rushed forward to help him as the older man grabbed Bellamy. "Miss, are you hurt anywhere?" His voice was gentle, a complete contradiction to the hard look he had.

"I-I don't k-know," she whispered. Bellamy couldn't even think, let alone answer any questions.

"Okay, well we're gonna get you to the hospital and have them check you out. This may be a very hard question to answer, but did he sexually assault you?"

"No, but-but I think he was pl-planning to. I want to see my family. I need to know what happened to my boyfriend." Bellamy could feel herself getting stronger with every word that left her lips.

"Well, we've contacted the locals and it seems your family is all waiting for you at Beaufort General. We'll get you there shortly." He led her outside, found a blanket for her and settled her in the back of one of their cars. Bellamy was grateful that they left the door open for her. After being stuck in that dirty house the fresh air smelled so good. She winced when she saw her reflection in the window. Her cheek was swollen and her lower lip was split open. Bellamy wasn't going to complain, though. She was alive and that's all that mattered. Soon she'd be surrounded by the people she loved most in the world.

Bellamy watched as two men led a cuffed Jake out of the house. She recognized the one closet to her as one of the men in black standing in front of her in the house, but she couldn't see the other. Jake was shooting daggers at her as they led him to the back of a van. It was then that she noticed the other guy. Mark stood guard as the other guy must've strapped Jake in. When he turned, he saw Bellamy and slowly made his way towards her. She couldn't help the reaction to pull the blanket tighter around her shoulders.

"Hello, Bellamy, let me introduce myself. I'm Mark Jefferson, undercover agent with the DEA."

She watched his lips twitch as she felt her eyes go wide like saucers. "You-you're with the DEA?"

"Yep, we've been tracking Jake for about a year until I went in about six months ago undercover. Bellamy, I know what I did to you, but he had eyes watching me in the bar that day. I couldn't do anything to compromise the mission. I shouldn't even be telling you that, but I just wanted you to know that it tore me up doing what I had to do."

Bellamy stared at him, dumbfounded. Undercover Agent. She still couldn't believe it. Bellamy didn't want to try and understand what had happened. At least not right now while it was all so fresh in her mind.

"It was you I saw out of the corner of my eye? You're the one who took him down after I hit him?" she asked. She was still trying to wrap her head around the whole situation and everything that she had just learned. He looked at her with uncertainty in his eyes, but before he could say anything, another man called to him and tossed him what looked like a first-aid kit.

Bellamy had refused the ambulance that had come for one of her captors who got shot when he pulled a gun on the agents.

Mark opened the first aid kit and pulled out the swabs and some peroxide. He got down on his haunches in front of her. Mark knew he made her nervous because her eyes were looking everywhere but at him. "Bellamy, let me clean those cuts up for you?' He watched indecision and then resolve cross over her face. She simply nodded at him and scooted herself closer to the end of the seat. "Okay, this is gonna sting a bit, but I want to get it all cleaned up before we get you to the hospital." Mark grabbed her chin gently and started swabbing the cut on her lip. He stopped for a minute when she hissed at the pain. Mark dabbed a little ointment on her lip and then moved on to her cheek. He knew Jake was a bastard, but the way he hit this girl completely unnerved him. Bellamy had fire and fought back. It was something Jake was not used to. He was used to women cowering around him, and thanks to her quick thinking, they managed to subdue him.

After he cleaned the cuts he told Bellamy he'd be right back. One of the other agents, Agent Griffin, was riding along with him when he took Bellamy to the hospital. He had his reasons for taking her and not all of them were selfless. One, he wanted to speak to her family and explain what went down. Second, he wanted to talk to the locals and let them know what happened, but the main reason he had for going was because he wanted to see Stacy again.

One meeting was all it took for him to be hooked. There was just something about her and there was no denying the chemistry that was between them when they met. Granted, he didn't even know if she'd even speak to him after the whole incident at the bar the weekend before, but just to see those brown eyes again would be worth whatever she threw at him.

Bellamy watched Mark walk out of the house, followed by a man in black cargo pants, black t-shirt and some sort of vest over the top of his shirt. They both got in the vehicle she was sitting in the back of.

"Bellamy, this Agent Griffin. He's going to accompany us to the hospital," Mark said as he started the car.

Bellamy greeted the man and then sat back in her seat. Mark turned and gave her a reassuring smile before they turned around and started heading down the long driveway. He must've had the other agent come so she wouldn't be nervous around him. She still detested what he did to her, but he earned a little respect from her for trying to ease her discomfort.

The two agents talked quietly in the front seat while Bellamy blindly stared out the window. She'd seen the damage to her face earlier, but she had yet to see the rest of it. Bellamy was sure that she was covered in bruises from head to toe. Her thoughts drifted to Luke and how he was doing. She didn't know if she'd ever get the image out of her head of them kicking him. The groan that slipped past his lips after they got him with the taser again made her stomach roll, even now. Bellamy couldn't wait to wrap her arms around him and love him.

Chapter 21

Luke muttered thanks to the doctor as he left the room. Two cracked ribs and some deep bruising was the diagnosis from him. There was nothing that could be done for cracked ribs except for being careful and resting. They also gave him some plastic device that he was going to have to use a couple times a day to help him from developing pneumonia. It was gonna be a pain in the ass, but it was better than the ribs being broken and displaced. Otherwise he'd have to worry about a punctured lung.

He along with everyone else was waiting on pins and needles waiting for Bellamy to get there. They gave Luke's mom his discharge instructions and a prescription for pain medication. The ER staff told them they could wait for Bellamy to arrive, which was good because there was no way he was gonna miss her. Luke heard a big commotion in the hall, and when Ruth stuck her head out, she cried out and ran out of the room. He knew his girl was there. Luke watched everyone rush out of the room and decided he wasn't going to wait on the damn bed.

He could hear the happy chatter and cries as he eased himself off of the bed.

When he stood up, he lost his breath and bent over the bed, trying to breathe through the pain. He slowly stood up and when he turned, there she was standing in the doorway. Luke wanted to scream and commit murder when he saw what they did to her face. Her lip was split open and her cheek was swollen and black and blue. Bellamy's eye was practically swollen shut, but he had to remember she was alive and she was safe.

"Hey, baby," he said, and smiled through the pain as she ran to him and gently wrapped her arms around him. It hurt, but he didn't really care.

As soon as Bellamy felt Luke's arms wrap around her the tears started to come. They held each other for what seemed like forever. She knew she was probably hurting him, but Bellamy couldn't make herself let go of him. He was in a hospital gown and scrub pants. His pain was evident to her in the way that is breathing was shallow and his body rigid.

"Oh god, Luke, I was so scared. I didn't know what happened to you and I was frightened by what they might do to me." She looked up into his green eyes as he gently wiped at the tears that continued to fall.

Bellamy watched as he bent his head and gently touched his lips to hers. He was careful around the split in her lip. She savored that moment and felt his love for her through his kiss. Bellamy was grateful for their families giving them privacy for their reunion because she didn't want to share the moment with anyone else. She felt Luke pull his lips away and bury his face in her hair. The closeness she felt to him was indescribable and Bellamy couldn't have asked for more.

"Baby, I'm so glad you're okay. I was so worried." She could hear the hitch in his breath as he tried to talk.

"Shh...Luke, it's okay. We're okay." The pain etched in his face was heartbreaking. "Baby, why don't you sit if it's hurting you to stand?"

"No way, Bell. I'm not letting you go just yet," Luke whispered against the top of her head.

Bellamy went back to earlier when they were sitting together at the Bartlett Plantation having their much needed talk. It seemed like it happened days ago not hours. He'd forgiven her and in time the guilt she felt would hopefully dissipate.

She moved to sit down on the bed, hoping Luke would sit down, too. She knew he had to be in pain, but it was obvious that he didn't want her to see it. Men; they thought they had to be so tough and could never show weakness.

"Come sit with me," Bellamy said to Luke as she reached for his hand. As he slowly turned and just as he eased himself down onto the bed, they heard a commotion in the hall.

"What are you doing here, you son of a bitch!"

Bellamy looked at Luke and then at the doorway. She helped him up and when they made it to the doorway, she knew there was going to be problems. Stacy was being held back by Bellamy's brothers and Mark was walking towards them. She knew that no one knew yet that it was Mark that helped her.

"Stacy, please just calm down and I'll explain," Mark pleaded.

"I don't want to hear it, asshole! What the hell are you doing here?" Stacy couldn't believe she was face to face with the piece of shit again. He hit on her and got Stacy to invite him to hang out with them and it was all so he could get closer to drug Bellamy.

"Stacy, who is this guy?"

Stacy looked into Dylan's eyes when he asked. "He's the guy who drugged Bellamy."

Stacy felt Dylan's arm leave her and then Dustin as they both approached Mark. She stood there in shocked silence along with everyone else. No one could hear what the men were talking about, but it couldn't have been good, since Dylan was right in Mark's face. If Stacy was Mark, she'd be shitting her pants right about now. Mark was tall, but he was leaner than both Dustin and Dylan. Neither twin was heavily muscled, but they certainly looked it next to Mark's lanky frame. Bellamy ran quickly by Stacy to her brothers. She was talking rapidly, but Stacy could barely make out what she was saying. Why Bellamy would want to be anywhere near that bastard was beyond her.

From behind Stacy she could hear Charlie and Patrick's raised voices. She couldn't blame them for getting upset, but Bellamy's pleading voice broke through to everyone. They all fell silent as Stacy watched Bellamy stand next to Mark.

"Everyone, this is Mark Jefferson. He's an undercover agent with the DEA. Mark's the one who kept me safe while those men had me."

Stacy leaned against the wall in shock. The DEA? She couldn't believe it. So instead of being a regular liar, he was a professional one. She was glad she never did anything with him then, because Stacy had enough men in and out of her life that'd done nothing but lie to her. Aside from her father and uncles, there wasn't any man that she could completely trust. Stacy could thank the boy who took her virginity when she was 15 for starting that trend. She closed her eyes against those painful memories and pushed them to the back of her mind. When she opened her eyes, Dustin was standing right in front of her.

She schooled her expression and gave him a small smile. He reached out to rub her upper arm. "You doing okay?"

She gave him an embarrassed smile. "Yeah, sorry about that." Stacy looked around, seeing Luke and Bellamy talking with her parents while Mark and another gentleman all in black were talking to some men from the Sherriff's department. Luke's mom and dad were smoothing things over with hospital security.

Dustin touched her hand and brought her attention back to him. "Do you wanna get out of here? We can check on everyone later." The smile he gave her made her stomach flutter as she watched him walk over to his dad and whisper something in his ear. Stacy knew she should probably stay, but she really needed a good distraction and Dustin was the perfect person to help her with that. When he headed back towards her, he looked dangerous. He looked like some wild animal stalking his prey and she couldn't stop the tingle that shot from her breasts right to her pussy.

"Absolutely. I've had enough…drama for one day."

They started walking away from everyone when someone grabbed her arm, stopping her. She turned and tried to jerk away when she saw it was Mark. "Let me go, Agent." Stacy didn't even try to hide the disdain in her voice.

"Please, Stacy, just give me a chance to talk to you and explain. Five minutes is all I ask. Please," Mark said, pleading evident in his voice.

"Not now, Mark. Please just leave me alone."

"She asked you to leave her alone, man. She'll let you know if she wants to talk," Dustin said as he led Stacy away

Mark watched Stacy walk away with one of Bellamy's brothers and couldn't help but feel a little bit of jealously. Not that he had any right or reason to be, but he was. He'd never had that instant attraction to anyone before, but he had it for her, and once everything was over he'd just have to convince her to give him a chance.

***

Bellamy let one of the nurses take a look at her split lip and swollen cheek. They told her she didn't require stitches, but she'd need to be careful with her lip. The swelling in her cheek and eye would go down eventually and putting ice on it would help. Her mom and dad stayed by her side, with Travis and Brad blocking the door. They'd all been so relieved when they saw her walking down the hall when Bellamy got to the ER. No matter what, they all seemed to be an arm's length away from her. For once, people's protective nature towards her didn't bother her one bit.

Bellamy had informed her parents that Luke was going to stay with them so she could take care of him. Lola, at first, looked like she may argue with Bellamy, but changed her mind when Bellamy noticed Patrick whispering in his wife's ear. Maybe they saw the love Bellamy had in her eyes as she rubbed Luke's hair while he held her. They sat and waited while the nurse got Bellamy ready to be discharged as well.

Chapter 22

It was finally Independence Day, and a couple of days after the ordeal. Luke was still in a lot of pain. He had refused at first to take the pain pills they had prescribed him, but Bellamy begged him their first night home when Luke had gotten up to go to the bathroom in the middle of the night. Her parents had set up a twin bed for him in the family room to sleep in. Bellamy was going to take care of him at his house, but Ruth had begged her daughter to stay there.

She'd been sleeping on the couch to be near him if Luke needed her, and being the stubborn man he was, got out of bed by himself and couldn't help the pained moan that left his lips, waking Bellamy instantly.

She then proceeded to beg him to quit being stubborn and stupid. Luke would've been annoyed, but her eyes filling with tears made him suck it up and take the pills. Now, a couple days later he was taking them on a regular basis. He hated the fuzzy feeling they gave him, but it was better than being in excruciating pain. They didn't take away the pain completely, but they helped him sleep and made it somewhat bearable.

Dylan's party, which turned into just a backyard barbeque, had been the night before. Their parents invited just family and friends, but kept it fairly small. Luke had been stuck in a chair most of the time because it hurt to move. He hated to see his friend leaving, but this wasn't the first time that Dylan had been deployed. They sat together for a while and talked about all of the trouble they used to get into when they were boys. Dustin came and sat on the other side of Luke and joined the conversation.

"Luke, remember when Dylan made himself a fake ID?" Dustin asked as he gave his brother a pointed look. "That was the worst looking piece of shit I'd ever seen. That clerk in the liquor store up in Charleston looked at you like you'd lost your mind." The three men laughed together, but it made Luke tear up from the pain. He hid it the best he could. He didn't want the moment with his best friends to be ruined.

"It was probably because he handed her his high school ID first by mistake," Luke wheezed out. "I wish your brother and I wouldn't have been standing outside so we could've heard her chewing your ass," he said, turning to Dylan.

"Ha-ha. You guys are such assholes." Dylan's smile told Luke that he was being a good sport about it.

They reminisced for a while, and Luke knew he was gonna miss his friend. Dylan, god-willing, would be home in six to eight months and then he was done. He planned on helping with the family business once their dads retired. It'd be good to have him home for good. Even with Dylan being stationed at Parris Island, they still didn't see him a whole lot. Someday he hoped that Dylan would meet someone who could break through that hard-assed exterior he had. They all could see the shape he was in when he'd come home from a deployment. Each time it'd last longer and longer. He just didn't laugh a whole lot anymore. He'd always been the serious one, but in the last few years he took it to a whole new level. It was going to take a special woman to get through to him, but if it could happen for himself, it could happen for Dylan.

Luke scanned the Carmichaels' back yard until he found her. Bellamy was standing in the middle of the yard talking to Travis. Luke could see the affection that Travis had for her, the way he would lovingly stroke her arm and kiss her forehead as they talked. Luke would feel forever grateful to the man that helped Bellamy through such a hard time. Granted, he wished he would've been that person, but at least he knew she hadn't been alone.

Someday, he hoped that she'd be his wife and they'd start a family together. Bellamy was going to be an amazing mother and Luke wanted those children to be his. If the last few days taught him anything, it was that life was short and you had to grab on to what you wanted and never let go. That was how he felt about her.

Her face was still swollen and the bruise on her cheek was an angry shade of purple. Bellamy's lip swelling had come down some and the split seemed to be healing, but slowly. Luke had briefly talked to Bellamy about her moving home and hopefully moving in with him. He knew he was probably rushing her, but he couldn't bring himself to care.

Luke spent six long years thinking about their night together, and even though he hadn't treated her right and still dated other women, she'd never been far from his thoughts. He could feel his wallet in his back pocket and knew that before they could completely move forward Luke was going to show Bellamy the picture of their daughter. Luke had to be prepared for anything when that happened. Sure he should wait, but he wanted to move forward and they both needed some closure of the past and what they lost. He hoped to god it didn't push her away from him, but it was a chance Luke was willing to take.

***

Bellamy woke up early on July 4th to get ready to help her mom with the mini recital that the dance studio was putting on during the festival. She had smiled when she looked over at Luke sleeping on the twin bed. If he wasn't in so much pain Bellamy might've laughed at how ridiculous he looked on that small bed. He was sleeping without a shirt and Bellamy sucked in a breath when she saw the ugly bruising. The ER nurse told them it'd look worse before it got better and she was right. Bellamy didn't want to leave Luke, but her dad and brothers were going to be there to keep an eye on him.

After the recital, Dylan had asked Bellamy to go for ice cream. She was looking forward to spending some time alone with him before they all came back for the festivities. Bellamy knew that at some point Luke was going to be part of the conversation, but she hoped that it wasn't going to be bad. She knew that Dylan was coming to terms with them being together and now knowing the fact that Bellamy had been pregnant with Luke's child when she was eighteen. Bellamy just wanted to enjoy the time she had left with Dylan and not dwell on the past.

Bellamy stood off to the side waiting for Dylan to pay for their ice creams. He'd met her behind the pavilion where their mom's dancers were performing. The performances had been great. She was thrilled for her mom that she had an amazing group of dancers. It made Bellamy miss all of the dancing she'd done most of her life. Bellamy stayed hidden throughout the performances because her face was still a mess. She had to wear a ballcap and aviator sunglasses to help hide most of the bruise on her cheek.

Her lip was still swollen, but there wasn't much she could do to hide that. She was brought back to the present when Dylan came over to hand her the ice cream cone. They walked silently to the back booth and both slid into their seats.

Dylan smiled at his baby sister as she started eating her ice cream. It made him see red every time he thought about what those men did to her. She seemed to be holding it together well. Their mom thought that it probably helped that Bellamy was taking care of Luke. Luke did tell Dylan in the morning that he thought Bellamy was having a bad dream the night before. He said she'd been thrashing around on the couch and even cried out a bit, but Luke managed to get her settled down by sitting next to her, stroking her hair.

Dylan reached across the table and grabbed his sister's hand. "How are you holding up, brat?"

She gave him a lopsided smile. "I'm fine, just tired. I think I wake up every time Luke moves in his sleep."

"Well, why don't you let me take the couch tonight and you can sleep in your own bed. You need your sleep, too."

He watched as Bellamy thought about it. Dylan knew that she didn't want to be far from Luke, but she was dead on her feet. He couldn't see them right now because she wouldn't take her sunglasses off, but their mom had told him to watch her, that she was exhausted and had dark circles under her eyes.

No matter how old Bellamy was he'd always worry about her.

Bellamy smiled at her brother the best she could without hurting her split lip. She didn't want to be far away from Luke, but Dylan was right. Bellamy had slept lightly the last few nights because she was afraid that Luke would need her and she didn't want to have a repeat of the first night.

"You know, I may have to take you up on that. It'll give you guys a chance to talk before you leave." Bellamy couldn't help but look down at her hands as she said the last part. Dylan was reporting to the base tomorrow and then they were leaving the day after that. She could feel the tears beginning, but tried to hold them back.

"Bell, don't get upset. You know I've been deployed before and I've come home. But while we're talking about this, we might as well get the hard stuff out of the way."

Bellamy braced herself because she knew what was coming. The last time he was getting ready to leave he sat down like this with their parents.

She watched him pull a piece of paper out of his pocket. "This here is my bank account number. I've filled out all of the necessary paperwork that if I don't come home the money is to be split between you and Dustin. There'll be at least fifteen grand for each of you. Do whatever you want with it, but I'd love it if you used that money to start your life with Luke. Dustin already knows about it, too. I've rewritten my will and signed my POA. They're in a fireproof safe at Mom and Dad's, the combination is also on this piece of paper. Dustin's been given the names and numbers of who to call to make sure I make it home."

Bellamy couldn't help the quiet sobs that left her body. She hated this. Sure she respected her brother and what he was doing for their country, but it still didn't make it any easier. Bellamy felt him slide into the booth next to her and wrap his arms around her.

"Shhh…brat, don't cry. You know I'm gonna do my best to make sure I come home to y'all." Dylan tilted her chin up so he could look her right in the eye, but he had to take her sunglasses off first. He could see how red her eyes were and how young and fragile she looked. It broke Dylan's heart to see her looking like this, but he knew she was strong and that she'd move forward with her life.

"Promise me you'll take care of Luke. I've seen the love he has in his eyes for you. Hold on tight and don't ever let go of that. Marry him, have lots of babies and don't ever take anything for granted because you know what it's like to lose something so precious." Dylan wiped the tear that ran down Bellamy's cheek. "Bell, if something happens to me, take care of Dustin. Find him a nice girl that will help settle him down. I know he tries to act like sex is all he wants, but Emily hurt him. I don't know when or how, but she turned our brother into the man-whore he is now."

They both shared a sad smile at Dylan's last statement, because Dustin used to be the sweet romantic kind of guy, and then his freshman year of college it changed. He never treated women badly, but he never saw them more than a couple of times. They'd just turned thirty-one and it was high time for Dustin to find a woman worth keeping around. Dylan didn't want him to turn into a cliché, the eternal bachelor was not supposed to be it for Dustin. Now himself, that was another story. He was too messed up to ever be worth anything long term to a woman.

"I promise to take care of Dustin," Bellamy whispered. "But when you come home, and you will, he's all yours." Bellamy wrapped her arms around her brother and they sat in the booth together for a long time.

***

Bellamy carried out a platter full of snacks for everyone. Her family, Luke's and several of their friends gathered on her parents' deck and backyard to watch the fireworks that would be starting as soon as the sun set. Stacy helped carry out another platter while Brad and Travis helped with the drinks.

She caught sight of Luke sitting with her brothers, Zach and Skeeter. He crabbed and hollered earlier when Dustin and Dylan insisted on helping him walk out onto the deck, but his mom had come in and gave him a talking to.

Bellamy finished setting up the food and went back inside to freshen up. As she made her way up to her room she heard a noise coming from her parents' bedroom. It sounded like her mom and she was crying. Bellamy lightly tapped on the door and opened it peering inside.

Her mom was sitting on the bed holding a picture frame and didn't notice Bellamy until she sat down on the bed next to her. Bellamy could see the picture in her hands, and she couldn't help but smile. It was taken at Bellamy's graduation from college. She was in her cap and gown, Dustin was looking like Mr. GQ and Dylan was in his dress blues.

"Momma?" Bellamy placed her hand on Ruth's shoulder. "Why are you crying?"

Ruth wiped the tears that were running down her face. She was always torn when Dylan got deployed. Ruth was so proud of him for what he was doing, but on the other hand she was scared to death that her baby boy wouldn't come home. She felt her darling girl grab her hand squeezing it gently.

"Oh, honey, I'm just having a moment. It's just hard knowing that I'm so close to having all my children home, and I pray that God willing your brother will stay safe and come home to us," Ruth said as she wrapped her arms around her daughter.

"I'll do my best to come home to you, mom," Dylan said as he and Dustin entered the room, joining their mom and sister on the bed.

Ruth reached out and grabbed each one of her children and pulled them into a tight embrace. They all sat holding each other until she noticed the love of her life walked in.

She was thankful that Charlie had forgiven her for everything that happened when Bellamy lost the baby. Ruth watched him as he walked over and grabbed the picture she was holding and smiled at it as he set it back on their dresser. He reached out a hand to her and hauled her up off of the bed.

Ruth felt her insides melt as he wrapped her in his arms and kissed her. She smiled against his lips when all three of their children started making gagging noises like they did when they were younger.

"Oh, y'all can quit it right now," She tried to sound stern, but it was impossible when she started giggling against Charlie's chest. Ruth shooed them out of the room and turned back to her man.

"You know he'll be as safe as he can be," he whispered into her hair.

"I know, baby. I know."

Ruth stayed locked in his embrace until they realized the sun was starting to set and soon the fireworks would be starting.

***

Luke smiled when saw Bellamy walking towards him. She was carrying a blanket and dropped it on the floor right next to the chair he was sitting in. Bellamy leaned down and brushed her lips softly against his. She sat on the ground next to his chair and laid her head against his thigh. Even with everyone around he could still hear her sigh when he rubbed a hand through her hair.

The first boom sounded followed by white light that looked like one gigantic sparkler. Everyone around him "oohed and aahed" over the show, but he couldn't take his eyes off of Bellamy. She stayed leaning against his leg, snuggling as close as she could get to him. Luke caught a whiff of the scent that was uniquely hers, something spicy and citrusy all at once. He reached into his pocket and grabbed the ring that his mom had brought with her earlier.

It was the engagement ring that his dad gave his mom so many years ago. He'd wanted to go shopping for one, but his injuries prohibited him from going anywhere. Luke had called his dad and asked him to go to the jeweler to find the perfect ring, but his mom had other ideas.

When he first laid eyes on it he knew without a doubt that that was her ring. It was a thin gold band with a princess cut diamond on top. Luke's dad had sold his car to buy the ring back when he was eighteen and proposed to Luke's mom.

His nerves kept getting the best of him. He knew he was probably rushing her, but he didn't care. They belonged together forever.

As the finale started Luke pulled the ring out of his pocket. Bellamy's left hand was resting on top of his thigh, so he gently picked it up and slid the ring on her finger. He felt her whole body freeze up as he held his breath, waiting for her to look at him.

She slowly turned her head towards him, surprise clearly written on her face. Luke could see the tears starting to fill her eyes. He watched her lift her hand and looked at the ring closely.

Luke took a deep breath, or as deep as he could take. "Baby, I know this seems very sudden and especially after everything that's happened. When I thought I'd lost you, it felt like my insides were being ripped out. All of the bad shit that happened between us seemed to fade away and all I kept thinking was you had to be okay, we had to be together, because I honestly can't see the rest of my life without you in it—right by my side. I know we have a long way to go before we can both have some closure. I want to wake up every day knowing that you're snuggled up to me with that citusy scent that seems to be a permanent part of you."

"I want to fill our home with as many children as you want because I can't see anyone else being the mother of my children than you. Please, Bellamy, say you'll marry me, because I've lost you before and I don't want to ever lose you again." Luke's palms were sweating and he waited on baited breath for her answer.

Bellamy couldn't tear her eyes away from Luke. Every beautiful word he said warmed her heart. She felt the tears slide down her face, and for once Bellamy was okay with it, because they were happy tears. He wanted to marry her. Bellamy wanted to pinch herself to make sure she wasn't dreaming. She knew her answer as soon as he had slipped the ring on her finger.

Bellamy pushed herself up on her knees and moved so she was in between his legs. All conversation seemed to halt around them, but she didn't turn away from Luke. She gave him what she hoped was a smile filled with all of the love she had for him. "Yes, Luke, I'll marry you."

He cupped her face and kissed her with a fierce possession that made her toes curl. She could hear all of the clapping and cheering behind them, but she kept right on kissing him. Right then and there, Bellamy knew that things couldn't get much better. She and Luke were finally going to get to start over.

Acknowledgements

To my husband Jim, for handling the house and kids when I was deep into writing mode, I love you babe. To my two boys, Ethan and Evan, you guys light up my life every day. No Ethan, I will not buy you a Bugati.

To all of my lovely co-workers who have listened to me talk about my writing on and off for four years, I thank you for your never ending support. I love you all!

To Matt Schnepple, from one of our local fire departments. Thank you for answering questions for me about different drugs and treatments. The information you gave me was great and very useful and thanks Michelle for hooking me up with a great resource.

Last but not least, thank you Jennifer O'Neill, President of Limitless Publishing. Thank you for giving me this wonderful opportunity to share my stories.

About the Author

A Midwesterner and self-proclaimed nerd, Evan has been an avid reader most of her life, but five years ago got bit by the writing bug, and it quickly became her addiction, passion and therapy. When the voices in her head give it a rest, she can always be found with her e-reader in her hand. Some of her favorites include, Shayla Black, Jaci Burton, Madeline Sheehan and Jamie Mcguire. Evan finds a lot of her inspiration in music, so if you see her wearing her headphones you know she means business and is in the zone.

During the day Evan works for a large homecare agency and at night she's superwoman. She's a wife to Jim and a mom to Ethan and Evan, a cook, a tutor, a friend and a writer. How does she do it? She'll never tell.

Facebook:
www.facebook.com/pages/Evan-Grace/626268640762539

Twitter:
https://twitter.com/Evan76Grace

Goodreads:
www.goodreads.com/

Made in the USA
Lexington, KY
16 December 2014